Above All Dreams
Dawn of Alaska
Book 3

Naomi Rawlings

Praise for Written on the Mist

"*Above All Dreams* delivers it all--drama, suspense, romance, and perfect themes about chasing one's dreams against all odds. Dr. Quinn meets the Alaskan frontier in this beautiful story of love and adventure. Naomi Rawlings does it again!"— *Roseanna M. White, Bestselling and Christy-Award Winning Author*

"Kate Amos is a masterfully portrayed character who wrestles with how to break through the barriers of discrimination and "glass ceilings" in a world of burly men, gold miners, trappers and sailors. I found myself captivated and couldn't put the book down as Naomi Rawlings delves into the dilemmas of establishing medical communities in far flung Alaska while finding love for Kate." *Susan Gorilla Benton, Educator and Book Reviewer*

"Naomi Rawlings has knocked it out the park again. She always does a great job blending character development and plot, but her newest novel about a female doctor in the 1800s, is masterful." *Erin Healy, Multi-Published Author and Fiction Editor*

"I always look forward to reading Naomi Rawlings books. She is an excellent storyteller with beautifully written characters and storylines."—*Jennifer Lonas, Editor and Book Reviewer*

"Above All Dreams is a great story with relatable characters that go through real-life issues. It's absolutely inspiring. *Karen Hardick, Editor and Book Reviewer*

"Naomi Rawlings' writing style stirs emotions in an incredibly positive way. The characters come to life and in your mind and heart. You rejoice, cry, and laugh right along with them. The books in her Dawn of Alaska Series are my very top favorites."
—*Keili Holmes, Book Reviewer*

Other Books by Naomi Rawlings

Dawn of Alaska Series
Written on the Mist
Whispers on the Tide
Above All Dreams

Texas Promise Series
Tomorrow's First Light
Tomorrow's Shining Dream
Tomorrow's Constant Hope
Tomorrow's Steadfast Prayer
Tomorrow's Lasting Joy

Eagle Harbor Series
Love's Unfading Light
Love's Every Whisper
Love's Sure Dawn
Love's Eternal Breath
Love's Christmas Hope
Love's Bright Tomorrow

Belanger Family Saga
The Lady's Refuge
The Widow's Secrets
The Reluctant Enemy

Above All Dreams

Published by **Naomi Rawlings LLC**

PO Box 134, South Range, MI 49963

All Scripture quotations are taken from The Holy Bible, King James Version.

The characters and events in this book are fictional, and any resemblance to actual persons or events is coincidental.

ISBN-13: **978-1-955356-42-8**

Copyright © 2024 by **Naomi Rawlings**

Cover art © 2024 by **Carpe Librum Book Design**

All rights reserved. No part of this book may be reproduced or transmitted in any form or by any means, electronic or mechanical, including photocopying and recording, or by any information storage and retrieval system, without permission in writing from the publisher. No part of this book may be used to train generative AI without written permission from the publisher.

Printed in the United States of America

2024—First Edition

To Ellie, for your sunny smiles, creativity, and the light you bring to everyone around you. I love you.

Description

Ever since she was a girl, Kate Amos wanted to be a doctor, a dream that made her leave Alaska and travel clear to Boston for medical school. The problem is, there aren't too many female doctors in 1886, and there are even fewer people who will let a female doctor treat them.

Fortunately for Kate, the only other doctor in the growing town of Juneau Alaska is drunk more than he's sober, and he doesn't know the first thing about medicine. So even though the townsfolk might not want a woman doctor to treat them, they don't have much choice.

Until Dr. Nathan Reid arrives in town.

Nathan has been tasked by the Marine Hospital Service to start a hospital in the gold rush town of Juneau, and he's excited to get started. His research on the area showed him the town was desperately in need of a competent doctor. But Nathan is only in town for a few minutes before discovering that Juneau already has a competent doctor. She just happens to be a woman.

A rather beautiful woman—who's worried he's going to take away her patients.

But when trying to save a man's life leaves them in a compromising situation, Nathan finds himself standing at the front of a church while Kate walks down the aisle toward him.

From a USA Today bestselling author comes a frontier family saga filled with a female doctor, a marriage of convenience, and a love that heals wounded hearts.

Want to be notified when my next book releases? Sign up for my author newsletter: http://geni.us/DHKH7.
(Subscribers also receive a free novel.)

1

Inside Passage near Juneau, Alaska; March 30, 1888

How did a man get a doctor to Tanana, Alaska, three times a year?

Nathan Reid shoved a hand through his hair, then sat back, ignoring the gentle swaying of the ship beneath him as it cut north through the waters of the Inside Passage, heading for Juneau. A swinging lantern hung from the ceiling above him, and with the gray daylight filtering through the cabin's small window, its glow cast just enough light for him to study the giant map he'd tacked to the desk.

The Yukon River sprawled across the map like a mighty serpent winding its way through the rugged terrain of Alaska. Even on paper, the river appeared vast, an artery that pulsed through nearly two thousand miles of wilderness before finally flowing into the Bering Sea. The tiny village of Tanana sat almost directly in the center of the river, at the confluence of the Yukon and Tanana Rivers, in the middle of a land filled with endless trees and mountains.

The people of Tanana had no doctor, not even a nurse. No one to provide medical care if anyone grew ill or became injured in that small town. The only way to reach it was by boat up the Yukon. But Tanana wasn't the only settlement in the interior without access to medical care. There were a handful of others located on the Yukon River and its tributaries, like Fort Yukon, Anvik, and Nulato.

If he wanted to get a doctor into each of these towns three times a year, then he'd have to create a route for a traveling doctor. It would work for the summer months, but what would happen if Tanana or Fort Yukon experienced a smallpox outbreak in the dead of winter? There was no way to get inoculations to the community, except perhaps by dogsled.

And how many people would die in the time it took a dogsled team to reach Tanana?

Nathan sighed. He was probably wasting his time even trying to figure this out, because what were the chances he could find a doctor willing to spend his summers traveling up and down the Yukon River, and his winters dogsledding over the frozen route?

And what was the likelihood he could find a boat that would transport this doctor in the first place? The government didn't have any ships that traveled up the Yukon River.

Nathan tossed his pencil onto the desk and crossed his arms. Maybe it was best to just station a doctor in Tanana and not have him travel.

But then how would Fort Yukon and Anvik get care? And what about Fort Selkirk, which sat farther up the river in Canada? He doubted anyone with a medical bag had ever walked its streets, let alone someone distributing smallpox inoculations.

Nathan blew out a breath, then rolled his neck, which was growing tense from spending too many hours hunched over the map.

"It's raining again. Can you believe that?" The door to the small passenger cabin opened, and Nathan turned to find his partner, Dr. Victor Ellingsworth, stepping inside and closing the door behind him.

He pulled his wide-brimmed hat off his head and hung it on the peg by the door, revealing a head that had more skin than gray hair underneath.

A stream of water ran from the brim onto the floor, and Ellingsworth scowled down at the puddle. "I swear that's all it does here. Rain."

"It's supposed to rain." Nathan shifted in his chair again, trying to make the crude wooden frame a bit more comfortable to sit on. "Didn't you read the journal article I sent you on the climate of Southeast Alaska? The meteorologist who wrote it says the Pacific Northwest should be classified as a temperate rain forest. The water from the ocean collects and forms clouds that hit the mountains and cool quickly due to the cold air from the Arctic, which causes frequent and heavy rainfall. The meteorologist claimed that this part of the Alaskan and Canadian coasts is one of the wettest regions in the world."

"Yes, well, the water doesn't need to collect constantly, does it? A bit of sun isn't too much to ask for." Ellingsworth rubbed a hand over the bald spot on the top of his head, as though the pale skin would do anything other than turn bright red if it got a hint of sunlight.

Nathan shifted his gaze to the cabin's single, small window, which revealed they were passing a small island covered in rock and trees. "I think it's rather lovely. There's something majestic about mountains rising out of the sea in every direction you look, even if they're always shrouded in mist."

Ellingsworth snorted. "As though you would know. You've barely been on the deck."

Nathan rubbed the back of his neck, which still felt stiff despite his stretching. If only he had time to spend on the deck, watching the scenery and getting acquainted with the land that was to be his home for the next three years. "I keep promising myself I can spend some time up there after I figure out how to get a doctor to every village in Alaska three times a year."

"Don't tell me you're looking at that dratted map again." Ellingsworth crossed the cabin to Nathan's desk, rainwater still dripping from the cuffs of his trousers. "How many times do I have to tell you? This is a fool's mission. Alaska's too big. You'll never be able to provide medical care for all the inhabitants."

"It's not a fool's mission. If we can get the surgeon general to give us two more doctors—"

"Two more doctors?" Ellingsworth frowned. "You've already asked for five to be sent to this godforsaken place, and now you want two more?"

Nathan tapped his finger against the small dot that marked Tanana's location on the map. "The Yukon River is going to need its own route for a traveling doctor. And there's no way for me to get a doctor up to Barrow three times a year. I'll have to permanently station one who lives in the community."

Ellingsworth crossed his arms over his chest. He was a big man, and though his muscles had started to go a bit soft given his age, his chest was still twice as broad as Nathan's, his arms far more muscular. He was large enough and strong enough that he could walk into a room full of sailors and have every man there instantly pay attention. A rather useful skill for a person tasked with doctoring sailors.

"Those settlements have been getting along fine without

doctors for centuries." Ellingsworth gestured toward Barrow on the map. The village was positioned at the very top of Alaska on the coast of the Arctic Ocean.

How could the man say such a thing, especially about Barrow? "Have you forgotten the diphtheria epidemic that swept through Barrow last year? Or the bout of smallpox that swept through Anvik two years before that?"

Ellingsworth just shook his head, which caused drops of water to sprinkle across the map. "I appreciate what you're trying to do, Reid, but you're too optimistic for your own good. The Marine Hospital Service is just that, the *Marine* Hospital Service. We've got no business trying to provide medical care to every last person in Alaska, and I've told that to John more than once."

John would be Dr. John B. Hamilton, the surgeon general of the United States, with whom Ellingsworth was on a first-name basis. The two men had been working for the Marine Hospital Service for decades. While Dr. Hamilton had turned to a management role, Dr. Ellingsworth became known as an expert in communicable diseases. One might not be able to tell it by looking at him, but he'd been credited with saving over three hundred lives, most of it due to quickly establishing quarantine facilities during various disease outbreaks.

But disease expert or not, he was wrong about Alaska. "Someone needs to provide care to people in remote areas of Alaska, just like someone needs to provide care to remote regions of the Louisiana Bayou and Appalachia and the Texan Desert." Nathan stood, his chair scraping against the wooden floor of the ship. "People in these places die every day because of things that a doctor in a city could easily treat."

"Then more doctors should go to those regions." Ellingsworth planted his hands on the desk, two meaty palms with thick fingers. "I have no problem with convincing doctors to go to those areas. What I'm saying is it shouldn't concern the Marine Hospital Service. We treat seamen."

"Not in Alaska. The surgeon general has tasked us with treating the general populace."

Ellingsworth shook his head and muttered something under his breath.

Nathan held in his sigh—barely. In any other circumstance, he would be grateful to work under such an experienced doctor. But to have Ellingsworth with him in Juneau, when the man didn't even agree with the MHS's goal? When he had no interest in providing care to people living in remote locations?

"We've been over this before, Reid. You've read the same reports I have." Ellingsworth turned and stalked back to the door, where he took off his oilskin coat and hung it on the peg beside his hat. "There's no difference in mortality rates between people in rural areas without access to medical care and people in urban areas."

"That's because diseases spread more rapidly in urban areas—too rapidly to control. Unless we can convince city planners to spread out the new houses and tenements being built, we have little hope of correcting that. But rural mortality rates are different. We can improve those if we simply provide access to—"

"You're not going to change the world. You might have talked John into this fancy new plan of yours, but like I've already told you, it's not the Marine Hospital Service's job to treat the people of Juneau or Sitka, let alone Indians living in villages that take months to reach. I'll give it six months before John revokes funding."

Six months? Nathan's blood turned cold. When he'd presented his plan to the surgeon general, he'd asked for five years to establish a system of care that treated not just sailors but the residents of Alaska as well.

The surgeon general said he could have three years. That didn't seem like remotely long enough, but he might have had a chance of succeeding—if the surgeon general had put him in charge of the project.

Instead, he'd selected Ellingsworth to lead it as chief medical director of Alaska.

Up until about a month ago, Nathan had been somewhat in awe of the man. How could he not be? Ellingsworth had treated enough diseases and led the MHS through enough outbreaks of cholera, typhus, and yellow fever on ships that he was something of a legend.

But within a day or two of being dubbed the chief medical director of Alaska, Ellingsworth had made it clear he thought MHS funds should stay focused on ensuring contagious diseases didn't enter the country through the sailors who traveled the world.

So even though Nathan had been the one to approach the surgeon general about the need for more medical care in Alaska...

Even though he'd come up with a plan to establish a hospital that would treat not just seamen but also the general populace in Juneau and bring five new doctors to Alaska...

He wasn't the one in charge of implementing any of it.

But Nathan wasn't going to let the plan fail that easily. He could still remember what it felt like to stand over his mother's grave as an eleven-year-old boy, still recall how her casket had looked as it was slowly lowered into the ground, still quote verbatim what the doctor had said when he'd pronounced his mother dead.

If you'd gotten to town faster, I could have saved her.

Nathan didn't care how big Alaska was, or how remote, or how difficult travel was in winter. Nor did he care how much Ellingsworth mocked him for studying his map rather than taking in the stunning landscape surrounding them. If he could save even one life by stationing a doctor in a remote place, then he'd have succeeded.

But he didn't intend to save just one life. He intended to save dozens, or maybe even hundreds, like Ellingsworth. And after he did it in Alaska, he'd convince the surgeon general to let him do it again in the Outer Banks of North Carolina and the swamps of Louisiana. In the thick Northwoods of the Midwest, and anywhere else that needed doctors.

He might not have been able to save his own mother, but he fully intended to save someone else's.

2

"This is Juneau?" Ellingsworth huffed, his wide-brimmed hat pulled low over his head, even though the rain had stopped, turning into a thick mist that cloaked the landscape. "I don't know how you talked John into this fool idea."

Nathan had to admit, standing on the wharf and surveying Juneau was nothing like disembarking a ship in San Francisco or Boston or New Orleans.

Townsfolk might have assembled to greet the ship, and dockworkers might have already begun unloading the giant vessel, pushing carts filled with cargo down the gangway. But unlike any of the other places where the MHS had established hospitals, there were no cobblestone streets or buildings with pristinely painted siding.

No. The entire town of Juneau seemed to be comprised of ramshackle log buildings, most of which still had bark on the logs, as though whoever had built them felt that peeling off the bark would have taken too much time.

Though to be fair, none of the more polished cities had a mountain sitting directly behind them. It was majestic, rising nearly straight out of the sea, with some of the town built on a narrow strip of even ground at its base, and the rest built into the mountainside itself.

"We should be putting a hospital in San Diego or Seattle," Ellingsworth muttered. "Those cities have larger ports."

Nathan held in a sigh once again. Sighing seemed like the only thing he ever wanted to do around the renowned doctor. "We've already talked about this. The MHS is in the best position to offer medical services to Alaska."

Or more accurately, they were in the *only* position to offer medical services, because the MHS was the only government agency that employed doctors.

Congress might have established the Marine Hospital Service with the intent of treating sailors and containing diseases from other regions of the world, but that was a hundred years ago, before the Louisiana Purchase or any talk of settling the West. Before Alaska had been bought from Russia.

With the purchase of all that land came greater governmental responsibility. But when it came to providing medical care, the US government had spent the past century ignoring the needs of rural areas and focused only on providing medical care to sailors.

"Six months." Ellingsworth shifted, his large form dwarfing Nathan's. "Even if John doesn't revoke your funding by then, I'm leaving. I want to be somewhere warmer before winter. And don't think I can't talk John into giving me a different position either. Now go secure rooms at the boarding house. I'll wait for our trunks."

Ellingsworth started down the wharf without waiting for a response. Nathan watched him for a moment as he headed toward the log warehouse where the cargo was being taken, his gait slow and steady despite the dockworkers rushing around him.

Why was Ellingsworth so set on only treating sailors?

What if the dockworker behind him stepped on a rusty nail while unloading the ship and developed tetanus?

What if one of the children darting around her mother's skirts got appendicitis later that evening?

Could Ellingsworth not see the plight of the people around him? Not understand that they might desperately need medical care a few hours from now? Or worse, that someone in this very town might have died last night, all because there wasn't a reliable doctor in Juneau?

Nathan gave his head a small shake, then pulled a piece of paper from his pocket with the directions the first mate had given him for the boarding house. They said he needed to go right, toward the heart of town, so he stepped off the wharf . . . and straight into a thick puddle of mud.

He blinked as the mud soiled not just his shoes but the hem of his trousers too.

No cobblestone streets. You're not in New Orleans or Boston or Washington, DC. You're in one of the wettest places in the world.

At least according to that journal article.

But the street hadn't looked terribly muddy. Was all the ground this soft? He could only imagine how Ellingsworth would react if he stepped into such a puddle.

Nathan extricated himself from the mud, only to find the ground beside the puddle was soft as well, just not so soft it swallowed half his shoe.

It brought back memories of another muddy road in a remote place filled with trees and mosquitoes—and his ma's stern voice. She'd tried to sound stern because he'd tracked mud into the house, but there had never been anything stern about his ma. She'd been all kindness and sugar and love.

He swallowed. It had been two decades since he'd heard

her voice, though the passage of time didn't dull the pain that washed over him whenever he thought of her, or of the wildflowers he'd picked to lay atop her casket as it disappeared into the ground.

Nathan drew in a breath, pushing the memories away. He was no longer a boy who loved playing barefoot in puddles, nor was he in the wilderness of Michigan on a remote section of Lake Superior shoreline.

He was in Alaska, and his first order of business was to procure lodging. So he headed down the street.

He didn't get far before a shout sounded from farther down the road, followed by the pounding of animal hooves. He glanced up to find a wagon with four people careening his direction. He dashed toward the side of the street, along with most of the other people in the road—never mind the second mud puddle he had to trudge through.

The wagon rushed past, the man on the bench fighting to control the reins while a panicked woman clutched two children beside him. Shouts and cries filled the air as more and more townsfolk became aware of the runaway wagon.

Dear Father, please let that man slow the wagon. Nathan tossed the prayer toward the heavens, then started racing after the wagon. A doctor would be needed if it crashed.

The wagon veered hard to the right, heading toward a building that looked to be the general store. Two older men sat on the porch playing checkers over a barrel, and a woman and her children were sitting on a bench, likely waiting to be picked up.

"Look out," Nathan shouted, his chest heaving.

Others called out warnings too. But the people on the porch hadn't noticed the commotion farther down the street, and time seemed to slow as they looked up to see the wagon hurtling toward them with only seconds to spare. The two men leaped from their seats, scattering checkers across the wooden planks of the porch, while the woman grabbed her children and dived to the ground, attempting to shield them with her body.

The wagon collided with the porch in a deafening crash, its impact sending splinters of wood flying and a wheel spinning off the wagon. One of the pillars cracked beneath the impact, folding forward so that it half rested on the corner of the wagon.

The porch roof sagged, then groaned. For one sickening moment, Nathan imagined it collapsing, all those boards and shingles crushing the people seeking shelter below. But then the creaking ceased, and though the roof sagged, the remaining pillars seemed to support its weight.

Nathan wasn't sure when he'd started running toward the accident. All he knew was that he was pumping his feet as quickly as he could, wishing for the medical bag that was with his other belongings. He couldn't do much with only the bandages, carbolic acid, and stitching needle in his satchel, but he had to at least try to help.

"Someone get the doctor!" a shout rang out.

But there was no doctor in town . . . except a drunkard. That was part of why the Marine Hospital Service had chosen Juneau for its next hospital. It would take forty minutes or better for the doctor at the Treadwell Mine across the channel to get to Juneau once he was sent for.

Nathan leaped onto the porch and skidded to a halt in front of one of the men who'd been playing checkers. He was clutching his leg, a large gash staining the thigh of his trousers red. "Here, let's put some carbolic acid on this and then bandage it. We need to clean the wound and stop the bleeding."

Nathan fished in his bag for the blue bottle of carbolic acid and a cotton ball. In truth, the cut might need stitches, but he needed to treat injuries in order of severity, and he didn't yet know how injured the wagon passengers were.

"It hurts!" A groan came from the other side of the wagon. "Someone help! My shoulder's on fire."

That sounded like a possible dislocation. Nathan quickly dampened the cotton ball with carbolic acid, then thrust that and a bandage at the man's friend beside him. "Clean his wound with the cotton ball and then wrap it. I'll be back in a minute."

Nathan crossed the porch and rounded the other side of the wagon. A woman and girl knelt on the ground, muddy but seemingly unharmed, but a man lay beside a wagon wheel, clutching his shoulder and groaning.

Beyond him, a boy sat propped up against the wagon, tears streaming down his face as he held his arm. "It hurts, Mommy, it hurts."

"There's Doc Prichard." One of the townsfolk standing near the woman gestured across the street, where an older man with graying hair and a medical bag in his hand stumbled toward the accident with the swagger of a drunken man, never mind it was only three in the afternoon. "Looks like you're in luck. The doc even had his medical bag with him in the bar."

Nathan took a step closer, about to offer his services, but the woman didn't give him a chance to speak.

"That man is not touching either my husband or my son." She jabbed a finger toward Dr. Prichard, her jaw tight. "Someone get Dr. Amos."

"Ma'am." Nathan took another step closer. "I'm a—"

"I'm here. I'm here."

Nathan's words were cut off by another female voice. Then a woman appeared from around the back of the wagon, followed by a towering, broad-chested man with red hair.

There was another doctor in town? Nathan frowned. Had

he just arrived? There was only supposed to be one doctor, a drunkard.

Nathan expected the man with the red hair to head straight toward the driver with the dislocated shoulder. But the woman got to him first, kneeling on the muddy ground without a care for her crisp blue skirt and white shirtwaist. In fact, it was the woman holding the medical bag, not the man.

Why was she . . . ?

Nathan forced himself to stay rooted to the floorboards of the porch as the woman probed the driver's shoulder.

The driver howled in pain. "I thought you were supposed to help me! Crazy woman doctor. Yer just makin' it hurt worse!"

Woman doctor? Nathan felt his jaw drop open. Was the woman in front of him a doctor?

No. The report the MHS had commissioned last fall had said nothing about a female doctor in Juneau. And besides, hadn't someone called for a man named Dr. Amos? Surely the woman's name wasn't Amos.

"I'm not trying to make it hurt more, Mr. Cartwright." The woman's voice was both brisk and authoritative. "I'm trying to ascertain the quickest way to get you out of pain."

"Laudanum," the man howled. "That's the quickest way. Just give me some laudanum. I know you got some in yer bag."

"I'll give you some in about thirty seconds." The woman's hands were swift as they moved over his shoulder, probing muscle and bone just like Nathan would do to determine how badly the humerus had been pulled from its socket.

The woman looked over her shoulder at the tall man whom Nathan only now realized had a tin star pinned to his chest.

Not a doctor, then, but a sheriff.

"Jonas, I need you to hold him. This is going to hurt."

"No," the driver whined, trying to clamber up into a sitting position. But that only caused him to howl in pain again. "Give me laudanum first, then fix it."

"It can be fixed in less time than it would take to get laudanum out of my bag, let alone give the laudanum time to dull your pain."

"Here, give him some whiskey." The drunk doctor ambled closer and uncorked a flask, then knelt on the ground and held it over Cartwright's mouth. "Open up, Jim."

Cartwright did as asked, and the drunk poured whiskey between Cartwright's lips until he started to choke.

But the female doctor didn't let anything about the whiskey disrupt her. In fact, she'd been moving the whole time, nodding to the sheriff as he knelt by the man's head and murmuring instructions about how to hold him. Cartwright was still trying to swallow his mouthful of whiskey when she gripped his arm and gave it a sharp tug.

Cartwright spit out his whiskey and screamed, dampening the front of the woman's shirtwaist with the amber liquid as a popping sound filled the air.

Then the man slid back to the ground, a hand splayed over his shoulder as his breathing slowed. "Feels better already. Thank you, Doc."

The woman didn't so much as flinch at the whiskey now drenching her chest, or even smile at the compliment. Instead she rolled her eyes and turned to the sheriff. "Give him—"

"I'm here." Another woman rounded the far side of the wagon. A woman with rich chestnut hair and green eyes—a spitting image of the female doctor. The new woman took in the situation in front of the wagon with a glance. "Do you need anything?"

"Mr. Cartwright dislocated his shoulder. Give him a small dose of laudanum while I treat Benny." The woman shifted her gaze, looking directly at the sheriff. "I suspect Mr. Cartwright was drunk while driving his wagon. I smelled whiskey on his breath before Dr. Prichard offered it."

The sheriff crossed his arms over his broad chest and moved his gaze to the brown-haired woman who'd been in the accident. She was still kneeling on the dirt but now had an arm wrapped around her son's shoulder. "Is that true, Mrs. Cartwright? Was Jim drinking?"

The woman twisted her hands in her skirt, then launched into an explanation of how the mining claim they'd staked was no good, with barely enough gold to pay for a sack of flour despite all the months of work her husband had put into mining it, so they'd packed things up and had decided to head back to Chicago.

Nathan let the words float past him as he watched the woman doctor work on the boy, who looked like he had a broken arm. Of course, he couldn't say it was broken without examining it himself. But she was going through the exact steps he would to determine whether a break existed and where it might be.

And all he could do was stand there and watch. To be fair, no one else seemed to be injured. The woman and children from the porch might have some bruises, but they were already making their way down the street away from the commotion. And the two older men playing checkers . . .

Nathan forced his gaze away from the lady doctor and turned. He should inspect that gash more closely and see if it needed stitches.

But the man was already limping toward him, holding out the bandage. "Thank you, sir. Appreciate your help. I put the smelly stuff from the cotton ball on it, but I'm gonna have Doc Amos here look at my gash before I wrap it up. Make sure it don't need stitches."

"Doc Amos?" he asked.

"Kate Amos." The man shoved his hand toward the female doctor. "The town doc. Didn't ya just see her fix Jim's shoulder? She's right good at patchin' everyone up, even if she's a woman."

Right. A woman doctor. In Juneau. Whom the whole town seemed to know, which meant she couldn't have just arrived.

So why hadn't she been included in the MHS report on Juneau?

The man limped down the steps, his friend beside him, leaving Nathan alone on the porch. He looked around again, scanning the area a final time to make sure no one else needed medical care. But it looked as if everyone had either gone back to shopping inside the general store or come outside to watch Mrs. Amos—or was it Dr. Amos?—fix up the—

Crack! Something snapped above him, and the pillar that had been propped up on the wagon gave way. An ominous groan sounded, and Nathan glanced up just in time to see an object falling toward him.

Then it slammed into his head, and his world went black.

3

Kate stared at the pages in front of her, trying to make sense of the words in the gray light filtering through the window. Of course, she might be able to concentrate a little better if the rocking chair she was sitting in didn't creak each time she pushed it backward.

How did her sister tolerate sitting still for so long and knitting or reading a novel? Not an article from the *New England Journal of Medicine* on head injuries or apoplexy or heart failure. No. Her sister read fluff.

And liked it.

Kate huffed, shifted again, then tapped her fingers on the arm of the chair and looked up. Her sudden need to fidget fell away as her eyes landed on the handsome, dark-haired stranger lying in the bed on the opposite side of the small room.

What brought you to Juneau, Mr. Reid?

And why did he stay on the porch of the general store after the crash, when everyone else had the sense to vacate it?

The door to the room opened, and her twin sister, Evelina,

peeked inside. "Oh, he's still sleeping. When I realized you were in here, I assumed he'd woken up."

Kate went back to tapping her fingers absently on the arm of the chair. "No, he's still sleeping."

Evelina stepped farther into the room, her rich chestnut hair cascading down her back in thick waves. "He's not unconscious again, is he?"

Kate glanced at the small clock hanging on the wall. "I roused him about forty-five minutes ago, just to make sure his head injury wasn't getting worse. He woke, told me his name and where he was from, and then went right back to sleep."

"Oh, really?" Evelina's green eyes lit with curiosity. "Where's he from?"

Kate frowned. "Washington, DC, most recently, but he gave me a whole list of places. Charleston, San Francisco, Norfolk, New Orleans, and Boston. And he might have said Chicago too. Oh, and somewhere called Marquette. Have you ever heard of it?"

Evelina shook her head. "No. But it seems odd for him to have lived in so many places. He doesn't look old enough to have traveled that much."

"I'd guess he's about thirty. Maybe he has a job that requires him to move every year or two."

Evelina looked at him for another moment, as though she was also trying to make sense of the conundrum before her. Then she sighed and turned. There was something graceful and gentle about the movement, about the way her shoulders rose and fell and even how she turned.

Then again, everything about Evelina was graceful and gentle.

Kate should probably hate her twin for the way she had such a calming effect on everyone around her. But her sister was far too kind to hate, and so the two of them were best friends, even if Kate often felt like a walking ball of destruction next to Evelina.

"Go. I'll sit with him for a spell." Evelina nodded toward the door. "I can tell you're feeling antsy stuck in here."

And that was why she couldn't hate her sister. Evelina was always doing things like this, always finding ways to be kind to others.

"Well? Are you going to leave or just sit there scowling at me?"

Was she scowling? Kate relaxed the muscles in her face—or at least she tried to relax them—but nothing inside her wanted to calm down. Not after being pent up inside this room for over an hour. Not when she knew so little about her new patient. And not while the image of that board hitting Mr. Reid's head kept repeating itself over and over in her mind.

"It's not your fault." Evelina crossed the room and rested a hand on her shoulder. "You understand that you can't blame yourself for his injury, don't you?"

How did her sister do that? Set her at ease without even trying?

Kate was quite certain the only kinds of emotions she ever evoked in people set them on edge. Unless, of course, she was doctoring them. Then people seemed happy with her, even if she was a woman.

She reached up and rested a hand atop Evelina's, and something about the simple gesture brought a small bit of stillness to her soul.

Then her mind drifted back to that afternoon, to the panic that had overtaken her when she'd realized the porch roof was about to fall. "If I'd seen him standing on the porch, I would have shouted at him to move."

"You were treating a broken arm."

Yes. And to be fair, the porch roof hadn't looked unstable.

One moment it seemed like the damaged pillar just needed to be reinforced, and the next, the entire roof had come crashing down.

Kate rubbed her forehead. "I still haven't thanked Jonas for saving him. I can't imagine how much worse Mr. Reid would be had Jonas not realized what was about to happen." After that first board fell and knocked Mr. Reid unconscious, Evelina's husband—better known as Deputy Marshal Jonas Redding—had realized the roof was about to collapse and pulled Mr. Reid off the porch with only half a second to spare before the rest of the structure came crashing down.

"Oh, that's what I was coming to tell you." Evelina snapped her fingers. "I learned your new friend's name."

"He's not my friend. And like I said, he told me his name when I woke him earlier. It's Nathan Reid."

"All right, but do you know what he does for a living and why he's in Juneau?"

Kate quirked an eyebrow.

"He booked passage north on the *Alliance* as *Dr.* Nathaniel Reid, meaning he's a scientist of some sort."

"Doctor?" She frowned. "What's he here to study?"

Evelina shrugged. "What do they all come to study? Either geology or geography or maybe biology. I think Mikhail said something about an expedition of botanists studying the flora and fauna of Southeast Alaska this summer."

"So where's the rest of Dr. Reid's team? And why isn't he in Sitka? That's where most of the expeditions leave from." It was the right time of year for scientists to start arriving but not the right place.

"I don't know, though you could wake him and ask. If he can answer the questions coherently, then his concussion can't be all that severe."

"No. It's best to let him sleep."

Dr. Reid had regained consciousness after being struck by the board and had maintained it while they moved him to her examination room, after which he'd fallen asleep. She'd already roused him once to see if his eyes were dilated, but there was nothing to indicate a serious head injury. "The journals are all claiming that while unconsciousness is bad, sleep aids in recovery following a concussion."

"Is that what you've been reading? A journal article about concussions?" Evelina glanced down at the book Kate hadn't bothered to close. "And here I hoped you'd picked up one of my novels."

Kate rolled her eyes. "I'm sitting still, aren't I? That should count for something."

"Yes, it should. But like I said, I'll sit with him a spell."

Kate looked at the stranger again, running her eyes down his lean body. He wasn't overly tall or broad of chest, not like Evelina's husband, Jonas, or their brother Sacha. But there was something lithe and strong about him, something that made her hate to see him lying there so weak, especially when he'd been on that porch after the accident trying to help others.

If only she had realized the roof was about to give way a few seconds sooner.

"Did Jonas arrest Mr. Cartwright?" she asked.

"He did, and Mr. Cartwright is none too happy about it, seeing how he planned to leave on the *Alliance*. Jonas says he'll need to pay to replace the collapsed roof before he can leave town. You can imagine how Mr. Cartwright feels about that."

Kate winced. She could, in fact, imagine the tongue-lashing Jonas would have received after telling a man with no money that he needed to come up with money before he could leave Juneau. Of course, it served the man right for drinking himself into a stupor and then climbing onto a wagon with his wife and children. "Just tell me Emma Cartwright has a place she can stay with the children."

"Jonas expects Mr. Cartwright to work for a few months over at the Treadwell Mine to pay back the general store. They have company housing, so there'll be a roof over his family's heads and food in their bellies. That sounds like more than they had up in the mountains."

It did. Gold fever was a real thing. Men made such a big deal of coming to Juneau and prospecting for gold, but she didn't know of a single man who'd struck it rich, and knew of only a handful who made enough money to live on. Most men left poorer than when they'd come, and the weather and isolation in the mountains could be particularly brutal on families.

But the Treadwell Mine on the opposite side of the channel was a full-fledged gold-mining and ore-refining operation. With tunnels that ran deep underground, the mine had hundreds of jobs available to anyone willing to work. Of course, workers had to deal with the constant stench from the chlorination plant and the ceaseless pounding of the stamps at the mill that crushed the rock from the mine so the gold could be extracted. It wasn't the type of place most men worked for very long, but the company did provide housing for their workers, so it would be a good fit for the Cartwrights until their debts could be paid.

"I just hope they're able to get back to Chicago soon," Kate muttered.

The bell on the trading-post door jingled, and she frowned. It was after hours, and they were closed for business, but they usually left the door open until dark in case someone came looking for either a doctor or the Deputy Marshal.

She pushed to her feet. "I should probably go check—"

"I'm looking for Dr. Nathan Reid," a thunderous voice boomed from the other side of the wall.

Kate glanced at her patient, who slept soundly despite the

noise, then straightened her shoulders and opened the door that led directly into the trading post.

A large man started toward her from where he stood in the center of the large room, his form almost tall enough to touch the top of the doorframe behind her. He had wide, strong shoulders but the thicker waist of an aging man. He was old enough to be Dr. Reid's father, but the man in front of her was as light-skinned as Dr. Reid was tan, and his face and chin had round, soft features. Everything about Dr. Reid's face and jawline was angular and firm.

"Well?" the man bellowed. Though given his size, perhaps his natural voice was simply ten times louder than most people's. "Are you going to tell me where Dr. Reid is?"

"He isn't accepting visitors tonight."

"Now see here, I'm Dr. Victor Ellingsworth, Dr. Reid's colleague, and I need to see him."

"You'll have to come back tomorrow."

"Step aside. I know he's behind the door you're blocking." The man leaned closer.

Whether he was intentionally trying to intimidate her with his large size or merely trying to get closer to his friend, she didn't know. But she straightened her shoulders and met his gaze. "I don't deny that. The answer is still no."

"Move. Now. I demand—"

"Nothing," Kate snapped, raising her chin. "You get to demand nothing here, because Dr. Reid isn't your patient. He's mine."

"I suggest you listen to Dr. Amos," a familiar voice said from the front door.

Dr. Ellingsworth turned toward the voice behind him, allowing Kate to view Jonas as he stepped into the trading post from the street.

"If Dr. Amos says the patient needs rest, then that's exactly what he'll get." Jonas crossed his arms over his chest, a chest that was more muscular than Dr. Ellingsworth's, even if the men were of similar height and build. "You can return tomorrow."

Dr. Ellingsworth huffed. "And who are you?"

"The Marshal, and I won't feel one bit guilty about locking you up for the night if you don't skedaddle. You heard what the doctor said."

"So that's how it's going to be?" The man looked between the two of them. "Fine. I'll return in the morning, but I fully expect to see Dr. Reid then."

He muttered something under his breath about obstinate female doctors before stomping off, the back of his neck bright red beneath his hat brim.

Jonas stepped aside, allowing the man to leave the building. Ellingsworth slammed the door behind him so hard the windows rattled.

Kate watched him storm past the window that overlooked the road before she finally blew out a breath, letting a bit of tension drain from her body. "Thank you. I was half expecting he'd try trampling me in an effort to barge into the sickroom."

"It shouldn't have taken my presence to scare him off." Jonas headed toward her, his expression grim beneath his short red beard. He wasn't a severe man, but he could put on a formidable front when he needed to. Both Kate and Evelina called the expression his Marshal face. "If he gives you any trouble, let me know."

"I will. For what it's worth, I believe the man is with a team of scientists, which means he should be leaving on his expedition soon."

"But not before your patient recovers and can travel with the rest of his team. How is he, by the way? Is his concussion severe?"

"It doesn't appear so, no." Kate explained that Nathan had woken twice and his eyes weren't dilated—all good signs—then she opened the door to the sickroom.

The moment Jonas spotted his wife, his entire face lit up, instantly transforming him from a serious Deputy Marshal to a loving husband. "There you are, sweetheart."

"Are you finished at the jail?" Evelina headed straight toward him, then pushed up onto her tiptoes and pressed a kiss to his cheek.

"I am." Jonas hooked an arm around her waist and pulled her closer. "Did you save me some dinner?"

Kate was tempted to roll her eyes. It didn't look like Jonas was half as interested in dinner as he was in Evelina. The two of them were utterly besotted. In some ways it was sweet, but there were certainly things she didn't enjoy about living with a couple who had been married less than two years.

"Jonas." Evelina giggled, her voice soft and breathy. "Stop. Kate's here."

Kate glanced toward the door, where Jonas now had his arms wrapped fully around Evelina and was nuzzling her neck. "Yes, Kate is here, and Kate can also hear you. Perhaps the two of you should go canoodle somewhere else."

She'd hoped to embarrass them, but Jonas's smile only grew as he stared down at Evelina. "Canoodle? That sounds like an excellent plan. Come on, sweetheart."

He tugged her toward the door, his eyes riveted on his wife. Kate just shook her head as the door closed behind them. Hopefully they made it into another room before they started kissing. The last thing she needed was someone stumbling into the trading post to find her brother-in-law smooching her sister. Again.

Kate moved back to her chair and picked up the journal article on concussions. She really should . . .

A groan sounded from the bed.

She was out of the chair in an instant. "Dr. Reid?"

"My head," he whispered, his hand moving to his forehead. "It hurts."

"You suffered a concussion."

"The lamp." He kept his eyes shut, his hand pressed to the top of his head, where the board had struck him. "Can you dim the lamp?"

She hadn't lit a lamp. It was still early evening. But she moved to the window and pulled the curtain shut, leaving the log room shrouded in near darkness.

"Thank you." The man breathed a sigh of relief, even though he had yet to open his eyes.

"I don't suppose you have any phenacetin."

Phena what? Kate stepped closer to the bed. The other two times Dr. Reid had woken, he'd been lucid, but now he was mumbling gibberish. Perhaps his concussion was worsening after all.

"I'd prefer willow bark tea to laudanum," he said, his eyes still shut. "Do you have any of that?"

That comment at least made sense. She touched a hand to his forehead. Willow bark tea had been the first thing she'd intended to offer him. She didn't like giving laudanum to people with head injuries. While it dulled the pain, it also dulled their other senses, making it hard to determine if the symptoms of a person's head injury were getting worse or improving.

"Yes, I have willow bark tea and hot water upstairs. Let's get you sitting up, and then I'll fix your tea. Would you like some supper too?"

"Yes, thank you."

"If you can push yourself up, I'll reposition the pillows behind you."

Dr. Reid did as asked, planting his arms on either side of his body and rising to a sitting position.

Or rather, he tried to rise to a sitting position. But the moment he moved his head, he made a heaving sound.

Kate reached for the bucket she'd set beside the bed for that very reason.

But she wasn't quite fast enough . . .

4

Nathan didn't remember the last time he'd been so mortified—or in so much pain.

His head screamed at him as if a railroad spike was being slowly driven into his skull, piercing deeper and deeper and becoming more painful with each second he stayed awake.

But he was still lucid enough to realize he'd vomited on one of the prettiest women he'd ever seen. Not once but twice.

Because it had taken them two times to ascertain that any time he moved his head, he had an uncontrollable urge to retch.

To her credit, the lady doctor hadn't shrieked in outrage or stormed from the room. She'd barely flinched, just like she'd barely flinched that afternoon when the wagon driver had spewed whiskey all over her shirt.

After helping him sit upright and settling a bucket on his lap, she had disappeared for a few minutes, then returned wearing a clean dress and carrying a tray with willow bark tea.

The tea only made him vomit again. And he hadn't even tried touching the bowl of soup and piece of bread she'd brought.

"Don't fret," she said as he dabbed his mouth with the handkerchief she'd thrust at him. "Vomiting is a normal symptom of concussions. And while it can indicate a severe concussion, none of your other symptoms give us cause to think that your injury is worsening. Your eyes are dilating and . . ."

He didn't catch the rest of what she said because his stomach was roiling again, and he reached for the bucket for what was either the fifth or sixth time in the past half hour.

She must have realized what was about to happen because she stepped closer, took the bucket into her own hands, and held it for him. He wanted to tell her not to, that he'd prefer if she left altogether so he could be sick in private. But he had no time to get the words out before another round of heaving overtook him.

She waited until he was done, then set the bucket on the floor beside the bed and sighed. "You need to try lying down. Your head doesn't seem to like being upright."

He groaned at the thought of trying to move, though once again, he agreed with her assessment.

"Did you catch what I said earlier? You have a concussion, but your eyes are dilating and there's no blood in your ears. So I assume it's rather mild, even if your current symptoms have left you indisposed."

Her words flowed over him like a cool stream. Nothing he didn't already know, but there was something comforting in hearing her talk, explaining the symptoms of a concussion almost as though she was reading them straight out of a medical book.

Then she reached out and brushed a wave of hair back from his forehead. It was probably a clinical gesture. Maybe she was checking to see if he had a fever, or she simply wanted to keep his hair clean when the next wave of retching came. But the touch made something loosen in his shoulders and chest.

Was this how his patients in a hospital felt when he touched them? Who knew a simple brush of a hand against a forehead could have such a calming effect?

"Here, use this to clean yourself while I get you some water." Again, she stroked the hair back from his forehead, then tucked a fresh handkerchief that had been dampened with water into his hand.

He couldn't help feeling a bit humiliated as he stared down at it. A gentleman should be the one to offer his handkerchief to a lady, not the other way around.

"Thank you," he said. Or at least, that's what he tried to say. He wasn't sure the words emerged as anything more than a groan.

She stepped away from him, and he dabbed at his mouth, then at a few specks of vomit staining his shirt. He'd ask for a clean one if he thought he was done vomiting, but the pain in his head told him it was going to be a long night.

"Here you go." Dr. Amos was back a moment later, holding out a glass filled with cool water. She took the soiled cloth from him with little fanfare, once again unfazed by a mess that would cause most women to shrink away. "Take a small sip. We need to replace your fluids, but not in a manner that might rile your stomach."

Again, he did as she bade, and she waited patiently while he slowly sipped, then took the glass when he held it up.

"How . . . ? Are you a doctor?" he rasped.

Every last bit of her feminine softness evaporated at the question. Her shoulders stiffened, her chin came up, and the compassionate glint in her eyes turned to green steel. "I became a doctor the same way any man does. I went to medical school, then I apprenticed at a clinic."

That wasn't what he'd been trying to ask. He knew the path women took to become doctors. It wasn't all that different from the path men took, though it certainly involved going to a different medical school. While a class on heart conditions or apoplexy could probably be taught to both genders, classes on the reproductive system or female complaints certainly weren't appropriate for mixed company.

"But why?" he asked. "What made you want to become one?"

Had it been some type of personal tragedy, like what had motivated him to pursue medical training? Or had she simply wanted to do something different, something that not many women did?

"That's none of your concern," she answered stiffly. "Now if your stomach has settled, I'd like to lay you back down and let you rest until morning."

He retched two more times as she helped him move back into a prone position. Each time she handed him a clean, damp handkerchief to wash himself with afterward, but her movements stayed brisk and jerky.

Once she seemed convinced his stomach had settled, she bade him good night and closed the door behind her, leaving him to wonder why she'd turned so prickly.

She was a beautiful woman, but rather than doing what most women did and settling down with a husband, she'd entered a profession that was widely considered a man's domain. There must be a reason for it.

And the fact she hadn't given him an answer only made him more curious about her.

KATE HUNCHED her shoulders and ducked her head against the rain, never mind that it was pouring so hard the droplets pelting against her oilskin coat bounced off the waterproof fabric and up into her face.

Some days, living in Juneau meant a person was going to get wet, no matter what kind of clothing they wore. And today was one of those days.

She didn't care, though. She could dry off after she got home. Mr. Gibbons had arrived from Seattle on the *Alliance* yesterday, and the sooner she spoke to him, the sooner she could get back to the trading post to check on her patient.

Dr. Reid had been sleeping soundly when she left, a good sign he was recovering from his concussion, but she wanted to be back before he woke.

There was hardly a person about on the street, considering it was eight in the morning with rain coming down in sheets. But the dim light from inside the office of the mill told her Mr. Gibbons would be there, just as she expected.

She crossed the loamy ground toward the small office building that sat in the middle of the property, surrounded by two large warehouses. The sounds of whirring saws cut through the rain, growing louder the closer she moved.

She reached her hand out to twist the knob on the door, only to realize she should have worn gloves. The metal was both wet and freezing, and her palm slid against the knob before she clenched it tightly enough to turn it and push open the door.

"Dr. Amos." The young man—Spencer, if she recalled—who worked as Mr. Gibbons's clerk, pushed to his feet the second she stepped inside the building. "Is something wrong?"

He ran his eyes down her, as though it was the first time he'd seen someone in a soggy coat, never mind the two coats hanging on the hooks beside the door were both so wet they dripped puddles onto the floor.

"No, nothing's wrong. I just need to see Mr. Gibbons. I figured it was best to come early."

"But . . ." He glanced out the window, where a sudden gust of wind drove sheets of rain into the windows with even more force.

"Is he in his office?" Kate hung her coat and hat on an empty hook, then wiped her damp hands in the folds of her skirt. "Can I go in?"

"Ah, yes, he's there."

"Good." Kate strode across the plain floorboards of the sparsely appointed room, then knocked twice before pushing the door open.

Mr. Gibbons looked up from where he sat behind his cluttered desk, a pencil in his hand.

"Dr. Amos." The kindly man set his pencil down and stood. "What brings you by on such a stormy morning?"

Kate pulled the envelope she'd somehow managed to keep dry from her pocket and slid it across the desk toward Mr. Gibbons. "I can offer you five hundred and fifty dollars."

Mr. Gibbons picked up the envelope and peeked inside it, then set it back on the desk and took a long sip from his mug. "I told you the price was seven hundred."

"I'll have it by the end of summer. You know not everyone I treat can pay me, but I've been able to save a decent sum."

The businessman rubbed his brow. "I know I promised you that building, but I've had three other offers to purchase it since arriving in town yesterday—one of them at the price of eight hundred dollars and the other two at a thousand."

Kate's entire body turned stiff. "You're not going to sell it, are you? Juneau needs a medical clinic. You understand that more than anyone."

"That's why I haven't sold it yet, but you can't ask me to

wait forever. More people are arriving in Juneau every day. The value of that building is going up, and you're expecting me to hold to a price I agreed to last winter—and the price was generous then."

"Just think where your son would be right now if I hadn't been at the trading post last December." It was probably unmannered of her to bring it up. But it was true. His ten-year-old boy had needed an emergency appendectomy just before Christmas. It had been a brutally cold day, with icy winds coming over the mountains and snow blowing off the ocean, but she'd donned her fur cloak and boots and trudged through the snow to the Gibbonses' house, where she'd removed the enlarged organ from the boy before it burst.

Both Mr. and Mrs. Gibbons had showered her with thanks and a generous payment for her services. But rather than take the money, she'd asked if she could use it as the first of many payments to purchase the mercantile Mr. Gibbons was closing.

As a businessman who owned several mercantiles in Seattle, Portland, and Bellingham, Mr. Gibbons had moved to Juneau, opened up a store similar to those he owned in Oregon and Washington Territory, and hired a team of prospectors to go out into the mountains, hoping to add a gold mine to his list of assets.

But a year and a half later, the hope of finding gold had faded into the grim reality that all prospectors who came to Juneau eventually faced. There might be gold in the mountains, but there wasn't enough to repeat the California gold rush of the late 1840s or the Pikes Peak gold rush in Colorado a decade later, where a common man could strike it rich. No, the gold that surrounded Juneau had such low-grade ore that even if a man managed to find a vein, heavy machinery that cost thousands of dollars was needed to extract and refine it.

But Mr. Gibbons wasn't a dunce, and somewhere in the year and a half his team had been prospecting for gold, he'd realized what Juneau needed even more than gold—lumber. And so he'd built three giant warehouses that could keep uncut wood dry despite Juneau's constant rain, and he'd built another warehouse to house the sawmills needed to cut the wood. Then he'd hired both a manager and a clerk to run the operation, so he could spend most of his time down in Seattle and visit Juneau only a few times a year.

Somewhere in that time, he'd also realized that his store was never going to compete with the general store in town or the trading post the Amos family owned, so he'd closed up that building as well. He and his family had been preparing to leave town and be back in Seattle for Christmas, but then their son George had gotten appendicitis.

"Please, Mr. Gibbons." Kate leaned forward. "I'm just asking for a little more time, only until the end of summer. I already have most of the money. You know I'll be able to get the rest."

The man's shoulders rose and fell on a sigh. "It's not that I don't trust you, Dr. Amos, but I have a policy of requiring payment in full in any of my business dealings. I learned my lesson in that regard the first year I started a business, and it was quite costly. Can't you ask your brother for the rest of the money? We both know he has it."

He did, but she didn't want to bother Alexei. First, because he'd feel he had to say yes, even though he was pursuing several business ventures. And second, because she wanted to do this on her own. Alexei had already done enough for her and for Evelina and the rest of their siblings. He didn't need to sacrifice anything more for her.

"What if there's another boy who needs an appendectomy?" she asked. "Or a man who needs a bullet dug out of his shoulder after his firearm accidentally discharges?"

"Or a stranger who disembarks from a ship and then suffers a concussion while trying to help others after a wagon crash?"

So he'd heard about that. She shouldn't be surprised. The news was probably all around town.

The man took another sip of his dark coffee, then set it back down with a thud, his eyes pinned to hers. "I won't sell you the building for anything less than the seven hundred dollars we agreed to last Christmas, but I'll hold it for you until fall. I'll even give you an extra month and put the deadline at the end of September. If you don't have the money by that time, I'll sell the building to someone else. You can't expect me to keep my offer open indefinitely when buildings are fetching such a high price."

"It's a deal." Though she'd been hoping he'd sell her the building outright for the money she already had, she could hardly complain if he'd just turned down two offers for a thousand dollars.

Kate stood and held out her hand for Mr. Gibbons to shake. He eyed it for a moment, then gave a slight shake of his head and reached out to take it.

She almost asked why he was shaking his head, but that was a gesture she inspired all too often when she was around men. Instead she exchanged a few more pleasantries with the man, asked after his wife and children in Seattle, then left the office and headed back out into the rain, squaring her shoulders against the downpour.

Ever since she was a little girl, she'd dreamed of being a doctor. She'd achieved that dream four years ago, only to realize that she'd had the wrong dream all along. Because it did little good to have a medical license when there weren't any patients to treat.

Moving to Juneau—a town with only a drunkard for a doctor—had solved that problem two years ago. But now the townsfolk needed access to an actual medical clinic, and she would find a way to secure that building, no matter the cost.

5

Nathan woke to the feeling of a hammer pounding against his head. He groaned, keeping his eyes shut and pressing a hand to the throbbing spot, only to feel a bandage wrapped over his hair. He shifted and tried to alleviate the pain, but the hammering increased.

"Are you going to marry my sister?" a voice said from beside him. Not the voice of a man or woman but someone younger.

"What?" Nathan blinked, his eyes springing open.

It was a mistake. The sudden light caused a fresh round of pain to sear his head, and he slammed his eyelids shut.

"Last time Kate stuffed a man in this room and took care of him for a few days, he ended up marrying Lina. Now Kate's the only one left—unless you want to wait until Inessa's old enough to get hitched. That would be about three more years."

"Ah . . ." Again he tried to open his eyes, and again he failed. The light was too bright for him to tolerate. And while there was incessant pounding inside his skull, he still couldn't help feeling as though he'd missed something—like maybe the first half of the conversation, with a person he couldn't even see but whom he guessed to be a boy.

"The lamp," he rasped. "Can you dim the lamp?"

Huffing sounded from beside his bed, then, "The lamp isn't lit, but I can draw the curtains."

"Please," he mumbled, pushing himself into an upright position on the bed.

The sound of footsteps and the whisper of moving fabric indicated the boy was doing as he asked.

Nathan rested for a moment against the head of the bed, then tried peeking his eyes open a third time. The light didn't blind him, probably because there wasn't much filling the room, just a dim, gray half light that trickled in from a small crack in the curtains.

"Thank you," he said to the person he had yet to see.

"You still haven't said whether you're going to marry Kate."

Nathan moved his head in the direction of the voice. Slowly. So as not to trigger any nausea.

He found a native boy of maybe eleven or twelve. The dark color of his hair and eyes and the bronzed tone of his skin left no question as to his heritage. But the boy wasn't dressed as a native. His hair was cropped in the standard haircut of most white boys his age, and he wore white men's clothing.

"Well? Are you going to marry Kate or not?" The boy's eyes bored into him, two accusing black pools.

"Ah . . ." Why did the lad keep going on about him marrying the doctor? And why was he calling Dr. Amos by her first name? Had he said she was his sister?

No, that hardly seemed possible given the obvious differences in their heritage. He must have misheard. "I'm not planning to marry anyone at the moment. Do you mind fetching Dr. Amos, though? I'd like some willow bark tea."

"That's what Jonas always asked for too. And then he up

and married Lina." The boy's eyes narrowed further, and he crossed his arms over his chest. "Why are you in Alaska? Are you running from the law? Hiding from someone? Is Nathan Reid really your name?"

"Ah . . ." He rubbed the top of his head, where, for some reason he couldn't explain, the pounding seemed to be subsiding despite the interrogation. "Yes."

The boy's eyes became even more fierce. "Who are you running from? What crime did you commit?"

"Yes to the name. It's really Nathan Reid. Dr. Nathan Reid. That's the only thing I was saying yes to."

The boy huffed, as though he didn't believe anything Nathan had just said.

Nathan sighed. It seemed a bit ridiculous to give a child his reason for coming to Alaska, but the last thing he needed was for rumors to spread around town that he was running from the law. "My name is Nathan Reid, and I'm here to—"

"Ilya." The door opened, and a soft voice filled the room. Then Dr. Amos stepped inside, and Nathan found himself swallowing. Her hair was down this morning, falling about her shoulders in soft brown waves that held the barest hint of red, and she wore a purple dress with a ruffled collar that made her look kind and gentle. The choice of clothing seemed a bit at odds with the practical, efficient woman from yesterday, but he wasn't complaining. This version of her was lovely in a different way.

"What are you doing in here?" Again, her words were gentle, even though they held an underlying hint of rebuke as she looked at the boy. "Kate told you to leave Dr. Reid alone."

Kate? He blinked. Wasn't that Dr. Amos's first name? And wasn't the woman standing in front of him Dr. Amos? It sure looked like her.

A memory knocked at the back of his mind, something

from yesterday just before the roof had collapsed. Another woman had arrived, a woman who looked awfully similar to the doctor.

"You better get Jonas." The boy—Ilya, it seemed—shoved a hand in Nathan's direction. "He's running from the law."

"No. Wait. I'm not a criminal." Nathan held up his hands, hoping the gesture made him look innocent. "I'm here on official business. I swear it."

The woman turned to the boy, her face stern. "Ilya, why would you say such a thing?"

"I have to make sure, Lina. Last time Kate brought someone here, he ended up marrying you. What if this fellow sets his sights on Kate? One of us needs to ask him some questions."

"Sit." The woman pointed to a chair on the opposite side of the cramped room. "Seeing how you have no proof that Dr. Reid is a criminal, you can sit there until you're ready to apologize for making such a bold accusation."

Nathan expected the boy to instantly turn to him and apologize, but instead he huffed again, then tromped to the chair, his arms still crossed over his chest and his jaw hard. He plopped himself down in the plain wooden chair with an exaggerated sigh.

The woman shook her head, then turned and stepped closer to the bed. "Please forgive Ilya. He can forget himself sometimes. Kate had a quick visit to make this morning, but she should be back shortly."

"Are you and the doctor twins?" He pressed a hand to the top of his head, where his pain had started growing worse again.

The woman's face lit into a beautiful smile. "Yes. Kate's older by about three minutes. My name is Evelina Redding, by the way. You're more than welcome to call me Evelina."

Evelina. It was a beautiful name to suit a beautiful woman.

But Nathan couldn't exactly stop his mind from drifting to a different beautiful woman he wished was standing beside him.

"Your sister is a good doctor."

Her smile only grew. "One of the very best, though not too many men realize that."

It was impossible not to realize it. Someone without any medical training might only be able to see that Dr. Amos was a woman with a medical bag. But a doctor would be able to spot her expertise in a handful of seconds.

"How are you feeling?" Dr. Amos's sister reached out and rested a hand on his brow, likely checking for a fever. "Do you think you can keep down some breakfast?"

He winced. The doctor must have told this woman about how sick he'd been last night. "I better not try any food. My head is still quite painful."

"Kate won't let you leave the sickroom until you can eat a meal and walk on your own."

He'd figured as much—yet another thing that made her a good doctor.

The door opened again, and he looked toward it, hoping to find Dr. Amos, but an Indian girl stepped inside. Nathan guessed she was maybe fifteen or sixteen. She wore her hair in two long braids down her back and had on a green dress that looked similar to the type of dress he'd see on any white girl of that age.

A tall, muscular man followed her into the room. Nathan instantly recognized him as the sheriff who'd helped Dr. Amos at the scene of the accident yesterday.

"There you are." The sheriff moved toward Evelina and wrapped her in his arms, then planted a soft kiss on the top of her head. "Sorry. I got called away just after dawn. But I'm back now."

The sheriff grinned down at her, then lowered his mouth and kissed the woman, right in the middle of the room.

Nathan averted his gaze.

"I'm sorry about my sister." The girl stepped to the bed. "She and Jonas have been married for only a year and a half and, um..."

"They're always like this." Ilya rolled his eyes, still seated on the chair. "If I'd known, I would've begged Lina not to marry him."

"Your sister?" Nathan looked at the two youths, then looked at the white woman still caught in her husband's arms. So he hadn't misheard earlier?

"Half sister," the girl said. "Evelina's father remarried after her mother died."

Ilya hopped off the chair and came to the bed, even though he'd yet to apologize. "Our ma was Aleut. But she's dead now too—like everyone else."

The girl elbowed her brother. "Everyone isn't dead. Alexei, Sacha, Mikhail, and Yuri are all still alive, and Evelina and Kate, of course. Just not our ma or their ma, or Pa or Ivan."

"Ah . . . thanks for explaining." It seemed like the type of thing he should say, even though he hadn't understood half of what the girl told him. That was far too many names to keep track of, even when his head wasn't pounding. "Wait. Is everyone you just listed in your family?"

"Of course," the girl replied.

"I didn't realize Dr. Amos had such a large family." Or one that was quite so complicated.

"Her real name is Ekaterina," Ilya said.

Ekaterina. He rolled the name around in his head. It suited her. And it also appeared that she was Russian. From what he knew of Alaska, most Russians had moved back to Russia after

Alaska had been sold to America, but evidently not the Amos family.

"But she won't let no one call her by her Russian name." The boy tilted his chin in a defiant manner that reminded Nathan of Dr. Amos. "She insists we call her by her American name, since Alaska is part of America now."

Almost as though they could conjure her up by thinking about her, the door opened again, and Dr. Amos stepped into the room, her sharp eyes taking in the activity with a single glance.

"What's going on in here?" She crossed her arms over her chest. "I thought I told everyone to let Dr. Reid rest."

"I was making sure we could trust him." Ilya narrowed his eyes at Nathan again. "I still think he might be a criminal."

This drew the attention of the large man with the sheriff's badge. "What makes you think that?"

"Last time we had a stranger stay here overnight, it was you. And you lied about your name and were running away and trying to hide out in Alaska."

The man settled a large hand atop Ilya's head, then mussed his hair. "You make it sound like I was running from the law. I just wanted a fresh start."

Fresh start from what? Nathan wanted to ask, but there was too much noise in the room now, too many moving bodies, too much chaos.

"Excuse me," he mumbled, then reached for the waste bin and proceeded to retch in front of everyone.

6

Where was that dratted shipping manifest? She'd just had it a minute ago. Kate shifted the stack of papers on the counter of the trading post, searching for the manifest that contained a detailed list of the cargo that the *Alliance* had dropped off yesterday afternoon.

Ah, there it was, underneath the ledger she'd been filling out, not at the bottom of the stack of old manifests.

She slid the paper out from beneath the ledger and had just started recording the supplies that had been delivered when the bell on the trading-post door jingled.

"I'm visiting Dr. Reid today," a man's voice boomed. "And you're not going to stop me."

Kate looked up to find the large form of Dr. Ellingsworth filling the doorway.

She rubbed her forehead with the eraser on the end of her pencil. She didn't have a valid medical reason to keep the imposing man away from his associate today, though she was half tempted to try just because he was so belligerent.

"Keep your voice down and your visit short. He's still

recovering. Loud noises and sudden movements are particularly disruptive for him."

The man humphed, then tromped away, heading toward the small examination room.

Kate went back to working on the ledger. Yuri would be coming to town next week, and he'd want to take the ledgers from their trading post here in Juneau back to Sitka for Alexei to go over. That meant all inventory needed to be accounted for, along with sales transactions.

It was mind-numbing work, almost as bad as knitting or sewing or cooking, but someone had to do it.

Raised voices sounded from the sickroom, and she frowned. Did Dr. Ellingsworth have to defy every last request she made? Surely she wasn't expecting too much by having him speak quietly.

She left the ledger and headed around the counter toward the sickroom. She'd just peek her head in and remind Dr. Ellingsworth to—

"Don't tell me you're waiting for that charlatan to release you," his voice boomed through the door.

Kate halted, every muscle in her body turning stiff. It wasn't the first time she'd been called a charlatan, but she had to fight off the desire to ram her fist into something each time she heard it. She wasn't some snake-oil salesman who went from town to town selling fake elixirs that promised to heal every complaint a person could imagine. She was a trained doctor with a medical degree and a list of healthy patients.

Which this Ellingsworth fellow might know if he spent all of thirty seconds asking her about her credentials. But he couldn't be bothered, could he? He took one look at her, saw she was a woman, and assumed she couldn't possibly be a good doctor.

The bell on the trading-post door jingled again, and Kate

turned to find a man with a worried look stepping through the doorway. He carried a child of five or six in his arms.

"I'm lookin' for Dr. Amos. Can you tell me where to find him?" His voice wavered as he shifted the child in his arms. "My son stepped on a nail yesterday. Today the wound is all red and puffy, and Cyrus can't walk."

Kate moved closer, her eyes latching onto the obvious injury on the bottom of the boy's foot. It hadn't been wrapped with a bandage, leaving it open to bacteria and infection. True to the father's words, it was red and puffy.

She was about to reach out and touch Cyrus's foot, but the man took a step away from her, cradling his son tighter against his chest. "Where's the doctor? Are you his nurse?"

"Oh, I'm sorry. No, I'm not Dr. Amos's nurse. I'm Dr. Amos."

The man frowned. "But yer a woman."

"Yes, and I'm also a medical doctor. I trained at the New England Female Medical College. Take your son into the second room there while I grab my medical bag." She pointed toward the room, then turned and started toward the sickroom where she kept her medical bag.

At times like this, she wished she had a clinic. Then she'd be able to treat the boy in an actual examination room while Dr. Reid rested in the sickroom. But seeing how she was still several months away from being able to purchase Mr. Gibbons's building, she'd have to make do with using Evelina's schoolroom. Fortunately, it was a Saturday and the room was available.

"I ain't lettin' no woman doctor treat my son!"

She paused, her hand on the doorknob of the sickroom. "No, please. I promise I can treat him. A nail wound isn't something to trifle with. If not disinfected properly, tetanus can develop, and that can be deadly."

"That's why I need to find a doctor."

"I *am* a doctor." Kate took a step back toward the man, afraid that if she stepped inside the room for even a second, he would disappear with his son.

"A different doctor. No woman is treatin' Cyrus. Now where's the other doctor?" The man glanced at the window facing the street. "Someone said there were two doctors in town but told me I wanted Dr. Amos. Clearly that was a mistake."

Kate had a sudden urge to rub her chest, where a deep ache had settled. She didn't know who this man had talked to, only that whoever it was hadn't been mistaken. "There is another doctor. His name is Dr. Prichard, but he might not be in the best condition to treat your son."

The man took a step closer to the door. "Just tell me where I can find him."

She sighed. "In the bar across from the mercantile."

The man's brow furrowed. "At two in the afternoon?"

"At nine in the morning, two in the afternoon, and eleven at night. He'll have his medical bag with him."

"But is he . . . ? Will he be sober?"

"No. That's probably why whoever you talked to said to come to me."

The man's lips pressed into a flat line, telling her there was no way she was going to get any nearer his son's foot. "If you're not comfortable with me treating Cyrus, then you should take him across the channel to the Treadwell Mine. Dr. Witcomb will be able to treat him effectively."

"Dr. Witcomb, you say?" The man looked down at his son, his features softening as he stared at the boy who hadn't muttered a single word during their exchange. "Thank you."

"Can I at least bathe the wound in carbolic acid before you go? It's a basic antiseptic that nurses sometimes use. And it will ensure no germs—"

"No." The man tossed the single word over his shoulder as he shoved his way out the door.

She balled her hands in her skirt as she watched the man pass the window with swift, determined strides.

Did male doctors ever feel like this?

It was one thing to have a person seek care elsewhere if she wasn't able to treat them. But it was another thing entirely to have the ability to treat a child, yet not be allowed to because she was a woman.

It was almost enough to make her wonder if God had made some kind of mistake when he created her.

God is able to do exceeding abundantly above all that we ask or think.

Ephesians 3:20 was her favorite Bible verse—had been since she was a child. She'd clung to it as a girl who dreamed of becoming a doctor, then again as a woman who traveled thousands of miles from her home to attend medical school. She'd quoted it to herself as she fell asleep each night and when she woke in the morning.

But lately the verse had fallen flat. It was one thing to say that God could do above all she asked or thought when she was training to do something unheard of for women.

It was another thing to get to the other side of that training, only to feel like nothing had come of it.

Dear God, can't you . . . ?

What? What could she possibly ask for? That God bring the man back so she could treat his son? That God would somehow turn her into a man so people would let her help them?

Instead she found herself praying that the man would seek out Dr. Witcomb and not Dr. Prichard. She'd lost a miner to tetanus just last fall. Like Cyrus, he'd stepped on a nail, but it had been too late to do much by the time she'd been called to the mine to treat him.

And once she finished praying for that, she prayed that one day someone would walk into her clinic and be excited when she offered to treat them, not offended that she was a woman.

"It's a perfectly good building, and this Gibbons fellow won't sell it to me. It's downright infuriating." Ellingsworth threw his hands into the air as he paced back and forth in front of Nathan's bed. "I don't know where we're supposed to set up a temporary clinic. Every other building in this town is being used in some shape or form. It's almost like having a building is more valuable than having gold."

Nathan looked away from Ellingsworth's pacing, which was doing nothing to calm the pounding in his head. Surely the man knew fast movements didn't help a person healing from a concussion. So why was he pacing? "I'll pay Gibbons a visit after I'm released. Perhaps we can reach some other sort of agreement."

"There's no agreement to reach." Ellingsworth whirled toward him. "He refused to sell."

Nathan pressed a hand to his aching head. "Then perhaps he knows of another building we could use, or perhaps he'll change his mind once he realizes we're here to establish a hospital. You said he thought you were a scientist?"

"Yes. It's the most ridiculous thing I've ever heard." Ellingsworth stalked to the small wooden chair on the opposite side of the room and crammed his large form into it. "Who assumes someone with the title doctor is a scientist?"

"A community that's used to hosting researchers, I imagine."

"It's still ridiculous. How many researchers can possibly be in Alaska right now?"

"A lot, from what I understand. Didn't you read the reports I sent you on Alaska?" Had the man read anything he'd given him on Alaska? "Every one of those studies was commissioned over the past five years, covering everything from geological formations to research on natural fish habitat and marine mammals. There're probably three or four expeditions scheduled for this summer."

"Fine, fine. Perhaps it's not all that odd for someone to assume I'm a scientist." Ellingsworth absently waved his hand, then stood. "Now get out of that bed and get your things. We don't have all day."

Nathan's hand slid up to the top of his head, where the pounding seemed to increase with each moment Ellingsworth stayed in this room. Did the man not realize he had a raging headache and was unreasonably tired? That such things almost always accompanied a concussion? "Dr. Amos hasn't released me yet."

Ellingsworth scowled. "Don't call her that."

"Dr. Amos?" Nathan arched an eyebrow. "Why wouldn't I call her that? She's a trained doctor." That much he was certain of, even though she'd yet to tell him where she'd gone to medical school.

Ellingsworth's mouth fell open for a second before he snapped it shut. "She's a woman."

Nathan pressed his eyes shut. His head hurt too much to deal with this. "You and I both know there are women doctors."

"Yes, who treat female complaints and crying babies. Do you know of any women doctors setting a dislocated shoulder and treating concussions?"

"Sure I do. Dr. Kate Amos. She did an excellent job assessing my condition last night. Just like she did an excellent job reducing Mr. Cartwright's dislocated shoulder and treating his son's broken arm."

Ellingsworth sighed, a great, gusty breath of air that was nearly strong enough to ruffle the curtains. "We'll discuss this back at the boardinghouse. Get out of bed."

Nathan winced. That would involve standing without projecting the contents of his stomach all over the room. "I'm not going anywhere at the moment."

Ellingsworth crossed his arms over his large chest. "Don't tell me you're waiting for that charlatan to release you."

"She's not a charlatan. I spent all of last night and half of the morning vomiting. My head hurts like the dickens—the pain has even increased during the course of our conversation—and I'm pretty sure if I stand up, I'll either faint or vomit. Maybe both."

"Did you get knocked in the head that hard?" Ellingsworth frowned, and Nathan could almost see the impatience draining from the man's body as a look of genuine concern crossed his face. "You say the pain in your head is increasing? Is there a candle somewhere? I want to see if your eyes are dilating."

"Dr. Amos already checked my eyes. They're dilating, and the overall pain in my head has gone down since yesterday afternoon, but noise and conversation exacerbates the headache."

The older doctor bent close to study his eyes anyway, then reached out and probed the lump on his head with gentle hands. "Any unusual drowsiness?"

"Yes, but I've been able to wake each time Dr. Amos has roused me."

"I didn't realize your injury was that severe. This makes me even more determined to get you back to the boardinghouse so I can keep an eye on you. I'll see if I can pay someone with a wagon to—"

"No, I'm fine here. Dr. Amos is doing a good job of taking care of me. I have food and a warm bed. It's quieter here than it would be at the boardinghouse, and I'm not in any danger of my condition worsening at this point."

"And here I thought that woman doctor was just being stubborn when she wouldn't let me visit you yesterday. Had I realized how injured you were, I would have insisted on treating you myself."

"You tried to visit yesterday?"

Ellingsworth rubbed a thick hand over his bare head. "Of course. We might not agree on everything, but surely you don't think me callous enough not to check on you after I learned you'd been knocked unconscious."

Nathan could almost picture it: Ellingsworth charging into the trading post, assuming he'd be the one to administer care, and Dr. Amos refusing him entrance. "I wish I'd been awake to watch that conversation."

The bit of softness on Ellingsworth's face dropped in an instant. "That woman is a shrew. And a charlatan. She might have a pretty face and pretty hair, but don't go getting any ideas. There's plenty of other women in—"

"I ain't lettin' no woman doctor treat my son!" A man's muted voice floated through the wall.

"No, please. I promise I can treat him. A nail wound isn't something to trifle with. If not disinfected properly, tetanus can develop and that can be deadly."

Nathan straightened as he listened to Dr. Amos's muffled response through the door. She was right, of course. Tetanus could turn deadly fast. The MHS lost sailors to it multiple times a year, never mind that they distributed bottles of carbolic acid to every ship and gave clear instructions that it was to be used to clean all types of wounds.

"That's why I need to find a doctor." The man's voice filtered through the wall again.

"I *am* a doctor."

Nathan closed his eyes. *Dear God, please do something to convince this man that Dr. Amos should treat his son.*

He opened his eyes to find Ellingsworth looking at him, even though voices continued on the other side of the door, with Dr. Amos trying to convince the man to let her treat his son and the man stubbornly refusing. Dr. Amos finally let the man know that he could find Dr. Prichard at the bar down the road, and the voices moved away.

"All right. Fine. The woman knows a bit of medicine, I suppose," Ellingsworth muttered in a voice that was unusually quiet for the blustery man. "Probably enough to wash that wound with carbolic acid. And you might have a point about wanting a hospital that treats everyone in the community. I still think trying to get a doctor to every village in Alaska three times a year is dunderheaded, but it's clear Juneau needs a good doctor."

No, Juneau was *supposed* to need a good doctor, but the town already had one. Nathan settled deeper into his pillows, laying his head back until he found himself staring at the rough wooden boards of the ceiling. "You should offer to treat the man's son. I don't trust Prichard to do it."

"I would, but your friend is sending the man across the channel to the doc at the Treadwell Mine. Can't you hear her?"

Nathan listened for a moment, his ears straining to hear past the silence of the room until he could make out the soft feminine voice pleading for the man to take his son three miles south of town and across the Gastineau Channel to receive treatment.

The man eventually agreed, and then the front door

jingled, likely the sound of the man leaving to find the doctor at the Treadwell Mine.

It made Nathan's heart feel heavy. Never once in nearly a decade of practicing medicine had a person refused treatment from him.

But how would it feel to be Dr. Amos? To be perfectly capable of preventing a deadly disease from taking hold of a child but not be allowed to do so, and all because she was the wrong gender?

Nathan rubbed a hand over his face, then met Ellingsworth's gaze. "About that wagon . . . Don't bother finding one. I'll stay here until Dr. Amos releases me, and that's at least another night."

"You're serious?" Ellingsworth thundered.

"Why not? Dr. Amos is clearly a competent doctor."

"She's a woman!" Ellingsworth started pacing again. "Don't tell me a woman can make as good of a doctor as a man. I refuse to believe it."

Nathan shifted his gaze back to the ceiling, not able to watch the man pace again. "She's done a perfectly fine job treating me thus far, and likely would have done the same with the boy a few minutes ago."

"You're only saying that because you're enamored with her looks."

"Visiting hours are over, Dr. Ellingsworth." A cool voice cut through the room, and Nathan pulled his gaze away from the ceiling to find Dr. Amos standing in the doorway, her arms crossed over her chest and her eyes shooting sparks of green fire.

Sparks that were probably a bit more mesmerizing than she realized.

"If Dr. Reid is going to recover, he needs rest, and he's

certainly not getting any with you here. I told you to keep your voice down and not make any sudden movements."

"He's well enough to come with me. I've procured rooms for us at one of the boardinghouses." Ellingsworth whirled on her, a giant of a man crowding a slender woman.

But Dr. Amos wasn't the least bit intimidated. She straightened her shoulders, raised her chin, and met the larger man's gaze head-on. "He's not leaving until he can walk across the room in a straight line without losing the contents of his stomach."

"He doesn't need to walk. I'll hire a wagon to transport him."

Again, the doctor's eyes flashed green fire. It was too captivating to look away from.

"No."

"Stop being so stubborn!"

"I'm not being stubborn. I'm just trying to be as good a doctor as a man. You know, so no one mistakes me for a charlatan." Her lips curled into a tight smile, and Nathan felt himself wincing.

Just how much of their conversation had she overheard?

"I'm certain no male doctor worth his salt would send home a concussed patient who can't walk yet." Her words were about as warm as a glacier, and they filled the room with a layer of ice.

Ellingsworth held her gaze for a moment, his large form still dwarfing her smaller one. Then he let out a huff. "Oh, fine. Keep him here if you're going to be a shrew about it. I'll be able to get more work done if I don't have to watch over someone else anyway."

And with that, he stomped from the room without bothering to say good-bye.

He did, unfortunately, slam the door behind him, and

Nathan closed his eyes against the sudden noise as a fresh burst of pain ricocheted through his head.

"I'm sorry." Dr. Amos was instantly by his side. "I tried to explain you needed quiet and rest, but I fear your friend's skull is made of granite."

That was probably a good way to describe Ellingsworth. The man might be a scholar when it came to communicable diseases, but he'd never won any awards for his bedside manner. "I'm sorry about how he treated you."

She shook her head. "Don't be. He's not the first person to claim I'm incompetent because I'm a woman."

How could she be so calm about it? So accepting of this unfair treatment that would likely disappear if she cut her hair and donned trousers and started calling herself Timothy? "You still shouldn't have to put up with his antics—or the antics of the man outside the room earlier."

"You heard that?" She grew still.

"Yes. I hope his boy gets the treatment he needs."

She turned and moved to the large hutch against the wall that appeared to hold most of her medical equipment and supplies. "I gave his father instructions on how to reach the doctor at the Treadwell Mine. As long as he gets taken there and not to Dr. Prichard, he should be all right. Dr. Witcomb does good work."

She returned from the hutch with a candle, a concave mirror, and a box of matches. "You appear to be feeling better this afternoon."

He flashed her a wan smile. "My head still hurts, but I'm sitting up without retching."

"Can you try eating some chicken broth and bread? I'd like to see if you can keep food down." She lit the candle and stepped nearer, studying his left eye carefully, adjusting the mirror so the light wasn't so bright he had to look away from it.

It brought her face entirely too close. He could smell the trace of perfume on her skin—a scent he didn't recognize but somehow seemed both sweet and flowery. He could also see the little flecks of dark green that mixed with the mossy-green shade of her eyes.

Her proximity shouldn't have made her seem lovelier. It should have drawn attention to a blemish on her skin or a faint scent of sweat, but instead it only made her skin appear creamier, her eyes more striking, her hair softer.

She moved the candle from his left eye to his right, and a whisp of chestnut-colored hair fell from her tight bun to dangle beside her ear. It was almost as though her hair was insistent on making her appear soft and feminine, even though she seemed to put effort into making herself look severe.

Or perhaps she was trying to look important. Authoritative. That would certainly make sense, given the way the afternoon had unfolded.

She finally stood back. "Good news, Dr. Reid. Your eyes are still dilating. Now hopefully you can keep down your food. Shall I go get it?" Her voice was clinical and efficient, but a soft woman lurked somewhere beneath her brisk demeanor. It had to.

And that only made him want to peel back the layers of Ekaterina Amos until he found it. "Yes, please, but you're not allowed to stand near me while I eat."

Her brow furrowed into a quizzical expression he could only describe as cute, even in spite of the tight bun and serviceable green dress.

"I've already soiled two of your dresses. And I'd especially hate to ruin that one."

She glanced down at the dress, the furrow in her brow deepening. "Why? It will clean as easily as the others."

"Yes, but those dresses didn't match the color of your eyes."

Once again she grew still, a faint blush creeping across her cheeks.

And those green eyes that had no trouble staring down a man twice her size suddenly couldn't seem to meet his. "Is that your way of complimenting me, Dr. Reid?"

"Nathan." His throat felt inexplicably tight as he spoke, and it caused his voice to emerge lower than usual. "You should probably call me Nathan, seeing how you've spent the past day cleaning up after me. And yes, this is my way of complimenting you. The green dress suits you well."

"Oh, I . . . um . . ." She shifted from one foot to the other, still not meeting his gaze.

How interesting. She should know what to do with a compliment. He couldn't be the first man to think she was lovely, nor could he be the first man to voice it. Yet he'd clearly made her uncomfortable, and he wasn't sure how to fix it other than by giving her something medical to focus on.

"So about that broth . . . ?"

"Yes, the broth! I nearly forgot." She spun toward the door in a move that was just as dizzying as Ellingsworth's pacing. "I'll be right back, Dr. Reid."

"It's Nathan," he called after her.

But she'd already slipped out of the room, leaving him to wonder more and more about the female doctor who could hold her own against Ellingsworth but who didn't know what to do with a simple compliment.

7

It took another four days before Nathan finally found himself headed toward the sawmill on the edge of town, in search of a man named Mr. Gibbons. He'd spent one of those days in the sickroom at the trading post, and the next two days he'd spent partially in bed at the boardinghouse, with Ellingsworth vacillating between hovering over him, complaining about Juneau, and fretting that they wouldn't be able to find a building to use as a temporary clinic.

Fortunately, the Marine Hospital Service hadn't given them a strict timeline to follow in Juneau, but if the hospital was to be operational for winter, then construction would need to begin in May. And that meant he didn't have time for another concussion, or a broken leg, or a bullet wound, or any other injury.

But now his headache was mostly gone, coming back only around loud noises or when he tried reading. With a few more weeks of slow, quiet evenings and no books, he'd be back to normal.

But unfortunately, the place where he was headed was

filled with noise, and the sounds of saws from inside one of the warehouses only grew louder the closer he came to the mill. In fact, by the time he crossed the soft earth in front of the office building and opened the door, a faint pounding was starting at the top of his head.

"I'm here to see Mr. Gibbons," he said to the clerk behind the desk. "Is he available?"

The young man stood from his desk. "Let me check. What's your name?"

"Dr. Nathan Reid. I'm here as a representative of the Marine Hospital Service."

"Just a moment." The man crossed the small space to one of the two doors at the back of the room, little wisps of sawdust from the floor floating in his wake.

The clerk knocked twice, then opened the door and exchanged a few words with the man inside before pushing the door farther open and gesturing to Nathan. "Mr. Gibbons will be happy to see you."

"Thank you." Nathan nodded toward the clerk as he passed and stepped into Mr. Gibbons's office. The room wasn't very fancy for a businessman who owned a growing list of stores in Oregon and Washington Territory and a sawmill in a boom town. Plain painted boards made up the floor and wall, and the large desk at the back of the room looked as though it had been built of rejected pieces of lumber with a giant knot or an uneven end that the mill couldn't sell. But at least the noise from the mill itself was a bit quieter, and the floor a little less dusty.

"Dr. Reid, I presume?" Mr. Gibbons stepped around the desk and extended his hand, his bushy eyebrows and mustache not quite able to hide the kindness on his face.

Nathan shook the man's hand. "Yes, Dr. Nathan Reid. Thank you for making time to see me."

Mr. Gibbons quirked an eyebrow at him. "Spencer here says you're with the Marine Hospital Service. Does that mean you're a medical doctor? Or are you a scientist?"

Nathan gave a small shake of his head. Ellingsworth had warned him everyone in town would assume he was a scientist, and even though the Department of the Interior was commissioning a constant stream of studies to better understand the territory they'd purchased, it felt odd to have people automatically assume he was a scientist. "I'm a medical doctor."

Mr. Gibbons looked him up and down, almost as though performing some sort of inspection. "What can I do for you, Dr. Reid?"

"I'm hoping for two things, actually. First, I need to place a rather large order for lumber. The Marine Hospital Service has decided to build a hospital here in Juneau." Nathan fished the blueprints for the building, along with an itemized list of building materials, out of his satchel and handed them to Mr. Gibbons. "As you can see, the facility will be quite large, and we are hoping to begin construction in May. In addition to the hospital, we also want a quarantine bunkhouse built on the far corner of the property. There might be times when we need to quarantine sailors, and it's best to do so in a facility separate from a hospital to mitigate risk of diseases spreading. Do you think you can have the appropriate amounts of lumber delivered by then?"

The man stroked a hand over his jaw as he studied the paper. "I should be able to have this to you in, say, four weeks' time. Are you planning to erect some type of structure to keep the lumber dry while the hospital is being built, or do you want the lumber delivered in increments as the building is being constructed?"

Nathan frowned. "I hadn't thought of that, though it makes sense, considering how rainy Juneau is."

Mr. Gibbons grinned. "Not from the West Coast, are you?"

Nathan shook his head. "I grew up in a place where snow comes by the foot in winter, but it doesn't rain for days in the spring and summer. I'll take the lumber in installments, provided you can keep it dry here."

"That's why I have so many warehouses, my friend." Mr. Gibbons clapped him on the back. "But I also suggest building some type of structure on site to house the lumber as it's being used."

"Right. I should be able to make that change fairly easily." He and Ellingsworth didn't have to report every last detail to the surgeon general and his staff, just the large ones. As long as the hospital was built before winter, they wouldn't receive any complaints.

He picked up the blueprint for the hospital off the desk but let Mr. Gibbons keep a copy of the material list. "Now there's another matter of business I'd like to discuss. I'm told you own the empty building on Front Street."

The man narrowed his eyes. "You're the fifth person to inquire about it this week. The building isn't for sale."

The fifth person? So Ellingsworth wasn't the only one who'd tried to buy it. "Ah . . . I'm not looking to buy it, just rent it for about six months. I need to set up some sort of temporary medical clinic until the hospital is operational."

"You want it for a medical clinic?" Mr. Gibbons stroked his mustache, but there was something stiff about the set to his shoulders now, and the kindly look was gone from his face.

"Just a temporary one." Was he doing something wrong by asking to rent the building?

Nathan pushed the thought out of his head. It was ludicrous. What businessman would complain about making extra money? "I'd need to add several walls to the first floor of the building so it can hold multiple examination rooms, but I'll be happy to see that the walls are removed and the building turned back into one large, open space on that floor after I leave. I'm told there's an apartment above the store? I'm here with another doctor, and two more will be joining me once construction gets underway. I'd prefer for us to share an apartment rather than let rooms at the boarding—"

"Do you plan to hire Dr. Amos to work at your fancy new hospital?"

"You mean Kate?" Nathan tilted his head to the side, not quite sure why Mr. Gibbons had brought her into the conversation. "Do you think I should?"

Mr. Gibbons released a laugh so hearty it filled every last crevice of the room. "If you call her Kate, she'll hit you on the head with a board all over again and give you another concussion. She goes by Dr. Amos, and she's quite adamant about that."

Nathan reached a hand up to cover the knot on his head. She'd given him permission to call her Kate, though, on that second day he'd been stuck at the trading post.

He could still recall the way she'd grown still for a moment, her eyes softening, then told him he should call her Kate. Her voice had been almost unrecognizable as she'd said it, sounding gentle and warm rather than efficient and clinical. It was almost like time had suspended around them for those few moments, and they'd been caught in their own little world.

He'd kept calling her Kate the next day as his headache faded and he'd started keeping food down. He'd called her Kate the day after that too, when she'd asked her brother-in-law to find where Ellingsworth was staying and make arrangements for him to move there.

And now he couldn't think of her as anything other than Kate—even if the rest of the town referred to her as Dr. Amos.

"What makes you think I should hire Dr. Amos?" Nathan

tried again. Clearly there was a reason the man had brought it up. "Is she well respected? Does she have a reputation in town as a good doctor?"

"She's an excellent doctor. Performed an appendectomy on my son last winter and saved his life."

An appendectomy? Nathan tensed, the breath inside his chest freezing.

But Mr. Gibbons kept right on talking. "Without her, George would be dead."

"Right." Nathan forced the word through his thick throat and offered the man a stiff smile. "How fortunate she was able to treat your boy."

In truth, Nathan had no trouble envisioning Kate performing an appendectomy, considering her skilled hands and efficient demeanor.

But an appendectomy of all things. His chest started to ache, probably because the blood inside it had frozen solid.

"I keep telling my wife it's a shame Dr. Amos is a woman." Mr. Gibbons shook his head. "Were she a man, I expect she'd be at one of the leading hospitals in the country, specializing in some medical field or another. Instead, she's here, in a place where people have little choice about whether or not they see a woman doctor. Or at least, they had little choice about it—until you."

The knot from the top of Nathan's head decided to double itself and reappear in his throat. Or maybe it sprang up in his stomach instead, because that suddenly felt hard too. "I don't like what you're implying. The town of Juneau is growing quickly. Surely there's room for both of us to practice medicine."

"Didn't you say you'd be bringing in more doctors?"

He had, yes. So many doctors, in fact, that there probably wouldn't be many patients left for Kate to treat—unless she worked for him. But seeing how this hospital was being built to serve not just sailors but the community and outlying towns and villages as well, perhaps there would be a position for a female doctor. He knew of several large hospitals in various cities that kept one on staff to handle feminine issues and treat children.

"I can see how partnering with her would be an asset." But talking Ellingsworth into hiring Kate? After the start those two had? "I'll . . . ah . . . I'll bring it up with my superiors."

"Good on you." Mr. Gibbons smiled, the stiffness leaving his body. "Now, about that storefront. Right now, the building is under contract for sale at the end of September. You can rent the building until then, and if the sale falls through and the MHS can still use it, I'll offer you first refusal rights. Do you have time right now to walk through the building? If you like it, we can discuss the details over lunch, then stop by my lawyer's office and have him draft an agreement."

Nathan raised an eyebrow. "You move quickly."

"Being slow in business never benefited anyone. Shall we?" Mr. Gibbons gestured toward the door.

"Of course." If things worked out with Mr. Gibbons, he just might be able to have the clinic operational by this time next week.

But as he followed Mr. Gibbons out the door and into the thick mist shrouding the town, he couldn't stop the image of a woman with chestnut hair and green eyes from rising in his mind.

She'd known he was a doctor when she treated him, hadn't she? She'd called him Dr. Reid numerous times. Surely she expected him to open up a medical practice of some sort, even if she didn't know it would be a hospital.

But the entire time he'd been at the trading post, she hadn't said a word about him taking her patients. She couldn't be that concerned.

Unless she'd assumed he was a scientist. What if she had no idea that he was a medical doctor?

He needed to go visit her and make sure she understood he was a doctor, needed to tell her that even after he opened the clinic and then the hospital, he had every intention of encouraging her current list of patients to keep seeking treatment from her.

But at the same time, Kate had just sent an injured boy three miles south of town and across the Gastineau Channel to get care. And while that might work for a condition such as tetanus and an infected cut, needing to travel three miles could mean the difference between life and death for something like a bullet wound.

It seemed that even with Kate living in town, the people of Juneau still needed better access to medical care. He wasn't going to apologize about offering it.

8

Alexei Amos adjusted the sails on the sloop, steering the sailboat with a small cabin through the shallow waters of the Gastineau Channel toward Juneau. He sighed as he glanced up at the sky, which shrouded the mountains in such a thick layer of clouds that he couldn't see the tops of them. Juneau was always so dreary. Stuck in a valley with mountains from the mainland on one side and mountains from Douglas Island on the other, the gold-mining town was constantly covered with dense gray clouds, since the moist air from the ocean always got trapped between the peaks.

It was the thing he disliked most about visiting. Sitka, where he lived, had its share of mountains and water and rain, but it was still sunny half the time, the wideness of the sound and proximity to the open ocean creating less opportunity for clouds to form between the mountains.

But seeing how he hadn't set eyes on the family that lived in Juneau since Christmas, and seeing how he wouldn't be staying in Juneau very long, he could endure a couple days of dreary weather.

Alexei pointed the nose of the boat toward an open slip along the wharf, then let down the sail . . .

And frowned.

A familiar canoe was tied to the wharf, though that wasn't the part that had him frowning. He'd expected to find his family's canoe here.

It was the skinny form of a twelve-year-old boy with tan skin and black hair climbing onto the wharf that he frowned at.

What was Ilya doing in the canoe during school hours?

The sloop slowed to a stop, gliding into place just behind the canoe. Alexei tied off the boat, then grabbed the ladder and took the rungs two at a time, hauling himself onto the wharf in record time.

"Ilya."

The youngest Amos sibling whirled around, a giant smile plastered across his face. "Alexei!" He darted forward, throwing himself at Alexei.

Alexei caught him, then swung the boy up into his arms, his muscles straining to heft the brother he'd once lifted with ease. "What has Evelina been feeding you? I swear you've put on twenty pounds since Christmas."

Ilya laughed, but even that sounded deeper than he remembered. "Lots of stew and bear."

It seemed as though Ilya had grown an inch since Christmas too. *That'll teach me to stay away almost four months.*

"I can see that, but shouldn't you be in school?" Alexei set his brother down and took a step back.

Ilya smiled again, his dark eyes bright with excitement. "Kate needed me to take medicine across the channel."

He raised his eyebrows. "It must have been a pretty big emergency for her to pull you out of school for that."

The boy shrugged. "Not that big of an emergency; otherwise she would have gone with me."

Alexei humphed. That's exactly what he'd been thinking.

Ilya slid his hand into his pocket, then rummaged around before pulling out a small, misshapen bit of gold. "Look what I found!"

"Uh-huh. I'm only going to get excited about that if you found it before school started. Because if you tell me that you skipped school to go prospecting, then I'll be confiscating the gold and giving you extra chores to do every day for the next week."

Ilya's eyes widened, and he stuffed the gold back in his pocket. "I didn't exactly skip school. Kate said I could go prospecting after I dropped off the medicine, and I found this new spot on Douglas Island. I had her permission."

"Did you have her permission to miss so much class time?"

Ilya winced, then looked away. "I didn't mean to. I didn't realize how late it was. And you don't need to worry about it hurting my future or nothin'. I know everything Lina's teaching."

Alexei shoved a hand through his hair. It wasn't the first time he'd heard Ilya whine about school. Ilya was too bright for the afternoon classes Evelina held for Tlingit children who were learning to read and write English. Inessa was in the same position, far too advanced for Evelina's lessons, but she sat in the classroom anyway, doing other, more difficult assignments.

Ilya, on the other hand, didn't want to do different assignments than his friends, but he was too advanced to do the same work as everyone else.

"You should come with me to Douglas Island." Ilya gripped Alexei's hand and swung him around toward the canoe. "I can show you what I found. The composition of the rock is interesting. There's a bunch of phyllite, but then I found a quartz vein with some pyrite and sphalerite, and then the surface gold. I'm going to head back as soon as school is done."

"No, you're going to stay and have dinner with your family, especially since we'll all be together."

The boy's shoulders deflated, and his lower lip poked out in a pout that assured Alexei his youngest brother was still more boy than man. "Can I at least go tomorrow after school?"

This was why school was nearly useless for the boy. Ask him to read *Swiss Family Robinson* and do a report on it, and it would take him six months. But he wouldn't be able to tell you half of what he read.

Ask him to read a geology tome, and he'd be mesmerized for hours. Then he'd spend his free time exploring the mountains and explaining the various rock compositions, how scientists suspected they'd formed, and if there might be any precious metals like gold, silver, or copper in them.

Sometimes it seemed like Ilya knew more about geology than the teams of geologists the Department of the Interior kept sending to Alaska for research.

But that still didn't mean he should be skipping class. Especially not at twelve years of age.

"Alexei."

Alexei turned to find Grover Hanover, the owner of the green grocery store, headed his way.

"Do you have a minute?"

"Sure," Alexei said, then nodded at Ilya. "Get to school. Now."

"But it's almost done for the day. Can't I—?"

"No. The only thing you can do is go to school. Do I make myself clear?"

The boy huffed and stormed off.

Alexei gave his head a small shake, then moved his gaze to

Grover. But he couldn't help keeping an eye on the boy over Grover's shoulder as he headed toward the trading post.

Alexei ended up speaking to Grover for longer than he expected. There had been a problem with worms in several of his most recent produce shipments, and Grover wanted to know if they could find another supplier in San Francisco.

Since Alexei was headed to San Francisco after his stop in Juneau, he agreed to spend time looking for a new supplier, but that led Grover into a rather lengthy explanation of just how Alexei might go about finding a new supplier, and what things he should look for before signing a shipping contract.

Alexei had been in town for almost an hour before he finally found himself heading toward the trading post across the street. It wasn't a pretty building—none of the trading posts his family had scattered throughout Alaska were—but it was large enough to hold everything from flour and cornmeal to leather saddles and furs to tents and pickaxes and gold panning supplies.

The moment he pushed open the door, the smell of leather and coffee and grain mixed together, making the trading post smell similar to the one they owned in Sitka. And in Ketchikan and Wrangell and, well, just about every other settlement in Alaska.

Kate stood at the counter, taking money from a group of men buying prospecting supplies, and he could hear Evelina's voice filtering through the schoolroom wall as she taught her students.

Kate opened the cash register and handed one of the men his change. "Have a good afternoon, gentlemen. Good luck with your prospecting, and remember we're always here should you need anything else."

They smiled at her, then muttered their good-byes. Alexei

held the door for them as they tromped out into the foggy afternoon.

"Alexei?" Kate blinked at him.

Clearly Ilya hadn't said anything about seeing him, but was it too much to expect his sister to smile when he greeted her? After all, they hadn't seen each other since Christmas.

"Is something wrong?" He headed toward her.

"I just . . . I wasn't expecting you. You didn't come because of my note, did you?"

"What note?"

"The note asking you—" Her lips snapped shut and she shook her head. "No, you wouldn't have gotten it. You would have left Sitka on Tuesday, right? And I sent the letter Monday." She peered over his shoulder at the door, as though expecting someone else to walk inside.

He looked over his shoulder too, but when the door stayed shut, he moved his gaze back to Kate. "Are you expecting someone?"

"Where's Yuri?"

He frowned at the mention of their youngest full-blooded brother, who was all of twenty-one. "In Sitka."

She blinked at him again.

"Why are you looking at me like that? We rarely come to Juneau together. One of us needs to stay home and run the shipping office."

"But Yuri is supposed to take me on my medical trip, the one we do every spring. I've cleared my schedule here and sent word to Ketchikan and Wrangell and Petersburg. The tribes are expecting me. Surely you remember."

"Of course I remember. That's why I'm here. To take you on your trip before I head to San Fransico."

"But—"

"Alexei!" The door to the schoolroom flew open, and Ilya darted toward him, a giant smile plastered across his face, as though they hadn't just seen each other at the wharf.

A group of children burst through the doorway behind him, indicating Evelina had just dismissed school. Ilya rushed forward to give him another hug.

"I hope you learned a lot during that last hour of school," he muttered.

A hint of red tinged Ilya's cheeks. "I just read my geology book. But don't tell Lina. She thinks I was reading *The Last of the Mohicans*."

Alexei shook his head, then opened his arms to Inessa, who stood waiting a few feet away. She moved gracefully into his embrace, her steps so soft and quick she reminded him of her mother, an Aleut woman who had been his father's second wife. She'd evidently passed down her athletic grace to Inessa.

"We were expecting Yuri." She gave him a squeeze, then released him. "But it's nice to see you too."

"Is it?" He slanted a glance at Kate. "I'm not so sure your sister's happy to see me."

"We're all happy to see you." Evelina stepped into his arms, her hug akin to being wrapped in a warm blanket.

"I'm perfectly happy to see Alexei," Kate said, raising her chin.

Evelina stepped away from him and laughed. "Then why are you glaring at him?"

"I'm not glaring, I was just expecting Yuri to accompany me on my trip, that's all."

Alexei crossed his arms. "You make it sound like I'm unable to sail a boat."

"It's not that."

"Then what?"

"Oh, fine." Kate snapped the account ledger closed with a thump. "If you want to know so badly, I'll tell you. I'm going to be treating patients on this trip."

"Yes. I know. That's the point of a medical trip, Kate."

"Yes, but you have the bedside manner of a toad."

His siblings erupted into laughter, the noise so loud it filled every last nook and cranny of the trading post.

"Did you hear that, Inessa?" Ilya wheezed. "Kate just called Alexei a toad!"

"I did not." Kate busied herself sorting through the stack of shipping manifests on the counter. "I said he had the bedside manner of a toad, and it's going to cause problems."

"And tell me, sister." Evelina dabbed her eyes with her handkerchief. "How does a toad behave at someone's bedside?"

"He sits there with a glower on his face and stares," Kate quipped, as though she hadn't even needed to think about her answer. As though she'd already spent a good deal of time contemplating how similar he was to a toad. "There's no smiling or presents for the children I treat, and he never, ever gets the patients to laugh."

"But Yuri does all those things," Inessa said, her voice hitching on another laugh.

"Yes." Kate sent him another glare. "He does."

So that's why Kate wanted Yuri to accompany her. He should have guessed. Yuri had never met a stranger—or a person he couldn't get smiling inside of thirty seconds.

Alexei could easily imagine Yuri setting a nervous child at ease so Kate could look down the child's throat or set a broken arm.

No one had ever accused him of setting people at ease. He was much better at setting them on edge. But that didn't change anything. "Yuri might make a better travel companion, but I have business to conduct in the villages where you're stopping, so I'm the one who'll be accompanying you. Though I'll try to be a bit less, er, toad-like."

Evelina straightened, her eyes filling with questions. "What kind of business?"

"We're changing the shipping route for the *Aurora*. The canneries we service will need to find a different shipping company to work with. This means the deliveries we make to the native villages around the canneries over the spring and summer will be condensed into one trip at the end of May. We'll still keep our typical October and February deliveries in place, but I wanted to personally inform the villages and cannery managers of our changes."

"You're changing the shipping schedule that much?" Inessa's eyes widened. "The Sitka Trading Company has been running that route for sixty years."

"Yes, but if we use the *Aurora* to run between San Francisco and Tokyo every summer, we can triple its profit margin. It's a business decision, pure and simple."

"I don't like it," Evelina crossed her arms over her chest. "That ship was built for sailing through icy waters. Shouldn't its primary route be in the north, regardless of the money it does or doesn't bring in?"

Alexei reached out and wrapped an arm around his sister's shoulder. He understood what she was saying. The *Aurora* had a special place in all of their hearts. He'd come up with the design while studying naval architecture in San Francisco, and the shipyard that his family owned in Sitka had built it the year after his parents died.

Over the past decade, the *Aurora* had become known for its ability to sail quickly and navigate through icy conditions. But other shipping companies had taken note and started commissioning similar vessels from the shipyard, built with six-inch-thick oak boards, an iron frame, and a double-lined hull, just like the *Aurora*. The outer hulls were all made of Australian ironwood too. In fact, the Revenue Cutter Service would be picking up their own double-hulled clipper—the URCS *Jefferson*—next week. They'd contracted for the ship to be built last summer, and its maiden voyage would be spent visiting the numerous native villages along the Alaskan coast this summer, even traveling up to Barrow. It would deliver medical supplies and food, as well as transport a doctor.

He couldn't complain about that. His family had been running those routes out of charity ever since Russia had pulled out of Alaska, and a part of him was happy to know that those responsibilities would now be overseen by a government agency.

But handing over those routes to the RCS also felt like the end of an era. It meant Kate wouldn't take a trip to Barrow with their brother Sacha this summer to treat the tribes that lived in the far north. It meant Sacha, who had captained the *Aurora* until he'd gotten married last summer, wouldn't be able to meet with the various chiefs and elders along the coast. It meant changes in so many ways, and while it was nice to know the Aurora would actually make them money this summer, his heart still felt heavy.

The door to the trading post opened, jingling the bell above it. Alexei turned to find a man in a three-piece suit stepping inside.

The man glanced around at everyone, then his eyes settled on Kate, and he swiped his hat off his head and took a step forward. "May I have a word, Kate?"

Kate? Alexei looked at his sister, waiting for her to demand that the man call her Dr. Amos. But the correction never came. Instead, Kate went to meet him by the door with a smile on her face.

An actual smile. Who was this stranger? And what had he

done to get Kate, of all people, to smile and let him use her first name?

"Don't worry," Ilya whispered in an overly loud voice. "He swears he's not a criminal."

"Oh, Ilya." Evelina huffed out a laugh. "Not that again. I'm certain Dr. Reid is an upstanding citizen. Leave the poor man alone."

"And just who is this Dr. Reid?" Alexei asked, not quite able to take his eyes off the stranger.

"He's a scientist of some sort," Evelina answered. "He came here on the *Alliance* but ended up with a concussion when he tried to help a family after their wagon crashed. He spent a few nights in the sickroom recovering before Kate declared he was well enough to leave."

"What's his first name?" Alexei tilted his head to the side, still studying the stranger. "Do you know?"

"Nathan."

Dr. Nathan Reid. Why did the name sound familiar?

Alexei watched them for a few more minutes. The man had a pleasant look on his face the entire time he spoke with Kate, and then he tried giving her something.

Kate shook her head and crossed her arms over her chest.

Rather than get upset, amusement lit the man's eyes, and the corner of his mouth tilted up into a half smile.

Kate stiffened in response, but that only made the man smile more. Then he said something else, tucked some bills into the crevice between Kate's two crossed arms, and left.

She stood there for a moment, staring at the door. Alexei couldn't see the expression on her face, but something about her stance gave him the impression she was at a loss for words, never mind she had a tongue as sharp as the fleshing knives sitting on the shelf against the wall.

She finally slid the money into her pocket, then turned and

came back to the group. But her shoulders weren't as stiff as before, and her smile crept easily back onto her face.

And that was enough to make Alexei wonder how much he didn't know about this Dr. Reid, the man who had somehow managed to turn his prickly sister soft.

9

Nathan strolled down the street toward the store that was already being converted into a medical clinic, his steps light. Visiting Kate Amos had that effect on him.

And it appeared that his visit had a positive effect on her too. She'd smiled at him and had even blushed when he'd thanked her for taking such good care of him.

But he hadn't made sure she knew he was a doctor. Hadn't told her he was in Juneau to establish a hospital. Not with her family there. That wasn't a conversation he wanted to have in front of a group of onlookers.

The Amos family was something of a legend in Alaska. More Russian than American in terms of heritage, they had called Alaska their home for over ninety years and owned a trading company and a shipbuilding company, both based in Sitka. The trading post, where he'd just been, was their post in Juneau.

The Amos sisters were something of an enigma. Kate might be a female doctor, but her twin sister, Evelina, had an equally unheard-of profession. She wasn't just married to the Deputy

Marshal; she was also a lawyer. She had even filed—and won—a lawsuit against the Department of Education over whether native parents could remove their children from Indian boarding schools.

If Nathan had to guess, he'd interrupted a visit from one of Kate's brothers when he'd entered the trading post earlier, but he didn't know which one. Alexei was the most well known, since he ran the trading company, but she also had a brother who was a rather famous explorer, and another who'd been a lifelong sea captain and was now building ships, and another who was . . . well, he wasn't quite sure what the next to youngest Amos brother did.

He'd have to ask Kate sometime. After he made sure she knew that he was a medical doctor and why he was in Juneau—and that he didn't intend to take any of her patients from her.

He needed to have that conversation sooner rather than later. Maybe then . . .

What?

What was he hoping would happen after he told her?

And what if, despite his best intentions, the new clinic and hospital ended up taking patients away from her, like Mr. Gibbons suspected?

Nathan rubbed a hand over his face. Alaska was so vast, and the medical needs so great, surely there was room for both a new hospital and Kate's practice. Yet there were parts of his conversation with Mr. Gibbons that he still couldn't wipe from his mind.

So he'd pay Kate another visit tomorrow. He'd wait until after work, then ask her if she wanted to go for a walk along the beach. Hopefully she'd say yes, and then—

"Reid. There you are." Ellingsworth stormed down the street toward him, waving a letter in his hand. "Where have you been? I've been searching all over for you."

"I stopped by the trading post to—"

"Never mind. It doesn't matter," Ellingsworth huffed. "There's been an emergency. I'm leaving town on the ship that's in port."

"You're leaving?" Nathan's gaze drifted across the street, where a three-masted ship was tied to the wharf. "Why? Where are you going?"

"There's been an outbreak of typhus at the MHS hospital in New Orleans. They're trying to keep it contained so it doesn't affect the general population, but the staff has it quite bad. It came in on one of the ships, then somehow spread to another ship, which turned around and came back to port about a day later when they realized they had an outbreak." Ellingsworth dabbed his brow with a handkerchief, his face turning paler with each word he spoke. "The hospital director has already succumbed, as have two other doctors."

"We've already lost three doctors?" He didn't like the sound of this.

"Yes. I need to replace the director, unless you want to do it, but either way, one of us needs to get on that ship. This letter was written over two weeks ago." Ellingsworth handed him the letter. "Heaven only knows how bad the situation is now."

"The MHS wants you to go? Not me?" He'd spent two of the last three years in New Orleans. It seemed odd that they'd ask for Ellingsworth rather than him.

"They don't care which one of us goes, but I've had typhus before and survived. That makes me more likely to survive it again, should I contract it. Have you had typhus?"

Nathan shook his head. "No."

"That settles it then." Ellingsworth plucked the letter out of Nathan's hand, hastily folded it, then shoved it back into the envelope. "Besides, putting a hospital in Alaska was your idea. You should be the one who stays to get it started."

Ellingsworth was right. The last thing Nathan wanted to do was walk away from Alaska now, not when he had that map at the boardinghouse filled with proposed routes for traveling doctors. Not after he'd just written the surgeon general to ask if seven doctors could be stationed in Alaska instead of five.

"I need to go pack. The *Thunderhead* is only going to be in port for a couple more hours." Ellingsworth spun on his heel, ready to race back to the boardinghouse, but Nathan held out a hand to stop him.

"Wait. One more thing. When you're in New Orleans, will you let me know if there are lice?"

Ellingsworth frowned. "Lice? Whatever for?"

"I read a journal article, and it noted how lice always seem to be present during a typhus outbreak. We know typhus spreads most readily in cramped living conditions with—"

"Don't tell me you think typhus is spread by lice." The large man rolled his eyes. "I thought I could count on your support of the germ theory. Now you think diseases are spread by insects rather than germs?"

"It's possible that the lice might carry the germs."

Ellingsworth just shook his head as he walked off, muttering something about not having time for such ridiculous nonsense.

10

Petersburg, Alaska; Two and a Half Weeks Later

Alexei made a terrible nurse. Not that Kate had expected anything different, since they'd already discussed he had the bedside manner of a toad. But she certainly missed having happy, easygoing Yuri on her spring medical trip.

Alexei, on the other hand, couldn't seem to stop glowering at her patients, even though he'd promised to be less toad-like. And he didn't even help all that much. He spent most of his time at each village visiting the chief or meeting with the cannery manager and explaining the changes to a route that their family had been running for over half a century.

But she couldn't complain about his whereabouts or bedside manner at the moment, because she was currently standing inside a longhouse with half a dozen other women, staring down at a heavily pregnant woman who was only a few hours away from dying.

X'unéi moaned weakly, her hands clutching her distended abdomen. "My baby. Please, save my baby."

Kate knew enough Tlingit to understand the faint, broken words, but according to the tribal midwife, this was X'unéi's third day of labor. After such a prolonged birthing, the baby would already be lost.

The shaman—the only male inside the longhouse—took the mother's hand and began chanting softly to one of the spirits, likely with the hopes that his invocations might aid in the delivery.

Two of the other women lit some cedar and began spreading a thin trail of smoke around the walls, which they probably believed would ward off evil spirits.

Kate couldn't claim to understand all the rituals that went along with a Tlingit birth. She only knew that unlike Americans or even Russians, the Tlingit regarded the birthing process as spiritual as well as physical.

But the look of sorrow on the lined face of Ldaneit, the midwife who'd overseen the birth of each child born in Petersburg for the past fifty-two years, confirmed everything Kate's medical training had taught her. No amount of chanting or burning of incense was going to save the baby's life. And probably not the mother's either.

"Let me check her," Kate whispered, kneeling down beside Ldaneit and raising the blanket covering X'unéi's legs.

It took her only a few minutes to see for herself what the midwife had told her when she'd first entered the longhouse. The baby's back was stretched across the opening to the birth canal. Not its head, which was the optimal position for delivery. Not its feet, which wasn't nearly as good of a position but usually meant the baby could still be delivered. Not even its buttocks, which was an even worse position for delivery but was still manageable.

But with the baby's back stretched across X'unéi's cervix, it was impossible to deliver the child.

"Have you tried moving the baby?" Kate rose and went to the basin of clean water, where she washed her hands, then rubbed them with carbolic acid from her medical bag.

"Multiple times," Ldaneit answered. "The mother screams in pain each time. Her stomach is too small for the baby to move. There is no fluid for the babe. There never has been."

"Are you sure her fluid hasn't broken?" Kate pressed a hand on X'unéi's abdomen for what was maybe the third or fourth time since she entered the longhouse. Given how prominently she could feel the baby, she'd assumed X'unéi's fluid had broken over a day ago.

But the midwife was shaking her head. "No. Her fluid never broke. She never seemed to have any. I could feel the babe for the whole pregnancy. I can try turning the babe again, but I'm worried it might cause bleeding."

A sickening knot twisted in Kate's stomach. So very little was known about what happened inside a mother's body during pregnancy. But it was possible for the uterus to rupture, and that meant certain death for both the baby and the mother. Unfortunately, trying to turn a babe too forcefully was one of the things that could rupture a woman's uterus.

X'unéi's eyes suddenly sprang open, and she clutched her belly, then released a low keening wail. Kate put her hand back on the woman's abdomen and felt the uterine wall hardening with the contraction. But there was no sense in telling X'unéi to push, because there was no way for the baby to descend into the birth canal.

"Get him out!" Agony laced the woman's voice. "Please. Someone get my baby out."

Kate settled her palm over the woman's hand and gripped hard. "The baby isn't going to be born the normal way. It's not in the right position for that, and we can't move it without causing bleeding. But there's a surgery I can do, one where I put you to sleep so you can't feel any pain and then cut into your uterus and take the baby out surgically."

X'unéi's brow knit, even though her eyelids were half closed with exhaustion. "Will the baby live?"

"I believe your baby is already dead." Her tongue tripped over the words, and only half because of her stilted Tlingit.

The shaman quipped something Kate didn't understand, his voice harsh, then he began another chant. But none of the other women inside the longhouse looked surprised by what she'd said. After three days of labor, they were hoping to save the mother, not the child.

X'unéi whimpered, a tear streaking her cheek. "If you don't take the baby out, I'll die too."

"Yes," Kate answered, even though the woman hadn't phrased her words as a question.

"Then do the surgery."

"I need to ask your husband."

X'unéi's eyes were already drifting shut as she said, "Tell him I want it. Tell him it's the only way."

Silence filled the large open space of the longhouse as Kate gave X'unéi's hand another squeeze; then she turned and walked toward the large double doors.

A man was standing just outside, his face pale despite his tan skin. "Were you able to help? What news do you have?"

Kate swallowed. "The baby is stuck."

"Are you sure?"

She pressed her eyes shut, wishing she could give him any other answer. "Positive. There's only one course of action, and if we don't take it, your wife will die along with your child."

Some of the men who had been standing nearby drifted closer, including Alexei and the chief. The chief went directly to X'unéi's husband and rested a hand on the man's shoulder. There was something familiar about the action, something indicating a close enough relationship that Kate found herself wondering if this might be the chief's son.

Which meant she couldn't mess up the surgery she was about to propose.

She took a deep breath and described the procedure, explaining that the baby was already dead, but if she didn't take it out, X'unéi would die too, and the best way to take the babe was to cut into X'unéi's uterus.

Some of the men looked aghast at her suggestion, but Kate explained that the uterus should heal fine, and X'unéi would be able to bear more children.

X'unéi's husband seemed to already understand it was the only chance to save his wife. When he finally gave his permission, Kate headed back inside the clan house, gave X'unéi some laudanum, then washed and sterilized her hands and did the same with her scalpel.

KATE LEANED against the railing of the sloop, staring at the village of Petersburg and the first in a series of three longhouses, where she'd spent most of the day. Night had nearly swallowed the structures and the mountains behind them, but not quite. Alexei had convinced her to come back to the sloop about an hour ago, after spending eight hours tending X'unéi and her precious baby girl following the caesarean section.

Part of her had wanted to stay in the longhouse all night, but having been kicked out of their beds for the past two nights, the rest of the clan wanted to sleep in their house, and she wasn't about to spend the night in a room filled with Tlingit warriors. So she'd left careful instructions with Ldaneit and had promised to return again at dawn.

Footsteps sounded on the deck behind her, and a moment later, Alexei leaned his elbows on the railing, surveying the mountains that cradled the small native village. "I can't believe the baby survived."

"Neither can I, not after such a long labor." At one point, when she'd rested her hand on X'unéi's stomach earlier that day, she'd thought she felt a slight movement. But then the babe had grown still, leading her to believe it was dead. Now, looking back on things, it made her wonder if a babe had trouble moving when the mother didn't have any fluid. If other doctors and midwives had also incorrectly thought that a lack of movement meant a babe had died.

Even now, hours later, she could still recall the feeling of joy that had surged through her when she'd pulled the baby through the incision, not to find a stiff child that was gray with the hue of death, but to find a pink, squirming girl who let out a long wail. The child was small but otherwise seemed to be healthy.

"I'm grateful the mother survived the surgery." Alexei stared into the night, likely at the shadowed form of that first longhouse.

Kate drew in a breath of air tinged with salt and sea. "Me too."

"If she had died, you would have been blamed for the death, and considering she's the chief's daughter-in-law . . ." The words hung in the air between them.

"I didn't have a choice," she whispered. "Had I not operated, they would both be dead."

"I know." Alexei tilted his head up, likely surveying the shadowed mountains that rose behind the small native village.

"Everyone in Petersburg knows. But they still would have viewed you as being responsible for the mother's death."

Kate fidgeted with a fleck of paint on the railing of the small boat. "Is there a point to this conversation?"

Her brother turned to face her, his dark eyes even more serious than normal in the growing night. "You're a good doctor, Kate. A very good one."

"And you're a terrible nurse."

Alexei's rusty chuckle filled the air for a handful of seconds before dissipating into the quiet surrounding them. "It's true. But my point is you should have an actual clinic in Juneau where people know they can find you at all hours of the day and night. I'll happily give you the one hundred and fifty dollars you need to purchase the store and the apartment above it from Gibbons."

She sucked in a breath, then held it in her chest for a solid minute, as though just as unsure what to do with the air as she was with what to do with his offer. She'd told him what she wanted the day they left Juneau. He'd known she wrote him a letter and sent it to Sitka, and he'd been insistent on knowing what it said.

He hadn't shown any sign of surprise when she asked for the rest of the money to purchase the clinic. No, his face had been as stoic as ever when he told her he'd consider it and then walked off.

But now he was offering her the money.

Because she'd proved something today by saving X'unéi and the baby? Because she'd proved something during the weeks she'd spent tending the injured and sick in the native villages scattered throughout the islands of Southeast Alaska?

"I don't want the money as a gift," she finally said. "I intend to pay you back."

"Why?" Alexei turned to her, leaning one elbow against the

rail of the gently rocking boat. "We're not that hard-pressed for money these days given how busy the shipyard has been. And you're part owner of both the Sitka Trading Company and the Amos Family Shipyard. Think of the money as your portion of the profits from last year."

"That just seems . . . messy."

"Why? I give Evelina and Sacha their cut of the profits each year now that they're both married. I know you're not married, but you have a valid reason for needing the money."

She stared out into the night, but the silence between them grew heavy.

"Have I done something to offend you?" Alexei finally asked. "Or do you really dislike me so much that you'll refuse an open gift?"

"It's not either of those things."

"Then what?"

She grew still for a moment, trying to find the words to explain the heavy burden inside her but not knowing where to start. "I want that clinic to be mine. Something I earned, not something I have because of a gift or because my great-grandfather started two companies. Does that make sense?"

"No."

She should have known he wouldn't understand. Why would he? He wasn't a woman fighting for a place in a man's world. He'd been born with an innate sense of business, then had inherited two businesses where he could use his abilities. He didn't know what it was like to be made fun of the second he left a room. To fight for even an ounce of respect from his peers. He didn't know what it was like to have a dream, yet spend his entire life having everyone tell him he'd never be able to achieve it.

"Let's try this." Alexei's voice was deeper than normal, filling the space between them and settling into the cracks and crevices of the sailboat. "I'll give you the money now, since you need it. If you want to pay me back, you can do that later, as your clinic grows. Will that suffice?"

"Yes, thank you." She looked down, not able to meet his gaze, though she didn't know why. She'd had no trouble meeting Dr. Ellingsworth's gaze when he'd tried storming into the sickroom in search of Nathan.

But now she found herself fiddling with that dratted fleck of paint on the railing again rather than looking into the eyes of the brother who'd paid to send her to medical school. "And I will pay you back. I'm not going to change my mind."

"I'll withdraw money from the bank as soon as we reach Juneau." Alexei pushed himself away from the railing, then paused.

She glanced up, and their eyes met for a brief moment in the dim light from the boat's lanterns. Something heavy and unresolved weighed down the air between them. Then Alexei gave a small shake of his head and left, his steps slow as he headed toward the small cabin at the front of the sloop.

Kate turned back to the town, where the last light of day had faded into darkness over the mountains.

She should be happy that Alexei had agreed to give her the money. A week from now, she'd be setting up her own clinic in Juneau.

So why did she feel like an awkward failure who'd never be able to stand on her own two feet?

11

Juneau; Four Days Later

They stayed in Petersburg for an additional three days. Kate had wanted to ensure there were no complications with X'unéi's incision or signs of infection.

Once Kate was certain that X'unéi would make a full recovery, she'd left the woman in care of Ldaneit, and they'd returned to Juneau.

True to his word, Alexei headed straight to the bank the moment they docked, and Kate now found herself tromping down the muddy streets of Juneau with a bulge of money in her pocket and her cloak pulled over her head to shield herself from the rain.

The deafening sounds from the mill filled the air, the only thing in Juneau not dampened by the rain. Well, that and the definite bounce in her steps and lightness in her heart as she opened the door to the office.

Chapter 11

The scent of sawdust greeted her as she smiled at the clerk. "I'd like to speak to Mr. Gibbons."

Spencer smiled back at her from behind his desk, then rose from his chair. "Of course, Dr. Amos. He's in his office."

"I heard at the bank that he's leaving tomorrow?"

"Yes. He'll be back again in the fall for a few weeks to check on the mill before the weather turns, and after that he won't return until next spring, unless there's an unforeseen problem, of course."

"I'm glad I caught him." And to think, if she'd tarried one more day in Petersburg, she would have lost her chance to purchase the building until fall.

Spencer rapped on the door, then cracked it open. "Mr. Gibbons, Dr. Amos is here to see you."

"Send her in." Mr. Gibbons bellowed from the other side of the door.

The clerk pushed the door open farther and stepped aside, gesturing for her to enter.

Kate couldn't help the smile that spread across her face as she crossed the room, pulled the banknote from her pocket, and put it on the desk. "There you are, Mr. Gibbons. Seven hundred dollars as asked."

He stared at the banknote on his desk and frowned. "What's this for?"

"The purchase of your building. I asked Alexei for the remaining money like you suggested. You're right. I shouldn't be depriving people of the kind of care they can get at a medical clinic simply because I don't want to borrow money from my brother. So here you go. The building is paid in full. Now all I need is for you to sign over the deed."

Mr. Gibbons was looking at her as though she'd lost her mind, or perhaps grown an ear on her forehead. "I can't sell you the building now. I've leased it through September."

"You what?" She tried to make sense of Mr. Gibbons's words, but they tangled in her mind, strange and nonsensical.

"Are you sure you still want the building?"

She straightened. "Of course I want the building. We talked about this before I left."

"Yes, but that was before either of us knew about the hospital opening."

"Hospital?" she sputtered. "There's a hospital? Opening where? Certainly not here in Juneau."

She'd heard rumors last summer that the Marine Hospital Service might build a hospital in Juneau, but nothing had come of it. "You must be mistaken. The MHS would never put a hospital in such a remote location. I'm not even sure the MHS realizes America owns Alaska. They probably think we still belong to Russia, for all the medical services they provide our ships."

Mr. Gibbons pinched the bridge of his nose. "Just how long have you been gone? And when did you get back?"

Kate shifted awkwardly on her feet. "I was gone three weeks. And I've been back for—" she glanced at the clock hanging on his wall—"forty-five minutes."

"So Alexei collected the money from the bank, and you came straight here?"

"Yes." She hadn't even said hello to Evelina yet. "Is there a problem with that?"

"It explains why you haven't heard the news. It's been all over town for the past two weeks, the only thing people have been talking about. The Marine Hospital Service hasn't just decided to build its next hospital in Juneau; it's also decided this hospital is going to have a community emphasis as part of a new trial program. It won't exclusively treat seamen. In fact, the assistant medical director is talking about taking medical care to every town in Alaska through the MHS. I assumed

Chapter 11   109

you'd heard and wondered if you would still want to buy my building in the fall."

"Yes, I still want it." The words emerged a bit harsher than she intended. And was it just her, or had the collar of her shirtwaist suddenly grown tight? "Where else will I have my clinic? Surely you don't expect me to keep my practice confined to that single room inside the trading post for the rest of my life."

Mr. Gibbons winced. "Don't take this the wrong way, but do you think you'll have enough patients to maintain a clinic with a hospital in town? A hospital with multiple other doctors on staff?"

Male doctors. That's what Mr. Gibbons meant, though he was kind enough not to say it.

She'd been through this before, not just in Boston, but also in Sitka. When given a choice between a female or male doctor, most people—even women—chose a male one. The only women who ever wanted to see her were the ones experiencing female issues, and sometimes they still elected to see male doctors.

Juneau had been different, though. People here had accepted her medical care—because they'd had little choice.

It was either her or Dr. Prichard, and only drunkards went to him.

"Perhaps the Marine Hospital Service will send a horrible doctor that no one trusts to treat them."

Mr. Gibbons quirked an eyebrow at her. "Did Dr. Reid seem all that terrible to you?"

"Dr. Reid?" she squeaked, the collar around her neck growing even tighter.

Dr. Reid, with his sincere words and kind eyes? Dr. Reid, who had told her to call him Nathan? Whom she'd given permission to call her Kate? Who had apologized profusely and then poked fun at himself for spending a full day retching after his concussion?

Who had come to visit her at the trading post and insisted she take an absurd amount of money for his treatment a few days after he'd been discharged?

"He's not a medical doctor, Mr. Gibbons. He's a scientist."

Mr. Gibbons eyebrows flew up. "Where did you get that notion? Certainly not from him. That man is a doctor through and through."

She thought back, trying to remember the conversations she'd had with Nathan. She'd assumed he was a scientist. But had he actually told her he was a scientist? Had he mentioned what field of science he studied?

Had she ever spoken to him in such a way that he would know she'd assumed him to be a scientist? Or had he thought, when she'd addressed him as doctor, that she believed he was a medical doctor?

"He's a doctor?" she rasped, her throat feeling as though she'd just swallowed a fistful of ocean sand. "A medical doctor? Are you certain?"

"A rather accomplished one. He's the assistant medical director for all of Alaska, appointed by the surgeon general himself. He's already started coordinating construction of the hospital building and an adjacent quarantine facility that's set to begin in May."

And he'd asked her for phenacetin when he'd first woken in the sickroom. She'd thought he was mumbling something incoherent, but he'd been asking for a medicine with pain-reducing properties. Because he was a doctor, and he knew the name of the medication to ask for. Why hadn't she caught it?

She straightened her shoulders and slid the banknote farther across the desk. "For the building. I still want it."

She wasn't going to shrink away and wallow because a

reputable male doctor was opening up another medical practice. She'd been treating the people of Juneau for two years. They trusted her. Surely they'd still seek her for treatment, especially if she had a proper building for her clinic.

Mr. Gibbons looked down at the paper. "You can't have the building now. You'll have to wait until the lease is up at the end of September."

The lease. She'd forgotten. Not that she could complain about Mr. Gibbons leasing it after she'd begged him for more time to come up with the money. But she didn't want to wait that long to open an official clinic, not with competition in town.

"Who did you lease it to? Perhaps they'll be willing to let another building through the summer so I can purchase yours now." It was worth going to the lessee and asking.

Mr. Gibbons dabbed the side of his head with a handkerchief, never mind that it was too cool for him to be sweating. "The renter isn't going to move."

"Why?" she whispered, a ball of dread growing in her stomach.

But the look on Mr. Gibbons's face told her what she needed to know, even before he spoke.

It was the perfect building for a medical clinic, not just because the first floor could be modified to hold two or three examination rooms plus a waiting room, but also because there was an apartment above it.

If she wanted to use it for that purpose, so would any other doctor.

But even knowing what Mr. Gibbons was about to say didn't prepare her for the pain that pierced her chest when the businessman finally opened his mouth and said, "I leased it to Dr. Reid."

Nathan looked at the woman sitting on the examination table in front of him and bit back a sigh. And to think when he opened for business two weeks ago, he'd been worried no one would come to his clinic. But the opposite had been true. It seemed he'd seen half the town over the past two weeks.

"Well?" Mrs. Trumball shoved her hand closer to him, her eyes riveted on her index finger. "What do you plan to do about my finger? I really do think it's broken."

The finger didn't have so much as a bruise. "My initial examination shows nothing to be concerned about. How painful is it?"

She blinked at him, her hazel eyes round and slightly too innocent, not filled with the look of agony that usually appeared when someone broke a bone. "Very painful. I'm certain I heard a crack when I hit it against the table while kneading bread dough."

A broken finger from kneading bread dough. Did she really expect him to believe that? "Your finger looks perfectly fine. Are you sure you heard a crack?"

"Quite sure." The woman fluttered her lashes at him.

"Let me take another look." Nathan pinched the finger between his own thumb and index finger, carefully moving from the tip down to the base, and pressing a bit harder than he usually would.

The woman didn't flinch once, let alone gasp in pain.

"How many rooms is the hospital going to have?"

Nathan refrained from rolling his eyes—barely. If he'd heard that question once, he'd heard it a hundred times. "I'm not certain. It has yet to be built."

"But don't you have blueprints? How will the builders know what to build without them?"

Chapter 11

He did have blueprints, tucked into the bottom of one of his trunks. And he knew exactly how many rooms the hospital would have without looking at the plans. But he wasn't of a mind to answer all the nosy questions the townsfolk of Juneau had.

"I'm still not sensing any kind of break. But if your finger is paining you that much, I suggest we tie it to the finger beside it and splint them both. That will provide the optimal opportunity for recovery."

"A splint?" Mrs. Trumball tugged her hand away from his and twisted her lips together. "Now that you mention it, some of the pain seems to have faded. Perhaps it's just a sprain?"

This time he couldn't manage to hold in his sigh. "Yes, perhaps. In that case, I recommend resting it for the remainder of the day, and possibly even tomorrow. After the pain fades, you can go back to using it normally."

"Thank you." She fluttered her lashes again, then sent him a smile so bright, he found himself hurrying toward the door.

Mrs. Trumball was a mother of three and married to the foreman at the mill, but Nathan had only learned that by asking around town after her first visit. In his office, she acted more like she was single than married—and she'd found reason to come to his office three times since its official opening two weeks ago.

Nathan stepped to the door and wrenched it open, only to find that three more people had entered the waiting room while he'd been examining Mrs. Trumball's finger. That brought the total to nine patients waiting to see him.

It was going to be a rather long day.

"Don't you think I should come back and have my finger checked again before I go back to using it normally?" Mrs. Trumball stopped beside him in the doorway, the narrow space causing her to stand far closer than was proper. "Just to make sure it really is all right?"

Nathan sucked in a breath through his nose, then blew it out through his mouth, long and slow. Perhaps he'd underestimated how much patience it would take to open a medical clinic to the public. Did Kate ever get asked to treat nonexistent injuries? If so, how did she manage to keep herself calm?

"I expect the pain to lessen on its own." Nathan squeezed past Mrs. Trumball and stepped into the waiting room, breathing a bit easier now that there was more space between them. "I only want to see you again if it grows worse, if your skin becomes discolored, or if your finger swells. Do you understand?"

The woman studied her finger, and he could almost see her imagining ways she might be able to discolor her skin without actually injuring the appendage so she could come back tomorrow. "Yes, thank you so much for your time, Doctor."

She opened her purse and held out two dollars. It was an exorbitant sum to pay for an office visit, but arguing with the woman while they stood in front of nine other people seemed worse than simply taking the money, so he slid it into his pocket—and hoped Mr. Gibbons at the mill paid his foreman a handsome salary.

"Who's next?" Nathan called before Mrs. Trumball could ask him another question about the hospital or concoct another injury.

A woman stepped forward in a light-blue dress edged with dark-blue trim. She carried a basket on her arm, and her blond hair was pulled back into a bun with a few tight curls hanging by her face. He'd seen her around town a time or two before, and though she was a bit thin and her bun was rather tight, she was always well dressed.

Had she come to his clinic to bat her lashes, swish her fan, and complain about pain in her little toe while asking questions about the hospital?

"I'm not here as a patient, Dr. Reid, but on behalf of the Presbyterian mission, I want to present you with this." She handed him the basket she'd been holding on her arm.

Only then did he look down and realize it wasn't filled with knitting to finish while she waited in his office; it held fresh-baked bread, cookies, and several jars of jam.

"Thank you." He took the basket and smiled.

She smiled back, but in a sincere manner, not a flirtatious one. "I'm Janice Thompson, one of two teachers at the day school for Indians."

"The day school for Indians?" The smile on his face felt a bit more genuine. "What a noble endeavor. I'm sure everyone appreciates your efforts to help instruct the greater community of Juneau."

Her smile grew wider. "Thank you. If there's anything you need concerning your hospital or new clinic, please ask. There are four teachers at the Presbyterian mission, two for the Indian school and two for the white school. But school will be out for the summer in May, so if there's a way we can help, please let us know."

Miss Thompson had come to his clinic out of a genuine desire to help? Not because she wanted gossip?

Perhaps she was worth getting to know better. "That's very kind. I already know we'll need curtains and blankets. If I provide the fabric, would you and the other ladies at the mission be able to . . . ?"

The door opened, and a familiar figure stepped inside. A familiar figure dressed in a serviceable blue skirt and white shirtwaist, with hair pulled into a bun that was too severe for the natural beauty of her face.

"Kate?" He hadn't seen her in several weeks, though he'd

heard she'd taken a medical trip to the various villages scattered throughout Southeast Alaska.

She paused in the doorway, her gaze catching his, trapping it. He wasn't sure how long they stood there, eyes locked together in front of everyone. It could have been two seconds or twenty minutes.

Finally her tongue darted out to wet her lips. "So it's true."

Her words were so soft, he could barely hear them, but they landed in the room with the force of falling boulders, large and devastating.

"I expected more from you, Dr. Reid." She spoke his name as though it was a curse, then her eyes swept the people in his waiting room. "And from the rest of you too."

Then she spun on her heel and strode out the door, her back straight and shoulders stiff.

"Wait . . ." Nathan attempted to take a step after her, never mind the basket weighing down his arm. But she was already gone, disappearing from the steps and hurrying down the street at a quick clip.

Nathan shoved a hand into his hair, trying to push aside the look he'd seen in Kate's eyes. It hadn't been anger, at least not at first. It had been pure hurt.

The anger had come a moment later, after her gaze had swept the people in the room.

"Don't mind her." Miss Thompson rested a hand on his arm, though her smile had turned tight. "I think you're doing wonderful things for our town. And not all the women in Juneau are as rude as the Amos women. Or as scandalous."

"Scandalous?"

"Yes." The woman sniffed, the lips he'd been admiring just a few minutes ago now pressed into a thin line. "Kate Amos is a female doctor. Do you know how inappropriate that is? The kind of things she would have needed to study in medical school? It's quite scandalous, I assure you. Not the type of profession any proper woman would enter."

"It's nothing of the sort." The middle-aged woman sitting in the corner made a swishing motion with her hand. "Dr. Amos treated me for the ague last year, and I got better in two days."

"She treated my son too," added the man on the bench against the wall. "I don't cotton to women doctors myself, but Dr. Amos sure ain't a bad one."

"Well, I agree with Miss Thompson." An elderly woman with a spray of flowers in her hat raised her chin. "There are some things a woman has no business doing, and being a doctor is one of them, right along with being a lawyer."

Right.

"I believe I'm next." A bearded man who looked to be a miner pushed himself off the wall and headed for the examination room. "So if y'all are done yammerin' about the Amoses, I'd like the doc to take a look at me."

"Of course." Nathan pulled his arm away from Miss Thompson—who was still holding on to it for some reason—then ushered the man into the room.

But as he listened to the miner's complaints about ringing in his ear, he couldn't quite seem to forget the look on Kate's face when she fled his waiting room.

Or shove aside the notion that even though she was a good doctor, she probably never once had nine townsfolk crowd into the trading post to wait for her to treat them.

12

Nathan's boots sank into the damp sand as he trudged along the deserted stretch of beach, his breath forming small clouds of mist against the gray air. Moisture clung to his coat and hat, pooling droplets of water on the oilskin despite the absence of actual raindrops. He shivered, muttering under his breath. Ellingsworth was right. There was never any sun in this stubborn, bleak town.

He'd thought about turning around several times, of going back to his apartment and making himself a cup of tea to warm the cold that had somehow worked its way beneath his coat and settled into his bones.

But Evelina Amos had told him Kate was out here somewhere on the cold, damp beach. And if she was stubborn enough to be out in this weather, then he was stubborn enough to find her.

He rounded a bend, and a lone person seated on a log came into view. Finally.

Mountains rose up on either side of her, some on the mainland, and some on Douglas Island, making her a solitary figure against the vast expanse of mountains and water.

"Kate!" he called out, his voice nearly swallowed by the heaviness of the air.

She didn't turn to look at him; she merely stiffened, her posture straightening. "Go away."

The command filled the otherwise silent beach, but he ignored her words, trudging forward until he reached the log where she sat.

He dropped onto it, the wet cold of the wood seeping through his trousers. "I'm not going anywhere. Not until we talk."

Kate sighed, turning her face away to stare out at the smooth, still water of the channel, the fur of her thick cloak seeming to shield her from the damp cold that gave him a constant urge to shiver.

He'd practiced a speech in his head, repeating the words over and over as he trudged down the beach. But now that he sat beside her, the only thing he could think to say was, "I'm sorry."

"For what?" She still hadn't bothered to look at him. "Leasing the building I was going to buy? Or starting a hospital? Or coming to town in the first place?"

"For not telling you I'm a medical doctor. I assumed you knew when you referred to me as Dr. Reid, but it's clear now that you and your family thought I was a scientist."

"Most newcomers here with the title doctor are."

"By the time I realized that and had the opportunity to address it, you had left town. I hadn't realized you were planning to do that either."

"It seems like an honest mistake, even if it was rather unusual." Kate kept her voice flat, sounding nothing like the determined energetic woman he'd met his first day in Alaska.

"I didn't realize you wanted to buy Mr. Gibbons's building."

She said nothing, which was somehow worse than if she were to beg him to let her have access to the building before September.

"I'll vacate it as soon as the hospital is operational," he offered.

"Thanks."

The single word was so dry, he suddenly found himself wishing for a canteen of water to moisten his throat. "Or maybe, instead of buying that building, you should come work for me."

Kate jerked her head in his direction—finally—her eyes round with surprise. "What?"

Ellingsworth would hate the idea, but Ellingsworth wasn't here, and he'd be able to write the surgeon general and explain the hire. The most prestigious medical doctor in the nation certainly wouldn't expect their first new employee in Alaska to be a female doctor, but there were numerous reasons to support bringing Kate on staff, one of them being her familiarity with the native villages.

And spending his days with a woman as lovely as Kate Amos wouldn't be a hardship. "You gave me excellent care during my concussion, and even after Dr. Ellingsworth returns, the hospital will need several more doctors. I'm officially offering you a position. You can start tomorrow at the temporary clinic. The two of us will work together."

He expected her to thank him. After all, he'd just come up with a way to avoid competing for patients.

But Kate's eyes flashed green fire. "No."

No? "But this is an excellent solution."

"I've worked for male doctors before."

She had? Nathan's heart gave a hard, solid thud inside his chest. "What happened?"

She looked away from him again. "They were more interested in how often I made them coffee than how often I saw patients."

There was more to that story. "Where did you—?"

"Did you tell Mrs. Trumball to loosen her corset while she was at your office?"

"Her corset?" Nathan frowned, heat creeping up the back of his neck. "What are you talking about? And why would I do such a thing when she came to me for a broken finger?"

Kate rolled her eyes. "Was it actually broken?"

"Let me clarify. She came to me for the same reason most people in town are coming to me. They're curious. They don't know what to think about me or the hospital, and they want to see how I'll treat them."

The firm set of her jaw only grew harder. "I've never had that happen. People only come to me when they're in desperate need of care and feel they have no other choice."

He had the sudden urge to squirm on the wet log. "I'm sure that was true at first, but surely after two years, people are more comfortable coming to you."

"Sometimes, not always. And I've never had nine people in my waiting room."

This probably wasn't the time to point out that she didn't have a waiting room. "Eight people. Miss Thompson wasn't there to be treated. She was giving me a welcome basket from the teachers at the Presbyterian mission."

Kate went stiff beside him, and Nathan found himself frowning again. "Is there some kind of disagreement between the two of you? She seemed quite pleasant at first, but her disposition changed once you entered the office."

"She doesn't think very highly of our family. And our

family doesn't think very highly of her. Whatever feelings you picked up on, I assure you, they are mutual."

"But why don't you get along? She works for the Presbyterian mission as a teacher at the Indian day school, and she—"

"Did she tell you that she won't let her students speak so much as a word of their native language in her classroom? And if they do, she raps their hands with her yardstick till they bleed?"

"Ah . . . no. She failed to mention that bit." And as unpleasant as that sounded, given the tight set to Kate's jaw, he guessed that wasn't the only thing the two of them disagreed on.

For some reason, he wanted to sit there and prod the rest out of her. Even though she was stiff as a fence post. Even though she'd met his eyes only a handful of times during their entire conversation. Even though everything about her prickly demeanor should make him want to run in the opposite direction.

Even though the invisible mist had turned into a drizzle, and the drizzle was now becoming a steady rain that dampened his neck and rolled down his back despite his hat and oilskin coat.

"So Mrs. Trumball . . ." Kate asked. "Did you tell her to loosen her corset? You never said."

"Are we back to her now? No. I didn't ask Mrs. Trumball about her corset. How do you know it was too tight?" That wasn't something he'd ever needed to deal with at any of his other posts—mainly because he'd been treating sailors.

"I saw her leaving the clinic, and her corset is always too tight. She's got a heavier form than Evelina and me, had a baby four months ago, and insists on keeping her corset cinched tighter than Evelina's. I'm concerned it might cause an organ prolapse."

An organ prolapse due to tight-lacing. Nathan scratched the side of his head beneath his hat. He'd seen a few articles on the topic in medical journals in recent years, but he'd never bothered to read them. Maybe he should dig them out. "I, ah, might be sorry I'm asking this, but how does one tell if a corset is too tightly laced?"

"Anything that reduces the size of a woman's natural waist is too tight. A corset, if it's worn at all, should be for support only, not for altering the shape of one's body."

"So Mrs. Trumball laces her corset tightly, but you and your sister keep yours looser?"

"Evelina keeps hers looser. I don't wear one." Kate paused for a moment, then pressed her eyes shut and covered them with her hands. "Oh, heavens, I shouldn't have said that, should I? And here I wonder why Janice Thompson complains about my lack of propriety."

She was right. Discussing her undergarments was far from proper. But he couldn't stop himself from running his eyes down her torso. Not that he could see any of it given the way the thick fur of her cloak draped her body, but he recalled how she'd looked in the sickroom in the simple green dress that matched the color of her eyes. He'd never have guessed she wasn't wearing a corset. She always seemed to bear a feminine shape with a narrow waist. Though her waist wasn't ridiculously small when compared to her chest and hips.

Not like Mrs. Trumball's waist.

Not like the waist of many of the politicians' wives and daughters back in Washington, DC.

Perhaps a lack of corset would be more noticeable on a woman with a heavier bosom, but he wouldn't know, because he'd never met a woman who admitted to not wearing one. "Why don't you wear a corset?"

She shot him a scathing look. "Because I like to breathe."

He felt his eyebrows rising. "Do you find they have that big of an impact on your breathing?"

"They limit lung expansion almost instantly, but that can be rectified as soon as a woman takes her corset off. The true danger lies in what happens if they're laced too tightly over a long enough period of time. They can misalign bones and displace internal organs, which will in turn affect a woman's ability to digest food. If a woman ever comes to you with complaints of indigestion, and her waist looks ridiculously small compared to the rest of her frame, the first thing you need to do is tell her to loosen her corset, not give her an elixir."

He surveyed her for a moment, the soft curve of her cheek, the slender column of her neck only half visible inside the hood of her cloak, the quiet intensity in her eyes. "This is all the more reason for you to work for me at the clinic. You're an excellent physician."

"I'm not going to work for you, but I suppose the polite thing to do is thank you for the offer, so thank you." She pushed herself off the log and stood. "Now it's growing late, and tomorrow . . . Well, I don't suppose I'll have many patients, will I? Perhaps I'll go over to the Tlingit village. There was an elderly woman who had the ague before I left. I should check on her. Or maybe I'll go up into the mountains. I haven't visited any mining camps in over a month."

"The miners let you treat them?" Nathan stood, the movement causing a cool stream of rain to trickle between his collar and neck and down his back.

"Sometimes yes and sometimes no. It depends."

"I'll go with you."

"Why?" She took a step back from him, her voice growing

terse once again. "So they know there's a male doctor in town and will start refusing treatment from me too? I'd wager they'll figure that out soon enough."

"That wasn't what I meant." He scanned the fog-shrouded mountains. Just how many camps were up in those mountains? It was his job to ensure medical care was provided for them, just like it was his job to ensure that remote native villages received medical care as well. All those goals fell under his purview as the acting medical director of Alaska.

But no one had told him there was already a doctor providing care in all those places.

"If you're concerned about my safety, it's unnecessary." Kate started down the beach at a clipped pace. "Jonas and my brothers don't let me go up there alone. And since Alexei is still in town, he'll likely be the one to escort me."

Nathan raced to keep up with her brisk stride, never mind her legs were shorter than his by several inches. "Do you find any commonality among illnesses that plague the camps? Like how sailors are susceptible to scurvy due to lack of fresh fruits and how coal miners suffer from lung disease? Are there any diseases that seem common among gold miners?"

She stopped walking and looked up at the mountains, her head tilted to the side. "There's probably a higher incidence of injuries and amputations, but I can't think of any specific diseases. If influenza is spreading in town, then a month later, it will reach the camps and sweep through everyone who shares the bunkhouse."

"I see." Nathan used the break in their walk to extend his arm to Kate, an unstated offer to let him escort her back to town.

She blinked at it for a moment but kept her hand at her side. "I'm not in need of company, Dr. Reid."

"'Dr. Reid'?" His eyebrows winged up. "I told you to call

me Nathan, remember? And you did. I recall it quite distinctly."

"That was before."

"Before what?"

She huffed and started walking down the beach again. "Before I realized you'd be setting up a medical practice in direct competition with mine."

"So now I'm back to being Dr. Reid?"

"Yes."

"Well, I'm still of a mind to call you Kate."

She slanted him a glance, sharpness flashing in her green eyes. "Is this some kind of test to see if I'm petty enough to revoke my offer for you to use my first name?"

He wanted to smile, but he managed to hold it back. "Not a test, but I'm curious as to your answer."

"No, I'm not that petty, but I won't complain if you call me Dr. Amos either. It would be the professional thing to do."

This time he let his smile break onto his face. "Kate it is."

She pressed her lips together into a flat line. "We're not friends, you and I. You'd do well to cast any notions of it aside."

Not friends? My, she was prickly tonight. Not that he could blame her, considering everything that had happened. "That just makes me more determined to win you over, Ekaterina."

She jerked her gaze toward him. "How did you . . . ?"

"Ilya told me. Was it supposed to be a secret?"

She crossed her arms over her chest. "I did not give you permission to call me that, nor will I ever, so I suggest you wipe that name from your mind."

"Just like I need to wipe any idea of us ever being friends from my mind?"

"Yes. Exactly like that."

He grinned. And heaven help him. Her stiff posture and clipped tone just made him want to call her Ekaterina again.

But he tamped down the urge, because it had been a long day, and Kate probably needed a bit of kindness in her life, even if she wasn't feeling particularly kind herself. So he extended his arm to her again. "May I escort you back to town this evening as your 'not-friend'?"

"My 'not-friend'?" She paused to look down at his arm once more.

"Yes, like you said. We're not-friends."

She huffed. "I have a rather strong feeling you misunderstood that statement."

"I assure you I didn't. I'm just quite determined to prove you wrong."

"I'm too stubborn for my own good. You realize that, don't you?"

But she reached out and settled her hand atop his sleeve anyway. Between her gloves and his coat, there were too many layers of clothes for him to actually feel her hand, but he could almost swear his body grew warmer just knowing she was touching him.

Medically speaking, it was ridiculous. He knew his body temperature was no different now than it had been ten seconds ago.

But there was a place inside him that seemed warmer anyway, so he rested his free hand atop hers and walked with her back to town, determined to learn as much as he could about his not-friend in the time they had left together tonight.

13

Juneau; Late May

Kate forced her gaze straight ahead, ignoring the hammering coming from the land to her left. It was an exercise in willpower she performed each time she walked down the waterfront. Of all the spots for Nathan to choose for a hospital, did it have to be smack in the middle of town? And right along the waterfront?

She supposed the location made sense, since the hospital would service the sailors on the ships that came into port.

But that made the hospital terribly hard to avoid, and it meant that while the building was under construction, hammering filled the entire downtown area.

Kate tucked the empty basket she carried closer to her stomach. Her thick fur cloak shielded both her body and the basket from the rain that had plagued Juneau for weeks on end.

She didn't want to think about how late in the year it was to still be wearing a fur cloak. But the weather hadn't seemed to get the message that spring was supposed to arrive, which meant the sky was just as thick and dreary now as it had been in February, and while they hadn't gotten any snow, the forty-degree temperatures caused her to breathe puffy white clouds into the air as she headed—

"Oh, goodness." Kate had rounded the side of a building, making a sharp turn away from the hospital, only to nearly collide with another woman. "I should have been paying better attention."

"You absolutely should have."

At the sound of the sharp voice, Kate looked up to find herself standing toe-to-toe with none other than Janice Thompson.

"Just because your last name is Amos doesn't mean you own the street. I highly encourage you to be more mindful of other pedestrians in the future." Miss Thompson humphed, pulling her own basket closer to her side. She didn't wear a fur cloak—she probably couldn't afford one on her teacher's salary—so she stood in a dark oilskin that shielded her from the rain, with an oilskin cloth draped over the top of the basket she held.

Kate didn't need to ask where the woman was headed. She made a habit of bringing lunch to the clinic and eating with Dr. Reid whenever she wasn't in school, and today was Wednesday.

Not that Kate cared. Dr. Reid could spend time with whomever he wished.

But Ilya had made a point of reporting on the man's every move each night at dinner.

"*Did you hear the crew that's supposed to build the hospital arrived today?*"

"*Dr. Reid had a line of patients out the door at lunchtime.*

There wasn't enough room for everyone even in that giant waiting room he has."

"The hospital crew has half the frame up already. How long do you think until they've got the whole thing built?"

"Miss Thompson showed up at Dr. Reid's office with a basket of food just in time for lunch today."

"Miss Thompson invited Dr. Reid to the Presbyterian mission for lunch after church yesterday. And he went. For the second Sunday in a row."

His reports on Dr. Reid's activities were so comprehensive that Kate was about ready to ship the boy back to Sitka and let Alexei, Yuri, and Sacha raise him.

Dinner last night had been particularly horrid. Alexei, after dropping her off in Juneau at the end of April, had taken a trip to San Francisco. He'd returned yesterday, and Ilya had filled him in on every last thing that had happened in Juneau while he'd been gone.

Unfortunately, all of the news seemed to center around a certain doctor with dark hair, a strong jaw, and kind eyes.

It wouldn't hurt so much, except that the number of patients who'd sought her out since Dr. Reid opened his clinic had dwindled to a handful per week.

Kate had tried to keep herself occupied by visiting the Tlingit village on Douglas Island or making extra trips up into the mountains to visit the mining camps. But she wasn't nearly as busy as before, and the hours she spent at the trading post without anyone calling on her doctoring skills felt like—

"Well, are you going to apologize or not?"

"Apologize?" Kate blinked, only to find Janice Thompson still standing in front of her, a pinched look on a face that would probably be beautiful if the woman ever learned how to smile.

"For nearly trampling me!"

"I'm sorry," Kate muttered, the words tasting like dust on her tongue. "I'll pay better attention next time."

"Good. Now if you'll excuse me, I need to bring Dr. Reid his lunch. We're very fortunate to have a doctor who works so hard serving the people of Juneau."

Kate wanted to say that there'd been a time when she'd worked hard serving the people of Juneau too—before Dr. Reid had come and taken all her patients.

But she couldn't argue the point about Dr. Reid being a hard worker. It seemed he was always working in one capacity or another, and it was almost enough to make her wonder if she'd been too quick to judge him that day on the beach. Too quick to turn down his offer of a job.

Not that she ever intended to work for a male doctor again, but everything about Nathan Reid seemed honest and genuine, including how he treated patients at his clinic.

She only wondered where that would leave her six months from now.

"Like I said . . ." Miss Thompson sniffed, her voice somehow biting without being overly loud. "I want to make sure Dr. Reid understands just how much the community appreciates him. So I baked his favorite pie."

The other woman shouldered past Kate, heading down the road with her head high and her shoulders stiff.

It was just as well. Had she mentioned her lack of patients since Dr. Reid arrived, Miss Thompson probably would have declared it a blessing from God and told Kate to use her extra time knitting or weaving baskets or cooking.

Kate started walking again, keeping her eyes on the white sign for the trading post at the end of the road. Once there, she'd find something useful to do, like . . . well, she wasn't sure. Maybe she'd review the ledgers with Alexei, or maybe she'd—

"Mudslide!" a shout rang through town.

Kate paused, trying to discern where the cry had come from.

Her eyes landed on two men on horseback barreling down the road. "There's been a mudslide north of town. Come quick. We need to search for survivors."

Kate's breath caught as the meaning of the men's shouts settled into her mind. A mudslide and a search for survivors.

Dear Father God, please keep everyone caught in that mudslide safe. After offering up a quick prayer, she broke into a run. She might not be strong enough to pull a grown man out of the mud, but she could certainly treat his injuries.

SHE WAS TIRED. She was wet. And she ached from her neck down to her toes. But that didn't stop Kate from trudging up the side of the mountain, searching for survivors in the massive swath of mud and debris that had torn down the mountainside. The mudslide had obliterated everything in its path, uprooting trees and snapping their trunks, filling in streams and caves and footpaths under mounds of earth and broken branches.

"Over here," Alexei called from somewhere above her. "I found someone. I think he might be . . ."

Alexei's voice trailed off, telling Kate what she needed to know, even though she started toward him. The thick, soupy mud beneath her clung to her feet with each step.

The rain hadn't let up all afternoon. It pelted the fur hood of her cloak and left droplets of moisture on her lashes and nose, making the ground that the volunteers searched even muddier.

Jonas reached Alexei before she did. He'd been searching a nearby section of the mountain, close enough to see and hear them but far enough away that they could each cover different ground. That's what the three of them had decided to do when they'd set off on their search earlier.

When Kate finally reached her brother, she glanced briefly down to find a middle-aged man with rough, weather-beaten features frozen in an expression of fear. A thick layer of mud caked the skin of his face, indicating he'd likely suffocated to death when the mud had torn down the mountain.

Kate bent down to close his eyes. Normally seeing a dead body wouldn't bother her. It was part of being a doctor. But she'd seen far too many bodies already today.

When they'd first reached the site of the mudslide, Jonas—acting as Deputy Marshal—had seen that a tent was set up at the bottom of the mountain to treat the men who were found alive. Dr. Reid had arrived just after the tent had been erected, and he was down there now, tending the survivors while Evelina and Inessa both helped with the nursing.

Dr. Reid had offered to let Kate run the tent instead of him, but she was happy clambering around the mountain with Alexei and Jonas, looking for people who needed to be treated before they could be moved. She'd rather be out moving and searching for people in need of help than waiting for people to be brought to her. Like the man with the broken leg that she'd splinted or the man who'd dislocated his shoulder against a tree.

Or at least, that's how she'd felt six hours ago, when she, Alexei, and Jonas had first set off up the mountain, but by this point, and with so many dead bodies, she wondered if she was doing any good.

"Let's take him back down the mountain." Jonas's voice sounded deeper than usual, rumbling against the constant patter of rain.

"Do we have to?" Kate asked.

Both her brother and Jonas looked at her, but Jonas was the one who spoke. "Why wouldn't we take him back to the tent?

He needs to be identified and given a proper burial. Then his family needs to be informed of what happened."

A shiver traveled up her spine despite the warmth of her fur cloak. "It will be dark in another hour or so. If we stop searching now and take him back down the mountain, it will use up the rest of the light. I'd rather spend the time looking for more survivors."

Jonas sent her a serious look that communicated his thoughts without having to voice them. He didn't think there would be any more survivors.

She couldn't blame him for thinking such a thing. The few men who'd survived had all been found in the first hour or two of searching.

"She has a point." Alexei scanned the ruined mountainside. "There's no harm in leaving the body here for another hour. We can carry it back down when we return to the tent."

"Kate, is that you?"

At the sound of the voice, Kate turned to find a solitary form trekking up the mountain toward them. She would have known who it was even without recognizing his voice. Nathan Reid wasn't a large man, and he certainly didn't have Jonas's muscles. But there was an air of strength and importance about him, even with his chest heaving from his trek up the mountain and his boots slipping in the mud.

"Shouldn't you be at the tent?" Kate picked her way down the mountainside toward him.

"Someone came to the tent and said there was a man in one of the caves up here in pain and wheezing. I'm trying to find him. He needs to be stabilized and moved before nightfall."

"Where's the cave?"

Dr. Reid shook his head, causing droplets of water from his hat to sprinkle his shoulders and chest. "I don't know. We found a man with a broken arm and hypothermia about a quarter hour ago, and I sent Pete down the mountain with him. Said I'd search for the cave on my own."

"That's a fool's way to end up lost." Alexei tromped down to where they stood, with Jonas beside him. "Especially if you're not familiar with these mountains."

Dr. Reid surveyed the carnage surrounding them, pausing briefly on the mud-caked body a few feet away, then brought his eyes back to meet hers. They were haunted with a weariness that went far beyond a tired body or aching muscles.

And she suddenly didn't have the heart to lecture him about continuing on alone, even if Alexei was right and he could have ended up lost and stranded on the mountain all night wearing a slicker that looked both too big and too thin to keep him warm.

"I'd have done the same thing," she said to her brother. "So would you and Jonas. We've got an hour at most to find that survivor. You and Jonas take the body down to the tent. Dr. Reid and I will look for him. I saw a cave not too far from here. Perhaps that's where he is."

"But what if you need to move him?" Jonas used his palm to wipe droplets of water from his cheek. "You're not strong enough to carry a man down the mountain, Kate."

"No, but we won't attempt to move a live man without a stretcher either. You'll pass more searchers on your way down. Maybe one of the groups will have a stretcher. Send them this direction."

Alexei studied her for a moment, droplets of water clinging to his dark lashes. She could sense he wanted to tell her something, but she didn't know what. She'd never been able to read her older brother the way Evelina could. He finally looked over his shoulder at the body and said, "Very well. You two best hurry."

It made her wonder if she'd done something wrong. Why

wouldn't he tell her what was in his brain the way he'd tell Evelina or Sacha or Mikhail?

The way he'd probably tell Jonas the moment she was out of earshot?

Things had been awkward between them ever since he'd given her money for the building. Or maybe things were awkward because she'd insisted on paying him back. Either way, the brother she'd always struggled to understand the most felt even more distant now, and she wasn't sure how to fix it.

"Where did you say that cave was?" Dr. Reid was already moving, not waiting for Alexei and Jonas to start down the mountain first or even give her a chance to tell them good-bye.

Even though he was clearly breathing hard, his gait was quick and lithe for someone who hadn't grown up climbing mountains, and she had to rush through the mud to catch up with him. "It's just up here and to the south. See? If you look hard enough, you can make out a rockface that didn't get buried in mud. I think it's on the edge of the mudslide's path."

"I see it."

They picked their way through the swath of debris that had torn down the mountain, stepping around uprooted trees and tumbled rocks. The labored sounds of their breathing filled the air between them, but Dr. Reid didn't speak. Instead he walked with his shoulders hunched against the rain, his head down so that most of the moisture pelted his hat, but she could tell that some of the rain dripped beneath the too-wide collar of his slicker.

He had to be half frozen given the temperature, but he gave no indication he was cold as he trudged toward the cave.

"How many people did you treat down at the tent?" she asked.

He slanted her a glance, tiredness filling his eyes. "Not

nearly enough. There were far more dead bodies than survivors."

"Most of the people we came across on the mountain were dead too."

He held her gaze for another moment, then straightened his shoulders and strode toward the cave. He reached it a few seconds before she did, his long strides able to cover more ground. By the time she stepped into the opening, he was already shaking his head. "He's not here."

Kate surveyed the cold, dark space. "Perhaps there's another cave farther up the mountain, more in the path of the mud? We don't have much longer to search, though." She stepped back out of the cave and into the rain.

"I hate these types of disasters." Dr. Reid came up beside her, his footsteps making sucking sounds against the fresh mud. "The suffering always seems so senseless."

Kate wiped a smear of mud from her cheek with the back of her gloved hand. "I know what you mean. I learned to be a doctor so I could help people, but with something like this . . ."

She shook her head, looking out over the ravaged landscape. She'd trekked up this mountain before, and on a sunny day, it was beautiful, the mountainside covered in thick green forests with sparkling water flowing down the creek beds and the gentle peak of the mountain climbing into the sky.

". . . It makes me feel just as helpless as I felt as a six-year-old watching my friend's mother die," she finished.

"Is that what prompted you to become a doctor?" Dr. Reid asked quietly.

"Yes." Her throat felt unbearably raw as she spoke the word.

"What did she die of?"

"Puerperal fever." Her reply was nearly drowned out by a

sudden increase in the rain's intensity, the drops hitting the ground with enough force that mud splattered their boots.

But the sudden downpour didn't take Dr. Reid's eyes from her. If anything, his gaze only seemed to soften. "So it was preventable. I'm so sorry."

"Yes, or at least I know it was preventable now. The death didn't seem preventable at the time." And that only made the situation more tragic, at least in her mind. Had she been newly back from medical school, had she been the one called to deliver the baby and not the doctor in Sitka, things could have ended very differently.

Like they had for X'unéi.

"By the time your friend's mother got sick, nothing could have been done. The preventable part happened during either labor or delivery." Nathan's voice held a gentleness that carried through the rain. "Or at least that's the theory I subscribe to, that germs cause puerperal fever."

She hadn't realized he held to the germ theory—not all doctors did—but somehow she wasn't surprised. He seemed too good of a doctor to believe that diseases were spread by foul air or imbalances in the body. "Me too. That's why I wash my hands and all my medical instruments in carbolic acid before treating a patient."

She glanced over at Dr. Reid again, only to find that he was looking at her from beneath the brim of his water-drenched hat once more.

Or maybe he'd never stopped looking at her. Maybe he'd been looking at her this entire time?

The thought gave her the sudden urge to fidget. "Why are you looking at me like that?"

"Like what? With a smile? A smile isn't an insult, Kate."

She bristled. "I know that."

"Do you, though? Because you seem rather intimidated by

my smiling at you. And I was smiling a moment ago because I was thinking that this is rather nice."

"You think this is nice?" She spread her hands to encompass the pounding rain and ruined mountainside.

"Not the mudslide or the people who died today but the fact that you're talking to me after avoiding me for weeks."

"I haven't avoided you once."

One of his eyebrows winged up. "Really? That's strange, because I've made a habit of stopping by the trading post twice a week to ask after you. Each time one of your sisters tells me you're too busy to meet, and they'll pass on the message that I stopped."

"I can't help it if I'm busy."

He smirked. Actually smirked! The scoundrel.

But at least he had the courtesy not to point out what they both knew, that he'd been far busier with his medical practice than she'd been with hers. Instead, he said, "Are you really so busy that you haven't had a spare hour where you could stop by my office and see what I wanted? It's been over a month."

"I know what you wanted."

"What?"

She pressed her lips together. The question felt like a trap. The first thing that sprang to mind was that he wanted to offer her a job again, but what if he'd wanted something else? What if he'd wanted to take her on another walk down the beach, or invite her for a picnic, or even invite her to tour his clinic after it had closed for the day? What if there'd been a new medical breakthrough he wanted to tell her about? What if . . . ?

"Kate."

Something about how he said her name had her pausing and turning to look at him. The moment she did, she wished she hadn't. His eyes were soft, his lips tilted into that faint half smile again. And he was watching her in a way that made her feel rather warm inside, never mind the cold rain.

It was almost enough to make her start calling him Nathan again.

"I'm not your enemy," he said. "You know that, right?"

Her throat turned thick. Why was he telling her such a thing? Of course he was her enemy. He'd come to town and taken her patients. Not all of them, but enough that she was starting to feel useless again, like all her work earning her medical degree, all her skills as a doctor, weren't valid.

"We're not friends either. I told you that on the beach that night."

"You did, but unfortunately, you won't give me a chance to be your 'not-friend,' even though I've been trying."

Not-friend? Were they back to that? "I don't want you to be my friend or 'not-friend' or 'not-enemy' or anything in between. I just want . . ."

She huffed. What? What did she want?

"What do you want?" he said, almost as though he could read her thoughts.

For him to go back to Washington, DC, and never return, because then she could have her patients back.

But that was a ludicrous thing to hope for, because now that the MHS had decided to put a hospital in Juneau, they'd just send someone else to replace him.

"Can you tell me?" He took a step closer. "Is there something I can do to make things better between us? To make your situation easier and—"

The soft look suddenly dropped from his face, and he swung his gaze away from her, focusing on something higher up the mountain. Then he grabbed her arm, jerked her around, and started running back in the direction they'd just come. "Another mudslide. Hurry!"

She heard it then, the cracking sound of trees being uprooted from the earth, and the loud, deep rumble of dirt dislodging itself higher up the face of the mountain.

His hand dug into her wrist, his breath heaving as he yanked her toward the cave they'd just searched.

Kate's chest struggled for air as she fought to wrench her feet from the mud with each step she took. But the roaring grew louder, the trembling of the mountain fiercer.

They darted around an upturned tree and raced above a dislodged boulder, the mountain shaking beneath them. But she could see the cave ahead—that small promise of safety—if they could reach it in time.

Dr. Reid glanced up the mountain a second time. When he looked back at her, his face had turned pure white.

She didn't have the courage to look up the mountain too, not when the roaring told her everything she needed to know. The mudslide was almost on top of them. But they were just about to the cave. Maybe thirty more seconds, then twenty. She found herself counting steps next. First six more, then five, then four. And . . .

Dr. Reid reached the cave before her and gave her arm one final yank. She tumbled inside, colliding with the solid strength of his chest a split second before a crash covered the mouth of the cave and shrouded them in darkness.

The angry roaring continued, only now the noise was dampened by the mud and sticks and earth blocking the opening.

"Alexei," she rasped. "Jonas. Evelina. Inessa. The tent. Everyone at the bottom . . ."

"I don't think it will hit them." The deep sound of his voice rumbled out of his chest and into her ear. "This one looked smaller. I think most of it occurred on a new section of mountain, not the part hit by the first slide. We were caught on the edge. Maybe we could have tried outrunning it had we gone the opposite direction, but I knew this cave was here. It seemed like the safer choice."

Safe—except for the fact that Dr. Reid was shivering uncontrollably.

She pulled a hand from beneath her warm cloak and rested it on his chest, only to feel the rain coating his oilskin coat. "Just how wet are you?"

She couldn't see his shrug, not with the darkness surrounding them, but she somehow sensed it.

"Considering we're going to be trapped here for the night?" His teeth chattered as he spoke. "Too wet. Far too wet and far too cold."

She patted his chest until she found one of the buttons to his slicker, then unfastened it and the one below it before slipping her hand inside the coat to see for herself how wet he was.

She jerked her hand back a second later. "You're soaked! How did you get this wet? And why were you traipsing around the mountain with such a poor coat? Being a doctor doesn't somehow make you immune to hypothermia. You should understand that."

Again, she felt his shoulders move up and down on a shrug, even though she couldn't see the gesture. "I gave my slicker to one of the men we dragged out of the mud a few hours ago. He was soaked and shivering, and I was warm and dry. The new slicker I grabbed back at the camp was too big, but I didn't realize just how big until I set off again in search of the cave. I got wetter than I realized."

Wearing an overly big slicker could certainly get a person wet, but usually not this wet. Based on his story of giving his slicker away, she guessed he was already soaked before agreeing to search for the wheezing man in the cave.

Why hadn't he said anything?

But she knew the answer, had seen it lived out time and again since she'd returned from her medical trip. Dr. Nathan Reid was more concerned with helping others than with his own well-being. All good doctors were.

And were she in his situation, she probably would have done the same thing to treat someone else's hypothermia.

"You need to take your clothes off," she muttered.

"I need to find a way to warm up is all."

"Yes, which means taking your clothes off."

"Moving helps with body heat. Maybe we should start digging our way out. It sounds like the mudslide has stopped."

She listened for a moment but heard no rumbling, nor did she feel any shaking inside the cave. "Why do men always assume they're invincible? You're wet and shivering in forty-degree weather. I don't care how much digging you do, you'll be hypothermic in thirty minutes. Even if you can somehow stay warm enough not to die while digging your way out of the cave tonight, then what? You're caught in the rain, in the dark, on the side of a mountain, without a lantern. We need to wait until morning to attempt leaving, and that means we need to get you dry. Now."

He didn't argue as she bent down and unlatched her medical bag, and she could only hope a bit of common sense was starting to seep into his thick skull.

It took her a moment to find the side pocket she searched for in the dark, but she eventually slid her hand into the cloth pouch and pulled out both a match and flint rock.

She struck the match, and a small flame flickered to life.

"You have matches?" Surprise laced his voice.

"I don't head into the mountains without being prepared." She took a few steps away from him, scanning the deeper parts of a cave that looked to extend rather far back into the mountain.

Just like before, she found nothing other than cold, damp rock. "Unfortunately the matches won't do us any good without wood for a fire. I was hoping someone might have camped here previously and I missed some firewood at the back of the cave when we looked before."

"A fire." Dr. Reid rasped, his body releasing a harsh tremble. "That would warm me up."

The flame on the match had nearly reached her fingers. She shook it out, then dropped it to the damp floor and stepped on it before turning back to him. "You have to take off your shirt before you get any colder. You're probably on the verge of hypothermia now."

"Kate, no."

"I have a fur cloak. It's not big, but it's thick, and if we huddle together, it should keep both of us warm through the night."

"It's not proper."

"That's what you care about? Whether this is proper? We have no food or water, and we don't know if we'll be able to dig ourselves out come morning, or if there's another entrance to the cave somewhere. If there is, we have only my matches to light our way, and you're worried about having your shirt off when I won't even be able to see you." Why were men always so stubborn? "Even if I could see you, I assure you, it won't be the first time I've seen a male chest. I'm a doctor, remember?"

"You're making me sound ridiculous," he gritted through the sound of chattering teeth, but the whisper of moving fabric filtered through the cave.

"You *are* ridiculous!" Kate dropped her cloak from around her shoulders and began unbuttoning her dress. It had gotten damp, though with her cloak, she'd probably be able to stay warm enough. But not if she was trying to share her body heat. Besides, all the medical journal articles she'd read had said the same thing. Using a fire, a warm bottle of water, and many blankets were the most common ways to treat hypothermia. But the research also indicated it wasn't the fastest or most effective treatment method. Skin-to-skin contact was.

"Where are you?" Dr. Reid spoke into the darkness.

"I'm coming." She headed back toward his voice, careful where she placed each foot as she retraced the handful of steps she'd taken away from him with the match. "We should lay the cloak on the floor and then roll up in it. That way we'll have some kind of barrier between the cold rock and our bodies."

"All right," he muttered, but the strained tone of his voice told her that he was still uncomfortable with what they were about to do.

She spread the cloak anyway, then lay down a foot or so from the edge. "Come on, lie beside me."

He was slow going about it, but he eventually did as she asked, placing himself far enough away that they still weren't touching.

"Grab the end of the cloak and roll first. You're the one who's shivering." Though she was starting to shiver now too, with the cool air kissing her skin through the thin layer of her chemise and bloomers.

He rolled once, causing his body to bump against hers, and the skin of his torso was far too cold for her liking.

"Kate, stop touching me."

"Were supposed to touch. That's the point."

"Sharing body heat doesn't mean your hands need to skim up and down my bare chest."

Oh, that. Right. She pressed her hands to her stomach. "I didn't mean it like that. I was just trying to assess how cold—"

"I understand, but it's not necessary. Now are you going to roll with me or not?"

"Yes. Can you roll on top of me, then take me along with you?"

He muttered something under his breath that she couldn't quite catch, then rolled again, the weight of his body falling onto her for a quick moment before she found herself caught tightly between Dr. Reid and the cloak. Then he stopped moving, leaving them both on their sides facing each other.

"Are you at the end?" She'd been hoping they could roll up twice, but they would probably need a cloak the size of Jonas's for that.

"I am." Again, Dr. Reid's voice sounded strained. "What are you wearing?"

Oh, was that why he was acting odd? "My shift. My dress got wet. Not as wet as your clothes, but wearing it wasn't going to be helpful, especially if we're supposed to share body heat."

"You took off your dress . . . ? And you're not wearing a corset?"

"No. I never wear corsets. I already told you, they—"

"Stop talking."

"What?"

"I said stop talking."

"But why? We're stuck here together. We should talk about something, shouldn't we? To pass the time?"

"No." Again, that tight sound was back in his voice.

"Do you think it's working? I'm feeling warmer. Are you?"

His chest rose and fell beside her own, which certainly warmed her body, never mind that she hadn't been particularly cold.

"Yes. The shivering is subsiding."

"Good. If we can stay warm through the night, then I'm hoping we can dig ourselves out of the cave come morning."

He sighed, the movement causing his chest to press even

more tightly against hers before retracting. "How many times do I need to ask you to stop talking?"

"I don't know. We're stuck here together for the night. It seems we should find something to talk about so we can stay halfway occupied. I'd expect you would agree, Dr. Reid."

"It's Nathan now. You don't get to tell me to take off my clothes, then press yourself up against me for a night without at least using my first name."

Oh, drat. He had a point about that. "Fine. I'll call you Nathan. Happy?"

"Not exactly, but I'm willing to compromise. Now, please be quiet."

She sucked in a breath, then snapped her mouth shut. There was no reason for him to be snippy, not when she was just trying to make sure he stayed warm. Unless maybe he was tired. Drowsiness was a symptom of hypothermia, and if that was the case, then she needed to keep him awake and talking.

But his body seemed warmer now than it had a few minutes ago, and his shivering had nearly stopped.

So she did as he asked and simply lay there, with her head tucked into the crook of his neck and his chest rising and falling against hers. It had the oddest calming effect on her, almost as though the thoughts tumbling through her head wanted to slow themselves down for once and simply rest.

Almost as though a part of her liked being curled up with the man who was supposed to be her *not-friend*.

14

Nathan was warm all over. From the tips of his toes to the top of his head, every inch of him was deliciously warm. In fact, he couldn't remember the last time he'd felt so warm—or the last time he'd wanted to linger in bed for so long.

Something tickled his nose, and he reached up to scratch it, except he couldn't move his hand. Or his arm or even his leg. And he was pressed against something that felt just as warm as he was, and dreamily soft.

He cracked an eyelid, waiting for the room around him to come into focus. But it didn't. He could barely see anything. There was a single faint light coming from his left and . . .

The cave.

Memories from last night flooded his mind. He was in a cave on the side of a mountain, and the thing tickling his nose was Kate Amos's hair.

He turned his head to the side and found her face just a few inches below his, her head nestled between the crook of his neck and the top of his chest.

And oh, heavens, he wanted to kiss her. Just like he'd

wanted to kiss her last night when they'd rolled up together in her cloak—and not simply so she'd stop talking.

How could he not want to kiss her, with her silky hair falling against his chest and her soft body pressed against his?

He still remembered the way she'd trailed her hand over his chest. He'd known she'd just been trying to gauge the temperature of his skin to see if he was hypothermic. But the feel of her fingers had caused a shudder to ripple through him for a reason that had nothing to do with the cold. If anything, it had a warming effect on his body. Just like pressing himself against her had warmed him right up.

He'd read about this in medical journals, that the fastest way to treat hypothermia was with body heat, preferably skin-to-skin contact. Of course, he'd never intended to personally test the theory. And for good reason.

Because now he had a rather uncontrollable desire to dip his head and kiss awake a woman who thought he was her enemy.

Something sounded from the entrance to the cave, and he looked over to where dirt filled the opening. It seemed like the light in the cave was growing brighter.

A series of rhythmic thuds sounded from outside the cave. Could those be shovels moving dirt? And were there voices too? The noises were faint, but perhaps people had found them.

Kate's eyes fluttered open, and she looked around in confusion for a moment, then buried her face in his neck. "You're so warm."

Heaven help him. Her hair brushed his throat, and that gave him the nearly uncontrollable urge all over again to lean down and kiss her.

Instead he shifted slightly, dislodging the part of the cloak that was tucked between his body and the cold stone floor.

The movement only brought his mouth closer to Kate's.

"Come on." He tried to ignore how close her mouth was as he spoke. "We need to get up and get dressed. I think rescuers have found us."

Whoever was on the other side of the mud and debris blocking the opening to the cave must have heard him speaking, because a voice trickled into the cave. "Dr. Reid, is that you?"

"Yes, it's me," he called back.

"I found Dr. Reid!" the voice shouted.

More shoveling sounds filled the air, accompanied by shouts from farther away.

"Is Kate there with you?" the voice asked again, and it sounded awfully close.

"Alexei," Kate muttered, trying to disentangle herself from the cloak, but his weight was still pinning it down. "That's Alexei's voice."

She would know better than him. Though Alexei was something of a legend in Juneau, Nathan had only seen Kate's brother that first time he'd gone to the trading post hoping to talk to her and yesterday on the mountain. That was hardly enough time to memorize the sound of another person's voice.

"Yes," he called back. "We're both here and well."

He hopped to his feet. Where were his shirt and trousers? He could barely see the rocky floor in the darkness, but they had to be somewhere.

Nathan spotted something on the floor and headed toward it, but it was Kate's medical bag.

He turned and scanned the floor again, which was a little more visible this time, which was strange. He hadn't expected the shoveling to affect visibility inside the cave quite so much over the last thirty seconds.

There. His shirt had been right next to the cloak all along. But Kate's dress was spread out by her medical bag. He grabbed it and tossed it her direction. "Put this on, and hurry."

Chapter 14   151

He started toward his shirt, but crumbling sounded from the front of the cave, and the remaining dirt fell away without warning, leaving the entrance open to the sun.

He squinted against the sudden brightness as silhouettes of men moved into the cave.

"Kate? Are you all right?" Alexei's voice again.

Nathan stood frozen, cold air bombarding his bare chest. He couldn't see the shadowy men very well against the brightness of the sun, but assumed the first figure rushing toward them was Alexei and the larger man behind him was the Deputy Marshal.

But both men came to a stop a few feet away, and the excitement on Alexei's face morphed into a white mask of fury. "Why are you unclothed, Dr. Reid?"

"He was prehypothermic and needed to be warmed up." Kate pushed to her feet with a natural grace that seemed at odds with the fact she'd just spent the night sleeping on a cave floor. "Since we didn't have fire, we had no choice but to use the heat from our bodies to stay warm."

She kept talking, but no one heard her. Not him, not Alexei, not her brother-in-law, and certainly not the two other rescuers standing at the front of the cave. The only thing anyone was paying attention to was what she was wearing.

The dampness of the cave and their body heat had rendered her shift nearly translucent, clinging to her body in such a way that Nathan averted his gaze, though that didn't stop a burning sensation from climbing onto his cheeks.

"Where are your clothes?" Alexei pinned his gaze to Kate's face, his voice a deathly calm.

"Oh, they were wet." Kate sounded about as bored as if they were discussing knitting patterns. "We tried to spread them out on the floor so they'd dry, see?"

Kate held up the dress in her hands—the dress she hadn't

had time to don since he'd tossed it to her only seconds before the dirt in the opening had crumbled.

Nathan didn't move any closer to his own shirt. He couldn't seem to pull his gaze from the two men at the front of the cave. Strangers who were whispering to themselves, looking at him and Kate with shocked disapproval.

"Put your dress on, Kate," Alexei barked. "Now. And I highly suggest you get dressed too, Dr. Reid."

Nathan scrambled over to where his clothes had been lying, finding them still a bit damp as he pulled on his shirt and trousers.

But it was too little, too late.

It didn't matter that he could explain.

It didn't matter that there was a logical medical reason for how he and Kate had been found.

The only thing that mattered were the angry looks on Alexei's and the Deputy Marshal's faces, and the accusations flashing in the eyes of the other rescuers.

"How many times do I have to tell you? We were just trying to stay warm!"

Nathan watched Kate as she stalked from one side of Alexei's office above the trading post to the other, her pace so fast that the papers on the desk stirred as she whipped past.

"You weren't wearing a corset," Alexei shot back, his face set into the same hard glower he'd worn since they'd left the cave that morning.

"I never wear a corset!"

"Then maybe you should start." Alexei's voice seethed with a quiet sort of rage that left Nathan feeling colder than he'd been last night.

But her brother's chilling voice didn't seem to affect Kate. If anything, her voice got louder each time Alexei's got quieter. "Why would I wear a corset? In case I happen to get trapped in a cave again during a mudslide? Fine, I'll borrow one of Lina's the next time I go up the mountain. Happy?"

"No. And I don't care about what you wear the next time you go up the mountain." Alexei jabbed a finger at Kate as she strode past. "Because you'll be married by then, and if you want to prance around the entirety of Alaska in your underthings, it won't be my problem."

"Married?" Kate stopped her pacing, her shoulders somehow growing stiffer, which should have been impossible, since they'd already been stiff enough to balance a stack of the hospital's lumber on. "I'm never marrying, you know that. No man alive wants a doctor for a wife. Besides, a husband would just slow me down."

Alexei didn't answer. Instead, he moved his narrowed gaze to Nathan.

Nathan felt the back of his neck grow warm, but he pushed himself away from the wall where he'd been leaning ever since they'd entered the office. He didn't know how long ago that was, only that the two siblings had been arguing for quite a while, and loudly enough that anyone in the store downstairs was sure to overhear them.

In fact, at this point, he suspected half the town of Juneau had decided they needed to shop at the trading post just so they could listen to the argument.

Nathan crossed the room to Kate. "I believe your brother means you and I will already be married."

"What?" She grew suddenly still, as though the idea was only now occurring to her. "No, no. We can't marry. I . . . you're . . . there's . . . there's no need. Things aren't as bad as all that. Give it a few days. The rumors will blow over. They always do."

"I was in my drawers, and you were wearing a chemise and no corset." The situation had been beyond indecent. Alexei hadn't given him an ultimatum about marrying Kate, but he hadn't needed to. There was only one course of action for any honorable man to take. "Had it been just me and your brother and the Deputy Marshal, perhaps we could cover this up. But two other men saw you. It needs to be corrected, and marriage is the best way to do that."

"But I was only trying to warm you up. You were prehypothermic, and the journal articles say—"

"I know what the journal articles say, and you know what the journal articles say, but no one else in this town has ever read an article on hypothermia and the various ways to treat it. It's not an argument you can win with the rumors that are spreading." Nathan shoved a hand through his hair. How could she be so oblivious to the damage this would cause her reputation?

Kate's brow creased, and she shifted her gaze toward the window that overlooked the main road running along the harbor. "Are you sure? Do people in town know already?"

"The people in the tent on the mountain knew before the two of you had a chance to put on dry clothes." A muscle pulsed on the side of Alexei's jaw. "You're not a common prostitute, Kate. You come from a respected Alaskan family that holds shipping contracts with the US government. If something like this happens, people talk."

"But will the two of you really force me into marriage?" She looked between them, her usually determined eyes oddly vulnerable. "Even if I don't want it?"

What did Kate have against marriage? When they'd both gotten out of bed yesterday morning, neither of them could

Chapter 14

have foreseen the circumstances that were about to transpire. But as far as Nathan was concerned, marriage was only a matter of time.

He'd never met a woman like Kate Amos. Strong. Determined. Independent enough to think for herself and make her own choices rather than be cowed by what those around her thought or said.

And she was a doctor to boot.

He'd fallen half in love with her the day he'd stood on the porch of the mercantile watching her treat that dislocated shoulder, and the rest of the way in love the day he'd talked with her on the beach.

Of course, seeing how she wouldn't even talk to him at this time yesterday, he'd assumed it would take six months or better to convince her to love him back. But now they were both standing in her brother's office discussing marriage.

The problem was, she seemed just as determined not to marry as she was to be a doctor.

Was it him? Did she find something about him intolerable or repulsive?

He didn't think so. Her objection appeared to be more against the idea of marriage in general.

At least, that's how Alexei was taking her objections, because his shoulders had lost their stiffness, and instead of scowling, he was looking at Kate the way one might look at a newborn kitten trying to walk for the first time. "If you don't marry, then you'll have to leave. Not just Juneau, but all of Alaska. Word will reach Sitka by the end of the week."

Kate twisted her hands together. "But where will I go? How will I practice medicine? Surely you don't expect me to start over again somewhere else? That's too much. I don't want to leave Alaska again. I don't want to leave my family."

Nathan reached out and took her hand in his. "That's why

we're going to have a quiet wedding ceremony this afternoon." Ellingsworth was going to throttle him, but he didn't care. "And then you can come work for me at the clinic, and at the hospital when it opens."

"No." She jerked her hand away from him, her body tensing all over again. "Even if we marry, I still won't work for you. I'll never work for you."

"Why?" Nathan tunneled a hand into his hair. "It's the most obvious solution. You can still practice medicine, and the rumors will go away. We might not have had a proper courtship, but I'll make you a good husband."

"I don't want to marry." She threw up her hands. "Why won't either of you listen to me?"

"Because your choice is to marry or leave." Alexei pushed himself away from his desk and headed to the window, which looked out over the street below and beyond that, the wharf. "I'm not saying this to make you miserable. I'm saying it because it's how the world works. A ruined reputation for a woman isn't like being a doctor. It's not a fight you can win."

A great huff of air streamed from Alexei's lungs as he studied the street below for a few more seconds. When he turned around again, his gaze sought Nathan's. "What if Kate marries you, but she keeps her own practice? One that serves women and the nearby tribes. She already visits the small villages scattered along the coast at least once a year, the closer ones more often. There's no reason to give that up."

Nathan winced. "Ah, she's welcome to visit the villages as often as she wants, but you should probably know that an RCS ship is on its way from Sitka with a doctor and medical supplies bound for the villages in Southeast Alaska. After that, the ship will head north to the villages on the Aleutian Islands and the coast of the Arctic Ocean, culminating in a trip to Barrow at the beginning of August."

"You're sending a doctor to that many places?" Kate's voice was quiet.

"Yes, it's needed."

Her jaw quivered, and she blinked rapidly. And were those tears in her eyes?

"What's wrong?" He stepped closer.

She gave her head a small shake. "All those villages . . . It's my route. I used to . . ." She pressed her lips together, then ducked her head to stare at the ground.

She'd visited that many villages? He'd known she made trips to the ones near Juneau, but he hadn't realized she'd gone to the Aleutians. "Since you have experience working with the tribes, I can see if the MHS will hire you next summer to—"

"Stop." She held up her hand. "Just stop talking."

He sighed. He wanted to reach out and touch her, to settle his hands on her shoulders and bring her close enough that the faint scent of flowers and fruit twined around him. Maybe even wipe the sad twist from her mouth with a kiss.

But she'd moved away from him and was now staring out the window, her arms wrapped around herself in a lonely hug.

He rubbed the back of his neck and turned to Alexei. "This might not be the ideal time to mention it, but I'm wondering if we can place a doctor on your ship that travels up the Yukon River this summer."

Alexei's eyebrows winged up in obvious surprise. "You want to send a doctor up the Yukon?"

"Yes. Or more ideally, I'd like to station a doctor permanently in Tanana and devise a route that takes him to the villages along the river three times a year. But at the moment, the Sitka Trading Company is the only organization that runs any kind of vessel up the Yukon River at regular intervals, and getting a doctor on that ship—even if he can only make one stop at each of the villages—is still better than nothing."

"It's a wonderful idea." Alexei stroked his jaw, ideas churning behind his dark eyes. "I'm happy someone at the MHS is concerned about getting a doctor into the interior of Alaska, but the ship that runs that route is leaving Sitka next week. Can you have a doctor there by then?"

Nathan's shoulders slumped. "No." He'd only just gotten confirmation that Ellingsworth had sent a doctor to San Francisco for the route up the coast.

"I'm more than willing to take a doctor in the future. But we have a limited window of time when the river isn't frozen, and that means I can't delay the departure."

Kate whirled away from the window. "I'll go!"

"No." Both he and Alexei spoke simultaneously.

"Why not? It will get me away from the rumors." She rushed back across the room. "And the Athabaskans and Yupik won't care that—"

"Absolutely not," Nathan quipped, but his words were drowned out by Alexei, who was now shouting.

"You don't seriously expect me to send you on a route like that without one of your brothers on the ship. You know how difficult a voyage like that is for a man. You know things can be much worse for a female passenger. Just look at what happened to Maggie aboard one of our ships last year. I can't just throw a female passenger at the captain without warning and know you'll be taken care of."

Kate looked about ready to cry. She stood with her shoulders hunched forward and her gaze fixed firmly on the floor. Her hands were clenched at her sides, and a thick silence crept over the room.

Nathan had never seen her look so fragile. "I wish there were a simple solution." He stepped closer to her, but he didn't reach out and take her hand again. Nor did he tuck the wayward strand of hair dangling beside her face behind her ear.

Chapter 14

"You can still visit any of those villages however often you want. The routes I have planned take a doctor to the villages only three times a year."

She shook her head. "I was only going to half of those villages before. And I only made it to the ones nearby twice a year. I can't imagine they'd need more than three visits a year."

"I can." Alexei leaned against his desk, arms crossed as he studied his sister. "Had you not arrived in Petersburg when you did, X'unéi and her daughter would be dead."

"X'unéi?" Nathan looked between Alexei and Kate.

Kate kept her head ducked, leaving her brother to explain.

"When we arrived in Petersburg, we found a woman who had been in labor for three days. Everyone presumed the babe was dead and that the mother would soon follow, but Kate performed a caesarian section on the mother and removed the baby surgically. The little girl and her mother both survived."

Nathan smiled, warmth filling his chest. Those were difficult surgeries. Very risky with a high mortality rate. But if it had been the only way to save the mother, Kate would have felt she had no choice. He wasn't surprised the surgery had been a success either, not with Kate performing it.

"That's amazing." He had the sudden urge to wrap her in a hug and never let her go. He settled for asking her to look at him instead, and he waited until her green eyes peered into his before speaking again. "I want you to keep going to those villages. I don't care what kind of rotation the MHS doctor is on, or even if he's there at the same time as you. Those villagers know you, and it sounds to me like they trust you. Whether we marry or not, you can visit the villages whenever you want."

Maybe he was being a scoundrel for even saying such a thing. It wasn't as though she should need his permission to go to those villages. But he felt like he should give it anyway, like maybe it would help if he did.

And that just left him wondering once again why the report from the RCS captain last summer hadn't mentioned Kate was in Juneau and taking trips to the native villages.

"Thank you for your offer." Kate took a step away from him, wrapping her arms back around herself. "But I'm afraid going to the villages won't be the same now."

"No. Wait. Listen to me." He stepped closer again. "Just because you won't be the only source of medical care doesn't mean you have to stop providing it altogether. Promise me you'll keep providing it."

She shrugged away from him. "I don't expect you to understand."

She turned as though ready to head back to the window, but he reached out and rested a hand on her arm, speaking to her back. "I want you to know that as your husband, I promise to do everything I can to facilitate your doctoring. Whether that means finding an escort so you can visit mining camps or letting you go on trips to native villages or giving you a job at the hospital. However you want to practice medicine, I vow I will support it."

She sucked in a breath. He barely heard it, that soft intake of air. But when she turned to face him, that faint sheen of moisture was back in her eyes. "Do you mean it? Truly?"

"I do." He dropped down onto his knee, then reached out and took her hand. "Kate Amos, will you marry me?"

Her tongue darted out to wet her lips. And for a moment, one precious, wonderful moment, he thought she was going to agree to be his wife.

But then she pulled away, a hard mask falling over those watery green eyes. And while he couldn't read her thoughts, he knew the next word out of her mouth wasn't going to be yes.

Chapter 14   161

KATE SUCKED in a breath as she stared into Nathan's face. It held such sincerity that she had little choice but to believe him. But marriage between her and Nathan wasn't going to work.

Not that she wanted to explain why. She was better off seeing if she could get him to change his mind about wanting to marry her. She didn't want to leave Alaska over a few rumors, but she also didn't want to commit her life to a man who would have full legal control over her.

So she turned to her brother. "Alexei, tell him that he doesn't want to marry me. Tell him all the reasons why I'd make the poorest wife to ever exist."

Her brother raised an eyebrow. "I can't think of a single one."

The oaf. She clenched her jaw, then turned back to Nathan. "I promise you, a month into our marriage, you'd find yourself regretting your decision, and yet you'd be stuck with me for the rest of your life."

"And just why do you think I'd regret spending the rest of my life with you?" There was something soft about his voice as he dropped her hand and stood to his feet, something that told her she'd only made him more curious about her rather than pushing him away.

"I can't sit still, for one. I'm a ball of nervous energy and never learned how to relax."

"Really?" He cocked his head to the side, but the way he looked at her said her confession had the opposite effect than what she'd been hoping for. "How fascinating. What do you do when you're tired or have had a long day?"

"I keep moving until I fall into bed and sleep."

"It's true." Alexei headed around his desk, where he poured himself a cup of water from a pitcher. "You should have seen her when she was younger. Our father often took us with him on his ship, and Kate was a walking disaster. The rest of us enjoyed learning about the rigging and sails or seeing new places. We could all find things to entertain ourselves, but not Kate. She ran from one end of the ship to the other, knocking things over and tangling herself in ropes. Father would get furious and confine her to the cabin, but that only made things worse."

Kate winced at the memory. To this day, she felt a bit claustrophobic whenever she stepped onto a ship or boat, never mind that the wide open spaces of water and mountains surrounded her.

"I've seen children like that in my practice over the years. They have so much energy, their parents can barely tolerate it." Nathan was still studying her, almost as though she was a puzzle he was trying to work out in his mind. "But I've never met anyone who's confessed to such behavior as an adult."

"I'm just trying to warn you what you'd be in for if we married."

"But there are times when you're still. I've seen it."

"I can be still as long as my brain is busy, but I always have to be doing something. I can't just step onto the deck of a ship and find myself content to watch the scenery like Alexei or Sacha. I'm not like Evelina, who can just give a person a hug or sit and talk to them while they tell her all their problems. It might not look like it, but I have more energy than Ilya. I swear I do."

Nathan took a step closer. "So being this still while we talk . . . Is that hard for you?"

"No, because my heart is about to pound through my rib cage, and my brain is busy thinking about the ways my life is about to change."

Oh, drat. Had she said that aloud? What was wrong with her?

Alexei burst into laughter. "That's another thing you should know about Kate. She can't hide what she's thinking."

Nathan's mouth tipped up in a half smile that looked awful similar to the one he'd shown her last night in the rain, when he'd told her they weren't enemies.

Today his smile made her stomach want to turn inside out. He took another step closer, reaching for her hand and taking it in his own again. "The only question I have left is whether our children will be calm and studious like me or little bundles of energy like you."

Their children? Heat rushed to her face. "I . . . That is . . . I . . . um . . . I find this conversation highly inappropriate."

His smile only grew bigger. "We're about to be married."

"No. We're not."

"Yes, you are." Both Alexei and Nathan said together.

They were really going to make her get married, weren't they? Either that or leave Alaska. Nothing she had said so far seemed to deter either of them.

"It won't be that kind of marriage," she blurted, tugging her hand away from Nathan and turning toward her brother. "Tell him, Alexei, that if we marry under these circumstances, it won't be for love. We won't share a bed or . . . or . . ."—she waved her hand absently—"do any of the things that could result in children."

It was the wrong thing to say, because Alexei's jaw stiffened, and his eyes took on a serious edge. "Don't be such a child. Of course you'll share a bed. It will be your duty as a wife. You already heard Nathan promise to make you a good husband, and as far as finding you a spouse goes, Nathan Reid seems uniquely suited to handle your eccentricities. If anything, he almost seems to enjoy them. It's enough to make me think God is in this marriage, that even though the cause of it might be a bit unconventional, it's a match ordained by heaven. I'll give you two a moment to yourselves while I notify the priest that there's to be a wedding this afternoon."

"I . . . but . . ." She watched Alexei leave the office, then moved her gaze back to Nathan. Was it just her, or had the room grown suddenly hot? "Surely you want a wife who's willing to . . . who wants . . . that is . . . to participate in . . ."—Again, she waved her hand in the air, searching for words that couldn't seem to come—"wifely duties. And that's not me. I don't want, uh, any of that."

Nathan stepped nearer, close enough she could smell the scent of sandalwood and rain on his skin. "Not right away." His breath puffed against her ear, warm and slightly ticklish. "We'll take time to get to know each other first, but eventually . . ."

He let the word hang there and pulled back far enough to peer down into her eyes.

"Eventually what?" she whispered, almost afraid of what he'd say.

There was something soft in how he looked at her, something tender in how he reached out and swiped a strand of hair away from her face, then tucked it behind her ear. "Eventually I expect you to be my wife in every way."

She swallowed, the noise so loud it seemed to echo in the room. "What if I'm not ready?"

"Oh, there's no question about whether you're ready. But I'm a patient man, and I'll wait until you are."

"What if I'm never ready?"

"The woman who burrowed her face into my neck last night? Who grows suddenly and inexplicably still when I step too close?" The corner of his mouth tipped into another of those lazy smiles, and it made something pull low in her stomach. "You'll be ready one day, and I'm willing to wait until you are."

Kate wanted to tell him no, that she still couldn't marry

him, that it would never work. But then she looked into Nathan's dark eyes. They were so patient, so tender as they watched her, the look on his face so open and honest, it was almost enough to make her wonder if she could have a good marriage with this man, one like Evelina and Jonas's, or like Sacha and Maggie's.

"I still don't feel like I'm ready to be your wife," she whispered, the words barely audible above the pounding of her heart.

"That's all right." He raised her hand to his mouth and planted a gentle kiss on her knuckles, his eyes never leaving hers. "I'm ready enough for the both of us."

15

As girls, her sister Evelina and her friends had spent entirely too much time planning their weddings. Kate could well remember sitting in the parlor in their house in Sitka with other girls from church, talking about what their husbands would look like one day. They dreamed about the dresses they'd wear on the day they got married, about whether they'd curl their hair with a hot iron or weave a crown of wildflowers to wear atop their heads.

Kate had always found the topic boring. She'd always had more fun dreaming of splinting a broken leg or performing a surgery than joining the conversation around her.

Even when she'd been engaged in Boston, she hadn't put much thought into her wedding. It had always seemed so far off, and there had always been more pressing matters that needed her attention.

But now she was married to Nathan, and even if she'd bothered to plan her perfect day, even if she'd dreamed of it for years, it wouldn't have looked anything like what she'd experienced that afternoon as she stood with Nathan in front of a priest in the gingham dress she wore every third Sunday. Pledging her life away to a man she'd known only two months, she'd wondered if God would strike her dead at the altar for lying when it came to the part in her vows about loving, honoring, and obeying her husband until death.

But God hadn't struck her dead, which meant that after the wedding, she and Nathan attended the impromptu feast Evelina had organized. How her sister could come up with enough food in a few hours to feed half the town was beyond her, but she had. And people had stayed at the Russian Orthodox church for hours, laughing and eating until they'd grown drowsy.

Only then had Nathan said it was time to leave. He took her straight back to his medical clinic and was painfully gentle as he showed her around the various rooms downstairs, once again stating that he would hire her if she ever wanted to work for him. Then he led her up the stairs to the apartment they would share. It had two bedrooms—thankfully—along with a kitchen and sitting room.

But walking around the building only reminded her of what she'd lost by marrying Nathan—the chance to own this building herself. And she couldn't help but wonder how many other dreams she'd have to give up now that she had a husband.

They were passing the door to a third room when she stopped, peeking through the half-open door. "You have a map of Alaska?"

"Yes. In my office. You can go in if you'd like."

She pushed the door open to find a basic desk and filing cabinet, but those weren't the focal point of the room. Her eyes instantly went to the large map pinned to the wall. Anyone's would. The map was the size of three large pictures, and it had markings all over it. Most were lines and arrows, but some were tiny pushpins with tips that had been painted different colors.

It looked like one of the maps Alexei used to plan shipping routes, but this one would make her brother jealous. She'd never once seen him code his routes with different colors.

"What's this for?" She headed to the map. "Don't tell me you want to start a shipping company."

"A shipping company?" Nathan chuckled. "Heavens, no. I've got enough to do with my time already."

"So why do you have this map? Why are you putting together shipping routes?"

"Those are proposed doctor routes. Like I told you and Alexei earlier, I want to ensure the people of Alaska have access to a doctor at least three times a year."

Three times a year. It seemed impossible. The area around Southeast Alaska alone was a spiderweb of channels and islands and fjords, but the map sprawled so much farther, reaching into regions where the sun never rose in winter.

"I didn't realize just how big your dreams were." Or how much time he'd put into painstakingly figuring out the routes that would cover the largest number of villages with the smallest distance traveled. The map before her wasn't some whim that had been thrown together on a night of boredom. It represented months—or maybe even years—of studying the land, the villages, the ocean and rivers and coast. Why, he'd probably spent hours just painting the tops of all his pushpins so that each route could be represented in its own color.

"Yes, my dreams are rather big, aren't they?" His voice seemed a little lower than normal. "Tell me, as someone who's grown up here, do you think I'm a fool for attempting such a thing?"

"No," she rasped, slanting a glance at him. "I think you're a hero."

"A hero?" Surprise filled his face. "I'm nothing of the sort."

"Then what do you call this?" She nodded toward the map.

His shoulders rose and fell on a sigh. "Discouraging. The map makes Alaska look so small, like I can actually reach all the villages scattered across the wilderness. Like it should be possible to take seven doctors, put some of them on traveling routes and station some at a hospital in Juneau, and provide medical care to everyone in Alaska."

He tunneled a hand through his dark hair, which had a habit of falling over his forehead.

As his wife, she could brush it back whenever it got in the way, and no one would think anything of it. But she kept her arms at her sides.

"The map doesn't show the frigid temperatures that plague the interior and Arctic in winter," he continued. "Nor does it show the ranges of mountains upon mountains that stack atop each other along the coast."

"Your map covers over half a million square miles. Nothing about it is small." And the idea of reaching all those remote villages three times a year felt as challenging as charting stars in the sky.

"There aren't any roads. I feel like that's the most unbelievable part about this place. Over half a million square miles, and not a single road that connects one town to another, let alone a railroad."

"That's because the water is Alaska's road system. It always has been. Look." Kate pointed to Wrangell and Petersburg in Southeast Alaska, not terribly far from Juneau. Then she moved her hand up to touch Unalaska in the Aleutian Islands to the west, and Tanana on the Yukon River in the center. Finally, she pressed up on her toes and stretched her body until her fingers grazed the pushpin at the very top of the map. Barrow, Alaska. "It's all on the water. But while I see how you might be able to get a doctor to all these places one time a year, I don't see how you'll be able to get them there three times.

Especially not Barrow. It's accessible for only a few months every summer, when the ice melts in the Arctic."

"I want to station a doctor in Barrow permanently."

Her gaze snapped to his. "You do?"

And here she was, feeling bad for herself because she couldn't go to Barrow once a year, that she'd no longer be the only doctor to visit Petersburg or Wrangell. But Nathan had a much better plan to reach Alaska than she'd ever been able to come up with.

"Yes, sending a doctor there for a brief visit this summer is only a temporary solution. Next summer I'm hoping to move a doctor there. And I want the doctor I asked your brother about sending on the Yukon trip this summer to travel via dogsled up and down the river in the winter."

A dogsled route? She shouldn't have ignored him those times he'd stopped by the trading post. Should have sought him out to see what he'd wanted. Because had she known this . . .

What?

What would have changed? Seeing this map helped her understand him better, but it didn't change the fact that with Nathan's arrival, her doctoring skills were becoming less and less needed in Alaska.

"I'm trying to convince the surgeon general to post advertisements in Scandinavia for a doctor who can handle a dogsled team." Nathan rubbed the back of his neck.

"That's a really good idea, but you realize that each of the villages have a shaman, right? They might not provide medical care the way we think of it, but they've been treating tribe members for hundreds of years."

A muscle pulsed at the side of his jaw. "Yes, but those shamans don't have access to diphtheria antitoxins."

"I . . . No. I don't suppose they do."

"There was an outbreak in Anvik two years ago in

February." He stepped forward and touched his finger to a place along the western portion of the Yukon River. "Twenty people died."

Kate sunk her teeth into the side of her cheek. She'd known about the outbreak—news traveled among the tribes in Alaska—but she was surprised Nathan knew.

"The year before that, there was an outbreak of smallpox here in Nulato." Again, he touched his hand to the spot on the map that marked the small Athabaskan village on the Yukon. "Three quarters of the town died."

"There was?" She felt her eyebrows rise in surprise. "I hadn't known that."

"Yes. People in rural communities are far more likely to die prematurely than people in cities who have access to doctors and hospitals."

Yet another thing she didn't know. But how did he know it? Had they taught such things in his medical school but neglected to teach it in hers? "And you're determined to provide better access to the residents of Alaska to see if that brings mortality rates down."

"As you said, it seems impossible, doesn't it? To put a doctor in every place where one is needed."

It was certainly a big dream.

But there was something about the way he spoke, about the discouragement filling his voice, that had her stepping forward and reaching for his hand. She gripped it carefully. Tentatively. It was so much larger than hers. The skin of his fingers were rough from working with his hands, but not so rough they grated against her own skin.

"Don't say it's impossible. God is 'able to do exceeding abundantly above all that we ask or think.'" The verse rolled easily off her tongue. She hadn't even needed to think about the words.

But it had apparently been a long time since her husband had heard them. Or maybe he'd never heard them at all, because he turned then, his eyes searching hers out.

"When the Bible says that, do you think it's talking about bringing doctors to Alaska?" There was something intense about his gaze.

"Yes. It applies to that, just like it applied to me becoming a doctor."

"That's the verse you used to get you through medical school?"

"And *to* medical school, seeing how Boston is so very far from Alaska."

He shifted the positioning of their hands until she wasn't the one holding his but he was holding hers, his larger palm dwarfing her smaller fingers.

Then he gave her hand a squeeze, and it brought back memories of earlier that morning in the office when he'd somehow, inexplicably, convinced her they needed to get married despite her long list of objections. "Thank you for sharing that with me. It helps."

She gave him a small smile. "You're welcome."

But he wasn't looking at her any longer, even though her hand was still tucked into his. Instead his eyes were back on the map, not leaving the vast territory laid out in front of him.

And she couldn't help but think that with every doctor he found to station in a remote town or travel one of her routes meant one less place her services were needed.

She tugged her hand away from Nathan's and looked down to find several other maps on his desk. The top one was of Alaska again, and though the markings on it weren't as detailed as the markings on the big map, it still had the rough layouts of the routes. She moved it aside to look at the map underneath, expecting it to be of a smaller part of Alaska, like the Alexander

Archipelago, where Juneau was located, or the Arctic Circle or maybe even the Aleutian Islands to the west.

She found a map of islands, but they weren't ones she'd seen before. She frowned as she studied the long, skinny islands that protected the mainland to the west from the sea. "Is this the Atlantic Ocean?"

Nathan turned back to her. "Ah, you found my map of the Outer Banks. Yes, that's the Atlantic Ocean, and this is a section of the North Carolina coast."

"And these arrows, the lines . . . Does that mean you're planning routes for traveling doctors there too?"

He stepped closer and looked down at the map. "Much like Alaska, the people of the Outer Banks have an appalling lack of medical care."

"What about this one?" She grabbed the next map off the stack on the desk and held it up. She recognized it as the southern part of Louisiana, but it had lines and arrows drawn all over it as well. "Are you planning routes for Louisiana too?"

"For the bayou, yes. Again, they don't have much medical care."

She stared at the map charting the various inlets and swamps of the jagged Louisiana coastline, then glanced down at the final map on the desk, which had lines drawn all over what appeared to be the southern coast of Lake Superior. "I understand these places might not have much medical care, but are you going to have to leave Alaska to establish hospitals in all of these places? I thought the surgeon general had moved you here."

His hand on the desk grew still. "My assignment here is for three years, then I'm hoping to—"

"You'll have to leave?" She couldn't quite bring herself to meet his gaze, couldn't do anything but look at the map of Lake

Superior and Nathan's motionless hand beside it. "You're not staying here permanently?"

"No, Kate. There's nothing permanent about working for the MHS, especially not in my capacity as—"

"Why didn't you say something before we married?"

Silence filled the space between them. Outside a horse nickered and conversation drifted from farther down the street, but inside, the room was so still it almost felt wrong to breathe.

"You didn't realize I'd be leaving," he finally said, his voice whisper-soft. "And you want to stay with your family."

She wrapped her arms around herself and headed toward the window, where she wouldn't be able to feel Nathan's gaze boring into her. Wouldn't feel the urge to look up and meet his eyes.

"You heard me this morning. I chose to marry you instead of leaving Alaska. Had I realized you intended to leave one day . . ." Her voice shook, and she hated the weakness it showed. "You should have told me."

"I'm sorry. I didn't mean to keep it from you. I thought you understood . . ." In the reflection of the window, she could see him rub a hand over his jaw, then give his head a shake. "No. Why would you know that? I should have told you the position wasn't permanent, but honestly, Kate, considering everything else that was going on, the details of my job were the last thing on my mind."

She drew her gaze away from his reflection and stared out the window, where raindrops were collecting on the glass. Beyond that, two men in a wagon made their way down the road, likely heading to one of the bars.

"Three years is a long time." Nathan came up behind her, and once again, she watched his reflection in the glass as he rubbed the back of his neck. "Who knows what our relationship will look like at the end of it, or how much my plans for advancing medical availability will have progressed. Perhaps I can stay in Alaska longer. Perhaps I can see if the surgeon general will station me here permanently. Dr. Ellingsworth won't want to stay forever, and when he leaves, we'll need a new medical director. I wasn't planning on it being me, but it could be."

She turned to him. "But you don't want it to be. You want to go to these other places, to make sure the people living in all those small towns have access to doctors too."

His shoulders rose and fell on a sigh. "Yes. I'm not going to deny that."

She felt as though her heart had been ripped out of her chest, like her lungs had forgotten how to draw breath, like everything in the life she'd worked so hard to build for herself was crumbling in a way that could never be pieced back together.

"Would you like an annulment?" That thatch of dark brown hair fell over his forehead as he looked at her. "I'll understand if you do."

Was that an option? Part of her wanted to say yes. She couldn't imagine what her life would look like anywhere other than Alaska. The time she'd been away to attend medical school and work for Peter's father had been miserable.

But she was a walking scandal. The rumors about what had happened between her and Nathan in the cave were worse than she'd realized, and now the entire town knew they'd married to salvage her reputation. If she were to leave him the next day, after being forced to marry him in such a public way, that scandal would live on for decades.

It might be so bad that she couldn't return to Alaska ever. And not only that, but the rumors would ricochet to the rest of her family. She didn't want to do anything that might jeopardize one of Alexei's business contracts or Mikhail's expedition opportunities.

"I'm sorry. Truly I am." Nathan reached out and settled a hand on her shoulder, strong and warm.

The simple touch helped to calm her breathing and caused something warm to spread through her, just as it had earlier that day in Alexei's office.

"Please forgive me for not explaining everything this morning. It's not something I intended to keep from you."

"I know. I'd never accuse you of such a thing."

Nathan Reid was the opposite of deceitful. He'd promised her he'd make her a good husband, promised she could keep practicing medicine. And as crazy as it seemed, she believed him, even in spite of what had happened in Boston. But she still couldn't envision herself leaving Alaska.

"But do you want an annulment? I'll send word to the judge in Sitka in the morning if you do."

She looked up at him, into those soft brown eyes filled with an emotion she didn't want to think about. "Do you want one?"

"No. Never."

"Then we'll stay married." The words hurt as they wrenched from her, but they would hurt less than watching her family be humiliated because of her actions. "Now, please excuse me. I'm quite tired."

She turned and headed for the door, feeling the weight of Nathan's gaze on her. But he didn't ask her to wait or call her back, didn't say anything at all as she stepped out of the room and closed the door behind her.

His new wife was in her room crying.

On their wedding night.

Nathan rolled over on his back, staring up at the ceiling illuminated in the dim light from his lamp. *God, is this really what you want for me? For Kate? For both of us?*

That morning, the wedding had seemed like such a good idea. The rumors flying around town were terrible. As a man, he escaped unscathed, but Kate's experience had been a different story.

In the three-hour period between when he'd left the trading post and when he'd arrived at the church for the wedding, half a dozen people had asked him if Kate had been trying to trap him into marriage because she had no prospects. Two men had made comments, wondering just how many times he and Kate had been together before. And Janice Thompson had asked him if Kate was pregnant.

As if a woman could know that the day after she spent the night with a man.

Not that he and Kate had done anything that could result in pregnancy, but even if they had, they wouldn't have known for five or six weeks whether she was with child.

So Nathan shouldn't be surprised that his new wife was spending their wedding night crying in her room.

Another sob filtered through the wall, and Nathan pressed his eyes shut.

What was he supposed to do? Lie here and pretend he couldn't hear her?

He rolled onto his side, but more broken sobs filled the room.

Should he go to her? Try to comfort her? Tell her that their wedding wasn't something she needed to cry over? That he would make her a good husband?

How could he tell her that when he'd forgotten to explain the requirements of his job before they'd married? When he'd neglected to tell her that marrying him would still mean she'd have to leave Alaska—just not immediately?

But as he'd explained earlier, maybe his position in Alaska didn't have to be temporary. He could ask the surgeon general for permission to stay in Alaska after his three years were up.

But if he did that, who would bring better medical care to the Outer Banks or the Louisiana Bayou or the wild, forgotten shores of Lake Superior?

He'd spent years dreaming of how he might one day increase access to medical care not just in one region but across the country.

Surely God didn't want him to give up that dream for Kate.

But where did that leave him? Besides staring at the ceiling listening to his wife cry herself to sleep through the wall on their wedding night.

16

Nathan woke to the unusual sight of sunlight filtering through the small curtained window. It cast a warm glow across the room that was at odds with the heaviness in his chest.

How had Kate slept? He'd lain in bed listening to her muffled sobs until well after midnight, when it seemed she'd finally fallen asleep. And all the while he'd prayed that God would show him how to love his wife.

But just because he'd fallen asleep dreaming of a time when Kate would feel secure in his love for her didn't mean that she'd slept through the night or woken with peace in her heart. She might be even more upset this morning than she'd been last night.

He slid out of bed. A quick peek out the window told him that the sun truly was shining over Juneau. It was one of only a handful of days he'd woken to sunshine rather than clouds since arriving in Southeast Alaska, but perhaps it was something of a gift from God. A little token from heaven to show them both that God wanted to bless their marriage, no matter how poorly it had started.

The scent of coffee wafted into the room, along with the scent of food cooking. Flapjacks, perhaps, but the aroma didn't quite smell like flapjacks.

Kate couldn't have slept that poorly if she was already up and making breakfast. Perhaps the sun had put her in a good mood too. He quickly tossed on a shirt and slid on some trousers, then stepped into the hallway, following the inviting scents to the kitchen.

His new wife stood at the stove, her shoulders stiff and her back ramrod straight as she poured batter into one of the two frying pans.

Then she took what looked to be a thin, large flapjack from the second pan and slid it onto a plate. She smeared jam over the pancake before folding it, first in half, then in quarters so that it was now shaped like a triangle. She topped it with butter and a sprinkle of powdered sugar, then poured another round of batter into the hot pan.

Nathan stepped farther into the kitchen. "It smells delicious."

She jolted at the sound of his voice, quickly glancing over her shoulder before focusing back on the stove. "It's just blinis."

"Blinis?"

"They're Russian, like your American flapjacks but thin and filled with jam or honey rather than topped with syrup."

Russian food. Considering her family's background, he shouldn't be surprised, but somehow he was. "I can't wait to try it. Is that coffee I smell too?"

"It's in the percolator." Kate tilted her head toward the table, where a percolator sat atop a hot pad. Two cups also sat on the table. One had been filled with coffee, but the other remained empty. He moved toward it, filling the empty cup with coffee that he swore smelled twice as good as usual.

"Breakfast will be ready in about ten minutes." Again she spoke with that brisk sort of efficiency that didn't invite compliments or even conversation.

But she should be complimented. The food really did smell wonderful, and here she was, up before seven in the morning, preparing food for a husband who had shattered her dreams the previous night.

"You didn't have to make it for me. I could have made you breakfast." Honestly, it seemed like the least he could do.

Kate looked over her shoulder, eyebrows arched. "Are you good at making breakfast?"

"I've been a bachelor for over a decade. I can crack a few eggs and fry up some bacon, cook a chicken or a roast. But I won't complain if you want to make blinis." Nothing he made smelled nearly as good as that.

A small smile tilted the side of her mouth. "You don't even know if you'll like them."

"I'll like them." If for no other reason than that she made them at a time when he'd expected her to refuse to look at him.

"It seemed like the thing to do on the morning after our wedding . . . make my new husband breakfast." She turned back to the stovetop. "Oh, wait. Is there a problem with the time I'm making breakfast? Would you prefer it later? I can make it later tomorrow, but I need to get to the trading post early today. I want to sterilize my instruments before Mrs. Blakenly arrives."

"The trading post? You're seeing patients today?"

"It's the first Friday of the month. There are several women who come to visit. They're standing appointments."

"Yes, but are they coming? Today?"

"Why wouldn't they be?" She picked up one of the pans and slid the blini from one side to the other until she flipped it.

"It's the day after your wedding."

She set the pan back on the stove with a thud. "You promised I could still practice medicine."

He paused, his coffee cup halfway to his mouth. "This has nothing to do with you being allowed to practice medicine. The entire town knows we married yesterday, and most people will probably assume that we're a little, er, busy today."

Kate glanced over her shoulder, the small patch of skin between her eyebrows furrowed. "Busy doing what?"

He rubbed the back of his neck, which felt suddenly warm. "Ah . . . getting to know each other?"

She glanced out the window. "Oh. So do you want to go on a picnic after I'm done seeing patients? It does look rather nice out."

"I wasn't talking about a picnic." He pushed himself away from the table and came toward her, leaning against the hutch beside the stove so he could better see her while she worked. "I meant that most people probably expect us to spend the day in bed."

She dropped the pan she'd started lifting, and it fell back to the stove with a clatter. "Um, I hadn't . . . That is, I didn't . . ." Redness crept up the back of her neck.

Had anyone ever told her how darling she was when she got flustered?

"You said we weren't going to . . . to do that until . . . until I . . ."

"Your blini is burning."

"Oh dear." She jerked the pan off the burner and slid the thin pancake onto the plate she'd been using to hold the hot blinis while she smeared jam on them.

His mouth tipped into a smile as he studied her profile,

every last bit of her attention focused on the blini. "I don't expect to spend the day in bed, but I'm saying that your usual patients probably think that's where we'll be, and they might not stop by the trading post."

She smeared jam on the blini with a bit more concentration than the task required. "Were you planning on keeping your clinic closed today?"

"Yes."

"What were you planning on us doing?" She turned his direction, but rather than look at him, her eyes drifted around the kitchen. "We could give everything a good scrubbing. A doctor can't be too careful about keeping germs out of a waiting room. There's a cobweb in the corner there too."

"Or we could spend the day actually getting to know each other. Talking, telling childhood stories, sharing our individual plans for the future, and then discussing how we might incorporate each other into those plans so we can both still achieve our dreams." He took a step closer to her, then another, bringing their bodies near enough that her arm brushed his chest as she folded the blini into a triangle.

She jerked her arm back. "I don't . . . that is, I didn't . . ." She looked up at him, her eyes clouded with confusion, as though she'd suddenly lost the ability to think. Good. He liked knowing he could have that effect on her. She certainly had it on him.

But then she took a step away and turned back to the stove. "Do you mind sliding that blini onto the plate behind you with the others?"

He did as she asked while she poured more batter into the pan she'd just emptied. "I think I'll go to the trading post anyway. I don't want to risk being unavailable if someone needs me."

He couldn't quite explain the feeling that twined through

him. Disappointment, perhaps. Or maybe a bit of frustration. Or maybe it was simply the feeling of hope leaving his body, with nothing but emptiness to replace it. "All right, go to the trading post."

"Will you open the clinic?"

"If you're not going to be here, yes." It wasn't as though he had anything else to do. Though he didn't want to guess what kinds of rumors were going to spread with both of them opening their competing medical clinics the day after their wedding.

"Good." Kate gave a curt nod, as though she expected their plan would somehow solve their problems. "I'll be back in time to make dinner. Unless I get called away to a village or a mine. I'll send Ilya over with a message if that happens."

"Or I could make you dinner."

She looked at him again. "Honestly, Nathan, cooking for you is the least I can do after getting us into this mess."

"Then tell me what I can do to make our situation easier for you."

She didn't answer, just focused on flipping one of the blinis, then sliding the cooked one onto the plate beside him, slathering it with jam, and folding it before gesturing for him to move it onto the plate holding the stack of finished ones.

He sighed. "Don't pretend like this is easy for you. I heard you through the wall last night."

She paused over the stove as she was about to pour the final bit of batter into the pan. "I'm sorry I kept you awake."

He leaned against the hutch again. "That's not what I meant."

She poured the last of the batter into the pan. "I'm sorry about your wedding night too. I'm sure that wasn't the way you imagined spending it."

He reached out and rested a hand on her shoulder, then

waited until her gaze came up to meet his. "Don't worry about our wedding night. Our path is going to look a bit different than the one most married couples take, but we knew that going into the wedding."

She sunk her teeth into the side of her lip. "You don't resent me for that? I was the one who insisted we get undressed in the cave. You don't deserve to have the rest of your life ruined because of me."

"Ruined? Have you gone daft? My life's not ruined."

"But it is. I'm not going to make you a good wife. I don't like any of the normal wifey things. I can cook well enough, but I find it rather boring. I can't knit; I can barely—"

"Stop." He reached out to stroke a small strand of hair behind her ear. "If I wanted a wife who was going to do all the normal 'wifey' things, I would have married some other woman years ago."

That little groove appeared back between her brows. "You don't want a normal wife?"

"That seems a bit boring, don't you think? And let's be honest, I'm already boring enough for the both of us. I show up for work on time every day and work late when needed. I read journal articles and analyze medical statistics in my free time, and I spend my nights staring at maps and dreaming about how to get doctors to obscure places like Tanana, Alaska. I don't need to marry a boring woman. Why do you think I stopped by the trading post twice a week for weeks on end?"

She shrugged her shoulder away from his hand and turned back to the stove.

"I mean it, Kate. Marrying you didn't ruin my life. It just sped up the process of getting something I already wanted."

"You're serious?" Her voice held doubt as she slanted him a glance, never mind she'd picked up the pan to flip the blini. "You *wanted* to marry me?"

"I wanted to court you first. And then, perhaps, if my feelings kept growing, I wanted to propose."

She flipped the blini, then set the pan back on the stove. "I had no idea."

"You never gave me the chance to tell you."

"No. I don't suppose I did."

Their eyes locked for a moment, the scent of the cooking blini wafting around them while a raven cawed in the distance. They were so close he could feel her breath against his chin.

Part of him was tempted to lower his head a few more inches and brush his lips against hers.

How would they feel? Soft and sweet? Confident and strong? Warm and inviting?

But then she turned back to the blini, stared at it for a few more seconds as it finished cooking, and slid it onto a plate.

This time the feeling welling inside him was disappointment. There was no other word for it. Disappointment that they hadn't kissed. Disappointment that she hadn't given him any meaningful sort of response after he'd told her he wanted to marry her long before they found themselves trapped in that dratted cave. Disappointment that she'd rather go to the trading post and wait for patients who probably wouldn't come rather than spend the day with him.

Nathan turned and headed back to the table, where he'd hopefully be far enough away from his wife that he wasn't tempted to kiss her. He forced himself to sit and sip coffee while she spooned jam into the center of the final blini, folded it into a triangle, and sprinkled a fresh dusting of powdered sugar over the entire stack.

When she set his plate in front of him a minute later and sat down to eat, she didn't say anything more about their relationship or how things might change now that she was his wife. In fact, she didn't say anything at all, just bowed her head and waited for him to pray, then ate her blini with the same practical efficiency she approached everything else with.

A few minutes later, she stood, took her plate to the sink, washed the dishes, then headed out the door.

Leaving him to sit at the table with an ache in his heart, staring at the plate of untouched food she'd made for him.

17

Sitka, Three Days Later; June 4

After being gone for nearly three months, Alexei wanted to say it was good to be home. But considering the way Sacha—the brother closest to him in age—was glowering his direction from across the office, Alexei didn't feel all that welcome.

"So you just up and gave your permission for Kate to marry a stranger?" Sacha dragged a hand through his light brown hair, his large form pacing in front of the series of second-story windows that overlooked the shipyard he managed below. Alexei hadn't even visited the house yet. He'd gone straight to his family's office that sat above the Sitka Trading Company warehouse.

Sacha had seen the sloop dock and left the shipyard to greet him, but the smile on his face had turned into a scowl as soon as Alexei told him about Kate.

"Nathan Reid isn't a stranger." Alexei reached for one of the envelopes sitting on the edge of his desk, a desk filled with mail and reports and ledgers he needed to go through. "He's a well-respected doctor. I asked after him while I was in San Francisco. Turns out he worked at the marine hospital there five years or so ago."

"But this is Kate," Sacha growled, his voice taking on an unnaturally deep rumble. "She won't be happy with just any man."

"I'm not sure Kate will be happy with any man, ever. Not after what happened with her fiancé. But Nathan Reid seems rather happy with her, which isn't something I'd expected to see."

Sacha stopped pacing and turned, crossing his burly arms over his even larger chest. "Oh, so one man shows half an ounce of interest in Kate, and you marry her off?"

Alexei clenched his jaw. "That's not what happened. Her hand was forced."

"It looks like Alexei has returned, ladies." A familiar voice sounded from the stairs.

Alexei turned to see Yuri, the youngest of his full-blooded siblings, climbing the stairs to the office with three—no, make that four—women surrounding him.

What was his brother doing bringing that many women to the office, and in the middle of the day, no less? "Shouldn't you be working?"

"It's nice to see you too, brother dearest." Yuri shoved a thatch of dark hair off his forehead, then flashed him a wide, charming smile—the very smile that made every unmarried woman in Sitka simper when they saw it.

That smile was the most defining difference between them. That and the eleven-year age difference. But without those two things, a person might look at the two of them and think they were twins. Yuri wasn't broad of chest like Sacha or muscular like Mikhail. No, he was thin and lanky, with hair and eyes as dark as Alexei's. But Yuri's eyes were always shining and full of mirth.

Alexei should probably consider it a good thing that he'd given Yuri such a happy upbringing. That his eyes didn't need to be filled with seriousness, and his shoulders didn't need to carry the weight of their family's future at twenty-one years of age.

Yuri sauntered closer. "Tell me, Alexei, how have you been in the time you've been gone?"

"He married Kate off to a stranger," Sacha snapped.

The grin dropped from Yuri's face. "You what? Why would you go and do something like that to our sweet Kate?"

Alexei scowled. "He's not a stranger, and I had good reason."

"Did you just call Kate sweet?" the woman resting her hand on Yuri's arm asked. Alexei didn't remember her name, only that her father was one of the bureaucrats who worked in the former governor's mansion on the top of Castle Hill, which had been converted into an administrative building after the US purchased Alaska.

"She's got a heart of gold, I promise." Yuri patted the woman's hand. "Sometimes she just hides it under a few porcupine quills."

Alexei pinched the bridge of his nose, already feeling a headache coming on. Never mind he hadn't even been home an hour. "You never said why you have four women here during business hours. Did you hire them to help file papers?"

Yuri sent him another charming smile. "No. We're on the planning committee for Alaska Day."

"That isn't until October." Alexei pinched his nose even harder.

"But we need to start planning now." Another of Yuri's companions said, a smile plastered across her face. Alexei recognized her as Freya Eriksson. Her father owned the smithy in town. "There's going to be a meal and games and a dance in the big warehouse."

"A dance." Hadn't they just had a dance at Christmas? And there was already one scheduled for Independence Day. Did they need to put one in October too?

"Heard the committee is a bit bigger than usual this year." Sacha sent Yuri a wink, then lumbered to the table at the back of the room and poured himself a cup of coffee.

"What's that supposed to mean?" Alexei followed Sacha to the coffee. Something told him he needed caffeine if he was going to survive the rest of this conversation.

"I was tired of Mrs. Traverton always planning everything for Alaska Day," Yuri answered. "So when they had a meeting for volunteers last week, I showed up, and they put me in charge."

"They put you in charge?" Alexei nearly poured coffee on his hand. "How did that happen?"

His younger brother shrugged. "I said I would organize a dance if they made me the president, and everyone voted me in."

That blasted dance. He should have figured his brother would be behind it. Did anyone even like dancing?

"It's going to be so much fun." Freya pressed a hand to her chest, a giant smile on her face. "I can't wait!"

Right. Because most people . . . wait. What had Sacha said about the planning committee being bigger than normal this year? Alexei narrowed his eyes at the cluster of women around his brother. "Let me guess, the rest of you all volunteered for the planning committee after Yuri did."

The women all raced to answer his question, their responses piling up one on top of the other.

"Yes."

"Of course."

"We knew he'd need the help."

"This is going to be the best Alaska Day Festival that Sitka has ever seen!"

"I'm sure it will be." Alexei rubbed the back of his neck. "But as much as I hate to ruin your plans for the afternoon, Yuri needs to get back to work. You'll need to find a time outside of business hours to do your planning, like maybe in the evenings or on the weekends."

Yuri sent him a dark look, but he didn't care. His younger brother had to learn to be serious at some point, and that meant teaching him not to bring a gaggle of women to the office when he was supposed to be working.

"You four head over to the big house and start planning with Maggie. I'll come find you after a bit." Yuri flashed the women another of his disarming grins.

"Two hours." Alexei tipped his head toward the clock hanging on the wall. "You're not off work until five."

"Uh, Yuri came into the office at six this morning," Sacha said from where he casually leaned against the wall, watching the conversation with his coffee cup in hand. "And worked until two."

Alexei blinked at his younger brother. "You did?"

"Yes." Yuri's jaw hardened. "Do you have a problem with me working early?"

"I didn't realize."

"You ladies should still go visit Maggie over at the house." Sacha nodded in that direction. "She'll enjoy the company. Yuri will be over in a few minutes."

"Bye, Yuri," Freya wiggled her fingers at him before

flouncing toward the stairs. Fortunately the other women all followed without any extra prodding.

Alexei breathed a sigh of relief the moment the last of them disappeared down the stairs.

"You don't need to look so happy about sending them off." Yuri rolled his eyes. "They weren't harming anything by being here."

"They were a distraction." Besides, what was wrong with wanting the office to be a place of peace and quiet? He had enough business to attend as it was. The last thing he needed was for the office to become some type of gathering spot for the Alaska Day planning committee.

"Someday, Alexei, you're going to meet a woman who'll wipe that glower off your face and help you remember how to smile." Yuri crossed his arms over his chest, though given his lean frame and shorter height, he didn't look nearly as imposing as when Sacha crossed his arms. "I hope it's soon—for all of our sakes."

Sacha snorted. "I wouldn't hold my breath. His heart's as black as a pirate's."

Yuri smirked, but then his face turned serious. "All right, my black-hearted older brother. Tell us about this man you married Kate off to. He better not be a lout."

"He's not." Alexei picked his coffee up off the table and headed back to his desk. The mere sight of the papers scattered across it made him want to sigh. It would probably take him a week or better to work through everything.

"Is Kate all right?" Sacha asked. "I can't imagine she's happy about this."

"I think she will be in time. She's rather put out with me at the moment." Alexei took a sip of coffee, then told his brothers everything he knew about Dr. Nathan Reid, including his arrival in Juneau, the concussion Kate had treated him for, and that he seemed to be both well respected and well liked everywhere he went. He then told them that Kate couldn't seem to stand him—though that wasn't unusual seeing how he was a male doctor—and that he was renting the building she was trying to buy.

"He really did that?" Yuri interrupted, eyes dancing, as though he could imagine the scene playing out in his head. "This Nathan Reid fellow rented the building Kate wanted for her own clinic?"

Alexei sat back in his chair. "To be fair, he didn't realize Kate was trying to buy the building."

Yuri chortled. "Kate must have been furious."

Sacha's deep laugh filled the room too, and Alexei couldn't help the chuckle that rumbled up from his own chest.

"You should have seen her. She was in a mood, all right. Though I needed to go to San Francisco after dropping her off in Juneau, so I wasn't around to endure much of her anger. When I returned, she was a bit calmer, but then she and Nathan got caught in a cave during a mudslide."

Alexei went on to fill in the details, explaining that Kate truly appeared to be trying to keep Nathan warm. But when he and Jonas and two other men from town had arrived at the cave in the morning, the two of them had been caught in an impossible situation.

"Are you sure Nathan wanted to marry her?" Sacha asked. "That Kate seemed more put out about the wedding than him?"

"Absolutely. It made me think there would have been a wedding anyway, just six months or so down the road."

"I thought you said Kate hated him." Yuri moved to the table against the wall, where he passed over the coffee and grabbed a few of the Russian teacakes sitting on a platter.

"I think she would have softened with time." Alexei tilted

his head to the side, thinking back over the handful of interactions he'd witnessed between Nathan and Kate. "As I said, Nathan is well liked, and he's thought fondly of Kate from the beginning."

"I hope it works out for them." Yuri popped a teacake into his mouth. "Kate has so much energy, it'd be terrible if she marries someone who sucks it from her. I'm not sure I could stand to watch it."

Alexei rubbed his forehead, where his headache had settled into a dull throb. Despite the threats he'd given Kate after the cave debacle, he felt the same. There was something strong and bright and vibrant about her. "If Nathan Reid doesn't do right by her, I'll make his life miserable."

"Good." Sacha gave him a curt nod. "Now tell us about your trip to San Francisco."

"And do be quick." Yuri covered his mouth in a mock yawn. "I have ladies waiting for me."

Alexei rolled his eyes. "I was able to procure a better rate on the ironwood we're getting from Australia. And I met with Harold Farnsworth of Farnsworth Shipping. They're building two iron-hulled ships a year at his shipyard down in San Francisco, but they're getting requests for at least five. They can't keep up with the demand."

"Huh. Sounds like us with our double-hulled ships." Sacha took a sip of coffee.

"It does, but I have to admit, seeing the inner workings of a larger shipyard was quite helpful. My mind's brimming with ideas of improvements that we can start making to our own ships." Though he'd need to wade through the papers on his desk first. "Did anything important happen here while I was gone?"

Yuri's mouth clamped into a flat line and he looked at Sacha. "Tell him about Caldwell."

"Caldwell?" Alexei's body instantly turned alert. "What happened?"

Sacha took a long drag of coffee, then pursed his lips together before finally speaking. "Marshal Hibbs dropped the investigation into him."

"What?" Alexei shoved himself up from his desk. "No. He couldn't have. There's too much evidence not to press charges."

"Not according to the Marshal," Yuri said around another teacake. "He insists there's no evidence of a crime."

"He had false navigational charts drawn up and distributed." Alexei shoved his hand toward the shelf against the wall that held their navigational charts. "If that's not evidence of a crime, I don't know what is."

"Hibbs claims that a worker at the Revenue Cutter Service committed the crime." Sacha's hands flexed at his sides, then clenched into fists. "And the worker's the one being charged."

"But not Caldwell."

"Nope."

Alexei stalked to the window at the front of the office, the one overlooking the clear blue waters of the sound. But the peaceful view did little to calm the blood racing through his veins. "Is no one willing to hold this man accountable for anything?"

"Apparently not," Sacha answered. "Seems like everyone's so enamored with the money he pays them that he can do whatever he wants."

Alexei looked between his brothers, Sacha casually drinking coffee while he leaned against the desk, and Yuri popping teacakes into his mouth. "How are you both so calm about this?"

"We've had time to get used to the idea," Yuri said around another teacake.

Alexei narrowed his eyes. "How much time?"

Yuri took a moment to swallow his food before speaking. "About three months."

He stilled. "Hibbs dropped the investigation as soon as I left?"

"The day after," Sacha confirmed.

He stalked back toward the desk. Had the Marshal deliberately waited to drop the charges until everyone knew Alexei would be gone for several months?

Most likely.

Because had he been in Sitka, he would have been knocking on Marshal Hibbs's door that same day, demanding answers. Then he would have paid a visit to the Revenue Cutter Service and the governor of Alaska, demanding a more thorough investigation. Thousands of dollars' worth of damage had been done to ships that had gotten stuck or hit boulders in shallow waters last summer, all because incorrect navigational charts had intentionally been distributed to ships, and everyone knew who was responsible for it.

But Preston Caldwell was not an easy enemy to have. His family held power in Washington, DC, and had more money than they knew what to do with. They owned the sole right to hunt seals for their pelts throughout Alaska. And with a market price of ten dollars apiece, seal pelts were nearly as valuable as gold.

The pelts would be even more valuable if poachers weren't killing seals at sea by the thousands.

But instead of lobbying for stronger laws and better enforcement of poaching, Preston Caldwell had found his own way of punishing the poachers. He'd run their ships—and others—aground with false charts.

And now it didn't seem to matter that last summer Caldwell had confessed to it all. True, he said he'd intended to distribute the charts only to ships that were poaching. But somehow they got into regular circulation.

If Preston Caldwell were anyone else, he would still be looking at five years or better in prison. But Caldwell fancied himself above the law—and the Marshal dropping the case probably proved that he was. Or at least that he had enough money to pay off lawmen when needed.

"Does Rosalind have anything to say about the investigation into her father being dropped?" Sacha set his empty coffee mug down on the desk and looked at Yuri. "You haven't said."

"You've been talking to Rosalind again?" Alexei scowled at his younger brother. Of all the women for Yuri to befriend, surely he could pick someone other than the daughter of their biggest enemy.

"Don't look at me like that." Yuri shoved the thatch of hair off his brow again. "I'm not doing anything wrong by talking to her. She needs a friend. But no, Rosalind hasn't said anything one way or another about the investigation being dropped. Though maybe I'm paranoid, because now I feel like Caldwell will come after us for turning him in to the Marshal."

"He'll definitely come after us. He already tried it last summer." Alexei took another swig of coffee. It tasted bitter in his mouth. "A man like Preston Caldwell isn't going to forgive and move on."

"Oh, that reminds me." Sacha snapped his fingers. "We're going to have visitors in August, two senators from Washington, DC. They're doing a survey trip of Alaska, and one of the things they want to discuss is the seals. They've asked for a meeting. Maybe we can ask them to dive a little deeper into the inaccurate navigational charts."

Alexei raised his eyebrows. "Two senators? I doubt they'll do anything about the charts, seeing how one of Caldwell's cousins is also a senator, but I'm happy they've taken an interest in curbing the seal poaching."

"They're friends of Dr. Torres's, from what I understand. And we have them to thank that there are more revenue cutters patrolling the waters of Alaska this year."

As far as Alexei was concerned, Sacha should be thanked first and foremost. He was the one who had contacted Dr. Torres, a scientist from the Smithsonian Institution in Washington, DC, about coming to Alaska and doing a preliminary study last summer on the effects of hunting on the seal population. But when Caldwell had learned about the study . . .

Alexei's jaw clenched, and he shoved that thought from his mind. Some things didn't need to be revisited. "Having more revenue cutters is a good start, but it's not a ban on international seal hunting, or a lowered quota on legal hunts."

"No." Sacha rubbed his short-cropped beard. "But I'll take what I can get. Maybe more changes will follow. The letter asked to meet with both of us. Will you be here?"

"Should be. I'm planning to stay in Sitka for most of the summer, though now that Kate's married, I might go back to Juneau to check on her, just to make sure Nathan is treating her right."

"I'll do that," Sacha offered.

Alexei raised an eyebrow.

His large brother merely shrugged. "I haven't seen her since Christmas. Besides, I want to meet her husband myself."

It made sense. The two of them had always been close. Not quite as close as Kate and Evelina, but Alexei could understand why Sacha would want to look in on her. Besides, she'd probably be happy to see Sacha. She certainly fought less with him.

"I want to finish up the ship in dry dock first." Sacha gestured toward the windows overlooking the shipyard, where another double-hulled ship was only a couple weeks away from being launched. "But after that, I can leave and still be back before the senators arrive. I'll bring Maggie and the kids with me for a visit too."

"Can I go?" Yuri asked, popping yet another teacake into his mouth. The man had single-handedly cleaned off the entire platter.

"I don't know." Alexei thumped Yuri on the back. "Seems like you've got a dance to plan."

"He's right. You'd better stay." Sacha winked. "Wouldn't want any of your lady friends to die of a broken heart while you're gone."

"Can't you just pick one of them and get married?" Alexei asked.

"One." Yuri blinked. "You want me to pick just one? How am I supposed to decide which one? Or what if I pick one and then get bored with her after a bit? It's better to be friends with all of them."

Alexei raised his eyebrow. "Do *they* think that? Because I've got a feeling each one of those women would be thrilled to become your wife."

Yuri's lips flattened. "I don't want to marry any of the women who were here today, if that's what you're asking."

He said it in such a way that Alexei couldn't help but feel curious. "So who do you want to marry?"

Yuri just shook his head. "Doesn't matter. It'll never work."

Then he turned and bounded toward the stairs—toward the four women whom he didn't want to marry but who were all waiting for him.

18

Juneau; Three Days Later; June 7

No one was at the clinic. Again. Kate looked around the small room that had held all of her medical supplies since the day she'd first opened her practice in Juneau. Never before had it felt so empty.

Nathan's prediction about last Friday had been correct. No one had stopped to see her all day, not even Mrs. Blakenly. So Kate had expected the woman to be waiting bright and early Monday morning.

She wasn't. Nor had she shown up on Tuesday or Wednesday, and now . . .

A knock sounded at the door, and Kate jumped to her feet. But Evelina was the person who poked her head inside, not an actual patient.

"Do you want some lunch? I made extra."

Kate slumped back into her chair. "No."

"Is something wrong?" Evelina closed the door behind her and stepped into the room. "Why are you sitting in the dark?"

Kate shrugged. "Guess I didn't bother to open the curtains."

"You've been here for three hours. Surely you had time to open them, or at least light a lamp."

She had lit a lamp and left it on for the first couple hours she'd been in the examination room taking inventory of her supplies, but once it had become clear that Mrs. Blakenly wasn't coming, she'd decided to save a bit of oil. "If you're after more light, you'd better light the lamp. It's too dreary outside to let any in."

It had been dreary every day for weeks on end, except for the day of her wedding, and the day after it. Those days had been bright and warm and full of sunshine, almost as though the weather itself had been mocking her and Nathan. She was starting to wonder if they'd get any kind of summer this year.

Evelina moved to the window and opened the curtain, letting dim, gray light into the room, then sat on the sickbed, arms crossed over her chest as she faced Kate in the chair. "What's wrong? You've not been yourself since the wedding."

She snorted. "How am I supposed to be myself when I'm married to a stranger who's stealing my patients?"

"Don't be petty. You and I both know he's not stealing them."

No, he wasn't. But it made her feel better when she phrased it like that. Then she didn't have to acknowledge that her patients were intentionally leaving her to seek treatment from her new husband. "Mrs. Blakenly hasn't come yet this month. She always comes the first Friday of every month. So does Mrs. Zeller and her daughter, and Mrs. Ramsway too, but none of them have stopped by to see me."

"The first Friday of the month was the day after your

wedding, less than a week ago. I know you were technically here to see patients, but the women probably heard about your wedding and assumed you were busy. In fact, I think I recall seeing Mrs. Blakenly at your wedding dinner."

"Mrs. Zeller and her daughter Abigail and Mrs. Ramsway were all there too."

"So there you have it." Evelina gave her an encouraging smile that seemed far too nice and patient and kind. "They all assumed you were closed last Friday."

Kate threw up her hands. "Why did everyone expect me to be closed?"

"Ah, because it was the day after your wedding." Evelina's brow furrowed. "You're supposed to be busy—with your husband."

"No, I'm not."

"Yes, you are."

"What if the bride didn't want the wedding?" Kate launched herself from the chair and started to pace, never mind the room was too small for her to walk more than a handful of steps before she was forced to turn around and head the other direction. "Is she still supposed to be busy then?"

"Not everyone knows the true details of your wedding. You were caught in a compromising situation with a man, which has led everyone to believe you were compromised, that you may have even wanted to be compromised. And as such, they assume you and Nathan wanted to spend time together the day after your wedding, and the day after that, and likely the day after that." A flush crept across Evelina's cheeks. "Honestly, people might avoid requesting your services for a week or better. They probably all assume you're, er, occupied."

"But I'm not occupied." Her hands curled into fists at her sides. "And I wasn't compromised."

Evelina gave her head a shake, then pushed to her feet. "If

you keep this up, you're only going to make things harder on yourself. God is able to do abundantly more than we ask or think. That verse pertains to your new marriage just as much as it pertains to your doctoring."

Kate pursed her lips into a flat line. She didn't want to think about that verse, not even if she'd given it to Nathan when he'd shown her his map. It didn't seem to apply to her anymore.

Evelina took a step closer. "Alexei feels like you and Nathan are a good match, that God might even have his hand on your marriage."

"If Alexei is so fond of marriage, maybe he should find a wife." The words came out more sharply than she intended.

Evelina jerked backward. "I think you should go back to the clinic and have lunch with your husband instead of us. Do something to show you're making an effort in your marriage."

"I am making an effort in my marriage. I've cooked both breakfast and dinner every day, even when Nathan offered to do it for me."

"Nathan offered to cook you food?" A soft, silly smile crept across Evelina's face, and she pressed her hands to her chest. "That's the sweetest thing! You should definitely go back to the clinic and let Nathan know you're taking him up on his offer. Don't be afraid to let him do something kind for you. He's probably trying to show you how he feels."

Kate lifted her hands, only to let them drop back to her side. "What if I don't want to know how he feels?"

"Oh, Kate." Evelina wrapped her arms around her in a soft hug. "You can't keep fighting this. He's your husband. Don't you want him to love you?"

Was that what she wanted? Nathan's love? She didn't know. She felt so confused, like she couldn't tell which direction was up anymore.

Evelina must have felt her stiffen, because she tightened

her hug. "Sometimes I feel like you're your own biggest obstacle."

"You make this sound so simple." She let herself relax in Evelina's embrace. "But I don't know how I'm supposed to get close to a man who's planning to leave Alaska one day."

Evelina pulled back, concern lacing her brow. "He's leaving? Are you sure?"

"Very."

Evelina's arms were back around her again, burying her in yet another hug. "Did you know that before the wedding? Tell me you knew and still decided to marry him."

"No. I found out that night, after the reception." She pulled away from Evelina and told her twin how the conversation had gone, how questions about his plans for better medical care had led to her finding out that he was stationed in Alaska for only three years, and he didn't want to request to stay longer.

Not that she could blame him. He had a good reason for wanting to leave. But she couldn't imagine how it would feel to give Evelina an embrace like the one they'd just shared, knowing it might be three or four or five years before they saw each other again. Couldn't imagine how it would feel to say good-bye to Alexei or Sacha or Yuri, or even Mikhail, though she barely saw him.

Couldn't imagine missing such important parts of Inessa's and Ilya's lives as they grew into adulthood.

"I'll miss you after you're gone." Evelina brushed a tear from her cheek. "But I'll come visit every summer when school is out. I promise."

"It's still three years away. And I'm hoping that somehow, during that time . . ." She couldn't bring herself to finish the sentence, but she didn't need to. One glance at her sister told her that Evelina understood.

"I still think you should go back to the clinic and have

lunch with Nathan." Evelina wiped another tear from her cheek, then straightened. "Considering everything that's going on, it's even more important that the two of you give your marriage a good foundation. You should stay at the clinic for the afternoon and see if Nathan needs help there. If someone comes here in search of you, I'll send Ilya with a message. It doesn't take more than a few minutes to go between the two places."

Kate fiddled with the fabric on the side of her dress. "I can't work for him, Lina. You, of all people, should understand why."

"No." Evelina frowned. "I don't understand. Nathan promised you could practice medicine after you married. And according to Alexei, he even offered you a job."

Nathan had offered her a job, but at the mention of it, memories of a different doctor's office rose in her mind. One with expensive wallpaper and fancy furniture and polished wainscoting and solid oak floors.

One where her exam room was just as empty of patients as the room she currently stood in.

But the clinic itself hadn't been empty. It had been bursting —just like Nathan's clinic—yet she'd been allowed to see only two or three patients a day.

Kate wrapped her arms around herself. "I promised myself I wouldn't work for another male doctor, not ever again."

"But Nathan is nothing like Peter's father. Surely you can see that."

Could she? True, Nathan was far more honorable and trustworthy than either her former fiancé or his father, but that didn't mean she was ready to work for him. It didn't even mean she wanted to be married to him. The happiest she'd ever been in her life was before Nathan arrived in Juneau.

But Evelina had a point too. Kate couldn't go back and undo the past, couldn't change the night she and Nathan had spent in that horrid cave or how they'd been found the following morning. She was married now, and she could either spend the rest of her life resenting their marriage or figure out how to have a good one.

She was already making a point to cook Nathan breakfast and dinner every day, but if they were going to have the kind of relationship that Evelina had with Jonas, then she probably needed to give him more.

"All right. I'll have lunch with Nathan." She gave herself a decisive nod and started for the door.

"Ah, maybe try smiling while you're eating." Evelina hurried to catch up to her. "It might get you a little farther than that scowl."

Was she scowling? Drat.

"Is this better?" She gave her sister a tight smile.

Evelina chuckled. "I suppose, but it's still not as good as one of your real smiles."

One of her real smiles. Right. She could show Nathan that. Honestly, it wasn't hard to smile when she recalled him telling her that he'd already planned to court her before they'd been trapped in the cave, or that he didn't want a boring, normal wife, that he'd always wanted to marry someone like her.

It was when she thought of everything else that the smile faded.

"How's this?" she asked Evelina.

Evelina smiled this time, a big, beautiful, genuine smile that Kate knew put her own to shame. "It's lovely."

It wasn't nearly as lovely as Evelina's, but it was a place to start. Maybe one day she'd be able to smile at Nathan the way Evelina smiled at everyone, true and full, without any fear that the person she smiled at would turn around and hurt her.

But today wasn't that day. She reached for the doorknob. "Send Ilya if you need me here."

"I will."

Kate walked out of the exam room into the trading post, donned her oilskin slicker hanging by the door, then pulled her hood over her head and stepped into the gloom outside. It wasn't raining, but it looked like the clouds were going to let loose at any time. They hung low and thick over the town, filling the air with dense moisture.

She made her way down the muddy street toward the clinic, skirting around puddles. Just how would Nathan respond when he saw her? Would he be happy that she'd come home for lunch?

She could almost imagine the way his eyes would light up while a soft smile stole over his face. But what would he say? That he was happy to see her?

What would she say in return? *I thought I'd come home for lunch today?*

Something told her that Nathan would give her that look of utter delight no matter what she said. And that with him looking at her in such a manner, it would be easy to give him a smile that just might rival one of Evelina's.

Kate turned the corner and headed for the clinic. She'd nearly reached the bottom step when the door opened and none other than Mrs. Blakenly and Mrs. Ramsway started down the stairs.

"Mrs. Blakenly?" Kate's throat turned dry as she approached the woman. What was her patient doing here? Surely there was some sort of explanation. Surely she wasn't suddenly seeking care from Nathan instead of her. "Were you looking for me here? I'm still seeing patients at the trading post."

Perhaps the women didn't know. Maybe everyone in the town assumed she was now working at Nathan's clinic, and that's why no one had stopped by the trading post since the wedding.

"Kate." Mrs. Blakenly halted on the middle step, and Mrs. Ramsway stopped right behind her. A moment later, Janice Thompson and Tillie Metcalf, her fellow teacher at the Presbyterian mission, appeared in the doorway.

Kate tensed when she saw Miss Thompson but brought her gaze straight back to Mrs. Blakenly, who really did need to have her asthma checked once a month. "I figured you'd be at the trading post on Friday for our usual appointment. But when you didn't arrive, I thought maybe you assumed I was busy. But the office is open. I can even see you this—"

"Why would either of these good Christian women want to be treated by the likes of you?" Janice Thompson swept past the other women and down the steps, her back ramrod straight. "You're a disgrace and a scandal, trapping an upstanding man like Dr. Reid and forcing him into marriage."

Kate stiffened until her spine was every bit as straight as Miss Thompson's. "That's not what happened."

"No?" Miss Thompson chuckled, but there was nothing kind about the sound. "So tell me, were you or were you not found spending the night in a cave just north of town with Dr. Reid? I heard you were in nothing but your undergarments."

"Nothing inappropriate happened between us. We were searching for an injured man and ended up trapped and needed to fend off hypothermia. I'd have done the same for anyone, a woman, a child, another—"

"That's enough!" A booming masculine voice sounded from the top of the steps.

Kate looked up to find Nathan looming over them all with a cold look on his face. "Tell her she's wrong," she said. "Tell her there was a medical reason we did what we did in that cave. That it wasn't some sordid trap I laid for you."

"You never should have agreed to marry her." Miss Thompson whirled to face Nathan. "There are half a dozen women with good reputations who would have gladly married you even after what happened."

"There's nothing wrong with my wife's reputation. She's an honorable Christian woman, and I'm happy I married her. The thing I'm not happy about is having her good name falsely and incorrectly attacked, especially on the doorstep of our home." Nathan crossed his arms over his chest and widened his legs, and though he wasn't a large man, he still looked intimidating as he glared at the women. "Now it's best you leave. All of you. And if I hear any one of you disparage my wife again, I won't see you in my clinic."

The women all seemed to grow still, their eyes moving from her to Nathan and back again. Mrs. Blakenly was the first to move, passing by her without meeting her eyes. Mrs. Ramsway soon followed, then Miss Metcalf.

Janice Thompson was the last to pass, but she paused for a moment on the steps, her eyes blazing. "You're a disgrace to women everywhere. Dr. Reid might look at your pretty hair and eyes and not see the rest of it, but I do, and I'm not the only one. You're mistaken if you think any woman in this town will let you treat them again after how you behaved."

Was that why no one had been to her clinic this week? Kate licked her lips. Was Miss Thompson convincing the women of Juneau that they needed to stay away from her after the events that led to her wedding?

She could try explaining again that nothing inappropriate had happened, try telling Miss Thompson once more that she'd just been trying to treat Nathan's prehypothermia. But what was the point? The teacher had despised her from the first day she set foot in Juneau, and now she had a reason for her animosity that the rest of the town would accept.

"I said you need to leave, Miss Thompson." Nathan's voice echoed from the top of the steps.

Kate didn't need to look up to know the other woman slid past her. She could feel it in the coolness of the air that suddenly surrounded her.

Then different steps sounded on the stairs. Heavier ones. The air around her turned warm again, but there was no anger radiating from Nathan as he approached and wrapped an arm around her shoulders. "Let's go inside. Are you hungry? I can make you some lunch."

"That's what I was coming back for," she whispered around the lump in her throat. "Lunch."

"You want to eat with me?" His lips tipped up into that tender smile she'd known he'd give her.

But she couldn't muster up a smile in return, not even a tight one. "I'm afraid I don't feel like eating anymore."

His hand stroked her arm in a soothing gesture. "What did Miss Thompson say to you after I told everyone to leave?"

She almost didn't tell him, almost kept it bottled inside, but she found her mouth opening anyway and the words pouring out. "That I was a disgrace to women everywhere, and she'd see to it that no woman in town would ever seek treatment from me again."

His hand stilled on her arm. "Kate, that's not true. You are the very opposite of a disgrace. I know there are rumors at the moment, but they won't last forever. Soon the people of Juneau will find themselves remembering what they've always known about you. That you're an honorable woman and an excellent doctor."

She wasn't sure the people of Juneau had ever thought those things of her. At least not anyone besides him, and maybe the Gibbonses after she'd saved their son. But it was a kind sentiment. "Did you treat Mrs. Blakenly today?"

"For asthma, yes. Why?"

Kate shook her head. "She was my standing appointment from last Friday."

"I didn't know. If I had, I would have..."

She held up her hand. "You don't need to explain. I know you weren't doing it to hurt me." And the worst part was, Mrs. Blakenly probably wasn't seeking treatment from Nathan to hurt her either.

She had Janice Thompson to thank for that.

"Come in for lunch, please. I'd already made a sandwich when I heard voices out here. I can throw together another one in no time." Nathan wrapped his arm back around her shoulders and tried to urge her up the steps.

But Kate kept her feet rooted to the wooden planks beneath them and shrugged away from him. "No. I was being honest when I said I'm not hungry, and you'll have patients back here soon. I'll go for a walk on the beach instead, maybe look for some shells. The Tlingit girls love it when I give them shells after I treat them."

"Don't leave right now, not when you're hurting." He swept a strand of hair away from her face and tucked it behind her ear. "I can give you patients if you stay."

She tilted her head away from where his fingers lingered behind her ear. "We both know they won't want me to treat them."

His jaw hardened. "It doesn't matter. I'll make them see you anyway."

"No. This isn't your problem to solve. I'll go up into the mountains tomorrow. The miners are always happy to see a doctor, even if it's a woman."

She took a step back from him, but something in his eyes prevented her from taking another step back. They held her in place for a moment, almost making her want to accept his offer of lunch.

Almost making her believe that he could give her everything he seemed to promise.

Until she remembered that he planned to one day take her away from Alaska.

So she turned and left before he could talk her into changing her mind about lunch—or anything else.

19

Mountains near Juneau; Four Weeks Later; July 5

Heaviness filled Kate's chest as she studied the injury in front of her. The deep, jagged gash ran for several inches down the miner's shin, where his flesh had been torn open by the sharp edge of a rock. Tiny stones, flecks of dirt, and a few shards of glass littered the raw tissue.

"I didn't think it was that bad," the miner rasped, his words half muffled by his thick, bushy beard. "I swear I didn't."

"So you covered it with a bandage and expected a wound like this would heal on its own?" She tried to temper her words, but did the man not understand how life-threatening gangrene could be? That covering a wound before it had been properly cleaned would exacerbate his chances of contracting the deadly infection?

"I'm glad you came to visit today." The foreman of the Perseverance Mine, Jace Lidding, watched her from the side of the bunkhouse as she worked. "I had no idea he'd even fallen the other night. Two other miners helped him out of the mine when he couldn't walk on his leg today. I was going to send for a doctor, but then you walked into camp."

"I'm glad I came too." She studied the wound for a few more minutes, then raised her eyes to meet the miner's in the dim light of the bunkhouse. He was lying on one of the lower bunks, a sheen of sweat on his forehead despite the cool weather. "How long ago did you fall, Mr. Griggs?"

"Day before yesterday. Had a bit too much to drink after work, and I tripped. Cut my leg right good." He propped himself up on his elbows and glanced at his wound, then sucked in a breath and winced. "Hurts like the dickens, though. Don't remember it hurtin' so bad yesterday."

"That's probably because it wasn't infected yesterday." Kate uncorked the bottle of carbolic acid that she kept in her medical bag. "I'll need to wash the entire thing, and that will mean reopening the parts where infection is setting in. Then I need to pluck out the rocks, dirt, and glass. I'm afraid it's going to sting."

"Just get it cleaned," the man muttered. "Don't need to be gettin' no gangrene and losing my leg."

She repositioned the lantern closer to the edge of the bed and studied the wound again.

The edges of the gash were red and swollen, and pus had begun to accumulate at several points. But there was no unpleasant odor, and while the area around the injury was warm to the touch, the angry red hue wasn't spreading up his leg.

She reached down and plucked one of several handkerchiefs from her bag. "Mr. Lidding, do you mind holding Mr. Griggs's foot?"

"Of course." The foreman moved to the end of the bed.

"Aw, I don't need no one to hold me down, Doc. I can take a bit of pain." Mr. Griggs moved his leg away from Mr. Lidding, then hissed.

"I'm sure you can, but I do this for every patient with a leg injury. I hope you understand." She flashed the man a demure smile, one she used only when she was trying to convince a man to indulge her.

The miner smiled back from beneath his bushy beard. "Oh, fine then. Lidding can hold it. But I ain't gonna move none. You'll see."

"Yes, I'm sure I will." She sent him another smile, then uncorked the blue bottle of carbolic acid and poured a few drops onto his wound.

Just as she'd suspected, Mr. Griggs howled, his entire body going stiff before he tried tugging his leg away from the foreman.

It took the better part of an hour to clean the wound. Once she'd doused it in an initial splash of carbolic acid, she used her tweezers to remove every last bit of dirt and rock and glass. By then Mr. Griggs's howls of pain had tapered to a small stream of whimpers. But when she took her scalpel and cut into the pus-filled pockets lining the edge of the wound, then rinsed those with carbolic acid, the howling started up again.

At some point two other miners came into the bunkhouse to see what was going on, and Kate suspected Mr. Griggs would soon face an endless amount of teasing over just how tough he was.

"The bandages need to be changed four times a day until the wound stops bleeding," she told Mr. Lidding as she cleaned her hands, then started disinfecting her scalpel. "After that, you need to change them only twice a day, morning and night. And finally, you can move to changing them once a day when everything is starting to heal and it's clear no infection will set in.

Mr. Griggs will need to stay off his leg until it's good and strong again, probably two weeks."

Mr. Lidding took the roll of bandages she'd given him and placed it in the cupboard next to the door. "I'll make sure it's done."

She had no doubt he would. Jace Lidding ran a good camp. She'd been coming here to treat his men ever since moving to Juneau two years ago. He'd always been accepting of her doctoring and encouraged his men to see her when she made her rounds. But she'd been at the camp for well over an hour, and there weren't any other men milling around the bunkhouse waiting for an examination.

She slid her scalpel back into its leather case and looked at Mr. Lidding. "Who am I treating next?"

Mr. Lidding shifted his weight from one foot to the other. "Ah . . . there's a couple other men with complaints, but—"

"Where are they? Do you need to get them from the mine? Or are you expecting me to wait until their shift is over?" She didn't relish the idea of walking down the mountain after dark, but when she made rounds by herself, Mr. Lidding always escorted her home, ensuring she arrived safely back in Juneau.

"The thing is . . ." He rubbed the back of his neck. "The men are . . . They're . . . uh . . . they're wondering if your husband plans to make any trips to the camps."

"My husband?" Her brow furrowed. "Why would he visit the camps? Construction on the hospital is underway, and the clinic in Juneau is so full that he usually has more patients than he can see in a day. He doesn't have time to come up here."

"So if some of my men wanted to see him, they'd need to go down to Juneau?"

"I suppose, but why would they do that when I can . . . ?" Her words trailed off as the realization hit her. "Mr. Lidding, just what are you trying to say?"

He held up his hands. "Nothing. I'm not trying to say anything."

"Really? Because I've been treating the men of the Perseverance Mine for two years, and not a single one of them has ever complained about my doctoring—or sought out Dr. Prichard instead of me. Why would that suddenly change?"

He ducked his head. "You're a smart woman, Dr. Am— Dr. Reid. Surely you don't need me to spell it out for you."

She swallowed. "Is this what all the miners think? Does . . . does everyone want to see Nathan over me?"

Over the past month, Janice Thompson's attitude toward her had spread to the point where only a handful of the women of Juneau were seeing her now. But she'd still been able to visit the mining camps and native villages, and no one in either of those places had asked to see her husband instead of her—till now.

The number of miners needing treatment had certainly dwindled. At this time last year, she could spend an entire day in one camp. But this was the second camp she'd visited so far today. At the first camp, she hadn't had any patients, and if Mr. Griggs was her only patient here, she'd have time to visit a third camp before dark.

She whirled around and started shoving her supplies into her medical bag. They weren't all sterilized, but she didn't want to take the time to clean them now. She'd sterilize everything when she got home. Heaven knows she'd have plenty of time to do so. It wasn't as though anyone wanted her doctoring these days.

"Dr. Reid." Mr. Lidding stepped in front of her, then reached out and rested a hand over hers, pausing her frantic packing. "Kate. I'm sorry. It's nothing against you. You're an excellent doctor. You've saved at least three of my men's lives, probably more, over the past two years. And that's not counting

Griggs's, who was awfully close to getting gangrene until you came. I appreciate you coming here, and you're welcome back at the Perseverance Mine anytime."

"But no one will want to see me." She pulled her hand away. "Not unless it's an emergency, and I just so happen to be the closest doctor."

He sighed. "I don't personally have need of a doctor right now, but if I did, I'd let you treat me."

"How very magnanimous of you. Tell me, how many men do you have working for you right now? Thirty? Forty?"

"About thirty-five."

"And you're the only one willing to let me treat you?" Was that somehow supposed to make her feel better?

"I truly am sorry," he tried again, his eyes sincere.

She wanted to say that he should be sorry, that his men were oafs and clodhoppers who ought to be ashamed of themselves.

But were they?

Was there something wrong with a man wanting to be treated by a male doctor?

Was there something wrong with other people not trusting her medical skills simply because she was a woman?

It felt like there should be.

But maybe the problem was God. If she'd been born a man, none of this would be happening. People wouldn't refuse her medical treatment or look at her like—

"Let me walk you to the next camp." Mr. Lidding held out his arm for her, his blue eyes still filled with unspoken apologies.

She picked up her medical bag. "I'm not going to the next camp."

What was the point? They'd just ask that she send Nathan to treat them.

"Let me walk you down the mountain then."

"No, thank you. I'm not in the mood for company." She brushed past him and out the door into a watery sunlight dimmed only by a thin film of whitish-gray clouds.

He followed her anyway, tromping along the damp ground beside her.

She sent him an angry glare, but he just shook his head. "I promised Jonas. All the foremen and camp owners up here did. We're not going to let you traipse around the mountain by yourself."

"Fine." She squared her shoulders, clamped her mouth shut, and quickened her pace. The sooner she made it down the mountain, the sooner she could be alone.

NATHAN SURVEYED the building that would soon become the hospital. Construction had started almost two months ago, and already the building was framed, the roof was up, and boards had been nailed to the walls. Soon there would be windows and doors, then rooms inside the building.

And for the first time, not only seamen but anyone who was sick or injured could come and receive treatment.

Had there been a facility like this in Marquette, Michigan, where he grew up, his own life might have been vastly different.

His throat grew thick, and he swallowed, shoving the thoughts of his mother's death aside as he stepped through the framed rectangle that would soon become the hospital entrance.

The sharp aroma of sawdust filled the air, and the sound of hammers striking nails echoed from the second floor of the building. The first floor was little more than a large, cavernous space with beams where walls would eventually go. It was currently empty save for the foreman who stood near the back of the building, his body bent over a makeshift table littered with tools and cups of coffee.

"Tom," Nathan called over the hammering. He weaved his way through stacks of lumber toward the burly man.

"Dr. Reid." The foreman looked up, wiping his brow with a rag before gesturing to the building. "What do you think?"

Nathan couldn't hold back his smile. He could almost sense the good this building was going to do, almost see the walls up and the rooms filled with patients.

Almost feel the lives that would be saved.

It was enough to make his throat go thick all over again. "It's coming along much faster than I anticipated. How soon do you think we can start using part of the building? Is it possible to finish a few rooms right by the entrance and use those, even if the rest of the building is still under construction?"

Tom took a sip of coffee, then pointed to a section of the blueprints. "Suppose we could finish off the first floor and let you use that. I wouldn't recommend trying to use just a few rooms while everything else is still under construction, though, not with all the sawdust. Don't reckon you want someone with a cough breathing that in."

"Sorry. I suppose my excitement is getting the better of me."

"No need to apologize." The man clapped a meaty hand on his back. "This hospital is going to be a huge boon for Juneau. I'm told we have you to thank for it, that you're the one who convinced the surgeon general to put a hospital here in the first place."

Nathan shrugged. "This area needed better medical care. That's already apparent just by how busy the clinic is."

"You need anything extra from us, just let us know. The

crew is happy to help however we can, even if that means moving furniture or building beds after the construction is done."

"Thank you. I appreciate it." There was one thing he needed at the moment, but neither Tom nor anyone on his crew could provide it.

More doctors.

Ellingsworth had sent a doctor north on the route that the new RCS ship was taking, but what about the doctors who were supposed to be arriving in Juneau? The surgeon general had said five doctors could go to Alaska, and then Nathan had written a letter asking for two more. But he had yet to hear back from the surgeon general, even though he'd written that letter two months ago. But if the surgeon general was already counting him and Ellingsworth as two doctors, even with Ellingsworth gone and the doctor on the ship as a third, that still left two more doctors who should, in theory, be arriving anytime.

So where were they?

If Kate decided to start working for him, they could still probably staff an additional two doctors, bringing the total to eight. No one from the MHS was making trips to the mining camps or native villages yet. Originally, he'd assumed he could assign a doctor from the hospital to make those visits a couple days of the month, but there was almost enough work between the camps and the villages to employ a doctor full-time.

"Tell you what," Tom said. "Tomorrow I'll pull the crew down here to start finishing off the first-floor interior. If the windows come in on time, I'd say it'll be another five to six weeks before this floor is operational. Then we can move on to the second floor. Is that fast enough for you?"

"It's perfect. Truly perfect." Hopefully he'd have his two

other doctors by then, and Ellingsworth would have returned from New Orleans. Then they could start . . .

A familiar flash of blue caught his eye through the open space where a window would soon be placed. He recognized the serviceable blue skirt instantly.

Was Kate coming to see him? He leaned out the rectangular opening. "Kate! I'm in here."

She stopped walking and looked around, as though it took her a minute to recognize who was calling her, or where she was.

"I'll see you at home." Her terse words traveled across the distance to him; then she straightened her shoulders and stomped off.

He sighed. He hadn't exactly been expecting his wife to run toward him with open arms or gush that she'd missed him while visiting the mining camps, but would it hurt if she acted at least a little happy to see him?

Sometimes it felt like they hadn't made any progress since their wedding five weeks ago. Kate cooked for him regularly, but only because she viewed it as her duty, not because she actually enjoyed making food for him. There'd been a time or two when he'd almost gotten past the defenses she always seemed to erect, like the day she'd found her patients outside his clinic. But at the last moment, she pulled back, reinforcing the walls around her heart that were taller than the mountain behind Juneau.

It made him wonder if three years would be enough to break down those walls and woo her, to give their marriage the solid foundation they needed before he pulled her away from Alaska.

But what had put her in such a bad mood today? She'd been visiting mining camps, and she usually came home with bright, dancing eyes and stories to tell about her patients.

Had something happened? Perhaps someone she'd treated had died?

Nathan turned back to Tom. "I need to get home, but thank you for the update. I'll stop by again in a few more days. If you need me before then, you can find me at the clinic."

"Sounds good, Doc." Tom bent to make a note on the blueprints. "I'll let you know how things go."

"Perfect." Nathan left through the back door of the hospital—or rather, what would soon be the back door, since it was just a giant rectangle cut into the wall—then he headed down the street that led to the clinic.

He made quick time as he covered the few blocks that separated the buildings; then he unlocked the door and slipped inside. He'd intended to head upstairs to find Kate, but banging noises sounded from one of the exam rooms.

"Kate?" He crossed the waiting room and peeked inside. Sure enough, his wife stood there, the entire contents of her medical bag dumped onto the examination table beside a bowl of carbolic acid. She muttered a string of indecipherable words as she wiped down her stethoscope with brisk, jerky movements.

"Kate." He said her name louder, then stepped farther into the room.

She raised her eyes to look at him. Based on the tense set to her shoulders and the hardness in her jaw, he'd expected to find them hot with anger. Instead they were filled with tears.

"What's wrong? Did something happen?"

She pulled her gaze away and reached for her scalpel, wiping it down rather aggressively given the sharpness of the blade. "You need to schedule a day to visit the mining camps. That's one of the things you're supposed to do, isn't it? Provide medical treatment to remote locations?"

He rubbed the back of his neck. "Um, yes. But you're

already doing that. You head up the mountain at least once a week, and you're certainly capable of providing care."

"No, I'm not."

"What are you talking about? Of course you are. I've seen you—"

"It's not my skill that's the problem." She slammed the scalpel onto the table, then picked up her otoscope. "Not my training or the care I give. It's that I'm a woman. And now that everyone knows a male doctor is here—and that I'm married to him—they want you to treat them, not me."

His jaw clenched. "Did someone say something to you? Tell me who, and I'll fix it."

"It was good someone said something." Her hand trembled as she attempted to clean the pointed edge of the otoscope used for looking into a person's ears. "There have been fewer and fewer patients for me to treat each time I go to those camps. I didn't think much about it. Sometimes people are sicker than others. But then today..."

She hung her head, and the otoscope clattered to the table with enough force that the cone-shaped tip came off.

Nathan stepped forward and wrapped his arms around her. "I'm so sorry."

"It's not your fault," she spoke into his chest.

"It's entirely my fault. If I'd never come to Juneau—"

"Another doctor would have come. The town is growing too fast not to attract someone else. I should probably be grateful you're the one who ended up here. At least you respect me."

He stroked a strand of hair back from her face. "I know you say you don't want to work for me, but the offer is still open. There were half a dozen patients at the clinic today that I would have handed off to you. Maybe more. And those were just the ones I specifically thought about you treating."

Her already dull eyes grew even dimmer. "Let me guess. They were all women or children."

"Is there anything wrong with that?"

She pulled away from him. "It would be one thing if male doctors never treated women, but they do. So why can't I treat men? It feels like I'm being punished. That's why the idea of working for you, of being told which patients I can and can't treat, makes me feel itchy. Almost like I can't breathe."

He took a step back and tunneled a hand through his hair. This woman. Couldn't she trust him just a little?

He'd known that she hadn't wanted to work for him when they married, but to say the thought made it hard for her to breathe? "Have I done something to make you think you'll be miserable working for me? Something to make you believe I'll give you patients who despise you, or that I'll use your position in the clinic to hurt you in some way?"

She pressed her eyes shut, her shoulders slumping. "No. No. You've done nothing like that. It was all before, back in Boston. And it's not fair of me to project what happened with Peter at his father's clinic onto you."

"Peter?" The name tasted sour on his tongue. "Who is this Peter?"

"You don't know?" She jerked her gaze back to him, then blinked. "No, I don't suppose you would. He was my fiancé."

The words slammed into him. "You had a fiancé?" Why was he just now learning about this?

Kate shrugged, as though the fact she'd once promised her life to another man was barely worth mentioning. "We met in medical school. His father has a large, well-known clinic in Boston. You spent time in Boston, right? You may have heard of it. It's called Bosely Medical."

"Bosely Medical. As in the clinic run by Dr. Geoffrey Bosely?"

"Yes. That's the one."

He slumped into the wooden chair by the door. "You worked for the most prestigious doctor in Boston?" Again, why had no one told him?

"Dr. Bosely thought adding a woman to his staff would be helpful, that I could assist with certain complaints that male doctors had trouble treating, so I accepted his job offer. Why wouldn't I? After all, Peter and I were marrying in the fall. It seemed like the perfect fit."

Kate turned away, her arms wrapped around herself as she stared at a distant spot on the wall. "But the only people I ever saw were women who had complaints about their feminine courses or wailing infants the male doctors couldn't figure out how to treat. It didn't matter if other doctors' rosters were full or patients were waiting two hours to be seen, they never let me treat anyone other than women with female complaints and babies who appeared to have no medical reason for their distress. They wouldn't even let me stitch up a wound, and I promise you, I could stitch better than every male doctor there."

"So you left and came back to Alaska where you could practice medicine," he finished. He could see it playing out in his head, almost imagine how a man as prestigious as Dr. Geoffrey Bosely would treat Kate. It would have been little better than Ellingsworth had.

"I tried talking about the situation with Peter first, more than once, actually. But even though he said he couldn't wait to marry me, he wasn't of the opinion that I should see any other patients. In fact, he was rather adamant that once we married, I shouldn't see any patients at all, not even the handful of female patients who sought me out each week. He said I would be too busy attending society events with him and his family and raising our own children to work as a doctor."

Nathan's chest felt suddenly heavy, and a giant knot formed in his stomach. How could this Peter character have wanted Kate to stop working as a doctor? Anyone could see she was born to practice medicine. Her former fiancé couldn't have loved her all that much if he hadn't respected the abilities God had given her.

Nathan pushed himself up from his chair and crossed the room to where Kate now stood beside the cabinet that held medical supplies, putting everything she'd disinfected away.

He lifted a hand and rested it on her shoulder, waiting for her sad eyes to meet his. "I want you to know that you are fearfully and wonderfully made. That God created you in his image, and he didn't make any mistakes when he formed you. In Jeremiah 31, God tells the people of Israel that he loves them with an everlasting love. Did you know God has that same love for you and me? That God feels this way about all of his children? Even the ones who are women doctors?"

She reached for him, pressing her slender body tight against his and burying her face in his chest. "No one's ever told me that before."

"I'm not the one saying those things." He stroked a hand down the side of her head, where a lock of hair had fallen beside her ear. "God is."

"I don't feel like I'm fearfully and wonderfully made. I feel like I'm a mistake, like there's nowhere I fit, like I'll never belong."

"Look at me, Kate." He waited for her to raise her head and meet his eyes, even though he kept his grip around her tight. "There will always be a place for you by my side. You will always belong somewhere, because you're my wife, and you belong with me no matter where we go."

She blinked away a fresh round of tears. "Do you mean that?"

"Absolutely. And don't forget the promise I made on our wedding day either. I will never, at any point in my life, hinder you from treating patients."

Her chin quivered, then she tightened her grip around him and buried her face against his shirt once more. "Thank you."

Her shoulders began to shake, but rather than making him want to comfort her more, it made him want to growl. She shouldn't be crying over the simple promise that he would accept her for who she was and let her treat patients.

Those were basic aspects of being human, of being alive, not privileges that needed to be fought for.

When she'd objected to their marriage, he'd assumed she was being hardheaded. But in reality, she'd just been trying to protect herself from getting hurt the way she had in Boston.

Because if male doctors had restricted her access to patients in the past, why would she assume he was any different?

20

One Week Later

Nathan moved his eyes from the letter back to the smaller map of Alaska he'd unrolled across his desk. His eyes began to blur as he scanned the islands and mountains, the rivers and towns, so familiar he nearly had them memorized.

But it didn't matter how long he studied the map. He wouldn't be able to send a doctor to every town in Alaska, not when the number of doctors had just been reduced from five to four.

And to think he'd asked for seven.

The door opened without so much as a knock, and Kate swept inside, a slender book in her hand that he instantly recognized as the *New England Journal of Medicine*.

"Nathan, have you read this article about hypothermia and . . ." Her words trailed off as soon as she looked at him. "What's wrong?"

He sucked in a breath, then blew every last bit of air out of his lungs. "Nothing."

She crossed to the desk, her forehead pinched. "Don't tell me nothing. Clearly something's wrong. And here I've spent the past two hours assuming you were working on your plan for Alaska."

"I was. I am. I . . ." He propped his elbow on the desk and dropped his head into his hand. "Just read the letter. It explains everything."

She set the journal down and picked up the missive. A few seconds later, she slammed it on the desk. "That horrid, horrid man. He doesn't want to divert too many resources to Alaska this year? What does that even mean? Alaska probably gets less than one percent of MHS's yearly budget."

"It gets exactly one percent. That's what I begged Hamilton for when he tasked me with opening a hospital here."

"Well, it's less than one percent now."

Nathan scooted the letter closer, his eyes scanning the words for probably the sixth or seventh time that evening. "He didn't even acknowledge my request to have seven doctors sent here, and he should have received the letter sometime in May."

"Well, maybe if you write him a letter reminding him that you need seven doctors, he'll change his mind about giving you only four and decide to settle for five."

"Five isn't enough to do what I want. I've spent the past two hours staring at the map, and no matter what new routes I chart, it always ends up the same. I need seven doctors. Anything short of that, and I'm depriving entire regions of medical care."

Kate tilted her head to the side, her eyes lingering on the map. "Maybe you can have one doctor on staff at the hospital here in Juneau and spread the other three to different regions."

"One doctor here won't be enough. It's not enough now, and the hospital isn't even operational yet, just the clinic."

Kate pursed her lips. "Does the surgeon general say anything about when the other three doctors are coming?"

"One's already here, aboard the URCS *Jefferson* that's headed for Barrow. The next, Dr. Ellingsworth, will return as soon as the typhus epidemic has waned, which will hopefully be sometime this month."

"Is that how long it takes for an epidemic to move through an area? Three months?"

He blinked up at her. "Ah, it depends. If an epidemic is in a very small, controlled area, it can be as little as two months, but if an epidemic gets out of control in a large area like New Orleans, it can be half a year. It sounds as if the epidemic is under control though, but not finished yet."

"That makes sense. If there's a disease outbreak in Alaska, it usually takes about two months to work through a town, but our towns are small and isolated compared to New Orleans."

"They are indeed." Nathan sat back in his chair and looked back at the map on the wall. "But with one doctor already on the revenue cutter and Ellingsworth due to return at some point, that leaves only one more doctor position to fill, but it doesn't appear that the surgeon general is in a hurry to fill it."

Kate leaned a hip against his desk and crossed her arms. "I know you need more help here, but I won't complain if Dr. Ellingsworth never returns. That man can drive a person to insanity."

Nathan smiled, then gave his head a small shake. "You can't go around saying that. He's my superior, the chief medical director of Alaska. I'm just the assistant director who's filling his position while he's gone."

"But all this planning is your idea." She waved her hand toward the map.

"Yes, but I don't have the experience Dr. Ellingsworth does. He's established five new hospitals for the MHS over the past thirty years and is an expert in communicable diseases. The MHS has credited him with saving more than three hundred lives over the course of his career. I've helped establish only one hospital, and that was in a city, not in a remote area that was difficult to access."

Kate scowled. "There's no getting out of working with him, is there? What's he going to think of us being married?"

Nathan shifted in his chair. That was a good question. "He'll get used to it, eventually. If he doesn't find a way to leave first. He might have been assigned here, but he's not too keen on living in Alaska. Or delegating any MHS resources to anyone other than seamen." Perhaps that's why the surgeon general was reducing the number of doctors. Maybe Ellingsworth had written the man with his list of complaints about Alaska.

"Well, I suppose the lack of doctors from the MHS means people here will still need my services, so I'm not out of a job quite yet."

Nathan looked up to find Kate had moved to the large map on the wall behind him. She was staring at it, her eyes scanning the mountains and rivers and islands as though she could draw up an image in her head of how each one of the landmarks looked.

He pushed his chair back from his desk and went to her, settling a hand on her shoulder. "Alaska could have twenty doctors, darling, and people would still need your services."

The shoulder beneath his hand rose and fell on a sigh. "I'm not quite sure I believe that."

He removed his hand, but only so he could take her hand in his. "Fearfully and wonderfully made, remember. You are fearfully and wonderfully made."

She looked up at him. "You truly believe that, don't you? That there's a place for me in all of this?"

"I *know* there's a place for you, and I know exactly where it is." He ducked his head, putting his mouth beside her ear before whispering, "Right here by my side."

He pressed his lips to the place where her ear and jaw met.

He'd meant it as a sweet kiss, something to help her remember his words, but the moment he brushed his lips against her tender skin, she shivered.

Had he just found a ticklish spot? That wasn't something he'd learned in medical school. According to textbooks, the place where ear and jaw met were simply that, a place where the body's auditory system connected to its skeletal system.

But his wife's skin seemed extraordinarily sensitive right there. He reached out, gripping both of Kate's hands and tugging her into the crook of his body. Then he pinned her against him and blew on that tender place beneath her ear, which was still slightly damp from his lips.

She shivered again.

It only made him want to kiss her there a second time, just to ensure she'd have the same response.

So he did.

And sure enough, she trembled in his arms.

Interesting.

"What are you doing?" She writhed against his grip, but he was strong enough to hold her in place.

"Performing an experiment." This time he let the words puff on the damp spot just below her ear.

She squirmed again.

"Does that tickle?"

"Yes!"

He reached up to graze his thumb over the soft spot at the base of her throat. "What about this? Does this tickle?"

The way her body relaxed into his told him it didn't. So he bent his head and kissed her there instead.

She gasped again, going stiff for a moment before trying to wriggle away from him. "Nathan, stop this. I think it's time to conclude your experiment."

"It's not. I haven't discovered all the places you're ticklish yet."

"Is that what you're doing?"

"Yes. I suppose you could tell me where you're ticklish, but that doesn't seem like nearly as much fun as figuring it out for myself."

"I'm not sure I could tell you, actually. I'm not usually ticklish in either of those places."

She wasn't? Nathan dove for her neck again, but in doing so, he must have loosened his hold, because she squirmed away from him.

"Stop trying to tickle me! I have an idea about how to cheer you up, if you just give me the chance to tell you."

"Cheer me up?"

She raised her eyebrows. "About the surgeon general's letter?"

Oh, that. He'd nearly forgotten—probably because what they'd been doing had already cheered him up.

"And just how do you plan to cheer me up?" Did she want to go up to her room and continue the tickle game there?

"I'm going to treat you to pie at the hotel."

He blinked. "Pie?"

"Yes, sugar makes everything better."

"I . . ." He opened his mouth, then closed it. He'd much rather stay in the office, just the two of them, and go right back to what they'd been doing.

But he wasn't sure how much kissing his wife was ready for.

Yet she cared enough about his bad mood that she wanted to cheer him up. "Tell me, do you always have pie when you're upset?"

She waved off his question. "Of course not. Sometimes I have cake or custard or cookies. It depends on what's available."

"But you always have sugar."

Her shoulders rose and fell on a prim shrug. "Like I said, it makes everything better."

He smiled, feeling as though he'd just stumbled on a secret. Who would have guessed that the strong, determined woman he'd married had a soft spot for sweets?

"You'll feel happier after you eat some pie. I know it." She sent him a smile, true and genuine and full, not one of those tight ones she usually gave him.

"I'm sure I will." Not because of the sugar but because it was the first time Kate had offered to spend time with him in a way that wasn't just the basic, day-to-day life that married couples shared.

Because he'd discovered two new things about his wife that night: that she was rather ticklish when his lips were involved, and that she had a sweet tooth.

No woman would admit either of these things to a man she didn't trust.

He might be moving backward when it came to his medical goals for Alaska, but it seemed he was starting to move forward when it came to the woman God had given him.

21

Sitka; Four Days Later; July 16

Alexei pushed through the heavy double doors of the old mansion on top of Castle Hill and out into the misty evening. He moved swiftly, keeping his steps brisk as he ignored the headache that had come on after three hours of meetings with the governor and other officials.

Why did every bureaucrat in Alaska think the Sitka Trading Company was a charity shipping service? The prices they wanted to pay for having goods transported to and from various points in Alaska was insanely low, as if they thought he could pay his sailors with goodwill and warm thoughts rather than banknotes.

Alexei lengthened his stride, not quite able to leave Castle Hill quickly enough. Maybe once he got home, his headache would . . .

A familiar form appeared on the trail leading up the hill. Preston Caldwell.

Alexei pressed his lips together.

He couldn't avoid Caldwell, not without looking like an idiot and turning around. And he wasn't of a mind to move over to the far side of the trail and avoid eye contact like a chicken liver either. So he squared his shoulders and set his jaw as the man approached. "I didn't expect to find you walking around a free man when I returned to Sitka."

Caldwell paused on the trail, and a sudden gust of wind blew off the ocean. Alexei clamped a hand on top of his hat to keep it from blowing off.

But not Caldwell. The breeze didn't blow a single strand of his perfectly slicked hair out of place, nor did it ruffle the expensive fabric of his tailored suit.

"Were you expecting me to move back to Washington, DC, this summer?" Caldwell flashed him a sharp smile. "I assure you, Amos, I have no plans to leave Sitka. I find it suits me rather well."

"Yes, it would suit me too, if I had the lawman who oversaw the entirety of Alaska on my payroll." The words were out before Alexei could think to stop them.

Caldwell took a step closer, allowing Alexei to catch a whiff of his cologne. If money could have a smell, that was it. He bet one bottle could fetch a high enough price to feed an orphanage full of children in New York City for a year.

"I noticed the *Aurora* in the harbor last week." Caldwell's voice was deathly calm. "She's looking mighty fine."

The *Aurora*?

Alexei tried to keep his face blank, but he couldn't help the way his jaw clenched slightly, considering what had happened to his family's most prized ship last summer. Hopefully the movement was small enough Caldwell wouldn't notice. If he hauled off and punched Caldwell, the man would find a way to see he was locked behind bars, facing the prison sentence that should have belonged to Caldwell.

Alexei forced a smile onto his face that he hoped was dripping with as much condescension as Caldwell's. "Of course she's beautiful. Have to keep her looking nice seeing how everyone wants replicas of her—even the Alaska Commercial Company."

At the mention of his family's company, Caldwell's eyes turned hard. "That was my father's doing, not mine."

"Unfortunately for him, we're quite booked with other ships that have been commissioned." Alexei made a show of picking an imaginary speck of lint off his waistcoat. "We won't be able to get to those ships until sometime next year."

But the shipyard would eventually get to them, and Alexei would take the Caldwells' money because he couldn't afford to run his business in such a way that a powerful family like the Caldwells would have cause to ruin his reputation.

Sometimes navigating the ins and outs of owning a business in Alaska felt like swimming in a sea filled with sharks. There'd been a time when doing business had been straightforward and open, when people had appreciated both his family's shipyard and trading company.

But that had been the world his father, grandfather, and great-grandfather had lived in, back when Russia owned what was now Alaska.

But he wasn't going to fold his businesses and move away because Caldwell thought he could buy out everyone in Sitka. In another ten years, the man would be gone. Either the seals would be extinct or the price for the pelts would drop to the point where it was no longer lucrative to hunt them.

Alexei just had to survive until then.

"You say you won't be able to build my family's sealing

ships until next year?" A calculating glint flashed across Caldwell's eyes. "Tell me, Amos, what happens if you don't have a shipyard then?"

Alexei's stomach hardened into a tight knot. What was Caldwell getting at? Was he planning to jeopardize their shipyard the way he had the *Aurora* last summer?

Again, he fought to keep his voice calm, fought to keep any of the fear or worry he felt tamped down and let only his anger come to the surface. "That shipyard has been in existence over ninety years. I can't imagine any reason it would close in the next year. Can you?"

Caldwell sent him another sharp smile that didn't reach his eyes. "Then I look forward to seeing what types of vessels you build for my family. Now if you'll excuse me, I don't want to be late for dinner with Governor Trent. Good day, Amos."

The man strode off, the thud of his fancy polished shoes against the dirt path obnoxiously loud.

Alexei turned back toward home, his hands drawn into fists at his side. Dinner with Governor Trent. Did Caldwell have to tell him that? Just what would the two of them be discussing?

Something he should be worried about? Or was he simply not important enough to get invited to a fancy dinner with the governor?

Alexei quickened his pace as he strode down the hill. But the brisk walk did nothing to calm him, not with the threat to the shipyard lingering in his mind. Or knowing that Caldwell and the governor were having dinner.

He burst through the doorway to the house with a frown, then headed toward the scent of food and the hum of conversation coming from the kitchen.

He'd normally find such things calming as well, but not tonight.

"Sis, tell Finnan he has to give it back." Ainsley's voice

greeted him as he entered the kitchen. She was standing next to Sacha's wife, Maggie, at the oven, the girl's long red hair bound into two braids that dangled beside her ears. She'd placed her hands on her hips, every inch of her eight-year-old body filled with indignation.

"I'm playin' hide-and-seek." Finnan grinned from where he sat at the table with Sacha, tucked into his adoptive father's large lap.

"Try looking in the top drawer of the table in the parlor." Yuri took a sip of coffee from where he was sitting at the table beside Sacha. "Last time I searched for a pencil and paper there, I found it filled with various other, er, treasures."

Ainsely looked at her younger brother, a wide smile filling her face. "Thank you!" She rushed out of the kitchen door, nearly barreling into Alexei in the process.

"No!" Finnan wailed, scrambling off Sacha's lap. "Why'd you tell her?" He darted out of the kitchen, his stride no match for Ainsley's longer legs.

Maggie sighed as she set a steaming platter with roast beef, carrots, and potatoes on the table, her long blond braid swinging over her shoulder. "Yuri, did you really have to give away Finnan's hiding place? Who knows how long it will take to find wherever he decides to stash things next?"

Of all his brothers, Alexei never would have guessed that Sacha, the dedicated sea captain, would fall in love with a woman who was raising two half siblings. But here they were, a year after Maggie had walked into their lives—or more precisely, onto Sacha's ship—with Sacha happily married and the proud adoptive father of an eight-year-old girl and a five-year-old boy.

"That, and I'm not sure Ainsley really needs to keep a letter from a boy tucked in her pocket day and night," Sacha muttered. "Better to let her brother steal it."

"A letter from a boy?" Alexei looked between Sacha and Maggie. "Why is a boy writing letters to Ainsley? She's eight."

"You're just as bad as Sacha." Maggie walked behind Sacha's chair, then bent and wrapped her arms around his neck. "The letter is harmless, I promise. Boys wrote me letters when I was that age."

"Well, I certainly wasn't writing girls any . . . Wait." Sacha turned his head and narrowed his eyes at his wife. "Did you just say boys were writing you letters at eight? How many boys? What did those letters say?"

Maggie chuckled and pulled away from him. "Don't worry, luv. I didn't end up marrying any of them."

"If you ask me, eight is a bit old to start writing girls letters." Yuri winked at Maggie. "I was writing them by five or six."

Alexei snorted. "What did they say? 'You look pretty? Will you play with me at recess?'"

Yuri lifted his shoulders in a careless shrug. "Every man has to start somewhere. Which is why I find what came in the mail today so interesting." He pushed himself up from the table, and a big, catlike grin spread across his face as he slid something out of his pocket. "You got a letter."

Alexei crossed his arms over his chest. "Only one?" He'd been expecting at least a half dozen from the business connections he'd made in San Francisco.

"Oh no, you got nine total, boring business stuff, most of them. I dropped them in the basket on your desk. But this one?" Yuri smirked, his eyes bright. "It says it's from a Laurel Farnsworth."

Laurel had written him? Alexei felt his eyebrows shoot up, and he reached for the letter.

Yuri yanked it away. Of course he did. Because simply handing another person a letter like a grown adult was too much to ask of Yuri.

"Farnsworth?" Sacha scratched the stubble on his chin. "Isn't that who you went to visit in San Francisco? One of your former professors from school?"

"I visited the brother of my naval architecture professor, the one who owns the shipbuilding company. Laurel is his daughter." And she was horribly out of place amid the high society of San Francisco. She liked baking, much to the horror of her parents, who were quite convinced she needed to spend more time in the drawing room with her paints or practicing her singing if she was ever going to catch the type of husband they expected of her.

The type of husband her two younger sisters had already married.

She'd been awkward and uncomfortable in that fancy drawing room, so infinitely practical despite the wealth and opulence surrounding her that Alexei hadn't been able to stop himself from seeking her out and striking up a conversation.

Which had led to him paying a call on her the next day.

And the day after that.

"So tell me, big brother . . ." Yuri tilted his head to the side, a teasing glint in his eyes. "Do you have a lady friend?"

"I most certainly do not."

"How old is she?" Maggie asked as she set plates and silverware around the table.

"Old enough," Alexei quipped.

Sacha hefted his large form from the table, then peered over Yuri's shoulder at the letter before raising his gaze. "Are you serious about her? You haven't shown interest in a woman since—"

"Since Clarise. I know." Alexei looked at his brothers. They weren't going to let this go—now that Yuri had found the letter —and they likely weren't going to let him have the letter until he divulged everything either. "I don't know whether I'm serious about Laurel, at least not yet. I consider her a friend more than anything."

A friend he wanted to remove from a world where she didn't fit and never would. Watching Laurel in San Francisco was like watching someone try to shove Kate into a fancy gown and tell her she had to be content sitting in a polished room drinking tea all day without treating patients.

Kate would go crazy, and he was surprised Laurel hadn't.

"Just a friend?" Yuri finally handed him the letter, but the grin on his face only grew wider. "Are you sure?"

Alexei looked down at the envelope for a moment, his fingers tracing the elegant script. He opened it, then skimmed the contents quickly before tucking it into his pocket. He'd read it more thoroughly later, when dinner wasn't growing cold on the table and he didn't have three other sets of eyes watching him.

"Well, I haven't met Laurel Farnsworth . . ." Maggie propped a hand on her hip, a grin plastered to her face. "But anyone who makes you smile like that can't be all bad."

Was he smiling? Alexei stroked a hand over his jaw. He supposed he was, at least a little.

Ainsley and Finnan chose that moment to race back into the kitchen, Finnan holding a letter while Ainsley screeched after him.

It took a few minutes to get them settled and seated at the table, but Maggie managed to work some sort of magic on them. She was even able to convince Finnan that he needed to wash his hands.

"I think this is good for you, brother." Sacha leaned close and clasped him on the shoulder, his voice low. "It doesn't have to mean you forget Clarise or what she once meant to you. It just means you're not letting her hold you back anymore."

Is that what getting a letter from Laurel meant? Alexei slid into his chair, bowing his head as Sacha sat beside him and said grace. A minute later, he found himself serving Finnan roast beef and carrots, then dishing out food for himself.

But as conversation moved to his exchange with Caldwell, then to progress at the shipyard and Sacha and Maggie's upcoming trip to Juneau, Alexei couldn't ignore the feeling of the letter in his pocket.

Nor could he stop the name Laurel Farnsworth from echoing in his mind.

Or remember the last time a woman other than Clarise had put a smile on his face.

22

Juneau; Ten Days Later; July 26

Kate didn't make a formal decision to start working for Nathan. It just sort of happened.

One day he closed the clinic around lunchtime so he could treat the sailors on a ship that had come into port. She had been upstairs baking, but when a high-pitched wail sounded from the street and someone pounded on the door, she'd come running.

By the time Nathan had returned to the clinic two hours later, she had fully treated the boy who had fractured his arm so badly, the bone was protruding through his skin. That had included not just setting and splinting the bone but bathing the wound with carbolic acid, then wrapping it so it didn't get infected.

By the time she'd finished, other townsfolk had seen the clinic door open, and the waiting room had been full, so she started treating other patients. Only two had refused to be seen by her, one of whom was Janice Thompson.

And the smile on Nathan's face when he'd walked into the clinic and found her treating patients? It was so bright it caused her stomach to dip and her chest to feel light at the same time.

After that, she stayed around the clinic more often, treating a handful of patients each day and keeping the doors open when Nathan was called to a ship.

Then one evening, when a ship came in after dinner, Nathan invited her to go with him. And that was how she found herself standing on a ship with the handle of her medical bag clasped in her hand.

"Open up."

Kate watched as Nathan planted his feet on the floor of the swaying ship and prodded the jaw of the sailor seated on the stool in front of him. The first thing he'd done after boarding was turn the first mate's cabin into a makeshift examination room, something that was apparently standard practice among MHS doctors.

Now that there was an MHS doctor in Juneau, sailors on ships that came from other countries needed to be examined and declared healthy before they could disembark. It was a policy the government had instituted in an effort to stop diseases like typhus and yellow fever from spreading to the United States. The ship they now stood on, the *Voyager,* had been to Russia, Japan, and China since leaving San Francisco six weeks earlier, meaning Nathan needed to examine the sailors.

After traveling to foreign countries, her own family's ships were treated the same way when they arrived in a port with an MHS hospital, like Portland or San Francisco. Now Juneau would be added to the list.

"Aw, Doc. I ain't got no scurvy." The sailor seated in the

chair in front of Nathan jerked his chin away from Nathan's hand. "Been eatin' limes an' lemons, I 'ave."

"That may be, but I still need to inspect your gums." Nathan tapped the man's jaw. "Now open up."

"Who's the woman? I'll let her look in my mouth . . . iffin' she gives it a kiss first." The sailor with at least two missing teeth and a mass of unkempt hair sent her a smirk, and it was all Kate could do not to wince.

"That woman is Dr. Reid," Nathan said stiffly.

"Dr. Reid?" The sailor puffed a breath of air directly into Nathan's face, and he grimaced. "She ain't no doctor. She's a woman."

"I assure you, she's a doctor, and she also happens to be my wife, which means if you talk about kissing her again, I'll break your nose. Now open your mouth."

Nathan spoke so methodically and clinically that it took a moment for his words to register. When they did, Kate found her mouth falling open. Had he just threatened to—

"You done married her? Good on ya', Doc. She's a—"

Nathan didn't let the sailor finish. He grabbed his jaw, using both hands to pry it open. "Grab the mirror, Kate."

She didn't just grab the concave mirror sitting on the desk; she also grabbed the candle and placed it in front of the mirror. It was the best way to cast a beam of light directly into patients' mouths. A doctor could usually do it on his own, but not when the patient was unwilling to hold his mouth open.

"It's scurvy. A rather bad case of it." She'd already guessed as much due to the red blotches and bruising on the man's arms, but it was hard to make a concrete diagnosis without also inspecting his mouth.

Nathan released the man's jaw and bathed his hands in carbolic acid while the sailor loosed a round of complaints about Nathan trying to pull his jaw off and Kate not knowing the first thing about scurvy.

Nathan let the man ramble, making a show of methodically washing his hands, the mirror, and the candlestick in carbolic acid until the man was done.

When he finally spoke, he used that bored clinical voice he had, the one that left no room for argument and let everyone in the room know who held all the power. "The red blotches and bruising on your skin alone are enough to tell me you have scurvy. When combined with the pale color of your skin—which indicates your body is no longer absorbing iron due to a lack of vitamin C—and the sore on your arm that looks as though it isn't healing, I'm even more confident about my wife's diagnosis. Your poor breath further confirmed your condition, but it wouldn't be a thorough examination without a doctor looking into your mouth, which we did."

Nathan stepped closer to the man and crossed his arms over his chest. Though he wasn't large like Sacha or Jonas, there was still something intimidating about the way he glowered down at the sailor. "Now I expect you to apologize to my wife for insulting her doctoring. She trained at a prestigious medical school in Boston and is every bit as capable of diagnosing you with scurvy as I am. Do you understand?"

The man nodded, his eyes round as he looked at her. "Sorry, ma'am."

"Doctor." Nathan corrected. "She's a doctor."

"Sorry, Dr. Reid." The sailor glanced between the two of them, then looked down at the sore on his arm. "Am I . . . am I going to be all right?"

"You'll be all right if you up your intake of fresh fruits and vegetables. The greengrocer in town carries kale and dried seaweed. We'll make sure some of that gets delivered to the ship before you leave in the morning. As soon as you get to

California, you need to stock up on grapes and any other fruits you can find. You should be able to recover within the next few months, but only if you eat fruits and vegetables at every meal and stay away from warm climates." Nathan shoved his hand in the direction of the wheelhouse. "I don't know where this ship is headed next, but I don't advise you visiting any ports that see frequent outbreaks of yellow fever or typhoid. Being deficient in vitamin C makes it easier to contract other diseases."

The sailor's shoulders slumped as he stood from his chair. "I didn't know about the typhus part, Doc. I swear I didn't. Guess I'll start eatin' them vegetables the cook is always shovin' at me."

"Yes, I guess you should." Nathan quipped as the sailor left the room.

"Is that common?" Kate asked the moment the door closed behind the other man.

"What? The scurvy or the arguing?"

Both, really, but she didn't have time to answer the question, because another sailor entered the makeshift examination room. And once they were finished examining that sailor, another sailor entered.

All in all, they treated ten crew members, which included the captain, cook, and first mate. Four of them had scurvy, and two of the cases were quite severe. Nathan ordered the captain to stay in port tomorrow until he could get a delivery of kale, lemons, limes, and apples from the greengrocer. Since no one on the ship appeared to be carrying any contagious diseases, they were cleared to travel to their home port, San Francisco.

And just like Nathan had told the sailors who had scurvy, he also told the captain that his cook needed to incorporate more fruits and vegetables into the meals he served, and that the ship was prohibited from going to ports in South America, the Caribbean, or South Asia until all symptoms of scurvy had gone away and the ship was cleared by another MHS doctor.

Neither the captain nor Nathan were too happy when they parted ways, the captain because his shipping route was being restricted and Nathan because four of the sailors were sick with an easily preventable disease.

As they headed down the gangway and onto the wharf, Kate slid her hand into his, then laced their fingers together. "Thank you."

His steps hitched, and he looked down at their entwined fingers, then into her eyes. "For what?"

"For defending my doctoring." The sailor with scurvy wasn't the only man to balk at her helping with the examinations, but each time someone objected, Nathan had been quick to correct them.

"I should be the one thanking you." He squeezed her hand. "Without you to assist me, I would have been on the *Voyager* until midnight or later."

"Maybe so, but you didn't have to defend me. I could have helped just the same without you insisting they call me doctor. Everyone would have assumed I was your nurse."

Nathan stopped walking and turned to her. "But you're a doctor. Insisting people call you by a title you worked hard to earn is the least I can do. Besides, isn't that something you usually insist on for yourself?"

"Yes, but . . ." She shifted, entirely too aware of his dark gaze boring into her. "That is . . . It's just . . . I can't recall another doctor ever defending me quite like that. Or at least, not a male doctor."

Nathan swiped a strand of hair behind her ear, then let his hand slide forward until it cupped her cheek, his skin warm despite the cool evening air. "Then I feel a profound need to apologize for every other man in my profession. Especially for your former fiancé. He should have defended you."

He hadn't, not once, and the memory nearly brought tears to her eyes. But Peter wasn't the one standing before her. Nathan was.

Did he realize how handsome he was as he stood there with an errant thatch of hair falling onto his forehead and his dark hair and eyes and his firm, chiseled jaw? His features, including his straight nose, were just sharp enough to make him appear strong, but not so harsh that he looked severe.

Oh, how had she ended up married to such a handsome man? "I know I wasn't given much choice about having a husband after what happened in the cave, but of all the people out there, I'm glad you were the one I was trapped with."

A slow smile spread across his face, a smile that made him look even more handsome. Confound it.

"Is that your way of saying you're glad you married me, darling?"

"I . . . um . . ." She shifted from one foot to the other. Was that what she'd been trying to say? Her brain hadn't taken it that far.

If she had to be married, then Nathan was the only man she'd want to be married to.

But did that mean she was actually *glad* to be married in the first place? Glad that her future was forever linked to Nathan's? "You see . . . I . . . um . . ."

"Has anyone ever told you that you're cute when you get nervous?" His smile only grew wider.

"I'm not nervous. I'm just . . ." But she didn't get a chance to finish, because suddenly his lips were on hers.

They were soft and warm, and they tasted of rain and sea and . . . Nathan. That was the only way she could describe it.

There was a unique flavor underneath the salty tang of the sea that simply tasted of her husband.

He kissed her like that for a few seconds, with only their lips touching. Then his arms came up and wrapped around her, pulling her close in a way that made the cool night air contrast with the warmth of his body.

A shiver traveled down her spine, and she suppressed it by raising her arms and looping them around his neck, her fingers toying with the hair at the back of his head. She could stay like this forever, secure in his arms, with his body pressed against hers, his lips softly grazing her mouth as though he had all the time in the world to kiss her.

And maybe he did. After all, they were married. They could stand there and kiss for an hour or two, maybe even three.

Except Nathan chose that moment to pull away from her, the side of his mouth curved into a smile.

And all she could do was stare up at him, speechless, her lips still warm from the sensation of his mouth against hers.

"Don't look so shocked by the kiss, darling. I know you've been kissed before. You were engaged."

"It wasn't like that." Her voice emerged as a thin rasp. "No one's ever kissed me like that." Just like no other male doctor had ever defended her doctoring.

He leaned down, resting his forehead against hers. "Then maybe we should head home so we can practice kissing more."

"Do we have to wait until we're home?" The five blocks to their apartment suddenly felt like five miles.

"Yes, we don't want to—"

"Excuse me. Are you Dr. Reid?"

Nathan turned in the direction of the voice.

"Dr. Nathan Reid?" a man with graying hair asked as he approached. He was clad in a finely tailored suit, the charcoal-colored fabric crisp enough that it stood out against the long shadows and dimming light. He approached with a confident gait, his polished leather shoes somehow unsoiled by the muddy street and his gold pocket-watch chain glinting beneath the lanterns.

Two other men and a woman accompanied him, each dressed entirely too fancy for Juneau. The older of the two men had snowy white hair and a bushy mustache. He wore a pressed navy suit with a bright silk cravat knotted at his throat and had a polished walking stick that seemed more for show than needed to help maintain his balance. The second man, who looked to be several decades younger, was equally distinguished in a dark suit, his overcoat draped over one arm despite the chilly mist.

The woman walked slightly behind them. Her powder-blue gown was a swirl of delicate lace and soft fabric, and a spray of feathers adorned her hat. Though between how her hat was positioned and the growing shadows, it was hard to see her face. The one thing Kate could easily see was that the woman's waist was the expected eighteen inches that high-society women sought to achieve. But Kate couldn't lecture her about tight-lacing, because her entire body looked just as gaunt as her waist, from the narrow set of her shoulders and hips to the thinness of her forearms and neck.

Even though she couldn't see the other woman's face, there was something strangely familiar about her. Could they have met in Boston?

"Forgive me," the first man in the charcoal-colored suit said, glancing between her and Nathan. "I hope I'm not interrupting. I'm Senator Randolph, and I'm looking for a Dr. Nathan Reid. I was told you'd be conducting an examination on one of the ships in port." The senator glanced down at the medical bag that Nathan must have set down at some point during their kiss, because it was at his feet rather than in his hand. "Might you be him?"

"Senator Randolph?" Nathan stepped forward and shook the man's hand, a professional smile on his face. "Yes, I'm Dr. Reid. It's lovely to have you in Juneau."

The man laughed, a loud, booming guffaw that contrasted with the elegance of his suit. "It's all right to admit you weren't expecting us for another month. We thought it best to move up our survey trip so we could spend the rest of the summer on holiday. That, and by moving the trip up, we were able to convince Secretary Gray here to accompany us."

"Secretary Gray?" Nathan turned to the man with the walking stick, who appeared to be the oldest of the group with the snowy white hair and the bushy mustache, and held out his hand. "As in Jacob Gray? Secretary of the interior?"

Kate bit back a gasp. The secretary of the interior was here? In Juneau? This man was technically in charge of Alaska, though he didn't govern Alaska himself. He appointed the governors.

She'd known there had been some type of official survey trip of Alaska planned, but she'd expected some midlevel bureaucrats would come, not the secretary of the interior himself, especially not with two senators. And she hadn't expected they'd want to talk with her husband either. But the only thing Nathan seemed surprised about was the presence of Secretary Gray. Secretary Gray stepped forward and shook Nathan's hand. "I've read the reports you submitted to the surgeon general. It's good to know we have a doctor working for the MHS who's concerned about medical care in such a remote area."

"Thank you, sir. It's an honor to meet you. If there's anything you want to see while you're here in Juneau, just let me know."

"I want a tour of the hospital in the morning." The secretary seemed to have no trouble issuing his first demand. "I'd like to see for myself how the funds we appropriated for the project are being utilized."

"Of course," Nathan replied. "It's not finished yet, but it will give you an idea of how effectively we'll be able to serve this region of the country once it's operational."

"Excellent." Secretary Gray gave a firm nod. "You can find us at the hotel after breakfast."

Nathan turned to the youngest of the three men, a blond-headed man with only a hint of gray at his temples. "You must be Senator Wells."

Kate's head shot up. "Senator Wells?" She sidled forward, peering at the man. "As in Senator Theodore Wells?"

"Yes." The man's blond eyebrows furrowed. "I'm sorry. Have we been introduced?"

"No. I . . ." Her mouth hung open as she searched for words to explain.

"Evelina?" The woman beside him asked, turning her head to fully face them for the first time. Only then did Kate recognize the woman with pretty blond hair, blue eyes, and a delicate face. The woman Alexei had once fallen in love with and almost married.

"Clarise." She gripped Nathan's arm, suddenly feeling as though the ground was tilting beneath her feet. "What are you doing back in Alaska?"

23

"Tell me again how you know Senator Wells's wife?" Nathan held the door open for Kate, then followed her into the clinic. She crossed the parlor that served as a waiting room for their patients and headed straight toward the stairs leading to the apartment above.

"Clarise already explained it over dessert. Her father was General Charles Rothley of the US Navy. He governed Alaska for five years." Kate tromped up the stairs, her shoulders slumped, her steps twice as slow as normal, almost as though she was too weary to lift her legs high enough for each foot to reach the next step.

Once she reached the top of the stairs, she crossed the sitting room that served as their private parlor, then headed down the hall toward her room. Nathan followed her, half expecting her to protest, but she didn't. She simply started stripping off her gloves and removing the tailored jacket she'd been wearing over her dress.

"I just watched my wife—whom I happen to know loves

the pecan pie at the hotel restaurant—pick at her pie for the past hour while barely glancing up. And the senator's wife did the same."

"I suspect that's typical behavior for Mrs. Wells. Did you notice how thin she is?"

Clarise Wells did seem alarmingly thin, but that wasn't the point. Nathan draped his suitcoat over the back of Kate's desk chair and took a step toward her. "Last time we had pie at the hotel, you devoured it in five minutes, then asked if I wanted to split a second piece with you. Now tell me what happened between you and the senator's wife."

"Nothing happened between us. She's six years older than me." Kate moved her hands to undo the button on her sleeve, then paused, her fingers trembling. "But something happened between her and Alexei. Between her brother and Ivan, and . . ."

She gave her head a small shake, then her hand came up to cover her mouth.

"What is it, darling?" He crossed the distance separating them, tucking her into the side of his arm so he could hold her close while looking down into her face. "What happened?"

"She was Alexei's fiancée." She pressed her eyes shut, causing a teardrop to crest and bead on her lashes. "They loved each other so much. Sometimes I think he still loves her, even though it's been over ten years."

"That's what has you so upset? That you ran into Alexei's former fiancée?"

She shook her head, her eyes opening to reveal even more tears. "No. It's not just that. It's about what happened before, with Ivan."

"What happened? And who is Ivan?" It wasn't a name he'd heard before.

"Ivan was my brother," she whispered, somehow sensing his question. "He was second oldest, right after Alexei. But one night, during a bad storm, he went over to Clarise's house to deliver a message about their parents' ship arriving safely in port. Except Clarise's brother, William, thought Ivan was a thief coming through the back door, trying to rob them during the storm. And so he... he... hid behind the door and hit him in the back of the head with a frying pan. The coroner didn't think that alone killed him, but it caused him to stumble, and then he hit his head on the corner of the hutch, and between the two blows..."

Kate shook her head. "Ivan didn't make it, and our parents didn't either. They were lost at sea during that same storm, and their little sloop was found the next morning dashed against rocks about a mile from the sound."

Nathan stood there, the arms he still had wrapped around his wife feeling like lead weights. Of all the things she could have said, all the stories she could have told, he'd never expected this. He'd known her parents had died in a storm—the entirety of Alaska seemed to know that—but he hadn't known about Ivan.

"All our lives changed that night," her voice trembled, "but none so much as Alexei's. He was in San Francisco studying naval architecture, but he had to leave early and come home to run the businesses. With Ivan dead, he and Sacha were the only ones over eighteen, and Alexei took legal responsibility for the other six of us. Clarise eventually called off the engagement. Said she couldn't build a future with Alexei knowing her brother had killed his."

"I'm so sorry," Nathan tightened his arms around Kate, as though if he held her harder, he might somehow be able to ward off the onslaught of horrible memories. "Did her brother go to prison? I assume the charge was something along the lines of involuntary manslaughter."

She shook her head again. "The jury ruled Ivan's death self-defense. Both William and Clarise thought Ivan was a thief. There'd been an uptick in robberies in Sitka, and everyone was trying to figure out who was responsible. We even had things stolen from our house. And because of that, the jury wouldn't convict him. Or maybe it was because he was the general's son, and the jurors were afraid to go against the general. That's what Alexei and Sacha and Mikhail all think, but when it happened, I wasn't exactly old enough to understand those kinds of things."

How devastating for her family. Nathan stroked a hand up Kate's back, then down again, but her muscles still felt tense beneath his hand. "You said Clarise was the one to call off the engagement? That Alexei might still love her?"

"That's right." She sniffled, wiping a tear from her cheek. "Alexei still wanted to marry her, and at first Clarise said she wanted to marry him too, in spite of what happened. Then one day she was just gone. She left Alexei a note, saying she felt guilty over Ivan's death, and that she and William were going to stay with her aunt in Washington, DC. A few months later, her father was officially transferred to a new position in Washington, and her entire family left Sitka. None of the Rothleys have been back to Alaska since."

"I'm so sorry." The words seemed like a pitiful attempt at comfort, but he didn't know what else to say.

"It all seemed so far away and in the past." Kate sniffled into his chest. "And then Clarise showed up, and . . ."

He wanted to say that he understood, but he couldn't. He might blame himself for his mother's death, but he couldn't imagine how it might feel if one of Kate's brothers accidentally killed his mother. That would bring a whole new level of hurt into their relationship.

So he simply wrapped both arms back around his wife, held her close while she cried into his chest, and prayed his actions would somehow be enough to give her the comfort she needed.

24

The dreams came in waves, washing over Kate in the night while the heavens unleashed a deluge of rain that pounded against the roof and windows of the apartment.

She'd been thirteen on that fateful night, old enough to know the rain pounding against the windows of their house was fiercer than usual, old enough to know the white-capped waves crashing against the shoreline were too high and wild for the normally calm sound. Old enough to feel a growing sense of fear as she stayed up past her bedtime, huddled in the attic with Evelina and Yuri. Ivan, Sacha, and Mikhail were in the attic too, but they were fighting for a place at the window, trying to see through the driving rain to watch the entrance to the sound from the highest window in the house.

"A ship!" Ivan pointed into the growing darkness. "There. Do you see it?"

"Is it the *Gray Wolf*?" Sacha turned from where he'd been pacing and headed back to the window, where night was quickly falling.

"I don't know. It's too soon to tell."

"It's not the *Gray Wolf*," Mikhail said from where he leaned against the far side of the window. "It's too big."

"You don't know that." Ivan glared at Mikhail. "It could still be Ma and Pa."

"It's not," Mikhail replied in that flat, even voice he had. He never seemed to get upset about anything. "It's some other ship. Who else was caught in the storm?"

"Everyone," Sacha muttered. "It came out of nowhere."

That was true. It had certainly come out of nowhere, and it had been fierce. Pa and Ma were making a quick run to Hoonah, on the opposite side of Baranof Island from where Sitka was located. The day had started mild and sunny. No one had worried about the weather, and Ilya and Inessa were old enough that Ma had left them at home for Kate and Evelina to watch.

But about two hours after her parents had left, the wind kicked up, and clouds covered the sun. The wind only got worse throughout the morning and into the afternoon, driving frightfully big waves into the sound. Local fishing ships had started returning to the harbor early, and then other ships entered the harbor, large ones the size of the *Alliance* and *Halcyon* that wanted to wait out the storm in the calm waters of Sitka Sound.

Except Sitka Sound wasn't calm. The waves looked as wild as they usually did during a windy day on the open sea.

Ivan, the oldest of her siblings after Alexei, had gone down to the wharf to ask about conditions on the water and catalog the ships that came in. It seemed like the type of thing Pa would want to know after he returned—which ships were safe, if any ships were feared lost, if anyone was missing. At twenty years of age, Ivan was an experienced enough seaman that sailors would talk to him. Besides, Pa was training him to take over the trading company.

When Ivan returned a couple hours later, rain had started to fall, and he had bad news. Not only had the storm come out of nowhere, but it didn't show signs of lessening anytime soon. The fact it had just started to rain was a bad sign, indicating the full strength of the storm had yet to hit them, even though the waves were already wild.

So here they were, hours later, huddled in the attic, watching and praying and hoping that their parents would arrive safely back in Sitka, while Ilya and Inessa slept downstairs.

Or maybe they were praying that it had been clear how bad the storm was, even from the sheltered side of Baranof Island, and their parents had stayed put in Hoonah.

Or perhaps their parents were heading back to Sitka and had beached the small sloop somewhere along the shoreline when the violence of the storm became clear.

Of course, if their parents had done either of those things, they wouldn't know until tomorrow, which meant they'd probably spend the whole night up here, dozing off and on, watching through the darkness and rain for the lanterns hanging on the bow and stern of a little sloop as it entered the sound.

"I know the storm came out of nowhere, you oaf." Mikhail gave Sacha a shove, though Sacha didn't move so much as an inch. Her third oldest brother was huge, like their father. *The chest of a sailor, Otets* always said. "But who else would try to make it back to Sitka Sound? It has to be someone from town. Everyone else would have found another place to seek harbor by now. And it has to be someone with a large ship."

Ivan straightened. "Bet you it's General Rothley."

Kate wrinkled her nose. Of course it would be the Rothleys. It was always the Rothleys. Alexei was engaged to the general's daughter, Clarise, and whenever Alexei was in Sitka, the two of them spent all day sitting around staring into each other's eyes. One time Kate had even caught them kissing. She'd run straight over to the shipping office and told *Otets*, but all he did was laugh.

Fortunately Alexei was down in San Francisco learning how to build tall ships like the ones *Otets* owned. That meant he couldn't always be sneaking off with Clarise. But he'd be back for the summer soon, and then it would be all smooches and lovesick gazes for a whole three months before Alexei went back to San Francisco for his final year of school.

General Rothley had already given permission for him and Clarise to marry.

As far as Kate was concerned, the wedding couldn't happen soon enough. At least then, Alexei and Clarise would have their own house to smooch in.

"General Rothley took a navy ship and several sailors to check on some fighting between the Aleut and Tlingit north of here. Took his wife with him." Ivan pushed himself away from the window and started toward the stairs. "They were due back yesterday. I saw William down at the wharf earlier, and he was worried that something had happened to the ship."

"Where are you going?" Sacha said to Ivan's retreating form.

"To the Rothleys'. Mikhail's right. It's a navy ship, far too big to be the sloop, and William and Clarise will want to know their parents are back."

"Be careful out there," Mikhail called.

"Of what? The rain? It doesn't bite. I'll just come home wet." And with that, Ivan tromped down the stairs.

What she didn't know—what none of them knew—was that those were the last words they would ever hear their brother speak.

KATE WOKE to the feel of a warm body pressed against her back and the weight of an arm over her waist. She blinked, trying to get her bearings before remembering that she'd asked Nathan to stay with her last night.

And stay with her he had, wrapping his warm, strong arms around her while she'd cried over memories that were best left in the past.

But now morning was here, evidenced by the trickle of murky, gray light that filtered through a crack in the curtains despite the rain beating a steady pattern on the roof.

She slid out from beneath Nathan's arm, careful not to wake him, and slipped on her dress, not caring that it was the same one she'd worn yesterday. She needed to see her sister, needed the feel of Evelina's arms around her, needed to sit beside someone who would understand why she felt so devastated by Clarise's appearance in Alaska.

And of course, they needed to send a message to Alexei about Clarise heading to Sitka in a few more days.

So Kate moved silently down the stairs, then across the clinic waiting room to the door, where she pulled on her slicker, ducked her head, and barreled into the rain, mud splattering the hem of her skirt as she ran. At half past five, it was too early for most people to be up, meaning it took her only a handful of minutes to reach the trading post. She slid her key into the lock and let herself inside, then headed toward the stairs that led to her family's apartment.

What were the chances she could knock quietly enough on

Evelina's bedroom door that she'd wake her sister without waking Jonas?

Slim. Jonas woke at the sound of a pin drop. It was the lawman in him.

Even so, she'd have to risk knocking. Evelina would want to know about Clarise as soon as possible. In fact, she'd probably be upset about not being told last night.

Kate reached the top step, then turned the corner . . .

And ran straight into a broad male chest.

"Sacha?" She blinked up at her giant of a brother, his light brown hair highlighted with streaks of gold.

He was already wrapping his burly arms around her. "Kate! And here I thought I'd be the one paying you a visit first thing this morning. How did you know I was here?"

She shook her head against his chest. "I didn't. When did you get in? Why are you here? Is something wrong?"

He chuckled, the sound warm and deep, and Kate closed her eyes, letting herself soak in Sacha's familiar laugh.

Of all her brothers, Sacha had always understood her the best. Oh, she knew her other brothers loved her, but Alexei was always a bit too busy with his own plans to take time for her, as were Mikhail and Yuri. Sacha, on the other hand, always had time for a hug, or a story, or to simply stop whatever he was doing and listen to her.

Which is what she found him doing now, looking down at her with his patient gaze and a small furrow between his brows. "I wanted to come meet my new brother-in-law. Heard quite the tale about your wedding. But it looks as though there's trouble in paradise if you're here at half past five. And I can tell you've been crying. Don't try to deny it. What did that bounder do? Do you need me to have a talk with him?"

"No. It's not Nathan. He's kind and sweet and even

defends my doctoring. I'm sure he's a better husband than I deserve."

One of Sacha's bushy eyebrows winged up. "Then why are you so upset?"

She sucked in a breath and blurted the words out before she could think about them. "Clarise is here in Juneau."

"What?" Sacha grew still, his arms tensing around her. "Surely you don't mean—?"

"Yes, I mean it. Clarise Rothley—or rather, it's Clarise Wells now. She's married to one of the senators that came here on a survey of Alaska. She's in town for two more days, and then her husband and Senator Randolph are heading to Sitka, along with the secretary of the interior. He's in town too. They're supposed to meet with Governor Trent and then you. They said something last night at the hotel about legislation regarding seal hunting."

Sacha dropped his arms from around her. "I knew two senators were coming, but not Secretary Gray. And they weren't supposed to visit until the end of August. But I had no idea one of the men was Clarise's husband—or that she'd be with him."

The creak of a door opening sounded from deeper inside the apartment, followed by two sets of footsteps, one heavy and one light. A moment later, Evelina and Jonas stepped into the room.

"What's going on?" Evelina looked between them, concern creeping into her soft green eyes. "Kate, why are you here so early? Did something happen with Nathan?"

Kate swallowed. "Not with Nathan, no, but Clarise is here in Juneau, visiting the area with her husband, Senator Theodore Wells."

Evelina stilled for a moment, much like Sacha had done after hearing the news. Then the same horror that Kate had spent the past eight hours suppressing filled Evelina's eyes. "No. She's not. She wouldn't do such a thing."

"She's staying at the hotel."

"The nerve of that woman!" Evelina's hands balled into fists. "Why would she come here? Doesn't she realize Alexei's miserable enough already? Why bring her husband here to taunt him?"

"To be fair, she didn't realize any of us were in Juneau, and she seemed quite upset about seeing me," Kate answered. "But she's going to Sitka next. I have no idea if she knows Alexei's there, if she's doing this intentionally, or if she's assuming he moved on with his life the way she has."

Evelina set her mouth in a grim line. "We have to warn Alexei."

"That's what I was just telling Sacha."

A heavy pounding sounded on the door downstairs, and the four of them looked at each other.

"Someone's probably looking for the Deputy Marshal." Jonas tightened the sash on his robe, then lumbered down the stairs.

"Normally I'd write Alexei a letter." Sacha rubbed the back of his neck. "But the senators are supposed to meet with us, and everything I have on the seals is back in Sitka. I should probably pack everyone up and—"

"Kate." A sharp voice interrupted from the stairs.

She turned to find Nathan entering the room ahead of Jonas, his chest heaving and wet, dark hair plastered to his face. His eyes swept quickly down her, then traveled back up to land on her face. "Are you all right?"

She blinked at him. "Yes. Why wouldn't I be? I just came to tell Evelina about Clarise."

"Next time you decide to dart off at the crack of dawn, please leave a note." His eyes bored into hers, hot and dark.

"Oh. I . . . Were you worried? About me?" She licked her lips. "There's no reason. I'm fine."

"So you're the man who put my sister in a compromising situation?" Sacha balled his large hand into his fist and held it up. "Give me one reason why I shouldn't slam this into your nose."

Nathan tugged on the collar of his shirt. "Ah, I had no intention of compromising your sister. I promise. I just wasn't aware of how cold Alaska could be at the end of May, and then we were caught in a cave and—"

"Oh, stop it." Kate planted herself in front of Sacha and crossed her arms over her chest. "If you're going to be cross with someone, be cross with me. I'm the one who insisted he take off his clothes."

"Goodness, Kate," Nathan muttered from behind her. "Don't you ever learn?"

She turned and blinked at him. "Learn what?"

Nathan pinched the bridge of his nose. "Please tell me I'm the first man you convinced to undress in front of you."

"Hardly. I'm a doctor, and there was a medical reason for us to get undressed. Why can't anyone understand that?"

Everyone groaned around her, even Sacha, though the murderous look had left his eyes, so she wasn't going to complain.

Nathan reached out and extended a hand to her brother. "I'm Kate's husband, Dr. Nathan Reid. I take it you're the sea captain."

"Shipbuilder these days." Sacha didn't reach out to shake his hand, just crossed his arms over his burly chest.

Nathan dropped his arm. "What brings you to Juneau?"

"Heard a story about my spinsterish sister getting hitched, and I wanted to meet her new husband for myself. Make sure he's planning to do right by her." Sacha narrowed his eyes at

Nathan. "Seeing how you tracked her down in a rainstorm without bothering to put on a coat, you might be half decent, but still, I don't take kindly to men who trap my sisters into marriage."

"Nathan! Where's your coat?" Kate swept her gaze over him. He was soaked. Again. Hadn't he learned by now not to go traipsing around in the rain without warm clothing?

"I wasn't exactly thinking about a coat when I woke up to find you gone."

"I just wanted to visit Evelina." She gestured toward her sister.

Nathan pressed his eyes shut and rubbed his forehead. "I understand. Next time tell me first."

"Were you really that worried?" She stepped toward him and wrapped her arms around his back. Never mind his shirt was soaked through or that her own dress grew damp when he wrapped his arms around her. "I'm sorry. I didn't mean to frighten you."

His hold tightened around her. "I know. And I figured you were probably here, doing exactly what you're doing, but there was that bit of worry in the back of my head."

"I would have worried too, had I woken to find you gone without a note."

"Would you now?" He pulled back just enough to look at her. The hardness was gone from his eyes, replaced with something soft and warm.

It made her want to press up onto her toes and kiss him like they had in the street the night before, to twine her fingers through the hair at the back of his neck.

"Can the two of you stay for breakfast?"

At the sound of Evelina's voice, Kate jumped away from Nathan, then looked around the room to find Jonas, Sacha, and Evelina all looking at her.

"That way Nathan can have a chance to visit with Sacha and his family." Evelina sent them a bright smile.

Nathan took a small step away from her, as though he, too, had been lost for the briefest of moments. "If we eat early. The clinic opens at nine."

"I'll get started now. Kate, do you want to help me?"

She didn't. She wanted to stay by Nathan's side and listen while he talked to Sacha and Jonas.

But she followed her sister into the kitchen anyway.

HIS OWN FAMILY wasn't nearly as much fun as his wife's.

The thought sprang into Nathan's mind more than once throughout the morning, but the first time it appeared was when a little boy with a mop of red hair and a face full of freckles raced into the kitchen and launched himself at Sacha. A girl with similar red hair and freckles appeared a few seconds later, but she was both old enough and dignified enough to walk into the room rather than run.

Then Sacha's wife, Maggie, entered the room, and the burly man's face lit up. He rose from the table and gave her such a big hug that it nearly swallowed her, then she set to work helping Kate and Evelina prepare a Russian breakfast.

Kate had never told him that she had a favorite brother or who it was, but that quickly became apparent in the time he spent sitting at the Redding's kitchen table. There was an easiness between her and Sacha that didn't exist between her and Alexei or her and Jonas. And Nathan lost track of the times he saw Sacha sling an arm around Kate's shoulder or say something to her as she moved around the kitchen.

Then he realized he was jealous, blast it all.

Last night, it had seemed like some of the walls around her

heart were finally coming down. They'd kissed in the street, and then she'd let him comfort her while she relived one of the most painful days of her life. After that, she asked him to stay with her, and he'd held her in their bed while she drenched his nightshirt with tears.

But this morning, she preferred the company of her family to him, and it made him feel about six inches tall. Made him feel like the steps she'd taken toward him meant nothing compared to how comfortable she was with her family.

Sacha still looked as though he might ball his hand into a fist and start swinging punches any second, but he seemed to have decided on conducting an interrogation first. The man had spent the better part of half an hour questioning him about his doctoring, about whether he liked Alaska, about where he'd lived before Juneau, and about where he'd gone to medical school. If there was a question that could be asked about a man's life, Sacha Amos had asked it without apology.

The entire time, Nathan couldn't stop thinking about the way Kate had clung to him as she'd tossed and turned last night, or what it might feel like if he gave Kate a happier reason to cling to him, like when he had kissed her and pulled her into his arms before the Wells arrived. "Tell me, what does my wife like to do for fun? She's always so busy working that it seems like she doesn't know how to relax."

"I'm not sure Kate does know how to relax, but I like that you call her your wife." Sacha eyed him over his cup of coffee. "That you openly claim her as your own, even though you didn't have much choice about marrying her."

Nathan moved his eyes back to the burly shipbuilder. "I don't have any qualms about claiming her. I wanted to marry her before the mudslide."

"You did?" This from Jonas, who'd been mostly silent as he

sat at the table, sipping his coffee and listening while Sacha interrogated him.

"Why is everyone so shocked when I say that?" Nathan sent Jonas a scowl. "She's beautiful and talented, not a pariah."

"I'll be the first to admit Evelina and Kate are pleasant to look at, but when Lina opens her mouth, most people smile. When Kate opens her mouth . . ." Jonas shook his head. "Let's just say that most people come away with a scowl—or worse."

Nathan moved his gaze back to Kate, her long chestnut hair cascading down her back in thick waves, a smile both on her lips and in her eyes as she listened to something Maggie said. "The first time I heard her talk, I thought she was brilliant."

"Hang it all," Sacha muttered. "Alexei's right. You are a good fit for her."

Nathan refrained from rolling his eyes. Barely. "Great. Any advice on how I can convince her of it?"

Jonas chuckled. "Good luck. I don't think anyone's ever been able to convince Kate of a single thing. She can be a mite stubborn."

"She's not as bad as all that." Sacha's eyes softened in a brotherly sort of way as he, too, watched Kate. "She'll see reason—eventually. Sometimes it just takes her longer than others. She's been through a lot, certainly more than most women. But if you're patient, she'll come around."

Patience. The very thing he'd been praying for, but he was starting to think God hadn't given him enough of it.

"She's got a soft spot underneath that hard shell she shows the world," Jonas added, finishing the last of his coffee.

"I don't mind the hard parts," Nathan replied. "I don't even mind her sharp tongue. I like the fact she doesn't care about what other people think. It's refreshing."

"Well, blow me down." Sacha thumped him on the back.

"Don't tell Kate, but I might be glad that mudslide forced the two of you to get married."

"Oh, I thank God for that mudslide every day. I've already told Kate that I wasn't forced to marry her. I wanted to. The mudslide just sped up the process."

"You've her told that?" Sacha shook his head.

"Sure did. The morning after we got married. Why?"

The dour man who'd spent the morning glaring at him suddenly grinned. "Welcome to the family."

25

"So you really think this can be done?" Secretary Gray studied the map of Alaska tacked to the wall of Nathan's office. "That you can provide medical services for the entirety of Alaska with just seven doctors?"

"Absolutely." Nathan took a step closer to the map, then tapped one of the arrows marking the route around the Aleutian Islands. "By using traveling routes for two of the doctors, we can not only offer better access to care but also keep track of disease outbreaks and put protocols in place to control them, much like we do for ships that arrive in America with yellow fever or typhus."

"Huh." Senator Wells leaned back in his chair and puffed on his cigar. "Good on you, Dr. Reid. I have to admit, I expected you'd spend the day telling us we needed to put a doctor in each little town."

"No. I don't feel as though stationing a doctor in each town is the best use of our resources." Nathan met the serious senator's gaze. After giving the group a tour of the hospital that morning, he'd discovered Senator Wells was the most serious and difficult to impress. And his impression of the man hadn't changed.

The senators and Secretary Gray had met with the Committee of Public Safety for lunch and spent the afternoon touring Juneau. Then Nathan had met them at the hotel for dinner, after which they'd moved back to the clinic.

Or at least, everyone except Mrs. Wells had returned to his office in the clinic, even Kate. Mrs. Wells, however, had said she was feeling faint and had retired early.

"My goal is to get a doctor to each town three times a year, and much of that is possible using traveling routes. Can you see where I have the proposed routes marked here?" Nathan traced the route through the islands of Southeast Alaska with his finger, then lifted his hand and began tracing the route that would cover the northernmost section of the coast that extended above the Arctic Circle.

The surgeon general might have restricted him to only four doctors for the next twelve months, but funding could still be increased for next year, and he had every intention of convincing the secretary of the interior and two senators that more money should be designated for Alaska. Maybe then he'd be able to staff all seven doctors.

"The only town where I suggest stationing a doctor permanently is Barrow," Nathan added.

"Barrow." Secretary Gray's eyes instantly moved to the red-colored pin marking Barrow at the top of the map. Positioned far above the Arctic Circle on the shores of the Arctic Ocean, it was at the very tip of Alaska, the place where the land gave way to an endless ocean of ice that eventually led to the North Pole. One day an explorer would probably reach the North Pole. The icy waters made the small Eskimo town accessible by ship for only two or three months of the year when the ice finally melted.

"It's too remote to be put on a traveling route, but it's imperative we keep tabs on it. Last year a diphtheria epidemic ravaged the town. It killed twenty-seven people, twenty-one of them children. Those lives could have been saved if the tribe had access to the diphtheria antitoxin, but no one knew about the outbreak."

Nathan could still remember the feeling of horror that had washed over him when the surgeon general had sent him a copy of that report. Fortunately, the surgeon general had also sent him a letter telling him it was time to come to Washington, DC, and put together a plan to improve medical care in Alaska.

Nathan had been asking the man for five years to increase the medical care throughout the territory. He only wished the surgeon general had decided to act before so many people needlessly died from a preventable epidemic.

But without more doctors, there might still be another tragedy like the one in Barrow.

Senator Randolph took a sip of port, then cocked his head to the side as he took in the room. "There are many in Washington who feel the MHS should stick to the role it's had for over a century and remain focused on treating only the navy and merchant sailors. They say the backbone of the economy is our fleet of merchant mariners who import and export goods, and that we shouldn't do anything that would divert funds from keeping our nation's seamen healthy. What do you say to that, Dr. Reid?"

It sounded as though Senator Randolph had spoken to Ellingsworth about ten minutes ago, never mind that the man was still in New Orleans. "I say that a hundred years ago, when Congress created the Marine Hospital Service, they did an excellent job of protecting a valuable part of the American economy. But those senators and representatives couldn't have known how the United States would push for expansion or that our country would soon be acquiring vast tracts of land through the Louisiana and Alaska Purchases. Today that land is in the process of being settled. The problem is, settlers have little access to medical care, meaning they die from preventable illnesses and conditions like appendicitis or diphtheria or smallpox, while people in cities can receive the care necessary to save their lives."

"And you think the Marine Hospital Service should step in and fill this role?" Secretary Gray's hand stilled atop his walking stick.

"I think either the MHS needs to be expanded into an agency that oversees public health in general or a new agency needs to be formed that focuses on the health needs of the American populace. Those needs can look different in different places. In cities, the rapid spread of contagious diseases due to cramped living conditions poses a constant threat. Just look at any of the cholera epidemics we've had in the last thirty years in places like New York and Saint Louis."

Nathan let his eyes drift around the room. Everyone was watching him, even Kate, who had spent most of their conversation sitting in the corner thumbing through a medical journal. "On the other hand, settlers in rural areas face far different medical needs. But regardless of location, without a healthy populace, our country would do nothing but struggle. So it's reasonable to ask Congress to fund some type of organization that sees to public health. In fact, I think the money you invest in such an effort will easily bring a substantial return in healthier citizens who are able to work longer and pay more taxes."

"You certainly make a good case, Dr. Reid." Secretary Gray clapped him on the back, a grin spreading across the snow-haired man's face. "But I'm afraid it's time for this old man to retire for the evening. Let's resume this conversation over lunch tomorrow, shall we?"

"Yes, sir." Nathan extended his hand to shake the secretary's, then moved to the door, where he shook both of the senators' hands on their way out. "Thank you for your time."

"Meet us at the hotel at noon," Secretary Gray called over his shoulder.

The moment the office door closed behind the men, Nathan turned to Kate, who was still at the back of the room, but she'd set aside the journal and had stood from her chair, her hands twisted in front of her skirt. "I didn't realize you were the one who got my report."

"Your report?"

"From Barrow, about the diphtheria epidemic." She came toward him. "Walking into Barrow last summer was the most horrifying thing I've ever faced as a doctor. The tribe had lost so many people, and they didn't know why. And the worst part was that those deaths were preventable. Even without antitoxins, a simple tracheostomy is often enough to save the life of a person with diphtheria, but no one in Barrow knew that, let alone how to perform one."

He stared at her, every muscle in his body turning still. "You were the doctor who went to Barrow last summer?"

She searched his face, her eyes round and luminous in the evening light filtering through the window. "You didn't know?"

No. He'd known she traveled to the villages in Southeast Alaska, and her brother ran a shipping company. But as for the rest . . . "Did you go on one of Alexei's ships?"

"Yes, on the *Aurora*. Sacha was the captain, and he ran the Arctic route to Barrow every summer. He always took me, and we delivered whatever medical supplies the MHS sent. We stopped at Kotzebue Sound, too, and several other villages on the coast, but Barrow was the farthest and most difficult to reach."

"How did I not know that was you?" Nathan whispered, his throat suddenly tight.

A confused little grove etched itself into the normally smooth skin between her eyebrows. "Who else would it be?"

"Did you send a report the year before last too?"

"I've sent reports for three years. Ever since I returned from Boston. The first year I went, I was still living in Sitka. I moved to Juneau after that."

Nathan turned and headed to the filing cabinet. He opened the drawer and riffled through a few papers, then pulled out the reports from Barrow. The name Dr. E. D. Amos was scrawled across the bottom of the first report, and the second, and the third.

"I should have put it together," he muttered, half to himself.

"Are you sending diphtheria antitoxins to Barrow this year on one of your traveling doctor routes?" She stepped closer and peered at the reports in his hand. "Please tell me you're sending the antitoxins."

"One hundred and fifty vials." He set the reports on his desk and reached for her. "Enough for everyone in the town. And next year we'll send another hundred and fifty, because antitoxins don't last as long as inoculations and will need to be replaced by then."

She gave him a small, sad smile. "Thank you. I don't know how the tribe contracted diphtheria, considering how remote the village is, but I don't believe they spread it to anywhere else. The epidemic ran through the town at the very beginning of summer. It had been over for several weeks by the time we arrived on the *Aurora*."

"We were able to trace the origin to a ship from Russia that visited in June. An outbreak started in Provideniya last spring, and it's likely someone on that ship was infected."

She looked at the reports on his desk. "You can track where an epidemic starts?"

"We try. That's part of why we inspect ships that have been in foreign ports when they arrive in a city with an MHS hospital."

"And all of that is over and above what you're trying to do in Alaska, how you're trying to make sure everyone here has access to some kind of medical care."

He rubbed the back of his neck. "That's more of a personal goal that I talked the surgeon general into. As you heard tonight, not everyone likes the idea of taking MHS resources and using them on the general public."

"Sometimes I think that I don't deserve you, Nathan Reid. That you're far too good for me." She looked up from the papers, and only then did he realize how close they were standing, that the heat from her slender body was radiating into his chest, even though they weren't touching.

"And what am I supposed to think about you?" He inched forward, causing their chests to touch when she inhaled. "The woman who travels clear up to Barrow to treat a village of a hundred and fifty people? The woman responsible for having antitoxins sent there?"

He reached down, his hands wrapping around her rib cage, then hefted her onto the desk and stepped into the folds of her skirt.

"Maybe I'm the one who doesn't deserve you." His face was so close that her breath brushed his face. Then he leaned down and pressed his mouth to hers.

Her lips were gentle and warm, her body soft against his, and it took only a handful of seconds before she melted into the kiss.

into him.

He wrapped one arm around her waist, clasping her to him, and used his other hand to tilt her head to the side. He broke from her lips only so that he could rain kisses across her jaw and down her neck. Then he planted a single kiss in the place where her ear and jaw met and watched her lips part on a ticklish gasp before he covered them once more with his own.

He didn't know how long he kissed her, letting himself sink into the sweet warmth of her lips. He only knew that he was once again tempted to ask if he could lead her upstairs, to ask if she wanted to become his wife in every way.

But she was still hesitant with him in so many ways. Just that morning, she'd left him asleep in her bed and sought out her sister rather than ask him to accompany her. And he'd promised he'd wait until she was ready to ask for more.

So he kept his thoughts to himself and buried his feelings deep inside. And a moment later when he broke their kiss and offered to escort her to her room, he did so knowing that he'd close the door behind her and watch her disappear into her room without him.

26

Sitka; That Night

Alexei stared down at the letter in front of him. It was the second one he'd gotten from Laurel, though he'd yet to write her back.

It started by talking about how sunny and warm the weather was but quickly went into the new things she'd been baking in the kitchen. A local restaurant was interested in placing a standing order of blueberry tarts each week, but her father refused to let her sell any of her baked goods. According to Laurel, he seemed both insulted and offended at the idea.

Alexei closed his eyes and tried to imagine a world where he'd be insulted by Evelina getting paid for taking a legal case or Kate getting paid for treating a patient. He was proud every time his sisters earned money in their chosen professions. Proud they had professions in the first place and had gone to school to learn how to do something they loved.

He'd gone to school once to learn something he loved, naval architecture, studying everything from why cutters were so fast and barges were so slow to the best materials to build a ship to the best placement of sails or the best choices in boilers or both.

He'd loved those years in San Francisco learning more about a subject he'd always enjoyed and knew firsthand from all his years of sailing with his father. And he'd wanted nothing more than to expand the Amos Family Shipbuilders to Seattle and start building ships for the company there. But after his parents and Ivan had died, he'd been duty bound to return to Sitka. The one bright spot in leaving California had been Clarise. At least he'd been able to see her every day, even if things were strained, considering how Ivan had died.

But then Clarise had moved to Washington, DC, leaving him alone in a place he didn't want to be, with his schooling unfinished and his dreams for the future withering more each day.

Sacha and Mikhail had helped, but they'd all been so young, and when Sacha took to the seas and Mikhail started getting job offers to guide expeditions, Alexei hadn't told them no. He never would have dreamed of forcing them to stay in Sitka and help with the day-to-day running of their shipping company and shipyard.

When Kate turned old enough to go to medical school, he hadn't told her no either. He'd reworked his shipping routes so they brought in enough money to support both Kate and Evelina going to Boston together.

Then when Evelina had written him after two months of teaching school and told him she wanted to study law instead, he'd gone to San Francisco and come home with commissions to build two more ships to pay for the extra expenses.

He didn't regret it in the least. Not now, and not at any point in the past.

So how could Harold Farnsworth be upset that his daughter was a talented baker? How could a father do anything other than support his daughter's dreams?

If Evelina had shown an interest in baking rather than law, Alexei would have hunted down another ship commission and paid to send her to Paris, where she could study with some of the best pastry chefs in the world.

He stared down at the paper in front of him, nearly blank except for the words *Dear Laurel* and a brief description of the weather in Sitka at the top.

He couldn't remember the last time he'd written a letter that wasn't business or family related, but Sacha was right. It was time for him to move on. Time for him not to let what had happened with Clarise hold him back.

So he put his pen to the paper and began to write, not just a few simple lines about the ships they were building, but paragraph upon paragraph about how he wished she had the chance to go to Paris and study with a master pastry chef, and about how much he'd enjoyed their conversations in San Francisco. He finished the letter with an invitation for both her and her father to visit him in Sitka, where her father could see the shipyard, and he'd be able to spend more time getting to know Laurel.

When he finally lifted his pen from the page and fanned the drying ink, he didn't feel the least bit guilty about writing such a revealing letter. If anything, his chest felt a little lighter and his shoulders seemed a little less slumped. It was almost as though his entire being had been waiting for him to move past what had happened all those years ago.

~.~.~.~.~

. . .

Juneau; One Night Later

Boom! Boom! Boom!

Kate woke with a start, her heart hammering against her chest as pounding resonated through the building.

"Dr. Reid? Are you there?" A feminine voice called from the street below. "Open up."

Kate flung off her covers and scampered across the room to where her dress from yesterday hung on a peg. She had it on in less than five seconds and threw open the door, only to find Nathan skidding into the hallway, his shirt untucked and half the buttons lopsided.

"Sounds like there's an emergency." He waved for her to follow him. "Come on."

She didn't need to be told twice as she tromped down the stairs, her feet racing to keep up with his thunderous steps.

Painful wailing sounded from outside, followed by the sound of retching.

Kate skidded to a halt behind Nathan just in time for him to fling open the door.

"You have to help, please." Janice Thompson stood on the stoop, one arm propping up the hunched form of Tillie Metcalf.

Sarah Cutter, another teacher with the Presbyterian mission, stood on Miss Metcalf's other side, helping to hold up the woman who was clearly too ill to stand on her own. And behind them, Gertie Gillespie, the fourth teacher at the mission, stood twisting her hands together.

"Tillie was feeling ill this afternoon," Miss Thompson rushed to explain. "So she went to bed early, but she woke us half an hour ago with this wailing."

Almost as though on cue, Miss Metcalf clutched her abdomen and let out a low keening sound that brought a chill to Kate's bones.

"Here, let me take her." Nathan stepped through the doorway and into the rain, never mind he was barefoot, and hefted the woman into his arms.

"It hurts," Miss Metcalf moaned. "My stomach. I've never felt this much pain."

"Is the pain worse on one side?" Nathan asked.

Kate had a strong feeling it wasn't the woman's stomach but her appendix.

"It hurts here." The woman pressed a hand to her right side, then squeezed her eyes shut against what was likely another wave of pain.

Kate raced across the parlor ahead of Nathan, then flung open the door to the first of the examination rooms, which was large enough they could use it for surgery, and hurried to light the lamps around the room.

"Can you help her?" Miss Thompson trailed into the room.

"Yes, but she'll likely need surgery." Nathan laid Miss Metcalf on the examination table.

"Surgery?" Miss Thompson wrung her hands together. "How can you say that? You haven't even examined her."

"I don't care what they have to do, just make it . . ." Miss Metcalf's words faded, and a retching sound filled the room.

Kate rushed to grab the rubbish bin, bringing it to the woman's side a mere moment before she lost the contents of her stomach.

"How many times has she thrown up?" Nathan asked.

"Five or six times," Miss Cutter answered from where she stood in the doorway with Miss Gillespie.

Nathan waited for the retching to subside, then gripped

Miss Metcalf's hand. "I believe you have appendicitis, but I'm going to need to press on your abdomen to be sure."

The woman nodded weakly, sweaty brown hair plastered across her face.

Nathan's face was white as he examined her abdomen, starting by putting pressure on the top left and gradually moving the pressure lower and to her right. When he pressed just above her right hip, she screamed in pain.

Kate made a beeline for the cabinet that held the scalpel, forceps, carbolic acid, and other medical supplies while Nathan launched into an explanation of why an appendectomy was necessary and what it would entail. His voice held a small tremor as he spoke, which wasn't something she would have expected from him in an emergency, but she was too intent on disinfecting the scalpel to ask questions.

"Will the chloroform hurt?" Miss Metcalf asked.

"No. It will make it so you can't feel anything," Nathan replied. "You won't even realize what's happening to you."

"Then hurry." She clutched her side again, and fresh lines of pain wreathed her face.

"I have the chloroform here." Kate brought the tray of newly disinfected instruments to the table, then grabbed the bottle of chloroform, uncorked it, and dashed some onto a handkerchief. "I'm going to need to cover your mouth and nose for a few seconds. Is that all right?"

Miss Metcalf's frightened eyes met hers. "Just make me better."

Kate held the cloth to the woman's face. It took less than thirty seconds for her to fade into unconsciousness. The moment she did, Nathan grabbed the scissors from the tray of medical instruments and began cutting the center of her nightdress from the bottom up.

"Are you sure this is necessary?" Miss Thompson paced beside the table, her face just as white as Nathan's.

"Everything Nathan told her is correct." Kate met the other woman's eyes. "Your friend's appendix is swelling and getting ready to burst. If we don't remove it before it ruptures, she will die. There is no question about it."

"But he's cutting off her nightdress. It's indecent!"

"It's medically necessary." Nathan kept his voice calm and matter-of-fact as he methodically moved the scissors higher, until Miss Metcalf's abdomen was exposed. "I can't have fabric interfering with the surgery."

Kate handed Nathan the bottle of carbolic acid and another handkerchief, then nodded at Miss Thompson and the two other teachers. "Perhaps the three of you should take a seat in the parlor. We'll let you know when we finish."

"No." Miss Thompson dug her feet into the floor. "Tillie wouldn't want us to leave her alone while she's lost consciousness."

"There will be quite a bit of blood." Nathan swabbed the right side of Miss Metcalf's abdomen with carbolic acid, which stained her skin a sickening yellow.

"I'm staying." Miss Thompson tromped to the chair by the wall and sat.

"Blood makes me a bit squeamish." Miss Cutter looked around the room. "But I'd like to try to stay."

"I'll wait in the parlor." Miss Gillespie whirled around and raced out of the room.

"Do you mind closing the door?" Nathan asked Miss Cutter, who still lingered in the doorway, as though unsure whether she should actually step inside.

"Of course." She pulled the door shut, then headed to the open chair beside Miss Thompson.

"All right, let's proceed." Nathan drew in a breath, his hand trembling as he picked up the scalpel and looked down at Miss Metcalf's abdomen.

Kate waited for the trembling to stop as he touched the knife to her skin, but it didn't. If anything his hand only shook harder. "Is something wrong?"

Nathan's eyes came up to meet hers, his gaze raw. "It's nothing. I just . . ." He pressed his eyes shut and drew in another breath, but when he opened his eyes, his hand trembled just as badly as before.

She took a step closer. "What's going on?"

"You need to do the surgery."

"What? No!" Miss Thompson bolted from her chair. "She's not performing the surgery on Tillie. She can't. She's a woman."

"A woman who happens to be an excellent doctor." Nathan didn't so much as glance at Miss Thompson, just handed Kate the scalpel. "You do it. Please."

She wanted to ask why. Surely Nathan had performed surgeries before. He must have for him to be named the assistant medical director of Alaska. So what was happening?

But she didn't have time to figure it out, not when a woman's appendix was about to rupture. She moved to take Nathan's position in front of the incision spot, then held the scalpel to Miss Metcalf's skin and opened it with a clean, straight slice.

It took her about forty-five minutes to remove Miss Metcalf's appendix. Nathan stood beside her the entire time, clearing away blood when needed and giving Miss Metcalf additional doses of chloroform. When he wasn't doing either of those things, he still stood by her side, murmuring words of encouragement as the surgery progressed.

His hands stopped shaking at some point, and color gradually returned to his face. About fifteen minutes into the surgery,

Miss Thompson and Miss Cutter left the room. Kate wasn't sure if it was because the operation was too bloody or the teachers had decided they could trust her to complete the procedure, or for some other reason. But either way, she wasn't complaining about the women leaving, especially since that left her and Nathan alone to work together.

And that's exactly what they did, worked together. Nathan was so good at anticipating what she'd need that she barely had to talk. She didn't once have to tell him to administer more chloroform or ask for an instrument. It was as though he could read her every thought.

When it came time to close the incision, Nathan handed her a disinfected needle that had been threaded with thread he'd soaked in carbolic acid. "Do you want me to do the stitching?"

"Can you do a better job of it than me?"

He sent her a lopsided smile. "Probably not. Male doctors aren't exactly known for their small, even stitches."

That was what she'd thought. There was something good about being forced to learn embroidery as a girl, even though the task had always bored her.

"You did excellent, Kate," he whispered into the room. "Truly excellent. Not that I had any doubt about your abilities, but watching you with Miss Metcalf, you were incredible."

"I wasn't any more incredible than you would have been."

He was silent for a moment, his throat working as he stared at the incision she was quickly stitching up. "You were far more incredible. I couldn't stop my hand from shaking while I was holding the scalpel. Don't pretend you didn't notice."

"Why?" She paused her stitching for a moment and glanced up at him. "I've seen you with patients around the clinic. You're a good doctor. What happened tonight?"

He blew out a breath. "Let me go tell Miss Thompson and

the others that Miss Metcalf made it through surgery, and then I'll explain."

"All right."

Nathan washed his hands in carbolic acid a final time, then headed across the room, his bare feet padding against the wood.

Kate focused on finishing the stitches, then discarded the extra thread and washed the needle and scalpel in carbolic acid before finally washing her hands. Soft voices floated through the wall, and Kate half expected Miss Thompson and her friends to come inside, wanting to see for themselves that the surgery had been a success. But instead she heard the sound of the outside door to the clinic opening and then closing.

A few seconds later, Nathan appeared back in the room. "Miss Thompson says thank you."

"She does?"

"Yes, and it even appears that she meant it."

Kate brushed a strand of hair away from her face. "I assumed she'd be upset I was the one who did the surgery."

"I told her you were a better surgeon, at least as far as appendectomies go."

"Does that mean your hands don't shake that much for all surgeries?"

Nathan closed his eyes, then dragged his hand over his face. When he opened his eyes again, he looked straight at her. "My mother died of appendicitis when I was eleven. I didn't know enough to save her, and it makes performing the surgery now . . . difficult."

The air stopped in her chest, filling her lungs with a sensation that was somehow both sharp and heavy. "I had no idea. Why didn't you say something?"

He took a few steps to where the chairs sat against the wall and slumped into one of them. "I have two sisters, but they're both considerably older than me and were married when my mother died. My father was away on a trip, and we lived five miles from town, and..."

"And what?" Kate headed around the table and sat in the chair beside Nathan.

He shook his head, his Adam's apple bobbing. "I still remember the moment she went quiet. I'd made a bed for her in the back of the wagon and was trying to get her to town. She'd been wailing and crying and vomiting ever since she'd woken that morning, and then it all turned silent. No more sobs or screams, no nothing. I swear the silence settled over the trees and squirrels and rabbits, over everything around us. I didn't need to turn around and look in the back of the wagon to know what had happened."

"I'm so sorry." Kate reached up and touched her hand to his cheek, but he didn't look at her, just kept his head down and his shoulders hunched as he stared at the floor in front of him.

"I took my mother the rest of the way into town. I was only a half mile away when she passed, and I wanted to know, even as a boy, what had happened. Why she'd been fine the night before but woke up that morning in an unbearable amount of pain that ended up killing her. The doctor had known immediately and said he could have saved her—if I would have either sent for him or brought her to town sooner. But I hadn't known until it was too late."

Kate shifted in her chair. How heartbreaking. And terrible. The story might have taken place twenty years earlier and happened to a woman she'd never met, but it made her feel sick nonetheless. And it made her heart ache for the man seated beside her. "Is that why you became a doctor? So you could stop what happened to your mother from happening to someone else?"

"Yes. Not that I did a good job of stopping anything tonight, but I knew you were here, that you were the better choice for the surgery. If I'd been the only doctor, I would have found a way to perform it."

She reached out and settled her hand over his, where it rested atop his leg. "I have no doubt you would have pulled yourself together. But still, your mother, her death ... it's why you care so much about everyone in Alaska having access to medical care, isn't it?"

He didn't answer, just moved his gaze to Miss Metcalf, still under the influence of the chloroform. Then he turned his hand over and clasped hers in an iron grip, almost as though he thought if he held it tight enough, he could transfer some of the pain inside him to her.

She'd gladly take it, if it would help ease his burden. "It's why there's a whole list of places where you want the MHS to establish medical clinics, not just Alaska."

He blinked away something that might have been a tear. "The MHS will never be able to provide medical care to all families. Even with a hospital in Juneau, there are still families and mining camps more than five miles away. If someone gets appendicitis, they'll likely die. If someone gets shot or there's an accident while cleaning a gun or chopping firewood with an axe, the person will bleed to death before a doctor can be called. In a city, a doctor at least has a chance of arriving in time to make a difference. But what we're doing here in Alaska right now ..."

He scrubbed a hand over his face, and when he spoke again, his words were barely audible in the quiet of the room. "It's a start."

"Yes, it is. A much better start than anyone else has bothered trying in the twenty-one years that Alaska has belonged to America."

She understood now why he couldn't promise that he'd find

a way to stay in Alaska when the surgeon general eventually tried to move him.

Because he wanted to go make a difference somewhere else.

Because he wanted to prevent another eleven-year-old boy somewhere from needlessly losing a parent.

And as much as it hurt to think she'd one day have to leave the place she loved, she couldn't be angry with her husband for trying to save people's lives.

27

Juneau; Two Days Later

Spending all her energy avoiding a person could be rather exhausting, especially when she had little energy after performing an emergency appendectomy in the middle of everything. But that's exactly how Kate used the little energy she had left on the final day of the senators' visit. She stayed far away from Clarise Rothley Wells, never mind that the senators and Secretary Gray spent almost the whole day with Nathan. When the group toured the hospital, Kate kept busy in the clinic. When they observed the clinic, Kate went over to the Tlingit village on Douglas Island, and she'd even found time to visit a couple of the mining camps as a way of avoiding Clarise.

But since this was the senators' last night in Alaska, she hadn't been able to wriggle out of dinner.

Fortunately, Clarise seemed equally interested in avoiding

her and had spent the dinner with her head down, pushing food around her plate while the men talked.

Now that they were back in Nathan's office, Clarise hadn't made a single attempt to speak with her. She just sat in a chair by the window, her posture so perfect and dignified it could be studied in a finishing school.

"Just where do you plan to find doctors willing to spend their summers traveling around Alaska?" Secretary Gray had pulled out his monocle and was studying the map of Alaska.

"I'm hoping we can post advertisements in newspapers." Nathan moved to stand beside the secretary of the interior. "If necessary, we can station doctors already working for the MHS here, but I'd rather fill these positions with people who want to go, not people who feel like they need to or they'll lose their job."

"Do you really think you can find enough doctors to come to a land as rugged and untamed as this?" Senator Wells asked from where he sat in a cloud of cigar smoke.

"Some people like living in Alaska. Just ask my wife." Nathan gestured to her, a smile tilting the edges of his lips. "She's been visiting the villages in Southeast Alaska for the past three years, haven't you, darling?"

Secretary Gray turned and faced her, his brow furrowed. "Yes, I should have asked before now. How do you like being a nurse for the Marine Hospital Service?"

"I'm not a nurse. I'm a doctor." The words were instant, flying from her mouth before she had a chance to soften them.

The room grew silent, and all eyes turned to her. Senator Wells even stopped puffing on his cigar.

"A doctor, you say?" Secretary Gray turned his monocle on her.

"Kate trained at the New England Female Medical College in Boston." Nathan came toward her, then reached out and gripped her hand, enfolding her suddenly icy fingers in the warmth of his. "She's been providing medical care to the tribes here ever since she received her degree. Then two years ago, after learning about the lack of medical care in Juneau, she moved here. She's only begun working for the MHS recently, once we realized our goals were aligned."

"And somewhere along the way, you got married." Senator Randolph finished, his gaze moving between the two of them.

"Yes. That too." Nathan squeezed her hand again, then smiled down at her.

His smile held so much tenderness that she suddenly found herself wishing they were alone in the office. Then maybe she could press herself onto her toes and kiss Nathan like he'd kissed her the other night.

"My wife sees a female doctor back home." Secretary Gray tucked his monocle back in his pocket. "She prefers that to seeing a male."

Kate swung her gaze away from Nathan back to the secretary of the interior.

"I see a female doctor too," Clarise said from the side of the room. It was the first time she'd spoken all night.

"I must admit, I didn't expect to find a woman doctor so far north." The secretary came around the desk toward her. "What do you think of Alaska? Do you ever find yourself missing home?"

Kate blinked at him. "Alaska is my home. My family is Russian, with roots in Sitka going back over ninety years."

"Your family's Russian?" The older dabbed his forehead with a handkerchief from his pocket. "Do you know the Amos family? They're from Sitka too."

From the other side of the room, Clarise sucked in a breath, but a quick glance at Senator Wells—who was still puffing on his cigar—revealed that he didn't seem bothered by the mention of the Amos family.

Kate tightened her hold on Nathan's fingers. Did Senator Wells know of Alexei, or what Alexei had once meant to Clarise? "I'm a member of the Amos family. That's my maiden name."

The secretary's eyebrows winged up. "The ship captain and explorer who've been sending reports to Washington are your brothers? And what was that woman's name? Evelyn Redding, was it? She brought a lawsuit against the minister of education. Is that your sister?"

The secretary of the interior knew of her family? Kate shifted her weight from one foot to the other. Why?

"Evelina is Kate's twin." Nathan tugged his hand away from hers, then settled it on the small of her back. "She and her husband live here in Juneau."

"Well, goodness, why didn't you say something sooner?" Secretary Gray looked between the two of them. "I would have liked to meet her."

"You want to meet Evelina?" Kate rasped.

"Of course I do." The secretary's lips pinched. "It's not every day the Department of Education loses a lawsuit."

No, she didn't suppose it was. As far as she was concerned, that only spoke to the stupidity of the minister of education insisting that a young native man couldn't leave one of his boarding schools, not even if the man's father had died and he was needed back at home.

But she kept her mouth shut and didn't offer to introduce the secretary of the interior to her sister. For all she knew, Secretary Gray had come up with the policy on Indian boarding school students. Indian relations certainly fell under his purview as secretary of the interior.

"Your brother is on our schedule of meetings for Sitka," the secretary continued. "Sacha is the one responsible for a study on the northern fur seal that took place last summer."

Yes, he was, but Kate hadn't expected the secretary of the interior to know her brother's name or be aware a meeting had been scheduled.

"And you provide medical care to the Tlingit?" The older man ran his eyes down her, then brought his gaze back to her face, where he waited for some kind of answer.

"Ah, yes, I visit the Tlingit villages. And the Aleut, Yupik, and Inupiaq ones. Or rather, I did before the MHS decided to send doctors on revenue cutters." She slanted a glance at Nathan. "It's unclear just what role I'll have once more doctors arrive in Alaska."

The secretary studied her for another moment. It was enough to give Kate the urge to squirm. When he finally looked at Nathan, she breathed a sigh of relief.

"I'm glad you pushed to get funding for establishing the hospital up here, Reid. It's clearly needed, and I have no doubt your plan will serve the area well. Should you need anything else from the MHS, don't hesitate to ask. As soon as I return to Washington, DC, I'll march down to the surgeon general's office myself and insist he instate funding for all seven of those doctors you want. And if he gives you any trouble in the future, let me know and I'll step in again. It's a shame we've gone so long in Alaska without better medical care, and it's clearly needed if this area is to be developed."

Kate felt a swell of pride in her chest. He'd done it. Nathan had convinced the man who held the final say on everything related to Alaska to increase his funding and give him seven doctors.

"Thank you so much, Mr. Secretary." Nathan reached out to shake the other man's hand, grinning from ear to ear.

In fact the whole room seemed to erupt into smiles. Well,

everyone except for Clarise. She'd slipped from the room at some point, and Kate wasn't sure where she'd gone.

"I'm more than happy to support your efforts to increase medical care in Alaska too." Senator Randolph moved to shake Nathan's hand, his face beaming.

"As am I." Senator Wells was too busy lighting a second cigar to stand and shake Nathan's hand, but he did offer a platonic smile. "The only remaining question I have is for your wife." His gaze traveled across the room to where she stood. "Tell me, Mrs. Reid. What's it like, doctoring Indians? We didn't have a chance to visit any of the savage villages for ourselves while we were here."

Savage villages? Every fiber of Kate's body turned stiff. Clearly the man didn't know about Inessa or Ilya—or her family's stance on accepting them as full siblings rather than sending them back to their mother's village in Unalaska. "You'll pass several villages on your way to Sitka. Perhaps you should stop and see one for yourself."

"That's a good idea." Secretary Gray tapped his walking stick against the floor as he headed to the map. "Any particular village you suggest?"

"I'm not going to a village filled with savages." Wells puffed on his cigar, filling the room with another round of cloying smoke.

"The Department of the Interior is just as responsible for the Indians as it is for the white men here." Senator Randolph took a sip of the port he'd been slowly nursing. "We should add a visit to our list."

"If you want to delay your trip to Sitka until tomorrow afternoon, I can take you to the village across the channel." Kate looked between Secretary Gray and Senator Randolph. "I need to stop there to check on a broken leg I splinted earlier today."

"By golly, you aren't considering it, Jacob," Senator Wells snapped.

"I'm more than considering it." Secretary Gray scratched the side of his head. "What time do you want to leave, Dr. Reid?"

Was he serious? Did the secretary of the interior really expect her to show him around a Tlingit village? "Ah, is seven too early? We should be done there by eleven, and then you can be on your way to Sitka."

Secretary Gray gave her a stout nod. "Seven works just fine."

"Clarise and I will stay at the hotel and have a relaxing morning." Senator Wells extended his legs out in front of him in a leisurely stretch that took up far too much space given the small size of the office.

Kate scanned the room for Clarise to see if she agreed with staying at the hotel, only to find she was still gone.

"I'll go to the village." Senator Randolph set his empty glass down on Nathan's desk. "Hate to come all this way and not visit one."

"You represent Virginia." Senator Wells cocked an eyebrow at his friend. "You don't have a single Indian reservation in your state, and neither do I."

"I actually have two reservations along the York River, but regardless of that, we still control the purse strings for Alaska, and I'd like to visit a village."

"Suit yourself." Wells pushed to his feet. "Reid, can I get a copy of the plans for the seven doctors and where they're supposed to be stationed? I'd like to take it with me."

"Oh yes. I forgot I asked for a copy." Secretary Gray said. "I want one for my records as well."

Kate used the distraction to slip from the room, her hands clenched into fists.

Savages. Of all the things people called the native tribes of Alaska, that was the word she hated most. The Tlingit, Aleut, Yupik, Inupiat, and Athabaskans weren't savage. They were merely different. They lived simply and valued art and beadwork more than money and land. There was nothing wrong with those things.

Why, if the boat that the senators and Secretary Gray took tomorrow wrecked and left the party stranded somewhere, they wouldn't be able to survive more than a week in the wilderness. But a Tlingit boy of eight or nine could survive indefinitely. There was something to be said for that.

Kate wasn't quite sure where she was going as she stormed through the clinic. She only knew that while she could handle Secretary Gray and Senator Randolph, Theodore Wells rubbed her the wrong way, and not just because he'd married Clarise.

But seeing how Nathan had succeeded in convincing the other men to support his plan to put seven doctors in Alaska, the last thing she needed to do was put that funding in jeopardy because she couldn't bite her tongue. She was better off leaving and going for a walk, getting some fresh air, maybe visiting Evelina. Yes, that's exactly what she would do. She'd go visit her sister and come back after the men were—

A noise sounded from the back door of the clinic, and Kate stilled. Was that retching? It sure sounded like it.

Rather than heading out the front door like she'd intended, Kate turned and headed down the hall that led past the little kitchenette to the back door. The retching grew louder, then seemed to subside for a moment.

Was it Clarise? Poor thing. The woman might be married to a lout, but Kate didn't wish retching on anyone. Hopefully it was something Clarise had eaten and not the onset of an illness.

Kate reached for the handle to the back door, about to turn

it, but the door opened on its own, revealing Clarisse in her dainty dress of powder blue and lace.

"Kate?" The woman's eyes widened.

"I'm sorry you're feeling poorly. Come lie down in the sickroom for a few minutes." Kate reached for her hand. "I'll fetch you a cool cloth and—"

"I don't need to lie down." Clarise jerked her hand away. "I just needed a bit of fresh air. The room was growing stuffy, what with all the cigar smoke from the men. I'm feeling fine now."

There'd been only one man smoking a cigar—Clarise's husband. Did he know the scent could make his wife ill? Unless... "Are you pregnant?"

"Good heavens, I hope not." Clarise's words were terse, her normally polite demeanor turning tense.

"I see." Kate let her eyes drift down Clarise once more, taking in the thinness of her shoulders and hips, the way her gown seemed to hang on her, even though a ribbon ensured it was cinched tight around her sickeningly small waist. Then there was how Clarise was acting, not even a little ruffled after being gone from the office for at least ten minutes to vomit. "Do you retch after every meal or just the largest one of the day?"

Something hard flashed in those crystal blue eyes. "I don't know what you're talking about."

"Don't you?" Because it was all becoming startlingly clear. Her only question was why. "So you're telling me that if I step outside and look behind the shrubs along the building, I won't find a pile of fresh vomit?"

Clarise moved to stand directly in front of the door. "Leave it alone. This doesn't concern you."

"I'm rather certain it does. This is a medical clinic, remember? And I happen to be a doctor."

"That doesn't make me your patient. Now if you'll excuse

me, I best get back to my husband." Clarise moved to step past her, but this time Kate was the one to block her way.

"What's going on? You can tell me now, or I can march back into the office with you and ask your husband how often you retch after you eat."

Clarise grew still, but her entire body radiated tension. "He won't care. If anything, he'll be happy once I explain it helps me maintain a eighteen-inch waist."

Kate didn't know who had set that ridiculous standard for women in high society, only that it must have been set by some oblivious man who thought nothing of the pain and suffering a woman would endure on his behalf. "This isn't healthy. Surely you know that. You have to stop retching after meals."

"So you'd rather have me tight-lace?" Clarise's eyes shot little blue flames. "At least this way, my waist is close to eighteen inches, and I don't need to lace my corset tight to achieve it."

"And you think starving yourself is better?"

"I don't have a drawer full of pessaries at home like my friends."

Kate felt like she was going to be sick. She'd treated a handful of women with pessaries back in Boston. Always rich, always of a certain social status. Working-class women couldn't afford to lace their corsets so tightly that their uteruses dislodged from their intended place and needed to be held inside them with a medical contraption. But upper-class women?

What made an entire group of women willing to sacrifice their health to look a certain way? Kate had never understood it. "Tell them to stop tight-lacing before their situations get worse. There can be infections, and if the prolapse gets bad enough, it can mean being bedridden."

"It's not as though any of us have a choice. This is expected where we live. No woman of any politician dares to show her face without an eighteen-inch waist. Some husbands even demand it within a couple months of giving birth." Clarise swallowed and looked away. "You might not think I listened to you all those years ago. You were so young, but even then you refused to wear a corset and warned everyone around of their dangers."

"You're right." Kate crossed her arms over her chest. "I never expected you would have listened."

"Well, I did. And I'm happy for it. I'm not sick like my friends. I don't have stomach pain after eating a rich meal or take elixirs filled with laudanum or use a pessary to keep my lady parts intact."

"No, but you're probably fainting. And the rough sound in your voice indicates damage to your vocal cords from all the acid they're exposed to from the constant retching. The dark shadows under your eyes tell me you're probably anemic. The pale shade of your skin indicates a vitamin deficiency. How much energy do you have? Do you need a nap every day?"

Clarise's body grew even stiffer, every muscle tightly coiling itself. "This isn't your concern."

No. It really wasn't. She would likely never see the woman again after today, so she turned to go. After all, there was little point in continuing this conversation.

But then she stopped and looked back at the woman with crystal blue eyes and light blond hair that had captivated her brother since the moment he first laid eyes on her all those years ago.

And she simply had to know. "Do you regret it? Your decision to leave Sitka, to walk away from Alexei?"

Clarise pressed her eyes shut, a bit of the stiffness draining from her shoulders. "I didn't feel like I had a choice."

"So even now, if you could go back in time and do things

over again, you would choose to walk away from Alexei and marry Theodore Wells?"

"No." Clarise shook her head. "Yes. I don't know."

"Do not tell me that man in there—the one who insists you have an eighteen-inch waist—is a better husband to you than Alexei would have been." Kate shoved her hand in the direction of Nathan's office.

Clarise looked stricken at the idea. "No, I'd never say that."

"Then why did you leave Sitka?"

"There are things you don't know."

Kate took a step forward. "Tell me."

Clarise shook her head. "I can't."

"It's been eleven years since Ivan died, and nearly that long since you left Sitka. Whatever happened, it's over and done. Surely you can tell me why you left."

"No, it's not over," Clarise whispered, her shoulders slumping. "It will never be over. And what does it matter whether I made the right choice all those years ago? I'm a married woman now with two children back in Washington, DC. My place is no longer in Alaska."

Kate took another step forward, bringing herself so close she could smell sour trace of vomit on the other woman's breath. "It matters because Alexei never recovered from what you did to him."

Clarise sucked in a breath, tears filling her eyes. "Don't tell me that."

"Why? It's the truth. Something that my siblings and I are reminded of each time we see him. Each time he doesn't laugh at a joke the rest of us laugh at or let himself have a single dance at a ball. You ruined his life the day you left."

"I didn't ruin anything." Clarise drew her shoulders up, though her eyes had taken on a dull, lifeless sheen. "Things were ruined long before that. But I can't tell you the whole of it.

All I can say is that Alexei would be far more miserable with me than without."

Kate shook her head. "Alexei would have forgiven you for anything, even after Ivan died."

"Stop, Kate. Please stop."

"No. I'm not going to stop. You're miserable married to that man. I don't care if he's a senator. He's made you miserable, and you shouldn't be. If you'd chosen Alexei, you would both be happy right now."

The woman in front of her—the one who'd seemed so small and broken just moments before—somehow drew herself up into a pillar as hard as granite and as cold as ice. "That's where you're wrong. I deserve far worse than my life with Theodore. So don't you dare look at me and feel pity. Everything I have, everything I am, good or bad, I deserve it all." With that, Clarise swept past her and down the hall.

Leaving Kate to wonder just what had happened that made Clarise decide she needed to spend the rest of her life suffering because of it.

28

Sitka; Three Days Later; August 2

"No. Absolutely not." Alexei made a slashing motion with his hand and shoved himself up from his chair, his blood boiling as he stalked in front of the governor's desk.

Both Governor Trent and Preston Caldwell sat back and stared at him from their comfortable seats inside the governor's office, but Alexei couldn't make himself sit, not with what the governor just said echoing through his mind.

"You can't just decide to relocate two entire villages of people because someone with money wants full use of an island." He shoved a hand through his hair. "Both on the Pribilofs and on Prince of Wales Island?"

"Three villages." Caldwell studied his hand from where he sat in the cushioned chair next to the one Alexei had just jumped out of. "There's one village on Saint George Island and two villages on Prince of Wales Island that need to be moved. Klawock and Kassan."

Kassan. Alexei had forgotten about that one. It was on the east side of the island. "Wait, are you telling me the Alaska Commercial Company needs *full* use of Prince of Wales Island? It's over two thousand square miles!"

Alexei felt ready to pull his hair out. Now he knew what Caldwell and Governor Trent had been meeting about a few weeks ago, and he had every reason to be worried, but not for the reasons he'd thought. He'd suspected Caldwell was going to try to undercut him somehow, maybe offer an unreasonably low price and steal some of the new shipping contracts he'd just signed with the government, or complain that he was violating some minuscule regulation and needed to be investigated.

Instead, Caldwell had decided he wanted to take control of two islands, one in the Bering Sea where the company that his family owned could legally hunt seals, and the other just south of Baranof Island where Sitka was located.

And part of that process seemed to be moving three Indian villages so he could have the islands all to himself.

Governor Trent set his pencil on his desk with a sigh. "We're not asking your permission, Alexei. We're asking if we can use your ships to move the natives. You don't have any say in how the land in Alaska is used."

"So it's already been decided? There's nothing I can do to stop it?" He felt hot enough he might just combust on the spot. Either that or fling himself at Caldwell and wrap his hands around the man's neck until he stopped breathing.

The death sentence just might be worth protecting three native villages.

"I don't see what the problem is." Caldwell took a sip of the brandy they'd been offered at the beginning of their meeting.

"The Alaska Commercial Company needs to expand, and we'd prefer to do so in a manner that guarantees we'll be free of any Indian interference. Both Prince of Wales and Saint George Islands have small Indian populations. Resettling the people there shouldn't be difficult."

"I'm sorry, did you just admit you want to remove people from their homes and claim it won't be difficult in the same sentence?" Alexei whirled on Caldwell. "Those villages aren't just their homes but their fathers' homes before that, and their grandfathers' and great-grandfathers'. Some of those villages have been in existence for hundreds of years. A businessman who's been in Alaska for all of three years shouldn't be able to force people like that to leave their homes."

Caldwell took another sip of brandy, his shoulders rising and falling in a careless shrug. "There are hundreds of inlets and harbors and coves that make a good setting for a village. They can resettle elsewhere."

"No. They can't. Or at least not in a place where they know the fish runs and black-bear paths, not in a place where they know where the salmonberries and thimbleberries grow so they can be harvested and dried for winter. And not in a place that has their longhouses. Or are you planning to have your men disassemble them and move the longhouses too?"

Caldwell rolled his eyes. "Don't be ridiculous. We'll move the savages into proper houses in their new villages. No need for an entire clan to all cram together in a single dwelling. Maybe giving them better houses will help them to be less savage."

Alexei's jaw clenched involuntarily, a muscle on the side pulsing. He wanted to explain how significant longhouses were to the Tlingit, that building a new one took over a year, not because the construction was elaborate, but because the artwork was. Totem poles and giant wooden doors would be carved and painted with symbols of the tribe, often a combination of wolves and ravens and whales. There had even been a time when dedicating a new longhouse meant sacrificing the life of a slave. That's how solemnly the Tlingit took their dwellings.

The practice of having slaves had faded, but that didn't mean Caldwell should somehow be able to relocate three villages of people.

"Preston has a valid point, Alexei," Governor Trent said. "I wish you'd take a moment to consider it rather than storm around my office. We'll be greatly aiding the Indians by moving them into modern houses—houses that Preston's company is offering to pay for. And we'll be moving them to more populated areas, where the men can find jobs and earn a living for their families rather than being forced to forage for basic necessities. Your insistence that everything should continue as it has for both the Tlingit and Aleut is shortsighted. If you truly cared for them, you'd want to see them fully assimilated into our society, where they'll be able to thrive in a way they can't while living in such primitive and remote conditions."

Alexei clenched his hand into a fist. "What if thriving means something different to the natives than it does to you? What if thriving means the villagers stay where they are and live as they have been? What if they don't want to move to a town, even if they get—"

The door opened behind him, and Alexei snapped his mouth shut as an older gentleman with gray hair entered.

Alexei expected to recognize the man. After all, not too many people would deem themselves important enough to barge into one of the governor's meetings, and it must have been clear they were having a conversation. He wasn't exactly trying to keep his voice down.

But he'd never seen this man before, let alone been introduced to him.

Governor Trent, however, shot to his feet, as did Caldwell.

"Secretary Gray!" Trent scrambled around his desk, his arm outstretched to shake the stranger's hand. "To what do I owe the honor of your visit, sir?"

Secretary Gray? Now the governor and Caldwell's actions made a bit more sense. Sacha had warned him the man was coming—right along with Senator Randolph, Senator Wells, and Wells's wife, Clarise.

Did that mean ... ?

His question was answered as the door opened further and two more men stepped inside, both impeccably dressed in dark, expensive-looking suits.

Then a woman followed, her eyes downcast.

The breath froze inside Alexei's chest, turning into a thousand jagged crystals of ice. Clarise. It had been almost eleven years since he'd seen her, and this wasn't how he'd envisioned meeting her again, not with his hairline sweaty from anger, his neckcloth askew, and hot blood pulsing through his veins.

She must have sensed his gaze on her, because she raised her head, her blue eyes tangling with his brown ones. She seemed to freeze as well, her face blanching white. Obviously she hadn't expected to find him in the governor's office.

She held his gaze for a handful of seconds, then ducked her head and slid her body demurely behind the younger of the two men who'd entered behind Secretary Gray.

Alexei assumed it was her husband, Senator Theodore Wells. He looked nothing like Alexei, with blond hair a few shades darker than Clarise's fair shade, and a dusting of gray at his temples. He was short but not particularly round or paunchy like so many politicians and bureaucrats.

Something hard lodged in Alexei's chest, and he had the sudden desire to excuse himself and bolt from the room.

The trouble was, everyone else was standing in front of the door. The men were all talking, exchanging introductions and handshakes and placating smiles. The conversation quickly made it clear that though Governor Trent and Caldwell had been expecting the senators, they'd arrived several weeks early. But neither of them appeared to have had any warning that Secretary Gray was coming.

Thankfully Sacha had returned to Sitka and warned Alexei about the visit two days ago.

"Preston, I saw your brother just before I left for Alaska. He sends his greetings." Senator Wells shifted closer to Caldwell, and the two of them entered a conversation about mutual acquaintances in Washington.

But the senator's small movement was enough to bring Clarise back into view. Once again, she kept her head down, her slender shoulders folded in on herself, as though she was trying to blend in with the wall.

It made him wonder just how much practice she'd had blending into the wall in the years she'd been gone.

He could stop himself from going to her no more than he could stop the tide from rising. She was another man's wife now. He knew that. Knew he had no business reaching out and touching the whisp of silky blond hair that had fallen beside her ear or inviting her for a picnic on the beach at low tide.

But that didn't mean there was anything wrong with talking to her. With asking if she liked living in Washington, DC, or why she was trying to blend in with the wall—something she'd never done when she'd lived in Sitka.

Please, God, give me strength. He sent the prayer to heaven before taking the last few steps that brought him to her side. "Hello, Clarise."

She slowly raised her face until their eyes met. But they weren't the same eyes he remembered. No. The eyes looking back at him were dull, as though the spark of life he'd once loved so much had been snuffed out long ago.

"I didn't realize you would be here." Her voice was whisper-soft against the louder conversations taking place. "Had I known, I wouldn't have come."

"Here as in standing in the governor's office? Or did you not know I was still in Sitka?"

"Sitka. You always said . . ." she swallowed. "You always dreamed of living in Seattle, or maybe even San Francisco. I assumed after I left . . ." Her words trailed off, the once vibrant blue of her eyes growing even duller.

"Someone needed to care for my younger siblings, to oversee the businesses."

"Yes, but . . ." She gave her head a small shake. "I'm sorry."

"For what?" That she'd come to Sitka? Or that he wasn't somewhere south of here, designing ships and building the business he'd always dreamed of?

"I beg your pardon, but who are you?" Alexei turned to find Senator Wells looking at him and Clarise, his eyebrows winged up. But there didn't seem to be anything possessive about the man's stance; he merely seemed curious as he looked between them. "Do you know my wife somehow?"

The question had been loud enough it stopped the conversation that Governor Trent had been having with Secretary Gray and the man he assumed to be Senator Randolph, and Alexei soon found five pairs of eyes on him.

Five, but not six. Because Clarise had gone back to staring at her shoes.

What was wrong with her? Where was the vibrant, happy woman he remembered?

"Well?" Senator Wells asked. "Do you know her?"

Now it was Alexei's turn to swallow. Did he know Clarise? No one here had been in Sitka eleven years ago. No one in the room knew their story. Sure, it could be unearthed if someone was of a mind to go digging, but it was something he'd much rather keep buried. After all, Clarise seemed to have moved on from him rather easily.

"We were friends once, when General Rothley was stationed in Sitka. I haven't seen your wife in over a decade."

"Ah, I see. Clarise, I didn't realize you'd have any friends left in Sitka. How nice that the two of you can catch up." The senator sent them both a patronizing smile, then turned back to Caldwell, ready to resume his conversation now that he'd given his wife thirty seconds of his time.

But Secretary Gray had other plans. He stepped forward, his hand outstretched toward Alexei. "Hello, I'm Jacob Gray, secretary of the interior for the United States of America. And you are . . . ?"

"Alexei Amos." He clasped Secretary Gray's hand. "Owner of Amos Family Shipbuilders and—"

"The Sitka Trading Company." The secretary cut him off, giving his hand a hearty shake. "You're the one responsible for that report about the seals that was sent back to Washington last summer, the reason we sent more revenue cutters to Alaska to control the poaching."

Secretary Gray knew about that? The back of his neck heated, or maybe that had more to do with the death glare Caldwell was sending his way. Still, he hadn't expected the secretary to know his family.

"That was my brother, Sacha. I believe the senators are scheduled to meet with him sometime during their visit."

"Oh, so you're not the ship captain? Which Amos brother are you, then? The explorer?" The man snapped his fingers.

"No. That can't be right. He's guiding the team of botanists I sent up the Stikine River."

"That's my other brother, Mikhail."

The secretary narrowed his eyes, thoughts churning. "I know who you are. Don't tell me. You're . . . you're . . . the one who gave the blankets to the Tlingit clan in Hoonah last summer. Was that you? And you're the one who gave the Marine Hospital Service that generous contract for delivering inoculations and medical supplies to all those remote Indian villages. Am I correct?"

"I . . . um . . ." Once again, Alexei found himself at a loss for words in front of this man. "Yes, that's me. And you'll have to excuse my surprise. I didn't realize anyone in Washington, DC, was paying that much attention."

The older of the two senators—Senator Randolph, he assumed—chuckled. "We can't help but pay attention to your family. Seems like any time a report about Alaska reaches my desk, someone from your family is named."

"Thank you, sir." Alexei extended his hand for Senator Randolph to shake.

"You're thanking me?" The senator chuckled again, a wide smile on his face. "I'm quite certain we should be thanking you. Alaska would be a bumbling mess without the government being able to hire your family for whatever needs arise up here."

"Our family's been in Sitka for almost a hundred years."

"And you understand every last thing about it." Secretary Gray cut in. "I have a check for you in my room. It came to my attention that you were never reimbursed for the blankets you gave to the clan in Hoonah last year. You only asked that your cost be replaced, but that hardly seemed fair, seeing how under normal circumstances those blankets would have been sold for full price, and now you've had to wait a year to get reimbursed.

So I added a bit extra to the check. Market price for the blankets, plus a gift."

Market price plus extra? Alexei had thought that money was lost. He glanced at Governor Trent, but the man was staring at his feet. It was just as well. Alexei had tried to get the governor to pay him half a dozen times, and that was just to cover the cost of the blankets.

"Don't look so shocked." The secretary slapped him on the back. "You staved off another massacre like the one at Angoon. Do you know how bad the press would have been had fighting broken out? How much it would have cost to send more soldiers and ships clear up here to quell the uprising? The least I can do is pay you extra for your troubles."

"Uh . . . thank you?" Alexei rubbed the back of his neck. Was the man concerned about the needless loss of Tlingit lives or the expense that waging a war with the Tlingit would cost?

Either way, Caldwell looked ready to murder him. Probably because his actions were the entire reason they'd needed blankets to appease the clan at Hoonah in the first place. A Tlingit man had been killed on one of the Alaska Commercial Company ships, and Caldwell had refused to compensate the clan for the loss of the man's life.

Alexei hadn't wanted the situation to escalate to the point that the clan felt it needed to take the lives of white men to compensate for their tribe member's death, so he'd procured the asking price of four hundred blankets and delivered them to Hoonah.

He'd had no idea his actions had drawn the attention of influential people in Washington, DC.

"So what conversation did we interrupt when we barged in here?" Secretary Gray tapped his walking stick on the floor. "Was it about the natives? If so, the two of you need to listen to this man." He nodded at Alexei. "Amos here seems to be an expert on Indian relations."

Alexei opened his mouth, then closed it, once again at a loss for words. An expert on Indian relations? Him? He had a relationship with the villages on the coast because his family had been trading with them for nearly a century.

That probably made him something of an expert, at least compared to the bumbling bureaucrats who knew nothing about Alaska but kept getting sent to Sitka.

"My family's company needs full use of two islands to better dry and tan our seal hides before taking them to market," Caldwell said. "We've decided on Saint George in the Pribilofs and Prince of Wales in Southeast Alaska. There are a total of three small Indian villages on the islands, and those residents will need to be moved to larger towns where they can find work. The ACC is generously offering to pay to build homes to rehouse all of the displaced residents."

"I'm against it." Alexei crossed his arms over his chest, meeting Caldwell's gaze. "I don't think anyone should be forced from their homes because the Alaska Commercial Company wants to use an island, nor do I see any reason why the ACC needs full use of Prince of Wales Island south of here. It's over two thousand square miles."

"Two thousand square miles?" Secretary Gray raised his eyebrows, then turned toward Caldwell. "I'm inclined to agree with Amos. You don't need full use of two thousand square miles for curing and tanning hides. At least, not unless you're offering to purchase the land outright. Is that what you proposed?"

Caldwell shifted his weight from one foot to the other, a look passing between him and the governor before he muttered, "No, sir. Governor Trent was going to simply let us use the land."

"How much is the proposed lease for?" The secretary turned to the governor.

The governor's face drained of color. "Ah, there wasn't going to be a lease. I was just going to let the ACC use the land."

"For no cost?" Secretary Gray tapped his walking stick on the floor again, with a little more force this time. "I agree with Mr. Amos. Those villages can stay where they are."

Alexei drew in a breath, the tension draining from his shoulders. He'd take the victory for now, though he wasn't sure whether he'd been able to convince Secretary Gray that the ACC didn't need to relocate the villages at all, even if the company did lease the land.

But that was a battle for another day.

Caldwell argued for a few more minutes, but the secretary was firm about wanting financial compensation for the land plus a signed agreement to build housing for any villagers who needed to be removed. And Caldwell didn't have the authority to agree to such a thing without first discussing it with the Amos family.

But when Alexei let himself out of the governor's office a few minutes later, his chest still felt heavy and his steps were slow. His family would be happy to hear about what had happened with the native villages and the secretary of the interior. But that didn't quite make up for seeing Clarise. He hadn't expected their first meeting would be fun, but he'd thought she'd at least be happy. Instead, she looked as though the life had been drained out of her.

"She's not my concern," he muttered to himself as he started down the road that led to the base of Castle Hill. She hadn't been his concern for over a decade.

But that hadn't stopped her from haunting his dreams, and

he didn't expect it would stop her from haunting them again tonight.

Only this time, the image that visited him while he slept wouldn't be young and lovely but a decade older, with worried lines etched into the skin around her mouth and dull, unrecognizable eyes.

And that made his heart heavy in a way he hadn't expected.

29

Juneau; Four Days Later, August 6

"So this is what it means to visit the mining camps." Nathan sucked in a breath, his lungs starving for air as he continued up the mountain path. "Not being able to breathe."

Kate turned back on the trail ahead of him, her movements three times as fast as his. "Do you need to rest? It's not that much farther."

That's what she'd been saying for the past hour, but Nathan was starting to doubt they'd ever arrive at the Perseverance Mine. "Clearly, I need to exercise more."

Kate didn't attempt to slow her steps at that pronouncement. If anything, she quickened her pace, plowing up a rather steep section of the trail. "I grew up hiking around the mountains. I suppose it's a bit of an acquired skill."

"I need to come with you every week so I can get proper exercise. I didn't used to be out of breath so easily, I assure you." Nathan scrambled up the steep section of trail after her, his lungs burning by the time the path evened out. He plopped down onto a moss-covered log, never mind the stain it would leave on his trousers.

The clouds were thinner this far up the mountain, providing only a weak barrier of white whisps between the log he sat on and the sun. The forest was a dark, dense green, with tall spruce trees that jutted up toward the sky and moss covering the rocks and ground.

It was a beautiful place to stop and rest, but Kate didn't seem to notice. She stood looking this way and that, as though waiting for something interesting to spring from the trees so she wouldn't be bored. She even tapped her foot.

"Are you ready?" She started pacing next. Because for some crazy reason, she didn't need to sit down after climbing straight up a mountainside for over an hour. "It's really not that much farther. Maybe fifteen minutes. I promise."

Fifteen minutes that would feel like fifteen hours. How did his wife do it?

"No. I'm not ready." He waited until she tromped by him again, then reached out and snagged her hand the second time. "Come here, wife. Rest a spell."

"I don't need to—ack!"

He gave her arm a hard tug, which sent her tumbling onto his lap. "You don't need to what?" He wrapped his arms around her despite her squirming.

"Nathan! Let me up. We need to get moving."

"Really? I beg to differ. Because I think we need to sit here for a bit, with you on my lap and your hair tickling my face." Her scent twined around him, that familiar aroma of sweet and flowery. He knew it wasn't rose or lavender or vanilla, like most women wore, but he still couldn't place it.

"It's not easy for me to sit still when there's something that needs doing."

"I know, but there's something that needs doing right here before we proceed any further. Something I need to tell you."

She stopped trying to pry his arms off her waist and turned to him, her eyes curious. "What?"

"You did an excellent job at the Tlingit village. Not just because Secretary Gray and Senator Randolph were there but because at some point since you returned to Alaska after medical school, you earned the trust of the people in that village. It was amazing to see, and it gives me hope that with doctors like you working for the MHS, my plan can come to fruition."

"It was nothing." She tried to shrug off his words and stand, but he tightened his grip again.

"It wasn't nothing. It was amazing, Ekaterina."

At the sound of her full Russian name, she looked back at him, her body relaxing in his hold.

"Don't let anyone ever convince you that what you're doing isn't important, that it somehow matters less than if a man were to do it. Do you understand?"

"Nathan . . ." The breath from her mouth tickled his neck.

"Yes, darling?"

She swallowed, and he could almost swear he heard it amid the quiet of the forest. "Thank you."

"I'm the one who should be thanking you." He dropped a kiss onto her forehead, then another beside her eyes. "And not just for helping me charm the men who've decided to give me funding." His next kiss landed on her cheek. "But for caring so much about those around you."

This time when he lowered his head, he planted his lips on hers, claiming her mouth in a kiss that gave his tired body a sudden burst of energy. He was gentle at first, slow to move his lips against hers, waiting for her to respond before he deepened the kiss. When her hands came up to curl in his shirt, he tilted her head to the side, giving him better access not just to her mouth but to the soft skin of her jaw and throat. Warmth spread through him, a heat that had nothing to do with their hike or the hazy sun filtering through the trees.

He wanted to sit there with Kate in his arms for the rest of the day. But a damp forest was hardly the place for anything more than a kiss. And certainly not the place for him to show his wife how much he was coming to care for her.

So he pulled back, noting the flush in her cheeks and the way her chest heaved. "There, now that we're equally out of breath, we can continue."

Her mouth dropped open, and she scrambled off his lap. "That was a dirty trick, Nathan Reid! Kissing me so I'd be out of breath."

It wasn't the reason he'd kissed her, but he wasn't sure she was ready to hear that just yet. So he chuckled instead, the sound of his happiness filling the forest as he stood from the log.

They continued up the path for a while longer, and this time Kate's estimate proved right. They actually did arrive at the Perseverance Mine within a quarter hour, and there were a whole host of men waiting to be treated.

By him. Not Kate.

She offered to examine the men several times, but only the foreman, Jace Lidding, agreed.

He thought about forcing some of the men to see Kate anyway, but according to the foreman, they'd been waiting a long time to see a male doctor, and one of the men had a sensitive issue he wanted only a male doctor to look at.

In town, the women were becoming more accepting of Kate after news of Miss Metcalf's emergency appendectomy spread. But there were still plenty of people who had always been skeptical of her as a woman doctor. And there were also people who didn't like the circumstances that had led to their marriage.

And now, given the choice between being treated by a man or a woman, the miners were all but shunning her too.

It was enough to make his heart heavy, but Kate willingly acted as his nurse, assisting him by bringing bandages and handing him his otoscope and stethoscope. But she grew quieter and more morose the longer they stayed, retreating into a shell that was so very different from the fiery woman he'd watched treat the Cartwright family after the wagon crash on his first day in Juneau or perform an emergency appendectomy in the middle of the night.

Was this what she'd been like in Boston? Had relegating her to work that was far beneath her skill level sucked the life from her?

They didn't leave the cook shack until after dinner, eating quickly before heading back down the mountain. Fortunately, hiking down the mountain was a mite easier than hiking up it. His lungs didn't heave to the point of pain, his legs didn't cramp, and he didn't need to stop every ten minutes or so to catch his breath.

"I'm glad it's summer," Kate said as she tromped along beside him. "Three months earlier in the year or three months later, and it would be dark by now."

"I didn't expect treating the miners would take so long." He surveyed the thick forest. In the dim light of the setting sun, the green was so dark it looked almost black.

"Neither did I, but you had five times the patients I normally do." She looked away, focusing on a break in the trees ahead. "I didn't realize how many men weren't coming to me before. It makes me wonder just what conditions have been going untreated."

Nathan reached out and grabbed Kate's hand, then stopped in the path, pulling her to a halt along with him. "None of that, Kate. What's our verse?"

"Which one? The one about me being fearfully and wonderfully made, or the one about me being created in God's image?" She tugged her hand away and continued back down the path, her shoulders slumped and her steps far slower than they'd been when trekking up the mountain that morning.

"The fact that no one at that mine except the foreman realizes how good of a doctor you are is a reflection on them, not on you," he tried.

Her shoulders slumped even more. "I suppose."

Not knowing what else to say, he continued down the path, matching his pace to hers until they emerged from the trees to find Juneau spread before them.

A rare break in the clouds allowed the sun to cast its unfiltered rays over the landscape, reflecting off the water and painting the mountains on Douglas Island a golden hue.

Nathan stopped for a moment and drank in the sight. "I wish there was a way to capture this, to remember how beautiful Juneau looks when the sun is out."

His statement at least brought a small smile to her lips. "Southeast Alaska is the prettiest place in all the world—when it's sunny."

Yes, he was starting to think it was.

"Look, there are two ships in the harbor." Kate nodded toward the channel. "Are you supposed to examine the sailors?"

He narrowed his eyes, studying the duo of tall ships at the wharf. "No ships from international ports were scheduled to come in." That was part of the reason why they'd gone up the mountain today rather than yesterday.

Though that didn't mean no ships had arrived. Accurately

predicting a ship's arrival date was akin to trying to predict which direction the wind would blow a month out.

"Come on, we better go see who's in the harbor." Nathan kept Kate's hand clasped in his as they made their way through the streets of Juneau. Though the town was normally quiet at this hour of the evening, the streets were busy tonight, the sounds of voices and the clomping of footsteps growing louder as they approached the wharf.

"Dr. Reid." One of the dockworkers stopped, the handcart he pushed laden with crates. He smiled at Nathan, then glanced at Kate. "And, ah, Mrs. Dr. Reid."

"Did these two ships just arrive?" Nathan asked.

"Within the past hour, both of them." He tilted his head in the direction of the ship that was being unloaded. "We're unloading the *Alliance*, but there was a doctor aboard that one. Now he's on the *Meridian*, though. He's examining the sailors, saying no one should unload anything on the ship until he's finished—not that anyone's listening—but you might want to see him. He keeps asking for you."

Another doctor? Had Ellingsworth returned? Or maybe the surgeon general had decided to send him a fourth doctor after all. Either way, it would be nice to have an extra hand around the clinic. "Thank you. We'll head straight there."

He tightened his grip on Kate's hand, tugging her through the maze of dockworkers toward the *Meridian*. As for whether they should be aboard the ship before the crew had been inspected, Nathan only restricted access to the cargo hold if it was apparent there was an outbreak on the ship.

He headed up the gangway, then stopped in front of the first dockworker he found. "I was told there's another doctor aboard? Where is he?"

"Over there." The man pointed toward the back of the ship, where the doctor was likely using the first mate's cabin as an examination room. "He's makin' all the sailors line up, see? He won't let 'em talk to none of us till he's examined them all. He threw a fit about us gettin' cargo out of the hold too, but Marshal Redding said it was fine, 'long as we don't mix with the sailors."

"Thank you." Nathan headed toward the back of the ship, dropping Kate's hand so they could separately climb the narrow stairs that led to the upper deck.

"Excuse me." He stepped around one of the sailors standing in line. "I just need to—"

"Reid!" Ellingsworth's unmistakable voice boomed from inside the cabin. "Where have you been?"

Nathan headed toward the cabin door, and the sailors had no trouble stepping aside so he and Kate could enter. "I was on the mountain with—"

"It's your duty to examine all sailors who arrive from foreign ports," Ellingsworth thundered. He was holding a stethoscope to a sailor's chest, but with the way he was shouting, he surely couldn't hear anything beyond the sound of his own voice. "Yet when the *Meridian* arrived, you were nowhere to be found."

Goodness. Something had put him in a mood. Just how many doctors and nurses had they lost in New Orleans? "That's because it's also my duty to visit the mining camps."

"As if the MHS has enough doctors or resources to be sending doctors to mining camps." Ellingsworth set his stethoscope on the desk behind him, then picked up the otoscope. "I'll be sure to write John and let him know that your desire to help the locals is already interfering with your ability to examine sailors."

So they were back to this argument again. Nathan heaved out a breath, then glanced at the sailor sitting on the chair in the center of the cabin. "Can you excuse us for a moment? Just go wait outside the door. Dr. Ellingsworth will examine you shortly."

The sailor scrambled to his feet and darted out of the cabin without a single word of objection.

Nathan turned back to Ellingsworth. "If you want to write a letter to the surgeon general complaining about how I'm handling my duties, you are more than welcome to. I've been in contact with him since you left, keeping him apprised of the situation here and the need for more doctors, but so far he's only seen fit to reduce the number of doctors originally scheduled to be here. I doubt he'll be surprised that I was expected to be in two places at once."

Nathan took a step closer to Ellingsworth, drawing himself up to his full height, which wasn't remotely tall enough to intimidate a man of Ellingsworth's size, but he didn't care. He'd been alone in Juneau, managing everything by himself for months. The man had no business returning to town and ordering him around like a child.

"Furthermore, you and I might disagree on how to best allocate our limited resources, but you are not welcome to accuse me of failing in my duties in front of others who know nothing about the MHS or our responsibilities. Juneau is a small community. Any disparaging remarks you make—whether about me or the MHS or the need to treat miners and natives—will quickly spread through town and have the potential to make our jobs more difficult."

"I never should have left New Orleans," Ellingsworth quipped.

"Then why did you?"

The older doctor pressed his lips together into a firm line.

The surgeon general must have sent him back here despite his protests. What a shame. Nathan would have gladly taken an inexperienced doctor straight out of medical school over

Ellingsworth and his stubbornness. The man was just going to cause problems.

"I see you've convinced her to be your nurse." Ellingsworth nodded behind him, and only then did he realize that Kate must have followed him into the room and not left when he'd sent the sailor away. "Good. At least you made a bit of progress while I was gone."

Nathan didn't need to look behind him to know that Kate's chin had come up, her shoulders went back, and fire was shooting out of her green eyes.

"John said you hired a doctor too. Where is he?" Ellingsworth looked around the room. "Did he go to the mining camps with you too? In the future, you need to split your duties, making sure one of you is here in case a ship comes in unexpectedly."

Nathan reached for Kate's hand, wrapping his larger fingers around hers, only to find them icy despite the warmth of the day. "Kate's the doctor I hired."

"You *hired* her?" Ellingsworth's shout was loud enough that every person on the ship was sure to hear it.

"I didn't just hire her. I also married her." Nathan's voice was steady, his stance firm as he met Ellingsworth's gaze.

"Oh, good heavens. You're serious, aren't you?" Ellingsworth yanked a handkerchief out of his pocket and began dabbing at his brow. "Did you listen to nothing I said before I left?"

"If you wanted me to listen, you should have given me good instruction, not bigoted claptrap. Kate's a local who was treating the residents of Southeast Alaska long before you or I were ever assigned here. Her work is excellent, and she already earned the trust of half the community before I hired her." It was trust she'd lost when the two of them had been caught in that cave, but she was slowly earning it back. "If you doubt me, feel free to write the secretary of the interior. He accompanied Senator Wells and Senator Randolph on their tour of Alaska. They visited the Tlingit village across the channel and saw firsthand just how valuable of an asset Kate is to the MHS."

Ellingsworth shook his head, eyes flashing. "John is going to hear about this."

"Like I said, Surgeon General Hamilton already knows." Nathan stepped forward, trying to keep his voice calm, but he wasn't going to tolerate this level of brutish behavior, not toward his wife, not toward sailors, not toward anyone. "I wrote him about hiring Kate weeks ago."

"And did he write back and tell you it was all right to hire a woman?" Ellingsworth flung his hand toward Kate, his voice nearly a screech.

"Yes. Or more specifically, the letter said that while it may be unconventional, meeting the medical needs of Alaska requires a bit of an unconventional approach, and that if I feel Kate is an asset to the MHS, I have full permission to hire her as long as I don't exceed my limit of four doctors." Nathan delivered the words clearly, his gaze holding Ellingsworth's in a way that left no room for argument.

A sharp knock sounded on the door, then it opened, and the large form of Jonas Redding filled the doorway.

"Everything okay? Someone reported shouting." The Deputy Marshal crossed his arms over his broad chest and glared straight at Ellingsworth.

"No. Everything is not okay. My colleague here hired that woman in my absence." Ellingsworth jabbed a hand at Kate.

Jonas raised his eyebrows. "I fail to see the problem."

"Of course you don't see a problem. You're not a doctor." Ellingsworth jabbed a finger toward the door. "Just ask any of the men out there if they want a woman to treat them, or a man."

Jonas looked at Nathan. "Do you want me to escort him off the ship?"

Nathan rubbed his forehead. It wasn't a bad idea. He didn't know what had happened in New Orleans, what had set the man off before he'd even arrived in Juneau, but at the moment, Ellingsworth was so agitated, he doubted the man could even perform an examination.

Yet he was going to have to work with the man until the surgeon general stationed one of them somewhere else, and Ellingsworth was his boss. The Deputy Marshal might be willing to listen to him over Ellingsworth, but having the other doctor forcibly removed from the *Meridian* would only hurt Nathan in the long run.

He drew in a breath, trying to find a semblance of calm, then looked at Ellingsworth. "Have you found any sign of disease on the ship?"

"No," the other doctor huffed, his shoulders losing a bit of their stiffness.

"Where was the ship most recently?"

This time Ellingsworth clamped his mouth shut.

"Russia," Jonas answered from the doorway. "And before that, Japan."

"Not ports known for outbreaks of yellow or dengue fever, or malaria, or any of the other diseases that spread easily in warm climates." Why was Ellingsworth so angry about him not being in Juneau when the *Meridian* arrived ahead of schedule if there had been little chance of disease aboard?

"There's an influenza in Russia that bears watching," Ellingsworth muttered, his face returning to its normal coloring rather than the mottled red that had covered it while he'd been storming around the cabin. "Looks like it might be a new strain. If you haven't received a letter about it yet, you will."

Nathan turned back to Jonas. "Are any of the sailors aboard ship coughing or vomiting? Is anyone feeling ill?"

"Not that I've seen," Jonas answered.

"Then it doesn't appear we're dealing with a Russian flu outbreak." Nathan leveled his gaze on Ellingsworth. "So do you want me to stay and help examine the men?"

"That depends." The older doctor shoved a hand at Kate. "Are you going to let that woman examine the sailors?"

"She has a name. It's Dr. Reid. And I'll let her examine whomever she wishes."

The man's lips pressed into a flat line. "Then no. I'll handle this by myself."

"Fine. We can discuss this further in the morning." Nathan spun on his heel, gripped Kate's hand, and nearly stalked from the cabin, but he stopped himself just inside the door and turned back. "Tell me one more thing before I go."

Ellingsworth sent him a bored look.

"Were there lice? On the ships? At the hospital in New Orleans? Did you find lice?"

The older doctor rolled his eyes. "I'm not going to feed your delusional theories by answering that."

"I'll take that as a yes." If there hadn't been lice, Ellingsworth would certainly be rubbing it in.

He turned and tugged Kate through the doorway, his thumb absently running across her knuckles.

She was silent beside him as he led her through the line of waiting sailors and out onto the deck, but that didn't comfort him. If anything, he wished she would have shouted at Ellingsworth, that she would have gotten into his face and told him she was just as good of a doctor as any man.

But instead, she'd stood there silently, almost as though the will to fight that had drained from her on the mountain might never return.

He raised her hand to his lips and planted a soft kiss on her knuckles. "I'm so sorry."

"It's not your fault," was all she said, letting silence surround them as they made their way across the wharf and down the road to the clinic.

But he felt like it was his fault, like if he'd said something more, if he'd defended her better, then . . .

What? Had he really expected Ellingsworth to capitulate and allow Kate to see patients then and there? Ellingsworth had been right when he'd said most of those sailors didn't want Kate to treat them. He fought with sailors about that each time he brought her onto a ship.

But that didn't mean he was unbothered by how Kate had been treated.

Dear God, what should I have done differently?

He could have forced the men on the mountain to see Kate, but that seemed akin to trying to pound a nail with the handle end of the hammer rather than the head. She was an amazing doctor, but he couldn't force people to start thinking that. They needed to see it on their own. So the best thing he knew to do was give her as many opportunities to practice medicine as he could. Half the town had already accepted Kate's medical care before he'd arrived, and she'd had an increasing number of female patients coming to see her since news had spread about Miss Metcalf's appendectomy.

But it seemed like they still had so very far to go. Maybe instead of focusing on how to get people to accept her doctoring, he needed to focus on showing her how much he loved her personally.

Because he did love her. He loved every last bit of the determined woman who'd refused to let Ellingsworth into his room after he'd suffered a concussion and who had begged to treat the little boy who'd stepped on a nail. He loved every last bit of the woman who would trudge up a mountainside to treat one or two patients and spend her summers sailing to the top of the world, just so the residents of Barrow, Alaska, could see a doctor.

He loved the woman beside him so much it hurt. But he didn't have the first clue how to give her the thing she seemed to need most—especially now that Ellingsworth had returned.

30

Sitka; That Night

Alexei readjusted his neckcloth as he left the crowded, stuffy room. Music swirled behind him, the notes from the stringed quartet the governor had hired for his elegant ball floating out into the hallway behind him.

He'd been too young to attend any balls back when the administrative building had been a mansion for the governor of Russian America, but something told him that no Russian governor would have been able to put on something more elaborate than the fancy dinner and ball Governor Trent had coordinated for the senators and Secretary Gray last night in Alaska.

He'd never understood why everyone loved dancing so much, not the casual dances that Yuri was always trying to convince some committee or other to host, and not these grand affairs where men dressed in their finest suits and women draped themselves in silk accentuated by heavy jewelry and ostrich feathers in their updos.

And that was precisely why he was escaping, at least for a few minutes. A man could only take so much dancing.

He turned the corner, intending to head to the end of the hall where a balcony would give him a bit of fresh air, but stopped when he found himself nearly on top of another person.

"Clarise?"

"Alexei." She ducked her head, not meeting his eyes.

She was dressed in a silk gown just as fine as any other in the ballroom, if not finer. It was a shade of silvery blue, the fabric shimmering subtly beneath the dim light of the hallway.

The dress was stunning, and if Clarise looked remotely healthy, it would have been one of the most elegant gowns he'd ever seen. But the embroidery on her bodice only served to underscore the unnatural thinness of her waist and rib cage, the gauntness of her shoulders, and the bony shape of her arms.

Did others see an emaciated woman when they looked at her too? Or did they notice nothing beyond the tasteful tiara and necklace set with light-blue gemstones that matched her gown? Did they see only her sophisticated chignon with soft curls that framed her face, and not the hollowness in her cheeks or the dark circles under her eyes?

She'd been in Sitka four days, but he'd seen her only that first day in the governor's office. Every other time he'd met with the senators and Secretary Gray—and there'd been numerous meetings—she'd been absent.

It was just as well, seeing that she was married. Were she still single, he'd have given anything to have a conversation with her, to ask her why she'd left, to ask her if she'd ever really loved him.

But she had a life now that didn't include him, and those things were best left buried.

Especially since he'd just sent a second letter to Laurel Farnsworth.

"I truly didn't realize you'd be here." She spoke with her head bent, her voice whisper-soft against the strains of music filtering into the hallway.

"I'm all but required to attend such events if I expect to do business with the government."

Clarise fidgeted for a moment, twisting her hands together in front of her. It was an action he was sure her husband would never allow. It made her look nervous and uncertain—two things Alexei never remembered her being before.

And it caused questions to swirl through his head. Was she happy in Washington, DC? Did she miss him? Did he ever appear in her dreams the way she appeared in his?

Hopefully not. What kind of life was that to wish upon a woman he'd once loved? He hoped she liked every bit of her life, that she was somehow happier there than if she had stayed in Sitka.

But the frail, anxious state of the woman in front of him indicated that wasn't the case. He'd seen how her husband interacted with her that day in the governor's office and again at dinner tonight, saw the painful thinness of her body and the dullness in her eyes.

She wasn't happy, nor was she the woman he'd once fallen in love with.

"Why'd you come on this trip? And don't tell me it's because you wanted a holiday with your husband." Alexei tilted his head in the direction of the ballroom. "He doesn't even remember you're here half the time."

She licked her lips, pale and pink. Those, too, were overly thin and not like he remembered.

And he'd kissed them enough that he remembered them well.

"The years I spent here were the happiest of my life," she whispered into the space between them. "I wanted to come back. To remember. But I didn't know you would be here, Alexei. I swear it."

"And had you known, you would have stayed away?"

Her brows pinched, her eyes filling with a sadness so deep that an ache opened up in his own chest. "I don't know."

"Well, whatever you were looking for here, I hope you found it." He straightened and offered his arm. "Here, let me escort you back to the ball."

She took it, her touch so light he barely felt it through his suitcoat. They walked in silence, retracing the steps he'd taken a few minutes earlier. He still intended to step outside for a breath of fresh air, so rather than enter the ballroom, he paused in the doorway, his gaze sweeping down the woman who had held his heart for far too long.

"There's food aplenty at the refreshment table. You should try a bit of everything. You might find something you like."

Her eyes shot up to his. "Is that your way of saying I'm too thin?"

"I . . . um . . ." Confound it. How was he supposed to answer that?

But his bumbling lack of an answer must have told her what she needed to know, because she offered him a faint smile —one that almost reminded him of all those years ago. "You're much more tactful than your sister."

Had Kate said something about how unhealthy Clarise looked?

"The smoked salmon is good," he croaked, memories swamping him. It had been her favorite food when she'd lived here, and he'd lost track of how many times he'd brought it to her over the years.

But rather than thank him and head off to try the salmon with a sparkle in her eyes, she pressed a hand to her stomach. "I find that food a bit too rich for me these days, but thank you for the offer."

He watched her gown shimmering beneath the lights and whispering along the floor as she headed to where her husband stood a few feet away from the punch table. Wells didn't even look at her when she came up beside him, let alone offer to dance with her. He was too engrossed in his conversation with the minister of education to even notice she'd returned.

The ache inside Alexei's chest widened. Not because he was terribly in love with the woman in the ballroom but because he barely recognized her.

And that somehow seemed worse than if the healthy-looking Clarise he remembered from eleven years ago would have waltzed into the room with a twinkle in her eye, then taken the arm of a husband who loved her so much he couldn't take his eyes off her and led him onto the dance floor.

"Is something wrong?"

Alexei jolted at the sound of the voice behind him, only to find Secretary Gray making his way down the hall, his walking stick polished to a sheen for the night's festivities.

"Nothing you need to concern yourself with," Alexei answered.

"That's good." The man thumped him on the shoulder. "I have quite enough to worry about. Wait here. I want to talk to you."

The secretary stepped inside the door of the ballroom, then gestured toward the senators across the room. A minute later, Senator Wells and Senator Randolph disengaged themselves from their conversations and headed toward them while Clarise stayed behind.

"Gentlemen, I found a more private setting for our conversation." The secretary started walking down the hallway, waving his hand for them to follow.

Another conversation? Hadn't the politicians discussed everything a person could possibly discuss about Alaska? For the four days they'd been in Sitka, the survey party had held endless meetings with the governor, Caldwell, the Revenue Cutter Service, and numerous other bureaucrats and businessmen that worked on Castle Hill, and that wasn't including the two meetings Alexei and Sacha had with them.

Alexei clamped his mouth shut and followed Secretary Gray first down a long hallway and then down a short one. This was a part of the mansion he hadn't been in before. It had once housed the Russian governor's private chambers, and he wasn't sure what the Americans used it for now.

The secretary stopped in front of a set of double doors, then opened them to reveal a large room with windows on both the north and west. Alexei guessed it had once been the governor's bedroom. The upper parts of the walls were covered in a rich navy paper, with deep oak wainscoting on the bottom half of the wall. Large drapes adorned the floor-to-ceiling windows, framing a picturesque view of the sound and the mountains rising out of the water beside it.

Secretary Gray moved to the polished table in the center of the room where a decanter and four snifters sat on a tray. "Would you men care for some brandy?"

Alexei rubbed the back of his neck. "Alaska is dry, remember?"

The secretary chuckled, pouring the liquid into all four glasses, even though no one had said they wanted any. "Does anyone really follow that regulation?"

No, they didn't, but it had still gotten his family into trouble last year. He hadn't touched a drop of liquor since, so he poured himself some water from the pitcher on the table instead.

The senators had no issue taking the brandy, though none of them seemed in any hurry to say why he'd been called into the room.

"I trust you men have enjoyed your time in Sitka." Alexei took a sip of his water.

"Of course," Senator Wells said. "I can see now why my wife speaks so fondly of her time here."

"Does she?" Alexei turned to the man. "Speak fondly of it, I mean?"

Wells took a sip of his brandy, then moved to stand beside the window, where the slowly setting sun was bathing the mountains and water in a deep golden hue. "Indeed. So much so that I wanted to see it for myself."

"What does she say of her time here?" Alexei couldn't stop himself from asking.

"That it's the most beautiful place in the world." Wells surveyed the landscape from his place beside the window. "She's not wrong. The mountains and water are splendid."

That was all Clarise had said of Sitka? Nothing about him? Or how happy she'd once been here? Nothing of the hopes and dreams she'd once had?

"You should send a painter here, Jacob." Senator Randolph glanced at Secretary Gray as he moved to stand beside Senator Wells at the window. "Someone needs to capture the beauty of this place. We can have prints put in the papers back home. Maybe if the people see it, they will understand why we paid so much for it."

They'd paid nothing for the purchase of Alaska. Something akin to two cents per acre, if Alexei recalled correctly. The land was worth far more, and he didn't understand why everyone he met from America always complained about how much Alaska had cost.

"Is there a reason I'm here?" Alexei finally asked, draining the rest of his water and setting the glass on the polished table with a thud.

Senator Wells turned back to him, still nursing his glass of brandy. "I wanted to ask you about your position on the Indians. I'm curious about why you don't think it's better to resettle the communities that live on Saint George and Prince of Wales Islands? To get them out of their longhouses and move them to somewhere they can have proper houses and work in a mine or a cannery?"

Alexei sighed. "If a tribe chooses to do that—if they want to leave the land they've been living on for hundreds of years and buy food at a market rather than hunt and fish and forage—then I have no problem with them moving. But the tribes are happy as they are. They don't want this life that you keep saying is progress, and I don't think anyone should force it on them."

"It's like I keep saying, Theodore. The best way forward is to educate the young." Secretary Gray lumbered to the elaborately upholstered chair at the end of the table and sank into it, snifter in hand. "That's why we've set up boarding schools, so we can assimilate the next generation of Indians fully into society. We can afford to let the parents cling to their old ways if we focus on the young."

"But what will happen to their culture if you do that?" Alexei sank into the chair beside Secretary Gray.

The secretary blinked at him. "I beg your pardon?"

"Their culture. Their carvings and beadwork, the way the village members all care for each other, and how families live together in generational homes. What happens to all that? Does it just get erased? If native girls learn to cook American food, what happens to the dishes their mothers and grandmothers used to make? If boys learn from American history books, what happens to the oral stories that have been passed down for hundreds of years from father to son? Do they fade away to nothing?"

Wells tapped his chin. "If only you weren't such an Indian lover."

Alexei stiffened. "What's that supposed to mean? I have two siblings who are half Indian. Of course I love them."

"It means that if things were slightly different, you'd make a good governor for Alaska," Wells answered.

Governor of Alaska? Him? Since when had that been part of their discussion?

Or did these men know something he didn't? Maybe Governor Trent was planning on resigning? He'd been in Sitka for just a year, but perhaps he was making plans to return to Washington, DC, and take a prominent position in the nation's capital.

"Yes, I quite agree with Theodore." Secretary Gray took the final sip of his brandy and set his glass on the table, then looked at Alexei. "You have all the skills I'd look for in someone to run Alaska, but politically speaking, you're a bit too honest and inexperienced. And your views on the Indians . . ." The secretary shook his head. "You'd be too accommodating. Why, you'd probably sign half the land in Alaska over to them if a tribe asked."

"It's their land." Alexei straightened in his chair. "They never gave up their claim to it, and they've never been compensated for it. You bought the land we're sitting on from Russia, but according to every tribe here, the land was never Russia's to sell. It's not as though Russia bought Baranof Island from the Tlingit."

"This is why we need a governor who can focus his efforts

on getting the tribes to agree to move onto reservations." Senator Randolph moved to the table, where he sat on the other side of Secretary Gray. "You and Theodore here want a governor who can grow the economy and minimize conflict with the Indians, but I say maybe we need to get these tribes onto reservations first, and if that results in conflict for a short time, then so be it."

Alexei stiffened. Was Senator Randolph saying that he wanted to go to war with the Indians?

"I'd rather keep the army out of it." Secretary Gray shook his head. "The relationship between the settlers and the natives in Alaska has been peaceful. If we start destroying villages and forcibly moving Indians to reservations, they'll retaliate, which means we'll need more army forts and soldiers scattered throughout Alaska to maintain peace. And you've seen how big Alaska is. That's a nearly impossible task."

The secretary tapped his fingers on the side of his empty snifter. "Besides, the Indians will sneak off their reservation land and massacre the settlers. They always do. News will get back to California and scare away settlers, and at a time when we want more people to come here. Our best hope is to convince the tribes to willingly move onto reservations in exchange for payment and goods."

"That will never happen." Alexei crossed his arms over his chest. "The tribes here know what's transpired with the tribes who've agreed to move to reservations everywhere else in the country. I don't care whether you're talking about the Tlingit, Aleut, Athabaskan, Yupik, Haida, or Inupiat, you'll never get a single chief or elder to sign a treaty that relinquishes their claim to their land."

"That's what I meant when I said you're not experienced politically." Secretary Gray slapped him on the shoulder. "Never give away all your cards when someone goes probing for information. Learn to hold your tongue, son. Reveal only what will help you win, not what will gain you enemies."

"He's right," Senator Wells said. "If the response you just gave came across in a report on Alaska, I'd recommend we stop doing business with both of your companies, even if you're the most qualified person to build our ships and deliver supplies to remote outposts. But I've met you and understand this is one small area where you're wrong, while having keen insight about almost everything else. Learn to hold your tongue if you intend to go anywhere in politics."

"But I..."

"Careful there," Secretary Gray warned. "What did I just tell you about holding your tongue?"

Alexei clamped his jaw shut. He didn't intend to go anywhere in politics. He wasn't a politician and had no desire to ever be one. He merely wanted what was best for Alaska. "I assume, based on this conversation, that Governor Trent is leaving?"

"At the end of September," Secretary Gray confirmed.

Alexei looked between the two men seated at the table, then up at Senator Wells, who still hadn't taken a seat at the table. "But you don't think I'd make a good governor?"

He could hardly believe the words that had just come out of his mouth. Did he want to govern Alaska? Since when?

"Wrong. I think you'd make an excellent governor," Secretary Gray replied, his hazel eyes serious. "Except for one thing."

Alexei felt his mouth go dry. "And that is?"

"I can't have a governor who refuses to put his Indian half siblings into one of our boarding schools."

The breath left Alexei's lungs in a giant rush, and something other than air filled them, something sharp and piercing and painful. "No. It's not happening. I'll never send Inessa or

Ilya away to a boarding school. They're my siblings. Part of my family, and I will raise them as such."

Secretary Gray sat back in his chair. "I know. And in your case, I understand. The children are being raised white, after all, not as savages. But I still can't appoint a governor who refuses to support our assimilation efforts."

Secretary Gray understood it because Alexei's siblings were being raised *white*? Alexei pressed his eyes shut. Did that mean he was failing somehow? Should Inessa and Ilya be learning more of their mother's Aleut heritage? Should he send them to spend the summer months with their grandfather in the Aleutians? Should Ilya be learning to hunt seals and whales from a kayak rather than studying geology in his spare time?

"You're right. I'm not a good fit for the position." Alexei stood, his chair scraping loudly against the polished floor while the water in his stomach from earlier turned sour. "I suppose that means our conversation is at an end."

Secretary Gray watched him, his eyes showing no hint of surprise. "You're a man of principle, Amos. I respect that. But we need someone who aligns more closely with federal policies and objectives to be the next governor of Alaska. Someone who will actively work to move tribes onto reservations and strengthen our Indian boarding school initiative."

"If you ever decide to change those policies and objectives to better serve the people of Alaska, let me know. I'll be happy to apply for the job." Alexei turned on his heel and stalked toward the door, yanking it open and letting it fall closed behind him with a loud bang.

He didn't bother to look back at Senator Wells or Senator Randolph as he left. He didn't want to see what he might find in their eyes. Derision? Disappointment? Condescension?

He was probably a fool for walking away from an opportunity like the one he'd just been offered. But he wasn't going to let himself regret his decision. Wasn't going to entertain hurting Inessa's or Ilya's futures for his own gain.

But that made him wonder . . . Just whom would Secretary Gray appoint as the next governor of Alaska? And how good of a job would the man do?

Because the wrong man in that position had the power to make things a living nightmare not just for his family but for the entirety of Alaska.

31

Juneau; Nine Days Later; August 15

"Otoscope, please, Mrs. Reid." Dr. Ellingsworth held out his hand for the instrument used to look in people's ears, his gaze riveted on the sailor seated on the wooden chair in front of him.

Kate planted her feet wide to steady herself against the gentle rocking of the ship tied to the wharf, then reached into the medical bag Dr. Ellingsworth had brought with him onto the ship.

His medical bag. He hadn't allowed her to bring hers.

"Well?" Dr. Ellingsworth looked over his shoulder at her in the dim light of the first mate's cabin. "Are you capable of finding the correct instrument, Mrs. Reid, or do I need to retrieve it myself?"

Her entire body turned stiff. He may have asked her to join him—or rather, insisted she join him—when a ship had come into port from Russia late in the day, but then he'd taken to calling her Mrs. Reid every chance he got. Not Dr. Reid.

And now he was insinuating she didn't know what an otoscope was?

She yanked the metal device out of the bag and slapped it into Dr. Ellingsworth's hand.

The man didn't bother to thank her, which was just as well. She wasn't sure she'd be able to hold her tongue if he uttered another insulting remark.

You can handle this, Kate. Take a deep breath.

She forced herself to drag air slowly into her lungs, then let it out just as slowly. She didn't know why she was letting Dr. Ellingsworth upset her. He wasn't any worse than the doctors she'd dealt with in Boston.

But that had been the biggest reason she'd left Boston, and Sitka after that. At least some of the people in Juneau had allowed her to practice medicine as she'd always intended.

But not now that Victor Ellingsworth had arrived.

Oh, why had she agreed to accompany Dr. Ellingsworth for these examinations?

Nathan was still up in the mountains, following up on some of the men he'd treated last week. And Jonas had gone with him, *To remind the miners that a lawman is in the area*, was what he'd said.

Apparently miners needed reminding of that every so often.

Kate had spent most of the day at the Tlingit village, leaving Dr. Ellingsworth to run the clinic by himself. She'd returned home in time to make dinner, but she didn't expect Nathan would be back until much later.

She'd been about to offer some food to Dr. Ellingsworth when he'd come storming up the stairs, saying that a ship had just arrived from Russia, and she needed to help him examine the sailors.

How foolish she'd been for believing she'd get to help in a meaningful capacity. Nurses were treated with more respect than Dr. Ellingsworth was currently showing her.

"Lantern." Dr. Ellingsworth held out his hand again, the otoscope positioned in the sailor's ear.

Kate grabbed it from off the table—it was already lit from when he'd looked down the previous three sailors' throats—and handed it to Dr. Ellingsworth with a lot more gentleness than she felt.

Only because she didn't want to set the ship on fire. She wouldn't feel the least bit guilty about burning the man's hand.

Dr. Ellingsworth peered into the sailor's ear. "You have an ear infection. I want you to put warm compresses of garlic and chamomile over your ear twice a day, but if it doesn't improve by the time you reach California next week, or if it gets worse, you'll need to seek out a doctor and perhaps get a myringotomy."

"What's a myringotomy?" the sailor asked, his forehead creased.

"It's when a doctor makes a small incision in your ear drum to allow the fluid to drain. The procedure is effective in treating the infection, but some patients report permanent hearing loss afterward, so I want to exhaust all other options first."

Kate released the breath she hadn't realized she'd been holding. She was slow to perform myringotomies for the same reason, but she hadn't expected Dr. Ellingsworth to care so much about a patient's hearing.

"Is there anything else wrong with me?" the sailor asked.

"Just the ear infection." Dr. Ellingsworth removed the otoscope from the sailor's ear and handed it back to Kate. "And the infection isn't very severe, which makes me hope the warm compresses will be effective. I'll have Mrs. Reid here prepare the compresses. Stop back by the cabin in about an hour to retrieve them."

Mrs. Reid. The small bit of kindness Kate had been feeling toward the other doctor evaporated with those two words.

"It's Dr. Reid," she whispered as the sailor left the cabin.

"Not to me," Dr. Ellingsworth retorted as he gestured for the next sailor to enter and sit in the chair. "Do you need instructions on how to prepare the compresses, or can you manage that by yourself?"

She offered him a sickeningly sweet smile. "I don't know. It depends on whether I can find the garlic and chamomile in your unorganized disaster of a medical bag."

Dr. Ellingsworth's lips flattened into a firm line, but Kate turned her back on him and stomped the three steps it took to get to the desk holding the medical bag.

She hadn't been lying about how unorganized the man's bag was.

She spent the next two examinations alternating between handing Dr. Ellingsworth whatever he asked for and searching for the supplies to put together the compresses. But by the time the sailor with the ear infection returned while they were examining the captain, she had three sachets that could alternately be warmed and held to the man's ear, plus another small bag with chamomile in case the sachets needed to be refilled. She assumed the sailor could get garlic from the cook.

"Thank you so much," the sailor said as he took the sachets. "I'll use one as soon as we finish unloading the cargo."

"That sounds perfect." She smiled at him.

"Yes, thank you both." The captain stood from the examination chair and turned toward Ellingsworth. "I appreciate you seeing to the health of my crew." He extended his hand for Dr. Ellingsworth to shake.

"No, thank you." The large doctor clamped his meaty palm around the captain's. "With the exception of one ear infection, everyone on your crew is healthy. There's no scurvy, no respiratory illness or flu running rampant. You're doing a good job."

Dr. Ellingsworth fumbled around in his bag for a moment, then handed the captain a bottle of carbolic acid. "Here. This is for your ship's cook. Use it to clean wounds and wash any instrument used to pierce the skin, like a knife. We find it greatly reduces the likelihood of gangrene."

Oh, drat. The man was giving the ship's captain carbolic acid too? Kate sighed. She might not like Dr. Ellingsworth, but she had to respect him at least a little. Nathan had told her that he was a knowledgeable doctor with decades of experience, and that the MHS estimated that he'd saved over three hundred lives during his time with them.

What a shame that everything else about the man was so off-putting.

The captain and Dr. Ellingsworth exchanged a few more words while Kate packed up their things. And no, she didn't wait to be asked. She just assumed Dr. Ellingsworth would deem himself too important to pack up his own medical bag when he could order her to do it.

She'd nearly finished when there was a soft rap on the open door, and a young sailor stepped inside.

A very young sailor. He couldn't have been more than twelve or thirteen and was likely working as a cabin boy. His face held a pinched look, and his arms were wrapped around his stomach.

"Ned." The captain frowned. "Are you all right?"

"Just coming for my examination." The boy's voice sounded thin and shaky.

"You didn't stop by already?" The captain raised an eyebrow at the boy.

Ned hunkered in on himself a bit more. "I wasn't feeling well."

"Have a seat. This will only take a few minutes." Dr. Ellingsworth pulled his stethoscope back out of his bag as the captain left.

The boy sank into the wooden chair without speaking. Dr. Ellingsworth listened to his heart, then looked down his throat and into his ears. "Everything looks fine, but you told the captain you're feeling poorly?"

Ned nodded. "I feel like I'm going to be sick."

Dr. Ellingsworth chuckled. "Still getting your sea legs under you, it appears. Tell me, how long have you been working as a cabin boy?"

"This is my first voyage."

"And you've been at sea for what, a month or so?"

"Yes, sir."

Ellingsworth rubbed his chin. "Have you had a fever at any point during your trip?"

"No, sir."

"What about a headache?"

The boy slowly shook his head. "No, sir."

"Like I said, it appears you need a bit of time to get acclimated to being at sea." Ellingsworth turned to stuff his stethoscope into his medical bag.

"Wait." Kate reached out and rested a hand on Ellingsworth's arm, just long enough to stop him before she pulled it away. "There has to be something wrong. This is more than seasickness, or he wouldn't still be nauseous now that the ship has stopped moving."

Dr. Ellingsworth glared down at her. "Could you try for one instant not to be the most hardheaded, stubborn woman I've ever met?"

She stiffened. "Not when I'm right. If you want to complain about me being stubborn and hardheaded, then do it when I'm wrong about something."

The man's eyes flashed. "Stick to what you know, *Mrs. Reid*—which clearly isn't treating sailors. Being in calm waters such as these or on land after being at sea for a month or better can lead to land sickness, the same as being at sea can lead to seasickness. The newer the sailor, the more likely it is to happen."

Kate's muscles grew even tighter. Her family owned a shipping company. She knew about land sickness—more commonly referred to as *getting one's land legs*—the same as she knew about seasickness. But something about this boy didn't sit right. He might not claim to have a fever, but his face was pale, and he seemed to be in a good bit of distress. "Can't you at least—?"

"That's enough, Mrs. Reid."

"It's Dr. Reid," she snapped. But she may as well have been talking to the ship's hull for all the attention he paid her.

She stepped closer to the boy and held a hand to his forehead. It felt clammy, but not feverish. "Is anything else wrong?"

She wished he would give her something, anything, that might warrant a more thorough examination.

But the young man merely shook his head. "I just want to lie down."

"Very well. Go rest. But if you haven't improved at least a little by tomorrow morning, send someone to fetch me. I don't like the idea of you leaving port feeling this poorly."

"No one else on the ship has any symptoms." Dr. Ellingsworth latched the top of his medical bag, then turned to face her. "Stop fretting like a woman."

"But..."

"But nothing. He's fine, and he won't need to see you

before the ship leaves port." Dr. Ellingsworth stalked out of the cabin without so much as a glance over his shoulder to make sure she was following him.

32

Juneau; One Day Later; August 16

"He hates me." Kate threw up her hands. Nathan dug his hands into his hair as he watched his wife pace back and forth in front of his desk, her steps so brisk the papers along the edge stirred whenever she stormed by.

"He literally hates me."

"I'm sorry, darling."

"He's treating me like a nurse, and I'm no such thing."

Nathan sighed. "I know."

She whirled on him, her eyes filled with green fury. "Do you really? Do you understand what it's like to be in an examination room, about to issue instructions to a patient with bronchitis, only to have another doctor barge in and declare your diagnosis wrong, then issue a different treatment?"

Nathan straightened. "He did that? Why didn't you come

get me?" He might not be able to change Ellingsworth's attitude toward his wife, but that didn't mean he would tolerate such brutish behavior.

"You were at the hospital site. But honestly, it shouldn't matter whether you're here or not. Because I shouldn't need to get you in the first place, nor should I expect you to solve my problems for me. He'll never respect me if I don't stand up for myself."

Perhaps that was true, but Kate sticking up for herself had only seemed to infuriate the man more.

Would the older doctor ever respect Kate? Or was it hopeless to ask him to see beyond her womanhood to her skill as a doctor? Ellingsworth had been in Juneau for ten days, and they'd been the most miserable days of Nathan's life.

Nathan had just come from a final walkthrough of the first floor of the hospital, and he couldn't even manage to smile about it. The floor was finished, and while they could start moving supplies and equipment over at any time, he couldn't imagine asking Kate and Ellingsworth to spend their lunch hour moving things. The two of them would probably kill each other if they had to spend more than five minutes in each other's company.

As though sensing they'd been talking about him, Ellingsworth burst through the doorway, his face red and his chest heaving.

"Your wife is a charlatan. I demand she stop practicing medicine immediately." He thrust a finger at Kate.

She stalked toward him, drawing herself up to her full height, which was laughably short compared to Ellingsworth's towering form. "I am nothing of the sort. You're just mad because you missed that bronchitis diagnosis."

Ellingsworth narrowed his eyes at Kate. "It wasn't bronchitis. It was pleurisy."

Kate planted her hands on her hips. "You're wrong, and I'll prove it in a week when Mrs. Mullins returns with every last one of her symptoms, plus a fever and difficulty breathing. You better pray it doesn't turn into pneumonia."

"Enough." Nathan snapped, but they were both too caught up in their argument to bother listening to him.

"I'm not here to talk about Mrs. Mullins and her pleurisy," Ellingsworth roared.

Kate stepped even closer to the large man, bringing them toe-to-toe. "I know, because Mrs. Mullins doesn't have pleurisy. She has bronchitis."

"I'm not talking about Mrs. Mullins at all." Ellingsworth thrust his hand toward the door. "I'm talking about the entire family that's crammed into my examination room with whooping cough. They said you treated their son last week."

Kate blinked. "I treated their . . . ? You mean Bryant Alston? The Alstons are here?"

"Yes, and every last one of them is sick."

"No, Bryant has asthma. I treat him every couple months. He was in last week with a cough, and—"

"The cough wasn't asthma. It was pertussis, commonly called whooping cough, in case you're unaware."

Kate didn't say that she knew the medical name for whooping cough—though Nathan was sure she did. She didn't say that assuming the cough was asthma was a simple misdiagnosis that could easily get mixed up when someone had a chronic condition like asthma.

Instead, she darted for the office door. "Excuse me. I need to go check on the Alstons."

"Oh no, you don't. They're my patients now." Ellingsworth tromped down the hall after her.

With a sigh, Nathan got up and followed, knowing that

whatever transpired in the examination room wasn't going to help the growing conflict in the medical clinic.

SHE WAS NEVER GOING to practice medicine again. Kate curled into a ball on her old bed—the one she hadn't slept in since marrying Nathan—and buried her head in the limp pillow. Light from the window filtered into the second-floor room that she'd once shared with Inessa and Evelina above the trading post, illuminating the familiar log walls, but Kate turned away from the brightness.

Maybe if she stayed here long enough, the bed would open up and swallow her. Then she wouldn't have to face the Alstons or the fact that her misdiagnosis had gotten an entire family sick. Then she wouldn't have to watch as the disease spread throughout Juneau, killing young children in its wake.

The door to the room opened, and Kate recognized the sound of Evelina's soft steps against the floorboards, but she didn't sit up or even look at her sister. She just stared at the crack in the wall where two logs fit together.

"I brought you some tea and cookies." Evelina set the tray on the bedside table.

"I don't want them."

"Kate . . ." A soft gust of breath whooshed through Evelina's lips. "Please don't do this to yourself."

"I'm not doing anything other than trying to sleep."

It was a lie. She wasn't trying to sleep. She was replaying every second of her appointment last week with twelve-year-old Bryant Alston in her mind, trying to figure out where she'd slipped up, how she could have assumed a disease as dangerous as whooping cough was asthma.

Had she asked the boy whether he'd had a fever or been

unusually tired leading up to the onset of his cough? Or had she just assumed he'd been feeling fine because he normally came to the office full of energy? He'd certainly had energy during his appointment.

His nose hadn't been any runnier than usual either, though the boy always seemed a bit congested, even in the winter.

Oh, if only she had taken that slight bit of congestion more seriously. Had asked if anyone else in the family was feeling tired or had a runny nose. Had taken Bryant's temperature just to ensure he didn't have a fever rather than using her hand for a quick check.

The bed dipped beside her, telling her that Evelina had sat on it. Then her sister's slender hand settled on her shoulder. "Everyone makes mistakes, Kate. Don't lie there and berate yourself over it."

"How can you say that?" She rolled over to look at her sister. "I might have gotten the entire town of Juneau sick, all because I missed a diagnosis. Do you know what will happen if the whooping cough spreads? How dangerous the disease is to young children? How many of them might die? What if it spreads to the Tlingit village across the channel, or to the Treadwell Mine? What if it goes into the mining camps and—"

"Stop it, Kate. You're not doing yourself any favors by lying here thinking such things. The Alstons mine their own claim as a family during the summer months and come into town only a handful of times. Maybe no one else was exposed to the disease."

"The likelihood of that is almost nonexistent."

"Well, that's what I'm praying for. And God is 'able to do exceeding abundantly above all that we ask or think.' Remember?"

Kate pressed her eyes shut. "That's the last verse I want to hear right now."

"Why?"

She didn't know why. The verse had brought her comfort for years. But over the past few months, it had felt like nothing more than a hollow promise.

"I suppose it's because God already gave me more than I ever expected to have." She opened her eyes, meeting Evelina's gaze. "He let me become a doctor, and I've been practicing medicine for four years, one in Boston, one in Sitka, and two here in Juneau. But not even God can help the fact that I'm inept at it."

Evelina's brow furrowed, her familiar green eyes filling with sadness. "Stop saying that. One mistake doesn't make you inept. All doctors misdiagnose things at some point. Just like all lawyers lose court cases. It's inevitable in both of our professions."

Maybe, but not all doctors made misdiagnoses that put an entire town at risk. "A better doctor would have recognized the whooping cough. A better doctor would have quarantined Bryant so the rest of his family didn't get sick, and then quarantined them in another location and monitored for symptoms. A better doctor would have—"

"That's enough." Evelina made a slashing motion with her hand. "I don't want to hear another word of this. When I decided to stop practicing law, what did you tell me? That I was talented and gifted and shouldn't run away from what God had called me to do. Well, now I'm telling you the same thing. You're talented and gifted and shouldn't be here, hiding in your old room and neglecting what God has called you to do. Especially not now, when there's a family that needs your care."

"But they don't." Kate sniffled, the tears she'd been refusing to shed finally spilling over onto her cheeks. "They don't need my care at all. They have Nathan and Dr. Ellingsworth to treat them, and I'm sure both of them will do a better job."

Chapter 32

"You can't say that."

"Yes, I can." She swiped at one of the errant tears. "They deal with disease outbreaks all the time. It's one of the main roles of the MHS. Did you know Dr. Ellingsworth just returned from handling a typhus outbreak in New Orleans? That's why he got called away from Alaska. I haven't dealt with a single disease outbreak. Ever. I know the protocols for quarantining the sick, but I've never actually done it."

Evelina just shook her head, a soft wave of hair catching on her shoulder. "You're being too hard on yourself, just like I was after I lost that court case. You can't let your past failures haunt you to the point that you give up on the present."

"It's not a past failure. It's a fresh one." And the only thing it made her want to do was give up.

A knock sounded on the door, hard and strong.

Kate turned her head, fully intending to deny whoever was on the other side of the door, but before she could open her mouth, it banged open.

"Kate's husband is here." Ilya bounded into the room. "He wants to see her."

Kate raised her gaze to find Nathan standing in the doorway. "I just want to be left alone." Her words broke over the sob welling in her chest. A sob she refused to release. Instead, she grabbed the bedcovering and pulled it over her as she lay back down, facing the wall once more.

Whatever Nathan had come to tell her, she wasn't sure she could take it. By now he likely knew how many people the Alstons had come into contact with over the past week, knew how big of an outbreak they were looking at containing. Knew how far along in the disease the Alstons were and the likelihood of everyone in their family surviving.

But she wasn't sure what she was supposed to do with the information once she had it, other than lie here and feel useless and sob into the pillow and think about never treating another patient again.

She felt Evelina shift her weight for a moment, then the bed straightened behind her, and footsteps sounded on the floor. A moment later, the door closed, and a bit of the tension coiling Kate's body left. She'd half expected she'd need to argue to get everyone to leave. But maybe she looked miserable enough that everyone had decided to leave out of pity. At least now she could . . .

Footsteps sounded in the room. Footsteps that were far too heavy for Evelina.

Kate looked over her shoulder to find Nathan standing beside her bed. "I asked you to leave."

"I'd rather stay." He looked tired, with shadows under his handsome eyes and lines around his mouth that she swore weren't there when they'd woken up that morning.

"I don't want to talk to anyone right now."

"I'm your husband, Kate."

"And Evelina is my twin, but that doesn't mean I want her here either."

He sat down on the bed, claiming the spot Evelina had just vacated. Except he was harder to ignore than her sister. The bed dipped more beneath his weight, causing her body to shift toward him until the scent of sandalwood wrapped around her. Until the only thing she could think about was how he sat beside her, the warmth from where his knee touched her back radiating into her.

"Why do you want me to leave?" His voice rumbled low and deep in his chest. "Because you made a mistake and your pride is hurt?"

"I put an entire town in jeopardy, a town I'm supposed to keep healthy." She stared blankly at the wall, not quite sure she could face her husband when she asked her next questions, but not able to ignore them either. "Do you know how bad it is? How many people have been exposed to whooping cough? Do we have any hope of containing the disease before it spreads to other towns?"

"Is that what you're worried about?" His voice softened, and she could almost imagine the softness in his eyes as he spoke, too, the tender way he was looking at her. "We have quite a good chance of containing it before it spreads to Juneau, actually. The Alstons have been working their claim by themselves for the past two weeks. They didn't come into town for any other reason than to see you. They didn't even go to the general store. Then as soon as more than just Bryant developed a cough, they came straight to the clinic."

She pushed herself up and turned to face him, brushing a wayward strand of hair from her face. "Are you sure?"

"Yes."

She'd been right about his eyes. They were soft and gentle and watching her with far more kindness than she deserved. "Do you know where they got whooping cough from?"

"They hired a prospector who worked with them for a couple weeks. They offered him thirty percent of whatever he found, but he quickly grew dissatisfied. He was getting over a cold of some sort when he arrived. They didn't think anything of it, but it's the most likely cause of whooping cough."

"Perhaps there's an outbreak somewhere."

"There's a small one in Seattle as we speak, but the most recent letter I've received says it appears to be contained."

She pressed her eyes shut. "Good. That's so good. But . . ."

"But what?"

She shook her head. "I still feel terrible, like it was pure luck that no one else was exposed. Like I should have done a better job at the appointment with Bryant Alston last week."

"Come here." Nathan positioned himself against the head

of the bed and held out his arms for her—arms that would feel strong and warm and comfortable—but she didn't move any closer.

"I told you I want to be alone."

He looked at her, a small muscle pulsing at the side of his jaw as the moment stretched between them. Conversation sounded from farther down the hall, followed by the thud of a door opening and closing. Outside the window, the unmistakable sound of a horse trotting by drifted up from the street. But silence filled the space between them.

"Are you happy that you married me, Kate?" His voice was low, his words wrapping around her in the quietness of the room.

"Happy?" She forced a little laugh. "What an odd question. You know very well that we were forced to marry."

"I'm not talking about how you felt the day of our wedding." He was deathly still as he spoke, his eyes two dark, probing orbs that seemed to take in everything about her. "I want to know how you feel about our marriage now."

She swiped that dratted strand of hair away from her face again. "Why?"

"Because I went into the marriage with feelings for you—feelings I told you about from the very beginning—and I expected that at some point you would start to return those feelings."

"I . . . I am. I do."

"Then why do you shut me out whenever something goes wrong?"

She sunk her teeth into her bottom lip, resisting the urge to squirm beneath the dark gaze she couldn't seem to look away from. "I don't know what you mean."

"Every time something goes wrong, you pull away from me. Today with the Alstons, when Ellingsworth returned, when

Clarise Wells arrived in Alaska. At the times I should be supporting you the most, you put a wall around yourself and refuse to let me in."

Did she do that? Truly? "I . . . I don't mean to. I guess I didn't realize that I was."

He leaned forward, his closeness shrinking the world to just the two of them. His scent—a mix of sandalwood and fresh air and rain—filled her senses once more, and she found herself glancing at his lips, then the strong column of his throat, and finally his chest. A chest that had held her several times since their marriage had started.

"Whether you realize that you're shutting me out or not, it's not something you'd be doing if you felt the same way about me that I feel about you. So that brings me back to my original question, which you still haven't answered. Are you happy that you married me?"

Everything seemed to grow still around her, as though time itself suspended. Except for Nathan's eyes. Those weren't still, even though the rest of his body was as stiff as the boards down at Mr. Gibbons's mill.

"I never planned to marry."

"I know, and again, that's not what I asked. My question is, are you happy that it happened anyway?"

Tears filled her eyes. She knew what he wanted to hear, just as much as she knew he didn't want her to lie. So the only thing she could bring herself to say was, "I don't know."

He looked at her for a long moment, and if she thought he'd been stiff before, his jaw and shoulders turned to pure granite as he pushed himself off the bed and stalked toward the door. "I guess that explains things."

She scrambled after him. "Wait. Don't go."

He paused but didn't turn to look at her. "Why would I stay?"

"I . . ." She licked her lips. "Because I want you to."

"Really?" His voice was as cold as the glacier north of town. "A few minutes ago you wanted me gone."

"Not like this. I don't want you to go like this."

He turned to face her again, but this time there was no tenderness in his expression, no understanding, not even any questions. His face was hard and flat. "I don't know what happened with you and your former fiancé, but I want you to know this: I love you, Kate. When we first met, I was intrigued by you, and possibly a little smitten. Then that morphed into genuine admiration and attraction as I watched you work. But now, after being married to you for nearly three months, I can genuinely say that I love you so very much."

For a moment she thought he would open his arms to her again, that he would pull her closer and tell her he loved her with tenderness in his voice and softness in his eyes. But he didn't. When he spoke again, he was just as cold as before, perhaps even colder. "The problem is, you don't love me in return, and I don't think you ever plan to. That would involve lowering your guard and trusting me, letting me in when you feel weak or vulnerable. And those are all things you're unwilling to do. So I think it's best if I honor your wishes and go."

"Nathan . . ." she croaked, her mouth falling open. But no other words came, because she didn't know what to say. Not even to the part about him loving her. She didn't understand why he would, didn't feel worthy of anything such a kind, honorable, good man wanted to give her, let alone his love. Not when she was such a mess. Not when all she ever did was make a muck of things and get into arguments.

Up until today, she'd at least been able to tell herself that she was a good doctor who saved people's lives, but she wasn't sure she could say that anymore.

"I see you don't return my feelings," he said, his voice still cold, his eyes void of any emotion. "I didn't expect you would."

He turned to leave again, then stopped to look back at her only after he reached the doorway. "One other thing I should tell you. Ellingsworth has decided to write the surgeon general and ask to be reassigned. He's hoping to leave Alaska before Thanksgiving."

She drew in a breath. "What? Why?"

"Because he doesn't like it here, and possibly because I told him I was through with him disrespecting my wife, that he needed to either find a way to get along with you or write the surgeon general."

"You told him that?" A fresh round of tears filled her eyes. "Even after I misdiagnosed the whooping cough?"

"As I said, every doctor makes mistakes from time to time. I hardly think one misdiagnosis in two years of working in Juneau should be held against you. And I think Ellingsworth was already debating asking for a different assignment."

Perhaps he was, but that didn't change the fact that Nathan had stood up for her and her doctoring once again, even though she'd never once asked him to.

She wiped at her tears with her palm. Could Nathan's willingness to stand up for her be one of the ways he was trying to show her how he felt? Could that have been his own form of telling her that he loved her? "I thought he didn't have a choice about being here."

Nathan's shoulders rose and fell in a stiff shrug. "He has more of a choice than most MHS doctors. He's been with the organization a long time and is on a first-name basis with the surgeon general."

"But you're encouraging him to go. For me." Her heart was hammering against her chest now, hard and furious.

"The constant arguing is hurting our ability to administer

medicine. He's a smart enough doctor to realize that. And I may have reminded him that Secretary Gray and Senator Randolph were both impressed with your ability to treat patients, particularly in the Tlingit village."

"Thank you. Nathan. Thank you so much." She went to him then, wrapping her arms around him in a hug, but he didn't hug her back, at least not the way he usually did. Instead, he pressed his arms around her for a few brief seconds before dropping them and stepping away from her.

"You deserve to practice medicine without prejudice, Kate. Whatever you do or don't feel about me, it won't change my opinion on that. Now if you'll excuse me, I need to make sure the Alstons have settled into the quarantine facility."

He turned and left, and she watched the door close behind him with a thud that felt far too final. He hadn't asked if she'd be home later that night, or if she was feeling any better after their conversation.

It was the first time he'd ever walked away from her without saying some type of good-bye, without doing some little thing that showed he cared about her.

Because their time together had been filled with small, constant gestures that showed he cared, little things that brought comfort to her life.

Little things she hadn't seen until now.

It made her wonder how many other things she'd foolishly discounted when it came to her husband.

33

Nathan stared at the silhouette of the hospital, complete with all its windows and doors installed. When he'd done his walkthrough that morning, he hadn't imagined he'd be using it by nightfall. It was just one room on the first floor for tonight, but the second floor was already close to being done, and the building would be fully operational in a few more weeks.

Tonight Ellingsworth was sleeping in one of the first-floor rooms so that he could keep a close eye on the Alstons. The Alstons themselves were all situated in the bunkhouse beside the hospital that he'd had built expressly for the purpose of quarantining the sick. He'd hoped the bunkhouse would sit unused for a year or two, but instead it would count as the first official time any part of the hospital was used.

He knew quarantining could save lives, but somehow he'd always imagined the first time he saw a patient in the hospital would be a little more dramatic. Perhaps digging a bullet out of a man's shoulder or performing a caesarean section. He'd always envisioned something fast-paced and life altering. Like the appendectomy Kate had performed.

At the thought of Kate, he turned and headed down the road toward the clinic. The sun was setting over the mountains, indicating it was halfway between dinner and midnight, and he'd skipped supper. But when he reached the door of the clinic, he couldn't bring himself to go upstairs and scrounge up a cold meal. Not without Kate.

She'd missed only a handful of meals with him in the few months they'd been married, and each time she'd missed them, it had been because she was seeing patients.

But not tonight.

The image of her standing in her room above the trading post rose in his mind. She'd looked so lost and forlorn when he left her, but what had she expected? She didn't feel the things for him that he felt for her, and it didn't seem like she ever planned to change that.

Like she even wanted to try.

What else could he do other than leave her alone as she'd asked?

Well, he supposed he could find another way to try proving that he loved her, but nothing he'd done so far was working.

Nathan looked at the stairs. He should head up them and try to eat at least a few bites of food, but the waiting room and the examination room the Alstons had been in should be scrubbed from top to bottom. The last thing he needed was to be responsible for spreading whooping cough throughout Juneau.

So he got a bucket and brush and set to work, but not even two hours of cleaning kept him busy enough to stop thinking about Kate.

By the time he finally trudged up the stairs for an extraordinarily late dinner, his back ached from spending so much time hunched over scrubbing the floor, but at least he felt a little hungry.

No sooner had he sat down at the table than he heard a door close somewhere downstairs.

Had one of the Alstons worsened? Had Ellingsworth come to retrieve more supplies? He scooted his chair back from the table, leaving his dinner to grow even colder, then headed toward the stairs.

But soft footsteps sounded on the treads, not Ellingsworth's heavy ones. A moment later, Kate appeared, her lovely, rich hair cascading about her shoulders in wild, tangled waves. Her eyes were puffy and red-rimmed and swollen, their light-green shade dulled by the sheen of tears.

She paused when she saw him, her throat working for a moment, then blurted, "I'm so sorry, Nathan. I've been a fool. Please forgive me."

The ground felt like it lurched beneath him, like he could no longer trust it to hold him upright.

"You're right. I haven't trusted you." She took a step forward. "You gave me every reason to, showed me over and over that you are nothing like Peter or Dr. Ellingsworth or any of the male doctors I worked with in Boston. But I ignored everything you did because it was easier to do that than to . . ." Her voice trailed off, and her throat worked.

"Than to what?" he whispered.

"Than to let myself feel things for you. I let myself love before, but it turned out very poorly, and—"

"I'm not Peter."

"No. You're nothing like Peter, and I should never have let my experiences with him and others cloud what you've been trying to give me."

He crossed the distance between them in two long strides, then crushed her against his body.

"I'm sorry," she muttered into his chest. "So very sorry. I know I can be prickly sometimes, but I never wanted to hurt you."

"Prickly?" He frowned, pulling back just far enough to look into her eyes. "You're one of the most lovable people I've ever met."

She laughed. "I am not. Evelina is lovable. She's soft and warm and kind. I'm brisk and confrontational and get so focused on what I'm doing that I forget to be nice."

"Kate, darling." He rested his forehead against hers. "I don't think any of those things when I look at you."

She peered up at him, eyes curious. "Just what do you see when you look at me?"

"I see someone who's fearfully and wonderfully made. Someone that God gave unique gifts to so that she could help others. Someone who—up until today—has been determined to use those gifts to the best of her ability, regardless of what others around her think or say." Nathan stroked a strand of hair behind her ear, then ducked his head and placed a soft kiss on her forehead. "That's what I think."

"And do you know what I think about you?" she whispered.

He gave a slow shake of his head.

"That I love you."

Something light filled his chest, and he knew he had to be wearing the most ridiculous smile.

He didn't care. "You love me? Truly?" He hefted her into the air.

She squeaked as her feet left the ground, but then she looked down at him, placing her hands on either side of his cheeks. "Yes. I love you. I'm a fool for not realizing it sooner."

"I love you too." He dropped her back to the floor, but only so he could crush her in his embrace.

"From here on out, I promise to be a better wife."

He nuzzled her neck "Do you now?"

"Yes. I'm going to start by being more open and trusting of you. And as for the other parts, well . . ." Her brow furrowed. "I'm hoping I can figure out how to be better at those too."

She looked so serious he had to stifle a chuckle. "Oh, so you don't know how to go about being a good wife?"

"I asked Evelina before leaving the trading post. She gave me a few ideas, so I'll start with those."

Of course she would. His serious, responsible wife. She probably planned to conduct some sort of experiment on what made a good wife before determining her next course of action.

But he had an idea how she could start being a better wife right at that very moment. "Was one of your sister's ideas that you should let your husband kiss you whenever he pleases?"

She blinked. "Ah . . . no."

"Well, a husband is supposed to kiss his wife. A lot." To emphasize the point, he planted a kiss on the tender spot beneath her ear.

She sputtered and gasped, then arched her head away from him, a bit breathless. "Evelina's ideas didn't have anything to do with kissing."

"No kissing? Did she say something about letting your husband carry you to bed?"

Kate glanced down the hallway, confusion filling her eyes again. "You want to carry me to our room? Why? It's only a few steps away."

He nuzzled his face back in the crook of her shoulder, where he planted yet another kiss. "If I carry you to our room, darling, it won't be so we can sleep."

"Oh, you want to . . . That is . . . Do you mean . . . ?"

Her tongue came out to wet her lips, and he smiled down at her. "For someone who's been medically trained to understand all the facets of childbirth—including conception—you get awfully embarrassed whenever I try to talk about it."

Her cheeks turned an adorable shade of red. "That's because it's not meant to be a topic of conversation."

"Oh, I think it is." He kissed the top of her forehead again. "Especially when it's discussed between a husband and wife."

"Nathan, wait." Kate pressed a hand to his mouth, stopping him from raining any more kisses on her face. "Are you sure about this?"

"So very sure. I've been sure since the moment I married you. The question is whether you're sure."

"In that case . . ." She reached up and wrapped her arms around his neck in that brisk, practical manner she had, then placed her lips on his.

He needed no further invitation to sweep her into his arms and carry her to his room.

34

Juneau; Eight Days Later; August 24

Kate made her way up the stairs, her feet practically floating. She'd felt that way ever since she and Nathan had . . .

Well, she wasn't quite sure how to describe it. Should she say that they'd resolved their disagreement? Or that they'd had an important conversation? Certainly she couldn't say that he'd taken her to bed and kissed her until her mind forgot how to form coherent thoughts, then . . .

Oh, good heavens. She had to stop letting her mind drift to inappropriate places, especially while she was working.

But Nathan didn't make such a thing easy. Every chance he got, he was tugging her into a closet or empty room and kissing her. Yesterday, when they'd been moving things from the clinic over to the hospital at lunch, he'd pulled her into one of the hospital rooms and asked if they could spend the hour break doing something that certainly wasn't consuming food or moving supplies.

And that didn't count the times he showed just how much he loved her before they fell asleep at night or when they woke in the morning.

If she'd had any idea how wonderful the full benefits of married life would be, she would never have been so stubborn and reserved with Nathan.

But it wasn't just the physical part of their relationship that had changed. They were talking more too, not just about expanding medical care inside Alaska, but about all sorts of things. What kind of house she wanted to live in one day and how many children she wished to have. They'd swapped worst-patients stories and their most embarrassing doctor moments. In some ways, it was starting to feel as though she'd married her best friend.

Her best friend who always wanted to kiss her.

So yes, she practically floated her way up the stairs to look for Nathan. The clinic was cleared of everything but the most essential supplies, and they were going to move the rest of those to the hospital over the weekend. She had no need to purchase the building for her own clinic now and would let Mr. Gibbons know the next time he returned to town. And the hospital would officially open on Monday morning.

Nathan was elated.

Kate reached the final step of the stairs and turned toward the kitchen, then stopped in the hallway when she heard the unmistakable sound of Dr. Ellingsworth's voice.

"It's a dream, Nathan. What you want for Alaska is never going to happen."

When had Dr. Ellingsworth gotten here? He hadn't seen patients at the clinic since the Alstons had fallen ill. Both he and Nathan had decided it was best for Dr. Ellingsworth not to treat patients at the clinic or on ships until the Alstons' whooping cough had faded and Dr. Ellingsworth showed no signs of contracting the disease. But he'd used his time at the hospital to set up the rooms and arrange the supplies she and Nathan had brought over.

And the Alstons were being released in the morning on the condition they go straight home and stay at their camp. All signs of whooping cough had faded, except for an occasional lingering cough that could last for several weeks. Both Dr. Ellingsworth and Nathan swore that the disease wasn't overly contagious at that point.

So what was Dr. Ellingsworth doing here? Hopefully something hadn't gone wrong with the Alstons.

"Look around you. This isn't a dream; it's a reality." Nathan's voice carried into the hallway, holding a hint of steel. "People need access to medical care, and we're providing it. We'll provide even more of it once the additional funding I've been promised comes through."

"You can't provide access for people on over half a million square miles of land with seven doctors, let alone the four you've actually been given approval for." Dr. Ellingsworth was always loud, but his voice seemed particularly forceful today.

Kate stepped into the doorway, ready to break up the argument before it got worse, but Dr. Ellingsworth was already talking again.

"I don't care how many senators you can convince of your plan or how much they like what you're doing here, if the surgeon general wrote you a letter saying he wants you back in Washington, DC, then you're the one who needs to leave, not me."

The breath stopped in Kate's lungs, turning cold and sharp. The surgeon general had written a letter saying he wanted

Nathan to return to Washington? Now? Before the hospital was even finished?

"Why do I have a feeling you're responsible for this?" Nathan's jaw was clamped tight, and his hands had a death grip on his desk. "Just how many letters have you written to him complaining about my work here?"

"It's not complaining to point out reality!"

"At least I'm trying to start hospitals. At least I'm attempting to address the health issues facing our country." Ice coated Nathan's words as he stared at Dr. Ellingsworth. "We've already saved six lives simply by being in Juneau and having the clinic open, and we've been here four months. Imagine how many more lives that will be in a year, or two, or three. But you found a way to pull the rug out from under me before anything lasting could be established, because all you can see is the health needs of seamen."

Ellingsworth threw up his hands. "Say what you want, but I'm not the one responsible for you getting sent back to Washington!"

"I don't believe you, and if you end up getting this program halted, there'll be blood on your hands from all the lives that will be lost. I hope you can live with that."

"I'm not—"

"Is that what your letters told the surgeon general?" Kate pushed down the churning in her stomach and stepped forward before Ellingsworth could launch into yet another argument. "That Nathan needs to leave Alaska now?"

Both Ellingsworth and Nathan turned to look at her in the doorway.

She stalked forward, bringing herself to a stop right in front of Ellingsworth, never mind that the man towered over her by at least a foot. "You might be a good doctor, but you're a horrible man. Everyone can see the good Nathan's doing here—except you."

Ellingsworth's eyes narrowed at her. "I'm not horrible. I'm practical. Appropriating MHS doctors and resources is complicated. The MHS can't give unlimited resources or top pick of doctors to every location."

"Kate." Nathan came around the side of the desk and rested a hand on her shoulder. "There's no point in arguing."

"But . . ." She had to argue. If she didn't argue, she'd end up crying, and Ellingsworth was the last person she wanted to cry in front of. "I thought we had three years."

It was closer to two and a half years at this point, but that was still almost a thousand days away. She wasn't ready to leave so soon. Not without Nathan seeing the hospital finished, not when leaving meant saying goodbye to her family and everything she'd been working for in Alaska.

The words tumbled around in her head, but her throat was too thick to speak, and all she could do was stare at Nathan.

"I'm so sorry," he whispered, his arms wrapping around her.

"Can't you ask the surgeon general if you can stay here permanently?" she asked when he released her.

Dr. Ellingsworth scoffed. "That's not how the MHS works."

"But . . ." What was she supposed to say? That her family and Alaska were more important to her than her husband?

After what she and Nathan had shared together the past week?

"When the surgeon general calls for a man to return to Washington, DC, he needs to go." Ellingsworth's voice turned a bit softer, but it was too little too late. There was no way kindness could make the situation better. "The only way your husband can stay is if he resigns from the MHS and decides to open up his own medical practice here in Juneau."

Was that a possibility? She glanced at Nathan, then moved her gaze back to Dr. Ellingsworth, since he was the one who was the most knowledgeable about how the MHS worked. "If Nathan does that, what will happen to the hospitals he wants to start in Louisiana and the Outer Banks and Marquette where he grew up? What will happen to all the people he wants to help? Is there anyone at the MHS who could take his place?"

Ellingsworth blinked, as though the thought had never once occurred to him, as though it was ludicrous to think there might be another doctor somewhere who had the same passion as Nathan for establishing medical care in remote places.

"It's best if I stay in the good graces of the surgeon general, Kate." Heaviness clung to Nathan's words. "It's both the fastest and easiest way to see better health care established in other places."

"But . . ." She felt like her heart was breaking, like it had cracked in two and was shattering into a thousand jagged, pointed shards.

She looked at her husband, with his straight nose and dark eyes and that wayward thatch of hair falling over his forehead. He'd spent the past week telling her he loved her each time she turned around, and she'd lost track of how many times she'd whispered those words in return.

Just that morning, they had seemed so unified. So together. So perfect for each other.

But nothing about their situation felt perfect now.

"Dr. Amos." Footsteps pounded up the stairs. "I need Dr. Amos."

Kate dragged her gaze away from Nathan and turned to find a Tlingit man standing in front of her. He was dressed in a linen shirt and bear-skin trousers with a brightly colored Chilkat blanket draped over his shoulders.

But she recognized his face, even though the worry etched across it caused her stomach to churn anew.

It was the chief's son from Petersburg, X'unéi's husband.

"Is something wrong with your wife?" she asked in Tlingit.

He nodded, then replied in Tlingit, "Yes, something's wrong with X'unéi, and the baby too. But it isn't just them. It's everyone on the ship along with those from my clan."

His words came so fast, she could barely make sense of them. "Ship? Did you just say there are sick sailors on a ship? And sick members of your clan in Petersburg?"

The man nodded.

Kate's heart thundered against her chest. "How many of them are sick?"

"Twenty or more from our town."

The thundering in her chest moved to her ears, until she could barely hear anything above the rushing blood. "Tell me what happened."

"It started after the ship arrived with three sick sailors. The shaman said it was bad spirits, he prayed an incantation to chase them away, but the next morning, one of the sailors was dead."

She turned to Nathan and Dr. Ellingsworth, translating everything the Tlingit warrior had just told her. "We have to go to Petersburg. Now. There's an epidemic that appears to be spreading throughout the town. It arrived on a ship, and one sailor has already..."

Before she could finish speaking, the Tlingit warrior's eyes rolled back in his head, and he fainted.

35

Petersburg, Alaska; Three Days Later; August 27

Nathan crouched beside the bed of furs where an elderly Tlingit man lay, his breathing shallow and labored. The longhouse's interior was dim, lit only by the flickering orange glow of a central fire that seemed too meek to fend off the dampness of Petersburg's air.

"Let's sit you up a bit, help you breathe easier." With careful hands, Nathan slid one arm behind the man's back and another under his knees.

The man mumbled something in response, but even if Nathan understood Tlingit, he doubted he'd be able to make out the words. They sounded like the incoherent ramblings of the dying, and he'd heard those enough in his years as a doctor to recognize them despite what language a man spoke.

Coughing echoed off the wooden walls as he moved the man into position. But then, coughing always echoed from somewhere. Too many were sick for the large, open space of the longhouse to be silent for long.

Nathan propped up the elderly man with an extra pillow and folded blankets to keep him upright. At this point, it was the only thing he could attempt that might keep fluid from completely filling the man's lungs.

But his breathing didn't ease with the change in position. Glassy dullness filled his eyes, and given the way that man's skin burned beneath the fabric of his shirt, Nathan had little hope that he would still be alive at this time tomorrow.

A fresh round of coughing filled the longhouse, seeming to come from everywhere at once. Nathan swallowed as he surveyed the large, rectangular building that had been filled with hale, healthy people just two weeks ago. Now nearly every inch of the communal space was occupied by the sick. Families huddled together on pelts, sweating and coughing while fever spiked in their bodies. Some of them vomited into buckets, some of them stumbled outside before the diarrhea hit. And for the ones too weak to move when their bowels loosed themselves, Kate had faithfully cleaned up the mess and told them not to fret.

It had been like this for the past three days. The Russian influenza that Ellingsworth had warned about had arrived in Petersburg with full force. He'd received a letter about it a few weeks ago, but nothing could have prepared Nathan for what they were now facing.

How a village or town could go from having over a hundred healthy inhabitants to nearly a third of them being sick in a matter of days was something he'd never understood. If anything ever made him feel helpless as a doctor, this was it.

Nathan stood and picked his way through the furs and woolen blankets toward the entrance of the longhouse. Kate was on the other side, tending a woman with two children, all of whom had come down with influenza symptoms that morning. He hadn't seen Ellingsworth inside the longhouse for a while. The other doctor had gone to check on the crew of the *Endeavour*. Everyone aboard it was sick, which Nathan had expected given the cramped living quarters on ships.

The old cook had died on his first night in Petersburg, but Nathan wondered if that was from the influenza or something else. The captain had told him the cook had a weak heart, and no one else had died nearly so quickly after contracting the illness. The rest of the sailors were all suffering the rather miserable effects of a cough, fever, muscle aches, and congestion.

But now that Ellingsworth had been gone for several hours, Nathan was starting to worry that another sailor had taken a turn for the worse.

He stepped through the doorway into the sunshine that seemed so at odds with the gloom filling the longhouse. He'd intended to turn toward the bay where the *Endeavour* was moored, but Ellingsworth stood only a few feet away from the entrance, staring at the ice-capped mountains to the north and the handful of jagged, bald mountains that jutted into the sky above the ice.

"How are the sailors?" Nathan came up beside him. "Did someone take a turn for the worse?"

"No. I think all but the cook will survive this, and I've half a mind to think he died of a heart attack during the night, not influenza. The cabin boy who brought us the epidemic will be back to normal in another day or two. He was up and moving around, asking if he could have extra food at lunch."

Their first survivor. That was encouraging. It showed there was at least a bit of light on the other side of all the sickness.

"After I left the ship, I checked on the chief briefly, but so far he seems healthy. Then I decided to stop by the tent and get some coffee before coming to the longhouse." Ellingsworth nodded in the direction of the two tents they'd set up side by side. One for Nathan and Kate, and another for Ellingsworth. "Coffee will still be warm, if you'd like some."

Nathan couldn't blame the man for taking a break—or needing a bit of coffee to keep himself awake. They were keeping one doctor on duty in the quarantine longhouse at all times, which meant they'd all gotten precious little sleep since arriving.

"I'm glad to hear the chief is doing well." The last thing they needed was for the leadership of the clan to be upended because of this disease. Though if the chief were to die, it looked as though his son was going to survive his bout with the influenza. His symptoms hadn't worsened into pneumonia, and he seemed to have a bit more energy and stamina that morning than he'd had for the past few days. His wife and daughter, whom Kate had saved back in the spring, were both progressing through the illness well too.

"This place. It's one of the most wild and untamed places I've ever seen, and yet it holds such beauty." Ellingsworth took a long sip of coffee, his eyes still riveted on the mountains across the sound, clear beneath a bright, sunny sky. "This view alone is almost worth enduring an epidemic. It certainly has a way of making whatever is happening here feel small, especially when the sun is shining."

Nathan surveyed the landscape, something he'd not taken the time to do as he'd run from one patient to the next. Petersburg was breathtaking. Unlike Juneau, which sat on a narrow channel sandwiched between towering, tree-covered mountains, Petersburg was in a bit of a natural opening, on a sound with mountains crowding it. These mountains were taller than the ones near Juneau, though, at least the ones across the sound near the Canadian border. Most of them were covered in ice with glaciers threading through them. But some of the mountains stood tall and proud, jutting toward the sun, with towering, rocky peaks that broke through the field of white.

Nathan pointed at an unusually shaped mountain peak, a hard, rectangular slab of stone that jutted higher than all the mountains surrounding it. "Kate says that one is called Devil's Thumb."

It wasn't visible in mist and rain, but today with the sun, it stood tall and proud.

"Kind of makes you wonder what the view might be like from the top, doesn't it?"

Nathan slanted Ellingsworth a glance. "Thinking of taking up mountaineering, are you?"

The man let out a grunt. "Perhaps if I'd seen this place when I was younger, before medical school and the MHS, I'd have been inspired to take a different direction in my life."

Nathan let his eyes drift down the older man's large form. As often happened with age, his body had lost a bit of its muscle tone. But at one time, he just might have been strong enough and determined enough to find a way to the top of the intimidating peak.

"I want you to know that I'm sorry, Reid." Ellingsworth pressed his eyes shut, then dragged a hand over his face.

Nathan frowned. Ellingsworth was apologizing? "For what? How you've treated Kate?"

The other man's eyes sprang open, and he frowned. "For letting the epidemic spread. When the *Endeavour* came to port in Juneau, I thought the cabin boy had seasickness. I swear I did. He didn't have a fever or a cough, nothing to make me think this would happen if I released the ship."

Ah. That. Ellingsworth had already apologized once, shortly after they'd arrived in Petersburg and he'd realize what ship had been carrying the influenza and who the first patient was. But he couldn't fault the man for wanting to apologize again. Something as heavy as this could weigh on a person's soul.

"No need to keep apologizing. It could happen to anyone." Though he wished it never did.

"I feel terrible." Ellingsworth sank to the ground outside the longhouse, then leaned his back against the rough wooden boards and set his coffee beside him.

"Don't let the guilt get to you. You did the best you could, and no doctor is perfect."

Ellingsworth grunted again. "I wish I'd listened to your wife."

"Kate?"

"She asked me to examine the boy further, was worried that he had more than just seasickness."

She had? "I had no idea."

"She didn't tell you?" Ellingsworth craned his head to look up at him.

Nathan pressed his lips together. "No."

The other man sighed, leaning his head back against the wall once more, his eyes focused on Devil's Thumb. "I assumed it was the first thing she'd have told you when we all realized it."

"We haven't exactly spoken much."

"Because you're busy treating everyone or because she's mad the surgeon general wants you back in Washington, DC, as soon as possible, and you'll be leaving Alaska as soon as we have this epidemic under control?"

Nathan swallowed. "I don't think she's mad, just hurting."

But their need to leave Alaska soon loomed between them, big and awkward and terrible. They'd been so close before, Kate had finally started trusting him, and they'd been working together and enjoying each other's company—all parts of each other's company—back in Juneau.

And now this.

They hadn't talked once about moving since they left the clinic, not on the trip to Petersburg and certainly not after they arrived. They'd been far too busy. But in some ways, it also felt like she'd put that wall back around her heart, and this time she'd built a mote around it as well, and then maybe put up a second outer wall, turning her heart into a fortress just as unscalable as Devil's Thumb.

"Ask her what she needs to make the move more comfortable, what she'd want in a house in Washington or wherever John sends you next." Ellingsworth's voice was unusually soft, floating on the breeze off the water.

Nathan shifted his weight from one foot to the other, still standing even though the other man sat. "Do you think that will help?"

"Do you know how many times Darlene and I moved over the years? Each time I promised to let her pick our next house and paid to have it decorated however she wanted. And once a year we went back to visit her family in Pittsburgh, no matter where we were or how far of a journey it was. They were small gestures, I'll admit, but they were enough to let her know I cared."

"That's a good idea."

"Trust me on this. There are a few things a man learns after being married for thirty years."

He supposed that was true. Ellingsworth had been married for a long time and had always seemed happy with his wife. Three years ago, she caught influenza, then pneumonia developed, and they hadn't been able to bring her back. Ellingsworth had spent over a month watching his wife slowly die, and it had devastated the skilled doctor.

"Just so you know, I don't hate that you're married."

Nathan looked down at the other doctor, who was feeling rather chatty for some reason.

"I think, by and large, marriage helps a man and brings a bit of balance to his life. And heaven knows, doctors need balance. It's the woman-doctor part I disagree with." Ellingsworth huffed, his chest rising and falling a bit heavily for someone who was seated. "But you seem rather smitten because of all the doctoring, and in truth . . ." The man sighed again, his chest laboring once more, as though it pained him to say his next words. "I've seen worse doctors. Much worse, even though they're men. Don't get me wrong. I still believe a woman has no place being a doctor. But if she's going to insist on it, well, your wife's not a charlatan. I shouldn't have said that when the Alstons came down with whooping cough. Any of us could have made that mistake."

Nathan supposed that was as close to an apology about Kate as he'd ever get out of Ellingsworth. "My wife inspires me and fascinates me. She makes me think about things in a new way. I know she's not conventional, but the conventional women from New Orleans and Washington, DC, and all the other places the MHS sent me over the years always bored me."

"Then talk to her about moving, see how you can go out of your way to make the move easier for her."

He pressed a palm to his chest, which seemed heavier now than it had a few minutes earlier. "I will."

Ellingsworth nodded, then wheezed, a slight cough rattling his chest. "I still feel terrible."

"About the epidemic? Like I said—"

"No. I feel terrible because I'm sick. I think I've gone and caught that dratted flu." Ellingsworth extended a hand toward Nathan. "You best help me up and to a bed."

36

Kate sat in the corner of the longhouse, her gaze fixed on the large figure lying on the bed of furs in front of her. The warm glow from the oil lamps cast flickering shadows across Dr. Ellingsworth's face, deepening the pallor of his skin and grooves of exhaustion. Night had fallen, and around them, the room buzzed softly with the labored breathing of the sick, the air heavy with the scent of incense the shaman was burning to ward off the evil spirits that had brought illness to the island.

Kate hadn't tried explaining to the shaman that the disease was likely spread by tiny microbes invisible to the human eye. She'd learned during her first year back in Alaska that it was always best to let the shaman perform his rituals while she administered medicine. If nothing else, the familiarity of the rituals brought peace to her patients.

But the incense was doing nothing for the boy of about seven lying two beds to the right. His lips and the tips of his fingers had been a dull bluish color when she'd stopped by his bedside a few minutes earlier, a sign that his body wasn't getting enough oxygen. And given the frail, reedy sounds of his asthmatic breaths, she wasn't surprised. She'd give him two, maybe three more hours. Evidently asthma didn't mix well with this Russian influenza.

Hopefully Ellingsworth would fare better than the boy, but at the moment, the man seemed frail and weak despite his large size.

"I thought I told you to rest." Nathan stood from where he'd been crouched next to an elderly man with pneumonia propped against the wall of the longhouse. He'd spent the entire day trying to strengthen the man's breathing. He'd sat him up, made poultices, even asked the shaman to administer an herbal treatment. But Kate feared the man had seen his last dawn, much like the boy.

Also like the boy, the villagers had said the elderly man was already sick before contracting influenza. In fact, Kate wasn't even sure he had it. If she were to guess, she'd say the man had developed pneumonia about a month ago and would be dying tonight, regardless of whether the Russian influenza had come to Petersburg.

But that still didn't make losing a patient easy.

Nathan picked his way toward her, stepping around the haphazard arrangement of furs and sleeping mats covering the floor until he reached her. "I remember telling you to go to bed about an hour ago."

"Yes, I remember that too."

He gave her a pointed look. "Then why are you still here?"

"I didn't want to leave."

Nathan sank down onto the floor beside her, settling himself so close their shoulders and arms pressed against each other. "If you get too exhausted, you'll end up like Ellingsworth. The best thing we can do is make sure each of us gets enough sleep."

"I agree. That's why I sent one of the healthy men to get

Evelina from Juneau. There are too many sick for the two of us to care for by ourselves."

He didn't say anything in response, just sat beside her, the heat from his arm radiating into hers as he looked out over the longhouse. "We'll probably all catch this new influenza strain, and the strong will survive while the weak won't."

She wanted to argue but feared he was right. "I think I might have already had it. Actually, I think my whole family did."

Nathan turned to look at her. "When?"

"Over Christmas. Alexei came home sick from a trip to one of the small towns deep inside Russia, and he ended up spreading it to all of us. We stayed home and kept to ourselves, but the course of the disease was much like some of the milder cases we're seeing. A cough and congestion, a mild fever. We all spent about five days in bed sleeping, then started feeling well enough to be up and around, though the cough and tightness in our lungs lingered. It makes me wonder if we caught it early, before it truly started to spread."

"I almost hope you did. That means I don't need to worry about you getting sick."

She understood what he meant. She still could get sick—and likely would considering the number of people she was treating—but she didn't need to worry about dying from the disease after having recovered from it once. No one in her family did.

A low, rattling cough loosed itself from Dr. Ellingsworth's chest, and Kate frowned. "I don't like how that sounds."

"Why?" Nathan leaned forward and rested a hand on the man's forehead. "His temperature is low, and he's not coughing nearly as much as the others. Those are good signs."

"No. Those only make me think he'll get worse. He's not

trying to clear his lungs. It's almost like he's giving up without fighting."

A pained groove appeared between Nathan's eyebrows. "I hope you're wrong. Ellingsworth is a strong man. He's survived both yellow fever and typhus, and those are very deadly."

"I hope I'm wrong too." She didn't want him dead, even if he was a stubborn brute.

She reached out and laced her fingers with Nathan's, wanting the comfort of him for at least a few moments before he sent her off to bed.

But instead of telling her that she needed to leave, he shifted closer, the scent of sandalwood wrapping around her despite the smells of incense and sickness filling the room. "I know we haven't had much time to talk since coming here, but there's something I'd like to tell you—no, need to tell you."

She started to pull away her hand. "If it's about leaving Alaska, then I'd rather—"

"I want you to pick out our house wherever the surgeon general moves us next, and I have some money set aside that we can use to redecorate it to your liking. If we're somewhere by the water, we can even buy a house that overlooks it. Maybe it will remind you a bit of Alaska."

She opened her mouth, not quite sure what to say. "That's very kind. Thank you." The offer didn't change how she felt about moving or take away all the reasons she wanted to stay, but it meant something that Nathan was willing to take her into consideration as they moved.

"And we can come back and visit your family every year."

She raised her eyebrows. "It will take at least ten days, probably more, to reach Alaska from wherever you're stationed. We'd have to be gone a month to six weeks."

"I don't care. If the surgeon general wants to move me from

Alaska early, it's the least he can do. I'll be firm with him on that."

"Nathan . . ." Her throat closed, making a reply impossible. Not that she knew what she wanted to say, other than he was once again being too kind to her.

"Just stop pulling away from me." He tightened his grip on her hand, which was still laced with his. "We're trying to move past that, remember? I know this is hard on you, but I still love you, and I haven't stopped loving you, even though I've been called away from Alaska. I hope you can say the same about me."

She stared down at their intertwined fingers, at the way his hand seemed to dwarf hers. "I still love you too. But I wasn't planning on needing to face this so soon. I felt like we were just getting to know each other."

"We still can get to know each other." He dropped her hand, but only so he could slide an arm around her upper back and pull her close. "This might be a hiccup in our plans, but I plan to spend the next fifty years or better married to you, and I also plan for the two of us to be happy the entire time."

She leaned her head against his shoulder. "There's a part of me that wants to beg you to leave the MHS and open up your own practice and stay here, like Ellingsworth said."

He stiffened. "Don't ask me to do such a thing. At least not yet. We should at least go to Washington, DC, and see what the surgeon general wants. If his plans are atrocious, if he's not going to let me establish better medical care somewhere else in the next few years, we can talk about coming back to Alaska. But that's not a decision we should make without first talking to the surgeon general."

"That's why I didn't ask. That and I know how much good you'll be able to do for people beyond Alaska if you leave."

He pressed a kiss to her forehead, then drew back, his eyes

searching her face. "I can tell there's still something bothering you."

There was, but she wasn't sure how to express it. Because even though she loved Nathan and was growing closer to him, even though she knew that as his wife she belonged at his side, she wasn't sure that she loved him more than she loved the life she already had in Alaska.

37

Petersburg, Six Days Later; September 2

Four mornings later, Kate woke up with a cough. She wasn't surprised, had been waiting for it, actually. The surprising part was that Nathan had somehow managed to keep himself from getting sick. He was washing his hands so rigorously in carbolic acid that they were stained orange, and he regularly stepped out of the longhouse to breathe fresh air, hoping that might help.

And maybe it did, because he was healthy as an ox, tending the sick for hours upon hours without stopping.

Kate, on the other hand, was tired and had a stuffy nose along with a mild cough. But she was well enough to work, even though Nathan frequently sent her back to their tent to rest. She spent the first day of her illness alternately resting and treating the sick, then left Nathan to cover the entire night shift by himself. She was resting in her tent again two days after getting sick when a commotion sounded outside her tent. She could tell by the chatter that someone new had arrived in the village. She hoped it was Evelina, but the voices and noise floating through the canvas of her tent told her the entire town was excited. And as much as she loved her sister, she couldn't imagine Evelina's arrival garnering that much interest.

When she untied the flap on her tent and peeked her head out, she saw that not just Evelina had arrived, but Jonas, Alexei, Yuri, and Inessa were all there too. And then there was Mikhail. She blinked, just to make sure her explorer brother was actually in Petersburg. But sure enough, he stood there talking to the chief alongside Alexei, his light brown hair hanging around his head in curls that would make any woman jealous. He must have returned from the expedition he'd been tasked with leading over the summer.

A few feet away, Yuri was standing in a crowd of warriors, a smile on his face while he chattered away. Off to the side, two older men were talking to Jonas, whose expression grew more and more serious the longer the two men spoke.

They weren't supposed to be here. She'd only asked for Evelina.

But they'd all come anyway.

And everyone's presence explained why it had taken Evelina so long to get here. After receiving the letter Kate had sent, Evelina and Jonas would have needed to go to Sitka to get the rest of their family, and they'd probably left Ilya there with Sacha and Maggie.

Inessa spotted her first, then said something to Evelina, and they both started her direction.

"Don't come too close." Kate held out her hand when both women were about twelve feet or so away. "I'm sick now too, and I don't want you to catch it."

"Your note said you thought we already had this flu," Evelina said.

"I think we did. But I don't want you to get sick all over again."

"Are you very ill?" Inessa asked, her face filled with worry.

"No, just a cough and a mild fever, and a bit of a stuffy nose, but not so sick I can't help in the quarantine longhouse."

Inessa nodded. "That's good. I'm glad to hear it." But she didn't look happy about anything, considering her face was still filled with worry. "Have you heard the news?"

Kate frowned. "What news? If it's happened since I got here, then no. News doesn't travel to Petersburg very quickly."

Evelina cast a quick glance over her shoulder at their brothers, all of whom were still talking, then turned back to her. "Governor Trent is leaving Alaska."

"Oh, well . . ." What was she supposed to say to that? Most governors in Alaska didn't last very long. "Is this something we're supposed to be upset about? Did Alexei like him for some reason?"

Evelina pressed her lips together for a moment before blurting, "Simon Caldwell is replacing him."

"Caldwell?" Kate's jaw turned hard. "Is he related to—"

"Preston Caldwell? Yes. They're brothers." Inessa's hands fisted in her skirt.

Kate pressed her eyes shut. Preston Caldwell had caused problem after problem for her family and the natives of Alaska. "How did that happen? Can Secretary Gray even do that? Doesn't he realize that Preston Caldwell thinks he's above the law already? What's going to happen when his brother gets sent here and becomes the law?"

Out of the corner of her eye, she saw Yuri break free from the crowd of men and start her direction. Alexei, Mikhail, and Jonas all noticed and headed her way as well.

Evelina must have realized that everyone was coming closer too, because she leaned forward. "Don't mention anything about the new governor to Alexei. He's furious."

He had every right to be furious. It was ridiculous that the brother of the most powerful businessman in all of Alaska would be made governor. Especially since the entire Caldwell family owned the Alaska Commercial Company, meaning the new governor, Simon Caldwell, had a financial interest in the ACC.

"How is anyone supposed to trust that the new governor will put Alaska's best interests before his family businesses?" she whispered.

"You sound just like Alexei," Inessa muttered under her breath.

"Kate, luv, why are you standing there all by yourself?" Yuri charged toward her, looking ready to sweep her up into a hug.

She held up her hands. "Don't come any closer. I've got the influenza, and I don't want to get you sick."

"You act as though that matters more than a hug." Yuri kept plowing forward, then wrapped his arms around her back and refused to let her go.

She sank into the warmth of his shirt, the scent of his cologne, the familiarity of her younger brother's arms that were neither too strong nor too weak. They were just Yuri.

"I love you so much, peanut."

She smiled at the nickname she'd hated growing up. Now it made her feel warm despite the chilly fall air. "I love you too, but you best release me before I cough on you."

"If you insist." Yuri dropped his arms and took a couple steps back from her, but he still stood closer than she preferred as a cough rattled her chest.

The moment she was done, Alexei stepped in with a hug,

and just like Yuri, his arms felt wonderfully familiar, even if everything about her oldest brother was stiff and severe, including his hugs.

"How serious is the epidemic?" he asked, scanning the village.

"About a third are ill. I don't know if the rest of the village will fall sick soon, or if the quarantine is working, but the sick are all in the last longhouse there." She pointed toward the final longhouse in a series of three, the brightly painted doors holding images of wolves and ravens and whales gave people little hint about the misery taking place behind them.

"What do you need us to do?" Evelina stepped forward for her own hug, and at that point, Kate gave up trying to resist any more hugs. She turned her face away, careful not to breathe on Evelina as she folded her into a soft embrace. Then she hugged Inessa, who folded her into a quick embrace, then Mikhail, who swept her up in a hug that was just as severe as Alexei's but for a different reason.

The closest brother to her in age was solid muscle. Lithe and sleek and strong, he had a body that allowed him to scramble up mountainsides and trek across the frozen tundra. There wasn't anything soft about him. Well, other than his eyes. They held an awareness that seemed to soak in everything around him, including her weariness and concern for the people of Petersburg.

"Let me show you to the longhouse." She turned away before Mikhail decided to ask a probing question she wouldn't want to answer, especially about her marriage, which he'd probably just learned about in the past week. "Nathan is working there, and he'll be happy for the help."

"How is he faring with all of this?" Alexei slowed his gait to walk beside her.

"He's stronger than me, that's for certain. I don't understand it. Nothing seems to faze him, not the people dying or the people recovering or the long hours. I expected him to fall ill by now. Instead, he's putting in eighteen-hour days or better, and I'm the one who's sick. With something I already had once."

"How much help does he have from the village?" This from Evelina, who was looking around Petersburg as they walked, likely taking in the lack of people and movement, with only a couple dozen Tlingit milling around.

"It's just him and me at the moment. Dr. Ellingsworth fell ill five days ago, and I took sick yesterday, though Ellingsworth is much sicker than I am. I've still been able to help, just not as much as before. Nathan keeps insisting I rest."

"No one from the village volunteered to nurse the sick?" Inessa glanced at the other longhouses as they passed, both of them boasting colorful doors that had been painted with various Tlingit symbols and stories.

"The rest of the clan offered, but Nathan and Dr. Ellingsworth refused. They said that after people fell ill and recovered, they could help, but they didn't want anyone else from the village introduced to the Russian flu."

"So it's just been you three all this time?" Alexei frowned but didn't say more.

Even so, she swore she could read his thoughts. *Why didn't you send word for us sooner? Why did you only send for Evelina when you asked for help? We would have come instantly had we known.*

Her throat felt thick. Why hadn't she sent for them sooner?

The unspoken questions hanging in the air between them sounded rather similar to another host of questions she'd been asked recently. *Why do you shut me out, Kate? Why do you shut me out whenever something goes wrong?*

"Do you have any idea how deadly this new flu is?" Jonas rubbed his beard. Everything about the stiff way he held himself indicated that he was there in his official capacity as a lawman, not a nurse. "Do we need to send warnings to any of the other villages?"

"So far only three have died, and all of them were either already sick or had conditions that complicated the disease, like asthma or pneumonia. But we have two inside the longhouse who have been sick for over a week and don't show any signs of recovering. They've developed pneumonia."

"Are the people who get pneumonia surviving?" Mikhail asked, his golden eyes meeting hers.

Kate twisted her hands in her skirt. "It's a bit soon to tell, as it can take a month or more to die from pneumonia, but I'm not hopeful they'll recover. So far about forty people have fallen ill. There are still another eighty in the town who haven't gotten sick, but we're having new patients come to the longhouse every day, meaning the disease is still spreading despite our quarantine measures. Nathan thinks it's only a matter of time before everyone gets this horrid flu, but at least everyone isn't contracting it at once."

Kate reached for the door, then paused and turned back to her family before opening it. "I just want to thank you all for coming. You didn't have to, but . . ." Her chest grew tight, and she knew better than to blame it on her fever. "But I'm glad you did."

Inessa stepped forward and hugged her again. "We're just glad you asked Evelina for help."

"Me too." Kate forced herself to smile, but it felt small and stilted. Because she suddenly couldn't imagine opening the doors to the longhouse and facing the illness and death inside without her family beside her.

But her family wasn't here because of her actions. They were here because of Evelina's.

In some ways, she'd shut them out as thoroughly as she'd shut out Nathan after their wedding.

Maybe it was time for that to change too.

38

The Amos family was wonderful. After only a day of them being in Petersburg, Nathan could see why Kate said she could never leave Alaska. They worked tirelessly, banding into two different groups with three of them taking shifts on and off. Everyone had come except Ilya and Sacha, and Evelina had dropped Ilya off in Sitka to stay with Sacha and Maggie while she collected the rest of her family.

Nathan had been hoping some of the town would be spared and the influenza outbreak could be contained, but they had seven more people come to the quarantine house that day, including the chief. It seemed another wave of influenza was hitting the poor town of Petersburg.

Nathan had written a letter to the surgeon general and sent it with one of the recovered warriors back to Juneau, where it would be put on a ship headed to Seattle and then sent by telegraph once it reached a large city. He'd done the same thing before leaving Juneau, saying he feared they had a Russian influenza outbreak in Petersburg, but he hadn't sent anything since. The surgeon general still didn't know that Ellingsworth had been ill for over a week.

Nathan reached out from where he sat beside the older doctor and covered Ellingsworth's hand with his own. The doctor slept on, the touch not stirring him from his heavy slumber as breaths rattled out of his chest. Breaths Nathan didn't like the sound of.

He leaned forward, pulling the stethoscope hanging about his neck up to his ears and holding the end to Ellingsworth's chest.

What he heard made him grimace. The telltale crackling of pneumonia was only growing worse, and Ellingsworth's breathing was more labored than it had been that morning, sounding high-pitched and wheezy compared to the deep, calm breaths of someone who didn't have an infection filling their lungs with fluid.

"Victor, no." Nathan hung his head, bowing it so deep that it nearly brushed the larger man's shoulder. "You have to fight. You can't let this disease take you. You've done too much, helped too many people."

A doctor as acclaimed as Victor Ellingsworth didn't deserve to die in an obscure Alaskan town no one knew about.

But the older man gave no indication that he'd heard anything Nathan said. His breathing remained the same, shallow and wheezy, his body caught in the deep, half-incoherent slumber of the seriously ill.

Had Kate been right? When Ellingsworth had first fallen ill, she'd said she was concerned by his lack of coughing. But every person who'd developed pneumonia alongside the Russian influenza had died. They'd yet to have a single survivor, and now that Ellingsworth had it . . .

"I believe it's time for you to rest, doctor."

Nathan raised his head from Ellingsworth's shoulder to

find Alexei Amos standing beside him. His shirt and trousers were wrinkled from spending too many hours hunched over the beds of the sick, and his normally smooth hair stuck up at odd angles.

But the controlled businessman didn't seem bothered by his disheveled appearance. He'd worked just as hard as everyone else in the family, making sure the sick got bread and broth and water, and holding buckets when a person retched.

"Well, if you're not of a mind to leave, I suppose I'll join you." The man sat on the floor beside him, then ran his eyes over Ellingsworth. "I take it you're not happy with your friend's condition."

Nathan scrubbed a hand over his face. "It's pneumonia."

Alexei let the heavy words settle between them before saying softly, "I'm sorry."

"I already have him sitting up. I can try a mustard plaster for his chest, but . . ." He let the words trail off. There was no need to finish. Mustard plaster or not, the man had little chance of survival.

He drew in a breath of damp air, fouled by the scent of sweat and sickness, then looked over at the dark-haired man beside him. "Thank you for coming. Had you and your family not shown up after Kate fell ill, I don't know what I would have done."

"You thanked me when we got here. You don't need to do so every day."

"Perhaps I want to."

That caused a small smile to tilt a corner of Alexei's lips. "You're family now. If you ever have need of something—anything at all—ask."

Nathan scanned the dimly lit room. Nearly everyone was sleeping at this hour, but Inessa was holding a cold compress to a woman's brow, and Yuri was helping a boy drink. The others were all either in the sloop or one of the tents they'd brought, sleeping after a long day of caring for the sick.

"I see now why Kate doesn't want to leave Alaska," he muttered.

Alexei raised an eyebrow, then waited a long moment before saying, "I didn't realize that was a possibility."

"I should have made it clearer before the wedding. But it all happened so suddenly that I didn't think to fully explain the nature of my job before we married."

"It sounds as though you're not permanently stationed in Juneau."

"The plan was for me to be here for three years, with a possibility I might be able to stay longer, but then I got a letter from the surgeon general telling me to return to Washington, DC, immediately."

"Immediately?"

"This epidemic is the only reason we're not on our way to Washington, DC, right now."

"She'll go with you." Alexei's voice was smooth and emotionless as it drifted across the sleeping bodies of the sick closest to them.

"Because she has to. Not because she wants to."

"She'll go with you because she loves you."

Nathan shook his head. "She says she loves me, and I know she does in a way. But I'm not sure that she loves me more than she loves your family, than she loves this." He raised his hand and gestured to the room. "Than she loves practicing medicine in Alaska. And I can't say that I blame her, considering how little choice she had about our wedding."

Oh, why was he saying this? And to Alexei Amos, no less? The man wasn't even a friend, let alone his confidant.

But it felt good to get the words out, to share the feelings that had been bottled up inside him for days on end.

Alexei didn't issue any judgment, even though it felt like he should. The other man simply watched him for a moment with dark, observant eyes. "She loves you more than she loves Alaska. She might not have realized it yet, but she will."

Nathan swallowed, thinking of how she'd stood in the center of the longhouse earlier that day, watching him through sick eyes as she hugged X'unéi and kissed her baby's forehead and sent them from the longhouse, fully recovered from the influenza. He'd caught her watching him again when she made rounds with the water bucket, and later when he checked patients' lungs with his stethoscope. "Did she tell you she'd rather follow me to Washington, DC, than stay here?"

Alexei snorted. "Kate doesn't tell me anything. But have you watched her lately? Really watched her?"

He couldn't keep his eyes off her. It felt like the only thing he did—watch her from afar.

"She listens to you rather than argues. She smiles at you. And she trusts you in a way that I don't think she trusts many other men. She might trust some of her brothers, but beyond that . . ." Alexei shook his head. "Men haven't been kind to her, like your friend Ellingsworth. I didn't realize how much damage all of that cruelty had done to her over the years. Not until I saw her here working with you."

"Do you really think she's that . . . damaged?" His voice cracked over the last word.

"I do now, yes. Yes. It makes me wish I had worked harder to gain her trust after she returned from Boston."

Nathan spread his hands. "I just prayed over and over that God would help me love her the way she needed to be loved. That's all I did, because there were times—still are times—when I didn't have the first clue what to do, or how to show her that I love her in spite of everything. That God loves her too. It hasn't felt like enough."

Alexei said nothing, just stared out over the room, his eyes seeming to absorb every last detail about the sick, sleeping people.

"I just keep wondering if I should have done something more. If there was a better way for me to show her that I love her, and I missed it somehow."

Alexei rubbed the side of his jaw. "You and me both."

Nathan jerked his head toward the other man. "What's that supposed to mean?"

"It means I've tried to protect Kate for years, but she never wanted my protection, not like the rest of my family wants it. She always seemed to feel trapped by it. I'm glad she's willing to accept it from you."

"She accepts very little from me." Though he could picture Alexei trying to protect Kate, all practical and serious and harsh. And he could just as easily imagine Kate tossing it back at his feet.

Because the woman needed kindness and love, not a list of practical actions.

"She accepts more from you than she does from anyone else, possibly even Evelina," Alexei went on. "I know she's been sick, but I've never seen her so at peace and calm while practicing medicine. She's comfortable with you. She trusts you. With you around, she knows she doesn't have to fight the world just to do the one thing she loves. I'm assuming that's because she knows you'll fight for her."

Was she really at peace around him? Was she really that calm? And all because she trusted him to defend her?

When he thought back to how fiery and defensive she'd been when treating his concussion, then thought about the way she tirelessly tended the Tlingit, even with a cough and fever, it almost seemed like he was thinking of two different people.

"Tell me." Alexei turned to him. "Is there a chance she's with child?"

The back of Nathan's neck turned hot. "I hardly think that's your business."

A wry smile tilted the corner of Alexei's mouth. "You forget, I was in the office above the trading post with the two of you the morning before you married. Kate was quite adamant your marriage would never include any activities that could lead to children, and you said you were willing to wait."

"So you're asking if I stopped waiting?"

"No. I'm asking if she changed her mind."

Nathan swallowed. "She did . . . right up until we got that letter from the surgeon general."

"I see." Alexei showed no surprise at his answer. No emotion at all, actually. And yet the man wondered why Kate was slow to accept his help. "It seems you and I are both in the position of needing to make difficult decisions."

Nathan narrowed his eyes, looking at Alexei again. "What decision do you have to make?"

"Oh, I already made my decision, though I'm not sure that's a good thing anymore."

"What happened?"

Alexei shifted, his jaw working back and forth in the dim light from the fire, as though he was debating whether to keep talking or get up and leave. "Do you know the new governor everyone is complaining about? Simon Caldwell?"

"Yes." It was the only thing he'd heard about since the Amoses had arrived. Kate had been furious. The entire family was. Or at least everyone but Alexei, it seemed. Now that he thought of it, he hadn't heard the man complain about the new governor once. And he was sitting there beside him, his face blank and emotionless, as though he didn't care whether the next governor was Simon Caldwell or a mouse or anything in between.

"I've met Simon Caldwell a few times in Washington," Nathan added. "His family has made some rather generous donations to the MHS in the past."

Alexei snorted. "Glad to know they can do something good with their money every now and then."

He shrugged. "They're known both for being generous, and for using that generosity to get what they want."

"That sounds a little more familiar." Again, Alexei stared out at the room, watching Inessa as she knelt to coax someone through a bout of coughing. "Secretary Gray offered me the governorship first. I turned him down."

"The governorship?" Nathan sat back.

"Don't act so surprised. I have a rather comprehensive knowledge of Alaska and good relations with nearly all the tribal villages. And I'm clearly capable of running a company. Do you think I'd do a poor job governing Alaska?"

"No," he found himself saying. "Not at all. You're different from the type of men usually chosen for such a task, but that's probably good."

"That's the conclusion I arrived at."

"So why did you turn the position down, especially if Secretary Gray was going to appoint someone your family despises to fill the role?"

"I didn't know who he was going to appoint." Alexei's voice deepened into a growl, his eyes narrowing. "Otherwise I might have reconsidered."

"I'm assuming you had a rather good reason for turning Secretary Gray down." Or at least, it must have seemed like a good reason at the time.

"I don't agree with the government's Indian policy for Alaska." The words dropped from his mouth, hard and stiff and unapologetic.

And they made complete sense. "I assume they want to put the Indians on reservations like they've done elsewhere?"

"That's part of it, yes."

"And you don't think the Indians will be better off entering into a peace treaty with the US government?"

"No."

Everything about the man went back to being cold and emotionless with that single word.

"But that's not the only reason I turned Gray down. Not the biggest one."

Again, Alexei's eyes tracked Inessa as she moved through the room, now bending to check the temperature of a boy who was tossing and turning in his sleep. It was the only thing about him that gave the barest hint of emotion. "They wanted me to put Ilya and Inessa into an Indian boarding school."

And just like that, everything about Alexei's situation snapped into place with perfect, vivid clarity. "So you turned them down. Of course you did. It might have seemed like you had a choice, but you didn't, not really."

"Like I said, I didn't realize Simon Caldwell was Secretary Gray's next choice for governor."

"Whatever this new governor does, I'm sure you'll find a way to protect your family."

Alexei's eyes turned to his in the darkness, the light from the fire sending shadows dancing across his face. "You say that with more confidence than I deserve. The Caldwells are very powerful, and I already worry that there are things going on that shouldn't be. To have two of the Caldwells in Sitka in different positions of power, one economic and one governmental . . ." His Adam's apple bobbed. "I might very well end up regretting my decision."

He might. But he would also survive it. Nathan knew that as surely as he knew the tide would rise tomorrow morning and fall tomorrow evening.

"All of this had a point, though. And I've gotten rather off topic." Alexei pinned him once again with those dark eyes, eyes that maybe weren't as cold as he thought. Maybe they were simply burdened with such heavy obligations that they didn't know how to ever look happy. "I don't know if it's truly best for you to leave Alaska in a week or a month or three years from now. Or if the best choice is to stay here and try to keep doing what you're doing, with or without the support of the MHS. Only you can answer those questions. But I do know that a great man isn't afraid to make sacrifices for those he loves. It seems like you've already done that with my sister. Just know that I expect it to continue, even after you leave."

It was a threat of sorts, but it only made Nathan admire the man sitting beside him. Not because Alexei was powerful or cunning or smart, though he was likely all of those things. But because this man had a deep love for his family and was willing to sacrifice much for their happiness.

It made him wonder what other things Alexei had sacrificed for his family in the past. And what else he might end up sacrificing in the future.

Nathan awoke the next morning to a hand pressed against his forehead. It was soft and cool, so he turned his head into it, then lifted his own hand to keep it pressed there.

Or rather, he tried lifting his own hand, but his arms felt unbearably heavy, as though they'd turned into weights in the night, as did his legs.

He tried opening his eyes, just to make sure it was Kate's

hand pressed to his head and not Evelina's or Inessa's, but cracking his eyelids against the morning light sent a bright slice of pain through his head.

The hand left his head, and he groaned, wishing she would move it back, but then the quilt rustled beside him, and he found a warm body pressed to his side, and the slender hand that had just been on his forehead slipped through a gap in his nightshirt and settled on his bare chest.

"You have a fever, dearest." Kate kissed the side of his face just below his ear. "I was starting to think you were stronger than the influenza, but apparently not."

"Just let me sleep. It will be gone by noon."

She chuckled softly, her body shaking against his. "Would you care to place a wager on that, husband of mine? Because the quickest fever to break has been mine and a couple of the children's, and it's taken two days, not four hours."

He groaned but couldn't think of a response, so he closed his eyes and drifted back to sleep.

39

Petersburg; Six Days Later; September 8

Kate pressed her eyes shut, willing the sound traveling through her stethoscope to go away. But it was there, a faint crackle that indicated pneumonia.

"Nathan." She removed the stethoscope from his chest and reached up to feel his forehead, but it was just as hot as it had been before she checked his lungs. "Don't do this to me. You can't get pneumonia."

His eyes blinked open, dull with fever. "I won't get pneumonia. Stop . . . worrying."

She pressed her lips together. The only thing she could do was worry. He'd told her his fever would break within four hours, but it was still raging five days later. He'd slept almost the entire time, and she'd only awakened him to coax the bare minimum of broth and food down his throat.

But five days was awfully soon to develop pneumonia.

Other patients, including Dr. Ellingsworth, had developed it after a week or longer. Unfortunately, everything about Nathan's bout with this wretched Russian influenza seemed more extreme than what others faced. His temperature was higher, he was sleeping more, and now his pneumonia had come on faster.

"I don't suppose you have any advice to help me treat a patient with pneumonia?"

Nathan's eyes fluttered open for a brief moment, then fell closed, but words rasped from his chest anyway. "Keep them sitting up as much as possible. Use cold baths to reduce fever. Keep hydrated with water and broth, use a mustard plaster on the chest, try eucalyptus tea and honey for the cough."

These were all things she was already doing. The problem was, none of them had worked on any of the other patients who developed pneumonia, not even Dr. Ellingsworth. He'd died two days ago. She'd told Nathan when it was clear the man had only a few hours left, and again after he passed, though she wasn't sure Nathan would remember being told. His fever had been so high, he hadn't been aware of much that was going on around him.

Kate set down her stethoscope and reached for his hand, her hold so tight he'd probably find it painful. "It's going to be all right."

But he didn't so much as open his eyes, let alone respond.

Two Weeks Later; September 22

NATHAN WAS GOING TO DIE. Kate sat beside him on a wooden chair Yuri had built for her when it became apparent Nathan was developing pneumonia. The longhouse was half empty now. The influenza epidemic seemed to have worked its way through the town in a little over a month since it arrived. There hadn't been any new cases in the past three days. After Dr. Ellingsworth's passing, she'd lost an elderly woman to pneumonia, which brought the total up to seven deaths.

And now she wasn't sure her husband was going to survive.

He slept sitting up, his back and head propped up with half a dozen blankets and pillows, but that did nothing to alleviate the fever that had spiked in his body yesterday, nor did the cold compresses on his forehead or the cool baths she'd given his chest and arms. His bare chest was stained yellow from the mustard leaking through the linen sack she'd placed the plaster in, the scent and sight of which she'd come to despise. She fed him bread soaked in broth every four hours and made him drink a cup of eucalyptus tea with honey.

For over a week, she'd thought her efforts might be working. His fever fell, and he was able to hold a conversation, ask about other patients, even grieve Ellingsworth's passing. Even though she could hear that telltale crackle in his lungs and the sounds of loud, harsh breaths whooshing in and out of him, he'd seemed to be beating the disease.

Until yesterday. His fever had shot up, and he'd been either unresponsive or unaware of his surroundings ever since. The strangest part was that his breathing didn't sound that labored, yet the telltale crackle of pneumonia was still there, lurking beneath his fever. And despite all her medical training and everything she had done, she feared she'd soon be burying her husband.

She bent her head, her grip tightening on his hand. "Nathan, please. You can't do this to me. You can't leave me." He was the most perfect man in the world. So kind and patient. Willing to let her practice medicine.

No, not willing, happy that she practiced medicine and

giving her a chance to do so at every opportunity. He had defended her countless times to skeptical male patients and Dr. Ellingsworth, and something told her that even if the surgeon general himself were to arrive in Alaska, Nathan would have no qualms defending her medical abilities to the most influential doctor in the country.

She could look another hundred years, and she'd never be able to find a man as perfect for her as Nathan Reid.

Alexei had seen that from the beginning. He'd tried to tell her that day in the office above the trading post.

She hadn't wanted to listen then, just like she hadn't wanted to listen to Nathan's gentle pleas that they marry. Just like she hadn't wanted to believe his promise that he'd let her keep doctoring.

If only she had realized how sincere he was. If only she'd been willing to trust him sooner. If only she'd understood how wholly good and kind and selfless her husband was. Then they could have had more time trusting and loving each other the way a husband and wife should.

Nathan had been willing to let down his defenses from the beginning. She'd been the one to ruin that. To hesitate. To be distrustful. To turn the short time they'd had together into something far less than what it could have been.

"Kate, are you all right?"

She felt a soft presence behind her, then Evelina's slender hand reached out to rest on her shoulder.

"I love him," she whispered, tears clouding her eyes. "I love him more than I love being here, more than I want to stay in Alaska, but I didn't tell him when it mattered most. And now..."

"Don't finish that sentence. He'll recover." Evelina opened her arms, then pulled Kate into a hug.

She went willingly. "You don't know that. The odds are

against him, and I don't understand why his fever is spiking, even though his lungs sound like they're improving. And when I look at what's happened to everyone else with pneumonia..."

She pressed her eyes shut against the tears threatening to spill out. "It's not that I can't live without him. I know I can. I did it for twenty-six years. It's that I don't want to. I remember how my life was before him. I still practiced medicine, yes, but it wasn't the same. Wasn't as rich and full as after I met him."

"I understand." Evelina ran a hand up and down her back in gentle, soothing motions. "I feel the same way about Jonas and practicing law and even teaching. Nothing in my life was as full as it could be—until I met him."

"Do you know how many times he's told me he loves me?" She sniffled, still clinging to her sister's arms. "More than I can count. But I didn't believe him, not really."

Kate pressed her eyes shut again, soaking in every last bit of comfort from her sister's hug. "He's so gentle and patient. So kind, so willing to give me whatever I ask for. And I'm a mess. I can never sit still, never let my brain slow down. I'm a woman who's a doctor, and I want to treat all people, not just screaming babies or women with certain complaints that make male doctors uncomfortable. I have to be the only woman in the world to even want such a thing, and part of me feels like this is all just some giant mistake. That I'm a mistake. That he shouldn't love me, and one day he'll wake up and realize it and want nothing to do with me anymore."

"Kate, no." Evelina pulled back from her. "You don't think that about yourself. Tell me you don't."

She raised her shoulders in a halfhearted shrug. "Sometimes I do. But do you know what Nathan told me when I said I was a mistake?"

Evelina shook her head, her eyes glistening with unshed tears. "What?"

"That I'm fearfully and wonderfully made. That I'm created in God's image, and he loves me with an everlasting love. And then Nathan would say that he loves me too. But I'm just not sure how to believe it deep down inside."

"Oh, Kate." Evelina pulled her back into her arms. "I had no idea you felt this way. Why didn't you say something?"

"So you don't think I'm a mistake?"

"No. I think you're exactly what you just said. Created in God's image, with a unique purpose in mind. You might not be good at sewing or have much patience in the kitchen. But I'm quite certain the God of the universe knew what he was doing when he formed you, that he wanted you to be different from everyone else. That he wanted you to be exactly who you are—a wonderful doctor who saves people's lives. And then he gave you a twin sister who loves you, and six other siblings who also love you. And finally, he gave you a husband who loves you.

"And do you know what's more?" Evelina continued. "I think Nathan loves you because of all the things you just listed, not in spite of them. He doesn't look at your quirks and eccentricities as something to be endured; he sees them as the reasons you're special. Your endless ball of energy captivates him. Your determination to carve out a spot for yourself in a world dominated by men inspires him. He'd be bored with anything less."

Would he? Perhaps. He'd told her the morning after their wedding that he didn't want a normal, boring wife. She hadn't believed him then; she'd assumed he was just trying to make her feel better. But what if he was being honest? "I'm still a mess, Lina. I make mistakes, I yell too much, I do impulsive things."

"That makes you just like the rest of us. Imperfect and flawed. A sinner. But you're still his light, Kate, imperfections or not. You keep his life from being a boring monotony of treating one patient after another with the same list of complaints."

"But . . ." She stared into her sister's eyes, ready to launch into another objection.

Except she had none. She'd offered up every one of them, some of them more than once. The only thing she had left to do was choose. Choose to accept that Nathan loved her in spite of her flaws. Choose to accept that God loved her too, that he had created her different from everyone else, but he'd done it for a reason.

And pray that God would allow the wonderful husband he'd given her to live.

40

She spent the evening on her knees praying and the night hours hunched over her Bible, reading beneath the flickering lamplight in her tent. By the time she arrived at the longhouse for her shift the next morning, she'd memorized Psalm 139:14: *I will praise thee; for I am fearfully and wonderfully made.*

And Genesis 1:27: *So God created man in his own image, in the image of God created he him; male and female created he them.*

She'd also read through the last part of the book of Jeremiah, just so she could understand how deeply God had loved the children of Israel when he said that he loved them with an everlasting love.

It gave her a sense of peace as she entered the dark longhouse with its cloying scents and stuffy air. But even though she'd spent a good deal of the night asking God to forgive her and praying that he would heal her husband, Nathan's fever had only climbed higher during the night, and the telltale crackle of pneumonia, though faint, still filled his lungs when she listened to his breathing.

"Inessa and I have been giving him cool baths every four hours, trying to keep the fever down." Evelina knelt beside her, her eyes tired and her mouth wreathed in subtle lines of fatigue.

"I believe you. It's just that it's not working." Kate pulled her knees to her chest and rested her forehead on them, trying to hang on to the peace that had been her companion through the night.

Dear God, what do I do? Is this really what you want for Nathan? For us? Is there something more I can try? Please show me. I'll do anything to spare his life. Anything at all.

She reached for her stethoscope again, slowly fitting the ends in her ears. She was about to press the other end to Nathan's mustard-stained chest when a long shadow fell over her.

"It won't sound any different than it did fifteen minutes ago."

She turned to find Mikhail standing at the edge of the makeshift bed. He'd come up suddenly, almost as though he'd appeared out of nowhere. But that was how Mikhail tended to move, like a mountain lion quietly stalking through the woods, only making his presence known when he wanted to reveal himself.

"I don't understand." She held the stethoscope to Nathan's chest. "It almost sounds like the pneumonia is getting better. His breathing sounds more normal, and the crackle is going away, but his fever just keeps climbing."

"I'll give him another cold bath." Evelina pushed herself up. "Let me get the bucket and sponge."

"No." Mikhail shook his head, his golden eyes pinned to Nathan. "You've given him hundreds of cold baths. If that was going to help, it would have already worked. You should stop them altogether."

Kate stiffened. "Why would you say that? Too high of a fever can cause seizures."

"The Athabaskans don't try to bring fevers down. They believe it's the good spirits warring with the bad in the body. That the higher the fever, the harder the battle. They let fevers break naturally."

Evelina's brow furrowed. "I've never heard of such a thing."

Neither had Kate. "You know there aren't good and bad spirits warring inside his body, Mikhail. There are tiny microbes we can't see called germs that bring about an illness."

This wasn't the first time she'd mentioned the germ theory to her family, but it was the first time Mikhail seemed remotely interested in it. He cocked his head to the side, then crouched down beside Nathan.

She wanted to say that every muscle of Mikhail's body was tightly coiled, like he really was that mountain lion ready to pounce. But sometimes she wondered if his muscles were simply always that tight, that it had something to do with the kettlebells and Indian clubs he used to keep up his strength when he wasn't leading an expedition. He wasn't as big as Sacha or Jonas, but he was probably stronger than both of them.

"Do these germs bring the fever with them," Mikhail asked. "Are they one and the same?"

"That's the theory, yes."

"What if the fever is good? Not brought about by the germs but because of them. What if the fever means the body is at war with the germs?"

"Like the Athabaskans believe?" Evelina asked.

Mikhail gave his head a quick shake. "The Athabaskans believe spirits are warring. But I'm just saying, if sickness is caused by bad microbes we can't see, perhaps fever is the body's way of fighting those microbes. When the fever finally recedes and leaves, the person is healthy."

Kate rubbed her temple. "That sounds preposterous."

Mikhail moved his sleek golden gaze to her. "Do you have any other ideas why the Athabaskan way of letting fevers break naturally seems to work?"

"Does it really work?" She sunk her teeth into her bottom lip.

"Usually, yes, but not always. Still, it seems like something to try, considering . . ." Mikhail didn't finish his sentence. He didn't need to. The weight of Nathan's illness loomed over them all.

And they'd tried cold baths, so many cold baths she'd lost count. What was the harm in trying something new, in letting Nathan's fever rise?

Possible seizures and brain damage and death.

But if they did nothing, he would die too.

"Do the Athabaskans do anything to treat pneumonia?" she asked softly.

"I can look in my journal. If they do, I'm sure it's a concoction of herbs, probably not all that different from the ones you've got in that mustard plaster. But it's worth checking." Mikhail pushed himself up and made his way quickly to the entrance of the longhouse.

"Are you sure about this?" Evelina turned to her.

Kate swallowed. "I can't just sit here and watch him die."

Evelina sucked in a breath, then blew out a long, slow stream of air. "I'd feel the same way if it were Jonas."

She reached out and gripped her sister's hand. "Just pray that it works."

41

Petersburg; Two Days Later

Nathan blinked against the darkness surrounding him. The dim flicker of fire somewhere in the room caused shadows to dance against a rough wooden wall and filled the rafters of the ceiling above with a smoky haze.

Where was he? Why did his muscles ache and his chest feel as though a weight sat atop it? He scanned the empty bed of furs next to him. Another bed of furs lay on the floor beyond it, also empty.

He drew in a breath, but his throat felt raw and dry, his breath raspy and painful. Where was he? Why was he . . . ?

"Nathan?"

At the sound of the soft voice, he turned his head to find Kate seated on a wooden chair beside where he lay.

She dropped from her chair to her knees beside him, then

reached out and brushed the hair from his brow. "Are you awake? Tell me you're awake, dearest. Tell me you—"

"Water," he whispered, his voice cracking over the word. "I need water."

"Of course you do." She pushed herself to her feet and rushed off. To where, he didn't know. She moved too quickly for him to track with his eyes. All he knew was that he wanted her back. That very instant. He would have gone for an hour or better with his parched, painful throat if it meant she'd stay by his side.

But she was back half a minute later, once again dropping to her knees beside him, her chestnut hair a tangled mess about her shoulders.

"Here, drink." She wrapped an arm around his shoulder, raising him up a bit higher than the pillows and blankets already propped behind his back. She held the wooden cup to his lips with such practiced ease, it made him wonder just how many times she'd helped him drink over the past . . .

"How long?" he asked after his first sip of water. "How long was I sick?"

She paused. "Three weeks. I thought . . . That is, I didn't think . . ." She shook her head, giving him another sip of water. "I'm just happy you're awake."

He glanced down at his chest, stained yellow from what he assumed was mustard poultices. But a reddish-brown paste had been smeared atop the yellow.

"What is it?" He slid a finger through the dried paste.

"Devil's club and onion."

"Devil's club?" He'd never heard of such a thing.

"It was Mikhail's suggestion. The native tribes use it for illnesses."

"It appears to have worked."

"I'm so very glad." She sniffled, her green eyes filling with tears.

He opened his arm for her, and she crawled beside him onto the pallet of furs, then laid her head on his chest, which still felt unnaturally heavy, but at least he could draw air.

"I love you," she whispered against his shoulder. "More than I love Alaska or practicing medicine or being with my family. I love you more than all of it. Wherever the surgeon general sends you, whenever he tells you to go, I want to be by your side."

Warmth filled him, and he couldn't help the smile that spread across his lips as he relaxed back into the pillows, his wife tucked safely against his side as he absently stroked her hair. "Had I realized falling ill would result in this, I would have endeavored to get sick sooner."

She sniffled again, her fingers curling against the bare skin of his chest. "Don't say that. Please don't say that."

He stilled, his hand only halfway through the silky lock of hair he'd been stroking. "Just how ill was I?"

"I thought you were going to die. Your fever spiked, and you barely responded when I tried talking to you, and I thought . . ." She slid her hand to the very center of his chest, never mind the dried herbs. "Mikhail was the one who figured out how to treat you. We kept giving you cold baths, trying to control your fever, but he said to let your temperature spike and see if it would break on its own. He said the Athabaskans do that, and it sometimes works. So that's what we did, along with the devil's club and onion. But I was so scared I would lose you, and that made me realize . . ."

She scooted herself higher on the pillows, pulling away from the perfect spot on his shoulder.

He was about to protest, but then she rested a hand on his

cheek, cool and slender against his flushed skin. "I really do love you, Nathan. So very much."

He turned his head farther into her hand and kissed her palm. "I love you too."

"I know that now, and while I knew it on some level before, I didn't fully realize it until you were sick."

"You didn't realize that I loved you?" How could she be so uncertain of it? He reached out and took her hand, folding it in his. "I'll find a better way to show you, darling. I'll do something—"

"No, even though you've shown me, and told me, time and again. But I had to accept it before it could be real to me. I suppose it's like us with God. God loves us with an everlasting love. But for his love to do any good in our lives, we have to accept it first. Except I felt like I didn't deserve the love God wanted to give me, or the love you wanted to give me. I'm awkward and different and odd, the last thing a woman is supposed to be."

He swallowed, his throat aching in a way that had nothing to do with influenza. "No, love, you're perfect."

She smiled through watery eyes. "I'm the farthest thing from perfect. But I'm still created in God's image. I'm still his child. And I'm exactly the person he wanted me to be, even with my oddities and imperfections. And so I decided it was time to stop fighting, time to stop telling myself I didn't deserve to be loved and accept that I'm fearfully and wonderfully made. That I'm created in God's image."

Nathan felt his face curve into a smile. "So you listened."

"Eventually." She smiled in response, but her eyes still glistened with unshed tears. "Though I'm afraid it took me a little longer than it should have."

"I love you in spite of your stubbornness."

"I know. But I want you to know that I meant it when I said

I love you more than everything else. I don't care where the surgeon general sends us next. As long as I'm with you, I'll be happy."

He reached out and brushed a messy, tangled lock of hair away from her face, then slid his hand deeper, until it cradled the soft skin of her neck. "I hate asking you to leave your family. The lot of you are so strong together. I can write to the surgeon general and ask him—"

"No." She pressed a finger to his mouth. "No. I won't tether you to Alaska. My life's dream was to be a doctor, and I am. God's already given that to me. Yours is to provide better medical care for the entirety of America. There's no question about which dream will do more good for more people, about which one matters more."

Nathan swallowed, staring up into the beautiful green eyes of the woman God had dropped into his lap one rainy Alaskan morning. The woman who loved him fully and deeply. The woman who was willing to make the kinds of sacrifices for him that Alexei had just made for Inessa and Ilya.

It might have taken several months for Kate to come to love him so deeply, but he would have waited ten times longer if necessary. Because there was nothing in this world as precious and hope-filled as the future they could now share together.

42

Petersburg; Two Days Later; September 27

Alexei stared beyond the calm waters of the sound toward the ice-covered mountains of the mainland. It was beautiful at this time of the evening, with the sun not quite setting over the mountains in the west and the water and wind nearly still. Senator Randolph was right about sending a photographer or painter or both to Alaska. He doubted people in America had any clue about the raw power and beauty of Southeast Alaska, and if they saw it, even in a photograph, they just might appreciate it more.

Soon he'd be exchanging this beautiful view for a different one. Everyone would be heading back to Juneau and Sitka in a few more days. The epidemic was mostly done, and they all needed to get back to work. There was no saying where the Russian influenza might spread next, but at least they'd gotten the town of Petersburg through the disease with only a handful of deaths.

But what would be waiting for him once he returned to Sitka? Would there be another letter from Laurel? Could she have agreed to take him up on his offer of a visit? Both she and her father might even be waiting for him when he docked.

Or Simon Caldwell might be the one standing on the dock as the newly minted governor of Alaska. The thought made his jaw tighten.

"There you are." Kate came up to stand beside him. "What are you doing on the beach at this time of night? Most of the town has settled into their beds."

Alexei scrubbed a hand over his face. "Just wanted a quiet place to think, but I didn't realize anyone was looking for me. Don't tell me Nathan's taken another turn for the worse." It had been horrible, watching the strongest woman he knew spend over three weeks at her husband's bedside, doing everything she could to save him from the disease that seemed determined to take his life.

Kate shook her head. "No. It's nothing like that. Nathan's continuing to improve. He should be fully recovered in another week. I was looking for you because I wanted to tell you that I'll leave your banknote with Evelina so she can bring it to you in Sitka at Christmas, since I won't be here."

He frowned. "What banknote?"

"For the building I wanted to purchase. There's no need to purchase it now that I'm moving. And even if I wasn't moving, there'd still be no need for me to have my own clinic now that I'm working for Nathan. I'll send a note to Mr. Gibbons explaining the situation before I leave Alaska."

He'd forgotten about the building. "Keep the money. Consider it a wedding present. Use it to buy something nice wherever the surgeon general sends you next."

She was quiet for a moment, her eyes scanning the beauty surrounding them. "I'll miss you all rather terribly."

He swallowed as he looked down at her. "I'll miss you too. But please take the money, and don't argue about it."

She looked at the ground, where she dug the toe of her boot into the soft sand. "I wasn't going to argue."

"You weren't?" His eyebrow winged up. "Are you Evelina posing as Kate, because I'm pretty certain my doctor-sister would spend at least twenty minutes arguing with me before agreeing to accept such a large sum of money."

Her teeth sunk into the side of her lip, and she peered up at him. "Is that really what you think of me?"

"I . . ." He opened his mouth, then closed it, at a loss for what he should say.

"I know I'm not as kindhearted as Evelina, but I want you to know that I appreciate you. I couldn't imagine having a better older brother. You paid for me and Lina to move to Boston, paid for my schooling, and supported me all over again once I returned home and found myself without work despite my new medical degree. A lot of brothers would never have supported a sister who wanted to do something so outlandish in the first place, but you didn't even blink when I laid out my plan to attend medical school, and I don't think I've told you thank you."

He stared down at her, not quite sure what had brought on her sudden bout of gratitude, or why the sister who barely talked to him was suddenly willing to share her feelings. "I never minded paying for you to go to medical school. I know what it is to have your dreams ripped from you, and I love all of my siblings too much to ever wish that on any of them."

The confession left him feeling a bit raw, almost as though he was standing in the governor's mansion with Clarise, facing the most painful years of his life all over again.

Kate's throat worked as she stared out over the sound, her eyes scanning the deep blues and purples of the growing twilight. "Like I said, you're a good brother, far better than I deserve. And know that I haven't been the sister you deserve in return."

"Don't say that."

"No. I want to say it, need to, really. I struggled for so long with how men treated me, specifically male doctors, and somehow in my mind, I told myself that accepting your help made me weak and dependent on you. In fact, I told myself that accepting anyone's help, even from my family, made me weak. But then you and everyone else showed up here to help with the epidemic, and Nathan and I talked about how I'm fearfully and wonderfully made, and it made me realize that accepting your help, your love, doesn't make me weak; it makes me stronger."

She turned to him, her eyes filled with an openness and vulnerability that he hadn't seen since she was a girl. "I wish I had figured this out before I needed to leave, but even though I'm moving away, I still want you to know how much I appreciate everything you've done for me over the years. I truly am blessed to have such a wonderful brother, and I'm sorry for shutting you out for so long."

He didn't know what had brought about this change. If he was going to guess, it had something to do with almost losing Nathan, but as he stood before her in the dying sunlight, there was only one thing he could do.

He reached out and took her hand. "Thank you for not shutting me out now. I promise I'll do everything in my power to maintain your trust in me, no matter how many miles separate us."

Then he pulled her into a hug and didn't let her go.

43

Petersburg; Two Days Later; September 29

Kate stood just outside her tent, the brisk morning air of Petersburg, Alaska, stirring the loose strands of hair around her face. From where she stood on the slight rise, she could see the village stretching toward the harbor, its residents milling around all but the last longhouse, which was still being used as a quarantine facility, even though there were only four patients inside.

For too many weeks, the village had been still, with far too many of the residents suffering from influenza. Those who were healthy had stayed hidden in their longhouses or had gone into the woods or to the beach to forage for food, and Petersburg had been hauntingly empty. But today the village was full of movement. To her left, men were preparing to leave for a hunt, and beyond them, a group of women was tanning a deer hide.

X'unéi was one of the women in the group, working alongside the others with her healthy babe strapped to her back as though the influenza had never happened.

Down at the harbor, the activity centered around a series of dinghies that had just rowed to the shore. A revenue cutter had arrived a quarter hour ago and was now anchored in the harbor, rocking gently against its moorings.

While Kate didn't usually hate the sight of a proud ship in the harbor, she despised this one. Mikhail had received a letter from Sitka only yesterday. The ship's sole reason for being in Petersburg was to pick up her brother and take him away . . .

At the wrong time of year.

As though sensing she'd been thinking about him, Mikhail emerged from the quarantine longhouse, wearing a fur parka that made him look more native than white. He carried a pack over his shoulder, and she didn't need to be close to know its leather was worn and soft, even faded in some places. How could it not be after the number of expeditions he'd brought it on?

Mikhail caught her gaze and headed toward her, his gait smooth and powerful, as though the pack he carried held mounds of feathers rather than the heavy supplies he'd need to head off into the wilderness.

"It's good to see the village looking so busy these days." He stopped by her side, somehow slinging the heavy pack off his shoulders in a move that looked as graceful as a ballerina's.

Kate threw her arms around him, burrowing into his thick fur parka. "I don't like the idea of you leaving on winter's doorstep."

His arms wrapped around her, hard and strong, just like his chest. "A team of botanists is lost somewhere up the Stikine River. Someone needs to go after them."

"Perhaps someone does, but it doesn't have to be you."

He raised a light brown eyebrow at her, his golden eyes seeming to soak in everything about her. "No? And who else would they send? Jack's already with them as the guide."

He spoke of Jack Ledman, who had grown up in Sitka right along with Mikhail. He was an excellent wilderness guide and explorer, though not as good as Mikhail. No one was as good as Mikhail. It was a fact acknowledged by everyone, from the bureaucrats in Washington, DC, to the frontiersmen who called Alaska their home, and it was why he kept getting more and more guide jobs that took him into the vast, wild interior of Alaska.

"Are you sure you have everything you need?" Kate looked down at his pack. Even though it was large, it looked too small to carry enough supplies to escort a team of missing scientists back to Sitka on the cusp of winter.

"Of course not." Mikhail grinned, his eyes practically dancing. "Part of the fun is letting the wilderness give me what I'm not carrying in my pack."

He meant things like food and water, or even a tent or coat made from a moose hide if needed.

"Watch out for grizzlies and wolves, and be careful of the temperature. It's sure to be below freezing at night in the mountains. If you start to get hypothermia, skin-to-skin contact and—"

Mikhail wrapped her in another hug, cutting off her words as he pulled her against his solid chest. "I'm going to miss this—your worrying and everything."

Kate held him tight, her throat closing against the sudden swell of emotion rising in her chest. "Just come back safe."

"I will." He stepped back, then picked up his pack. "You be careful too. Take care of that husband of yours. And try not to replace me with another annoying brother while I'm gone."

As though Mikhail could ever be replaced.

"Excuse me," a voice said from behind her. "I'm looking for Dr. Victor Ellingsworth. Do either of you know where he might be?"

Mikhail took a step back from her. "Kate can answer that for you, sir. I have a ship to catch." He held up his hand in a solitary wave, then turned and headed toward the beach.

Kate followed Mikhail with her gaze, praying it wouldn't be the last time she saw him alive. It was something she prayed every time he left, but never before had he been sent on a mission so late in the year. The expeditions he led always started in the spring, and for good reason. No one wanted to end up trapped on a mountain during an entire Alaskan winter.

"Well, ma'am, I'm assuming you can take me to the good doctor?" the man beside her said.

"Oh, um . . ." Kate turned to look at him. He was several decades older than she was, well into his fifties, or perhaps even sixty. He had a bushy mustache that covered his top lip and the sides of his mouth, and he was dressed rather fancily for Alaska in a crisp gray suit. "I'm sorry, but I'm afraid Dr. Ellingsworth passed about a month ago."

The man grew still for a moment, one side of his mustache twitching. "Victor passed?"

"We did everything we could to save him, but . . ." Her voice trailed off. She was unsure of what to say as the stranger in front of her attempted to fight his emotions. "Was he a close friend?"

"He was." The man's voice grew hoarse. "One of my closest, actually. We've known each other for over thirty years."

"I'm so sorry. We, ah, we buried him in the graveyard here. Would you like me to show you?"

"Perhaps in a bit. You'd better point me in the direction of Dr. Reid first."

The man had to mean Nathan, seeing how she'd never met him before. But Kate couldn't exactly let him walk away without knowing she was a doctor, especially not if he worked for the MHS. And since he'd asked for both Nathan and Dr. Ellingsworth, that seemed rather likely.

"I'm Dr. Kate Reid." She stuck out her hand to shake his. "Can I help you?"

"Are you now?" The man didn't take her hand. Instead his eyebrows rose, then his gaze swept down her. "How very interesting. Perhaps I should clarify. I'm looking for Dr. *Nathan* Reid."

"That would be my husband." She painted on her brightest smile, trying to pretend that the way the stranger was scrutinizing her was anything other than rude. "He's inside the quarantine house recovering from his own bout of influenza, but if—"

"Does that mean you expect him to make a full return to health?" the man interrupted. "Or do I need to worry about losing him like I did Victor?"

Kate felt her throat grow tight. "We expect him to return to full health within the week." She started walking toward the longhouse, and the stranger fell into step beside her. "His fever has broken, and he's lucid and talking, but I'm afraid his cough hasn't fully abated, and he's still quite tired after the pneumonia, so if—"

"He contracted pneumonia? Your husband?"

Oh, bother. Was this man going to let her finish a sentence? "Yes. In a few instances, maybe about five to seven percent of the cases, the Russian influenza progressed into a very serious pneumonia. We've yet to find a remedy."

"But Dr. Reid survived."

Kate nodded, blinking back the heat that still pricked her

eyes when she thought of just how close she'd come to losing him. "He's the only one, and we all consider it quite a miracle."

"I want to see him." The man strode past her toward the beautifully decorated doors of the longhouse.

"Wait." She raced ahead and planted herself directly in front of him. "This Russian strain of influenza can be quite serious, and if you haven't yet contracted it, I advise—"

"I want to see the quarantine facility and make sure it's adequate." The man glowered down at her, his mouth somehow firm even though half of it was hidden behind his mustache. "If part of the reason this influenza strain spread to so many inhabitants of Petersburg is due to failure to follow protocol, then I need to know. Otherwise, it looks as though our country has a highly contagious epidemic on our hands, and there are preparations that need to be made back in Washington."

"Washington?" Kate stepped away from the door. "You're from Washington, DC?"

The man didn't bother to answer. Instead, he yanked open the door and marched inside.

"He's over there, in the far corner against the wall." She pointed toward the bed of furs, where it looked like Nathan was awake, propped against the wall and talking to the boy she'd moved next to him yesterday.

When Nathan saw the man headed his direction, he slid back his covers and pushed himself to his feet. "Surgeon General Hamilton."

Surgeon general? Kate stopped walking. The man who hadn't been able to let her finish a sentence was the surgeon general of the United States?

Nathan started to extend his hand, then dropped it back by his side. "It's, ah, it's probably best if you're not in here. I'd hate for you to get the Russian influenza."

"As I told your wife, I wanted to see the quarantine facility and assess if there's anything that might be improved to better stop transmission of the disease."

"Oh, well, if that's your aim, go ahead." Nathan gestured to the open space of the longhouse. "I'm happy to hear any suggestions you might have for how to stop eighty-seven percent of a community from getting this disease."

"Eighty-seven percent?" The surgeon general muttered something beneath his breath, then looked Nathan up and down. "Lie down, Doctor. You look like you're about to collapse."

Nathan grimaced. "Thank you, sir."

The moment Nathan was once again propped up with pillows, the surgeon general fired off another round of questions. "Are you sterilizing your instruments with carbolic acid between each patient?"

"We are," Nathan answered.

"What about fresh air? I don't see any open windows."

"There aren't any windows to open. The Tlingit build their longhouses without them, but we've propped open the doors on some of the warm days."

Kate found one of the wooden chairs against the wall and dragged it over to where the surgeon general stood, then gestured for the man to sit. He didn't bother to thank her, just fired more questions at Nathan, so she sat in the other chair that was already beside the bed—a chair she'd spent far too many hours in over the past few weeks—then reached for her medical bag beside it.

"Did you allow any healthy villagers into the longhouse to nurse the sick and then send them back to their homes at night?" The surgeon general leaned forward, clasping his hands in front of him.

"No." Nathan shook his head. "Ellingsworth, Kate, and I

were the only ones treating patients until Ellingsworth got ill and Kate's family arrived. Kate's family contracted the Russian influenza last winter. Everyone survived, so we deemed it safe for them to help once we were down a doctor."

"Ah yes, Ekaterina Amos Reid, not only your wife but a doctor from the New England Female Medical College, and an MHS employee." The surgeon general turned to her once more, and this time he extended a hand. "It's a pleasure to officially meet you."

She set down the bottle of carbolic acid she'd been about to uncork so she could clean her medical instruments, then reached out and shook his hand. "It's a pleasure to meet you as well."

It was a lie, of course. Meeting the man was half nerve-racking and half terrifying, but she was determined not to let it show.

"I've received numerous letters about you. Are you aware of that?"

She shifted. "I was aware of some of them, yes." The ones she wasn't aware of had probably been from Ellingsworth, and she couldn't recall the man saying a single kind thing about her.

"I see," the surgeon general said, but rather than explaining what, exactly, he saw, he focused back on Nathan. "I had wanted you to return to Washington, DC, this fall to work on routes for traveling doctors in southern Louisiana. We're concerned about the typhus epidemic in New Orleans spreading through the bayou. But Ellingsworth's death changes that. Do you have any qualms about becoming the chief medical director here until spring?"

Kate nearly dropped the bottle of carbolic acid she was holding. Next spring? Did that mean they would have more time in Alaska?

"No, sir," Nathan answered, "though I'd like to—"

"Good, then that's exactly what I'd like you to do. Excellent work on the hospital, by the way. I toured it when the ship stopped in Juneau before coming here. I'm aware Ellingsworth was gone for most of the time it was being built. You did better than I'd anticipated with it."

Nathan blinked. "The hospital? Is it finished?"

"Yes, just last week. But I suppose you were in Petersburg and haven't had a chance to see it for yourself."

A smile filled Nathan's face. "The first floor was finished before we left. We'd been planning to open it on Monday, but ended up coming here instead. I'm looking forward to seeing it for myself and treating the first few patients there as soon as I return."

"I see. Well, like I said, you did excellent work. I'll be sure to make note of it in your file." The surgeon general sat back in his chair and stroked his mustache. "Now back to my plans for the spring. In March, Dr. Myles will be finished in Boston. I'd like to bring him here and make him the medical director of Alaska, then move you to the bayou. I know you've spoken with Secretary Gray and Senators Randolph and Wells. They returned from Alaska quite excited about your plan to increase the number of doctors here from five to seven."

"Four," Nathan snapped. "You took one of my doctors away because of funding issues, remember?"

"Yes, well, upon further reflection—and discussion with the secretary of the interior—I've decided I like what you've done with the routes for traveling doctors in Alaska. Next year, the Marine Hospital Service will be getting an increase in funding for the express purpose of expanding medical care to remote regions, not just in Alaska, but for the rest of the United States. I'd like you to head up this area of expansion."

So Nathan wasn't being called back to Washington, DC, because Ellingsworth had complained. He was being asked to return because the surgeon general had finally caught his vision. Pride filled Kate's heart, even though the new position would certainly mean they'd be leaving Alaska. She'd be grateful for the few extra months she'd have here, and then grateful for the new opportunities awaiting Nathan after they left.

"And seeing how we already have a facility in New Orleans and we're concerned about typhus spreading in the bayou, I'd like to see if we can create five or six routes for traveling doctors there." The surgeon general kept his gaze focused on Nathan, dropping information about the expansion as casually as he might discuss the weather, though she could see the excitement building on Nathan's face. "I'm hoping that will take only a year to develop, and then we can look at the Outer Banks region of the North Carolina coast. I actually have a list of several regions in need of medical care. Building hospitals that aren't on coasts will be difficult. That doesn't fall under our purview at the moment, but I want you to consider anywhere that there's a coastal area open for development—including Marquette, Michigan."

The world seemed to grow still around Kate. The fire stopped flickering, the ravens stopped cawing, even the hum of conversation outside dwindled until all she could hear was the roaring in her ears.

The surgeon general had just said Marquette. He'd offered Nathan the chance to build a hospital or clinic or some sort of facility in his hometown, giving him the ability to create a medical infrastructure that just might have saved his mother's life had it existed thirty years ago. Tears blurred her eyes, and not the sad kind. Nathan would be able to do a lot of good by leaving Alaska.

Chapter 43   449

She expected to hear him start gushing, to thank the surgeon general a hundred different times and stammer over his words. But he uttered the one word she never thought she'd hear.

"No."

She jerked her head toward him. What did he mean, no? This was his dream. And she'd told him she'd follow him anywhere. Did she need to remind him of that? In front of the surgeon general?

The surgeon general's mouth opened, then closed before opening again. "I don't understand. You've been asking me for this since shortly after I hired you."

Nathan pushed himself up higher on his pillows. "I'm happy to draft routes for traveling doctors. I can even go and visit the area while doing so, if I feel I need a firsthand look at things. But send Dr. Myles to New Orleans, or better yet, send him to Marquette so we can build a clinic as soon as next summer. He's as capable as I am of overseeing the establishment of a new hospital or clinic."

"Yes." The surgeon general blinked, the side of his mustache twitching. "Dr. Myles is quite capable. I won't argue with you there. But this was your vision, Reid. You're the one with a desire to expand medical care in remote areas, not him. Or has your vision changed?"

Nathan's tongue came out to wet his lips. "It hasn't changed, but I want to stay in Alaska. My wife is from here, and I've come to love this place, as wild as it is. I'm not convinced things will run smoothly just yet if I leave either. But as I said earlier, if you want to move forward with routes for traveling doctors, I'm happy to draft them from Alaska, much like I drafted the routes for Alaska while sitting in an office in Washington, DC."

Nathan's gaze shifted to her, taking on the familiar warmth

that seemed to fill his eyes whenever he looked at her. "Besides, I've come to believe my wife is a rather essential part of our medical plans here. She has inroads with the tribes through her family's trading company, and moving her away from here would set us back two decades in terms of establishing trust with the small, remote villages. Even if an Indian chief hasn't met her, he's done business with one of her brothers."

The surgeon general slanted a gaze in her direction. "Is what your husband says true? Do you have a good relationship with the Indians?"

"I . . . ah . . ." She rubbed the side of her head. "I think so, yes."

"This past spring she saved both a mother and baby in this very village by performing a caesarean section." Pride filled Nathan's voice. "You should have seen the greeting they gave her when she arrived to treat the influenza. We had the tribe's cooperation in establishing a quarantine facility not because Ellingsworth or I asked but because Kate did, and everyone here trusts her."

"I had no idea." The surgeon general swept his gaze down her, his face softening a bit. "It sounds like we're quite fortunate to have you as one of our doctors."

"I . . . um . . ." She shifted against the hard seat of the chair. "Not that fortunate. I'm a woman. A lot of people don't trust me to treat them. Especially not sailors."

"But the Tlingit do?" the surgeon general tugged on the corner of his mustache.

"Yes."

"And the Inupiat," Nathan interjected. "And probably all the other tribes in Alaska. Did you know she's the doctor who's been going to Barrow for the last three years? The one sending us those reports?"

Chapter 43   451

The surgeon general eyed her more closely. "You're the doctor who's been going to Barrow?"

Kate swallowed, suddenly feeling like she was on display. "Yes."

"Huh. I hadn't put it together until just now, but I suppose it makes sense."

She shifted. What made sense? She didn't understand.

"Would it surprise you to know that the doctor we sent to Barrow this summer had difficulty treating the Inupiat?" the surgeon general asked. "He had difficulty with the Aleut in Unalaska too, and the Tlingit in this very village, Petersburg. No one would come to him for treatment. They all kept asking for another doctor to come back, someone they trusted. A woman they'd watched grow up every year. I assumed this person the tribes kept talking about was a nurse. I should have realized it was my assistant medical director's new wife."

Kate held her breath, her eyes unable to leave the surgeon general's. The various tribes had all said that? About her? They'd been waiting for her to visit them over the summer?

"As you can see, that puts me in a rather awkward position of needing to find a different doctor for the route next summer," the surgeon general continued, his voice softening as his eyes met hers. "And yet, the exact doctor I need already is in my employ."

Kate's throat grew thick. Was he asking what she thought?

She shifted her gaze to Nathan, but he was grinning from ear to ear. "Of course they want Kate. She's an excellent doctor."

Wait... Did that mean...?

"I'll go with her, of course. As medical director of Alaska, it's imperative I see the territory." Nathan reached out and clasped her hand, warm and strong. "Perhaps we can bring a third doctor along, one that Kate can introduce to the various villages so that she doesn't need to go on such a long journey every year. I have plans for my wife that don't involve being separated from her for months at a time."

"Yes, adding a third doctor to the route next summer sounds like an excellent plan. We can think of it as a training period of sorts." The surgeon general reached into his breast pocket and retrieved a notepad and small pencil. "I'll make a note to allocate extra resources for that very thing."

"Or Nathan could go to Louisiana while I do the Barrow trip. We could split up over next summer to cover more ground."

Nathan's thumb brushed over her knuckles. "I'm not sure I can be apart from you that long, darling, but we'll keep that in mind."

"Send me a list of the proposed doctor routes for Louisiana over the winter." The surgeon general tucked his notebook back into his pocket. "We'll reassess and finalize our exact plans for you in the spring."

"But in the meantime, I'll stay on as medical director of Alaska." Nathan didn't phrase it as a question. He talked as though he already considered it a certainty.

The older man's eyes settled on where Nathan's hand linked with hers. "Of course. I can't think of a better person for the role. For either of the roles, really."

Kate's heart was so light, she felt as if she could float. She looked at her husband, tears filling her eyes while his hand still linked them together.

Exceeding abundantly above all she could have asked or thought or imagined.

God had done it not once, not twice, but three times over. First, he'd given her a way to become a doctor; then he'd given her a wonderful, adoring husband; and finally he'd provided an even better way for her to practice medicine than before. If she had tried imagining how her life would look ten years ago, she never would have guessed it could be so rich or full of love. But God had seen beyond her limited dreams and given her something far deeper and better than she'd ever hoped.

And she planned to spend every day for the rest of her life showing both God and her husband how grateful she was for her full and wonderful life.

44

Stikine River, Southeast Alaska; Four Days Later

Mikhail dipped the paddle of his canoe into the rushing waters of the Stikine River, his eyes scanning the rocky shore lined with pines and firs. A family of caribou grazed nearby, their breaths visible in the cold evening air. Beyond them, snow-dusted mountains rose in the distance, their white peaks evidence of winter's swift approach.

But he saw no signs of a canoe or dinghy, or perhaps even a fire on the beach. Nothing that indicated the place where a team of botanists had decided to leave the winding river that cut through the mountains and canyons of Southeast Alaska and Canada and venture into the forest.

He dipped his paddle in the water again, the muscles of his arms straining as he propelled his canoe and the one tied behind it against the current. If he didn't find evidence of a camp soon, he'd have to stop and set up his own camp for the night. Again.

He usually loved the stillness of the wilderness, the quiet. The feeling of being one tiny thing caught in a world that was so much larger and grander than him. But that feeling of peace had abandoned him today, just as it had yesterday and the day before that. Just as it had ever since he left his family in Petersburg, Alaska, at the end of the Russian influenza outbreak.

Perhaps that's why he had this disquiet in his soul. He'd witnessed too much suffering over the past month to think he could take on the wilds of Alaska as winter approached and return home unscathed. Or maybe it was his family. He wasn't supposed to be leaving them now, not on the cusp of winter. And not with Alexei hiding something.

Mikhail didn't know what his oldest brother was hiding, only that he'd been awfully quiet about Simon Caldwell becoming the next governor.

He glanced around the river again and sucked a breath of crisp, cold air into his lungs as he surveyed the wild beauty untouched by humans.

Would Simon Caldwell venture up the Stikine River in his new role as governor?

He snorted. The man probably didn't plan to leave his fancy office once he arrived in Sitka.

But what would Simon Caldwell do to this land if he saw the caribou, the trees, the towering mountains? Would he exploit it? Tear it up in search of gold and slash through the forests on a quest for lumber and furs?

Just come back safe. Kate's words from four mornings ago came back to him as he angled his boat toward the shore, heading toward a wide swath of rocky beach that would make an ideal camping spot for the night.

He'd never thought he'd see his oldest sister so happy, but

happy she was with her doctoring and her new husband and the obvious love growing between them.

But as he rowed his canoe onto the rocky beach, he wondered if that love would be enough to protect her and Nathan—or anyone else in his family—from what lay ahead now that Simon Caldwell was governor.

And he wondered if he'd be able to protect himself and the lost team of botanists from the perils of an Alaskan winter.

A NOTE FROM NAOMI...

Wow, sometimes God finds a way to give us our dreams, even when obtaining them feels impossible. I'm so glad both Nathan and Kate found ways to bring better medical care to the people of Alaska while also building a relationship of love and trust between themselves.

I know Nathan and Kate already have their happy ending, but I couldn't resist writing bonus scene about Kate's medical trip to Barrow. It'll give you a little glimpse of just how happy the two of them are a couple years into their marriage—and I think you'll love it. If you want to read it, follow the link below and type in your email, so I know where to send it. https://geni.us/AK3Bonus

*AND IF YOU want a head start on Kate's story, turn the page for a sneak peek.

Echoes of Twilight

Stikine River Wilderness, Alaska; October 1888

They were all going to die. The only question was how long it would take.

Bryony Wetherby dipped the wooden spoon into the pot over the fire and stirred the soup, trying not to think of how it steamed and swirled against the air that grew colder with each passing day. Trying not to think of how her fingertips were so cold they ached and the big toe on her left foot was numb.

And it was only October. Not November or December or January. Just October, and she was fighting frostbite.

"Bryony, come here and look at this." Her father's voice filled the campsite. "I think I found a new lichen."

Bryony looked up at where her father and Dr. Ottingford both crouched on the ground near a boulder on the outskirts of the camp. Behind the boulder, a glacial lake filled the valley, it's water a creamy turquoise color.

"I think it's a member of the *Stereocaulon* family." Her

father studied the lichen through his magnifying glass. "But I've never seen one before with a gray hue."

"Yes, I agree. It's definitely part of the *Stereocaulon* family." Dr. Ottingford, her father's research associate, said from where he kneeled on the ground beside her father.

"Hurry and grab that journal." Her father looked over at her, his brow furrowed into lines that showed his impatience. "Roger here will collect a sample to take back to Washington DC."

She almost asked her father what the point of recording anything about the lichen was, when it seemed more and more likely they would die in the Alaskan wilderness, surrounded by towering mountains and rocky valleys that didn't contain enough soil to grow any vegetation they could eat.

Six weeks. That's how long they'd gone on like this after their guide had died in a bear attack. At first they hadn't been worried. Her father and Dr. Ottingford had decided to collect samples for a few more days after they'd buried their guide. The Department of the Interior had commissioned their study on the flora and fauna of Southeast Alaska, and her father had wanted a chance to conclude the findings he'd been working on in the higher elevations near the Stikine Icefield.

But that was when they assumed they'd be able to find their way back to the river. Or to a stream. Or to anything that might lead them to the place they'd beached their canoes on the banks of the mighty Stikine River and headed inland.

"Bryony?" her father called. "Didn't you hear me? I need the journal."

"Come eat and I'll record the surroundings after dinner." Not that she could call the three handfuls of edible roots she'd thrown in the stew pot for dinner. It was flavored broth, at best, and not enough to sustain them through the night and into the morning. But it was the only thing they had.

"Get the journal." Her father's voice took on a stubborn edge. "This is too important to wait."

She sighed, then left the spoon in the simmering pot, grabbed the current book she was using to sketch her findings, and headed toward where her father and Dr. Ottingford were both crouched on the ground, studying the snow lichen with small, grayish-white leaves that covered a series of smaller rocks beside the boulder.

"Note how dense the coverage is, and that the leaves are more gray than white." Her father reached out and brushed one of the leaves with his finger. Then he continued to rattle off a list of observations about the size and shape of the leaves, how it grew in both sunny and shaded areas, and the density of the coverage.

Bryony held the pencil to the paper and recorded every detail he listed, then asked about the vegetation growing around it before finally sketching a picture.

"Create a more defined edge on the leaves. They look too feathery." Her father peered over her shoulder. "Don't you think the leaves need to be more defined, Roger?"

Dr. Ottingford carefully scraped a small sample of the lichen off the boulder and pressed it between parchment paper before straightening and looking at the journal. "Yes, make them a bit more distinct if you could, Miss Wetherby."

Bryony did as asked, waiting until both men nodded their approval and read over her notes before closing the journal. "Now can we eat dinner?"

Her father blinked, as though just now remembering that they needed to eat at least a few bites of food if they wanted to keep from starving. He got like this when he was focused on something, almost as though eating and drinking and not dying of hypothermia were all somehow secondary to studying vegetation.

"Right. Yes. Let's eat dinner." He scratched the side of his head. "What did you prepare?"

"A stew made primarily with roots." It was the only thing they could eat on the cusp of winter. The wild blueberries had ripened and died months ago, the fireweed stalks that could be eaten as young shoots were now brown and tough. And the glacier lilies, who's bulbs could be eaten, had also died. The only way to find food was to dig up the roots of various plants. Either that or hunt it, but that had been their guide's job, and they'd struggled to find food ever since he'd died.

"That's it? Root stew?" Her father raised a bushy white eyebrow. "I'm rather hungry tonight. Didn't we skip lunch?"

"Yes." And breakfast had been the same roots, only she'd fried in a pan over the fire rather than boiled them in a stew.

"Can't you make something with the jerky or pemmican? Maybe cook up some biscuits and fry it over the fire for sandwiches?"

She tried not to clench her jaw and tense her shoulders. Tried not to let the heat pricking the backs of her eyes turn into actual tears. Tried not to let the panic bubbling in her stomach creep into her voice.

But when she turned her gaze onto her father, she wasn't sure she succeeded in any of those things. "We ran out of pemmican two days ago and we sent the last of the jerky with Heath and Stuart when they went to find help."

"What about biscuits?" Dr. Ottingford's voice, which was normally dry and monotone, held a hopeful sound.

She sighed. "We ran out of that last week too. I told you."

"You did?" Father blinked again, his eyes large behind his spectacles. I could have sworn we had enough supplies to last us when Stuart and Heath left."

"We did, but we also assumed they'd be gone for about a week. It's been three."

"There, there, bug. Don't fret." He reached out and took her hand, then patted it as he'd done when she was a child. "I'm sure Stuart and Heath have found the river by now. Maybe they even went to one of those Indian villages to ask for help. It will all work out. You'll see."

"But what if it doesn't?" Bryony tugged her hand away from her father. "What if they slipped while trying to make it down a mountain? Or what if a grizzly bear attacked them too? What if snow comes tonight and makes passage out of the valley impassible?"

At this point, the only thing she could assume was that her brother and his best friend had perished in the wilderness right along with their guide. They should have been back well over a week ago.

And any number of things might have happened to them in this vast, beautiful, untamed land.

Why couldn't her father see it? How could he be so smart when it came to science, and so utterly clueless about everything else?

"We'll be fine." Her father reached out and patted her hand again. "This isn't my first expedition where something's gone awry. Roger, remember the time when we were in the Southwest studying the vegetation in the desert?"

Dr. Ottingford rubbed the bald spot on the top of his head, his eyes wide behind his own pair of wire-rimmed glasses. "Yes, I remember. We were able to find water before running out. It wasn't nearly as dire of a situation as our guide first thought."

That wasn't how she remembered it. It had seemed beyond dire, as though they'd been hours away from dying. She'd been accompanying her father on his expeditions since the ripe old age of eight—after her mother died. Before that, she'd assisted him by taking notes in the hothouse and sketching plants. But even though that expedition to Texas had been six years ago, she could still recall the terror she'd felt when their guide realized the creek they'd been planning to get water from was dry, and they had to look for another water source.

That had taken them four hours to find another creek.

But here they'd been lost in the wilderness for six weeks. Surely that had to be more serious than a four hour delay in finding water. Why couldn't her father see that?

"Your brother and Stuart made it back to the river. I'm sure they did. Help will be here any day." Her father turned toward the pot with steaming broth hanging over the fire. "I know a meal of boiled roots doesn't seem like much, but we'll be eating fish aplenty soon enough."

But what if Heath and Stuart got lost? Or what if they were dead?

"I know we said we'd stay here and wait for them to return with a rescue expedition, but I think we should leave in the morning." She followed her father back to the fire.

"No." Her father picked up one of the tin bowls beside the fire, then stirred the broth in the pot. "We said we'd stay here and study the vegetation until they returned. The last thing we need to do is move locations. That will make it impossible for them to find us."

"That assumes they're alive and well enough to lead an expedition back to us. And we don't know that they are."

Her father dropped the spoon back into the pot, his light blue eyes piercing beneath his bushy white eyebrows. "Do you truly think your brother is dead, Bryony?"

She shifted her weight on the uneven ground, her throat growing tight. She didn't want to think that. Didn't want to believe that what had once been a happy family of four, with two parents, one son, and one daughter, was now just a father-daughter team.

But what else was she supposed to think?

What—other than a major disaster—would possibly keep Heath from returning to them when he knew they were stranded in the wilderness?

"I don't know what to think, that's part of what makes me so worried. Part of what makes me think we need to leave in the morning." And hope and pray that they'd somehow be able to find their way through the towering mountains and winding valleys that had confused them for the past six weeks. "You can tell winter is coming. I know you can."

Almost as though confirming her statement, a brutal gust of wind blew down from one of the mountains, working its way beneath her wool coat.

"The girl does have a point, Atticus." Dr. Ottingford looked to the north, where the tallest of the mountains surrounding them towered over the valley with its snow-capped peak.

It should have been a beautiful sight, the majestic mountain with a turquoise lake at its base and a series of smaller mountains circling the lake. It had been beautiful, weeks ago, the first time she'd seen it. Before she'd realize just how lost they were.

Now it terrified her.

"We don't know what might have befallen Heath and Stuart, and the weather is turning." Dr. Ottingford gestured toward the mountain to the north, then dragged his gaze along the series of peaks that surrounded them to the east and south and west. "Half the time, the peaks are too shrouded in clouds for us to see them, and when we can, the snow line is always farther and farther down. We can't afford to be here when winter comes. The canyon we followed in here will become impassible with the first bit of snow."

Her father sighed, his large shoulders heaving. "I really do think Heath and Stuart will return, possibly with an entire team to guide us out. If we move locations, it will only be harder for them to find us. It might even prevent them from finding us at all. Leaving should be a last resort."

"It should, but like I said, we need to leave before the snow comes." Dr. Ottingford met her father's gaze. His voice was painfully calm as he spoke, not sounding worried or excited, like how he always spoke. "We don't know enough about the wilderness to survive a winter in these mountains."

"I think we should give it another week." Her father dipped the ladle into the pot and dumped the watery broth into his bowl. "If Heath and Stuart still haven't arrived, then we'll leave."

A week might be too long, but she wasn't going to be able to convince her father to leave his work. So she wrapped her coat tighter around her as another gust of wind swept into the valley and simply said, "Thank you."

Her father didn't respond as he wordlessly spooned the stew into two more bowls.

And Bryony couldn't help but wonder if staying an extra week meant she'd ever see home again.

Five Days Later

No RABBIT. Bryony stared at the noose she'd made with rope she'd twined together from cedar bark.

When she first decided to try snaring a rabbit, she'd realized she'd need to peel the bark off a cedar tree and soak it for a couple days until it became pliable enough to be stripped into pieces and braded.

But even after she'd made her own rope, she still hadn't

been able to she hadn't been able to catch an animal. Not today. Not yesterday. And not any day for the past four weeks since she first got the idea.

She'd moved the snare to several different places in the valley, but no matter what she did or how many times she tried, she couldn't catch a rabbit.

The snares that their guide, Jack Ledman, set all summer had brought in a constant stream of food. It had seemed like a simple thing to recreate to ensure that they didn't run out of food. Sometimes Mr. Ledman had set four or five snares a night, and they would all have rabbits come morning.

But she couldn't catch a single one.

Oh, what she'd give to go back in time to the day before Mr. Ledman had died and ask him how to snare a rabbit. Neither Heath or Stuart had known. She'd asked them both before they'd left camp to get help, and they'd looked at her as though she was daft.

They didn't know how to catch fish either, at least, not without a proper fishing pole and bait, and they had neither of those things.

This morning the snare had been set off, which made the lack of rabbit almost worse. For the first time in a week, they'd been close to having meat. So very, very close.

She tried to ignore the heat pricking the backs of her eyes and the lump in her throat. Tried to ignore the shiver that might be due to the damp, bitter cold, or might be due to the fact her stomach felt so hungry it was trying to eat itself.

She didn't know and didn't want to think about it. Just like she didn't want to think about the fact Heath and Stuart had yet to return with help. Or that she'd woken to a light dusting of snow on her bedroll that morning.

Instead she pushed herself off the ground, and forced herself deeper into the woods where she could dig more roots.

Hopefully the meager stew would tide them over for another day.

And hopefully God would answer her prayers about her brother and Stuart returning with help before nightfall.

He was following the wrong tracks.

Mikhail Amos hunkered into his bearskin coat as he strode up the mountain, stepping around fallen logs and boulders, trying to follow the tracks in the soft brown earth that were growing fainter and fainter in the drizzling rain. A gust of wind swept down the mountain, and Mikhail pressed his lips together. The wind was cold enough to bring snow, and all he could do was pray that somehow, by some miracle, the snow would hold off for a day or two, until he found the party of lost botanists he was searching for.

After two weeks of heading up the Stikine River until it crossed the border with Canada and exploring the mountains north and west of the river, he'd moved his search to the southern section of the river.

He wished he could say searching a new location had led to him finding the scientists, but he was still just as lost as to where they might be as he'd been when he'd left Petersburg two weeks ago.

This wasn't his first expedition into the uncharted Coast Mountains that ran from Seattle all the way up into the mainland of Alaska, nor was it his second or third. He'd been a guide for official government expeditions for the past eight years, leaving every April or May and returning every September.

He'd even accompanied teams of men on rescue expeditions two times before. But this was the first time he'd been charged with leaving by himself on the cusp of winter.

It was also the first time he'd gotten nowhere after two weeks of searching. It was almost as though the team of botanists had disappeared from the earth.

When he'd finally found a beached canoe and tracks on the beach, he'd been hopeful that following the tracks would lead to something helpful. The tracks were from a party of two, not six. But if the men were prospectors—most men roaming the wilds of Alaska were—and if they'd been searching the Stikine River Valley for gold the past month, they might have run into the botany expedition or at least come across some other tracks.

Following the men at least presented a chance that he might get helpful information about the lost botanists.

But he was staring to think these tracks belonged to the worst prospectors in all of history.

Any prospector who knew what he was doing would have gotten out of the mountains yesterday when the weather started to turn, knowing that snow was sure to follow.

But these men were moving deeper and deeper into the mountains. It was almost enough to make him turn around, but the tracks only looked to be a half day old at this point, meaning he'd likely overtake them by nightfall.

Hopefully they'd seen the party of botanists, because if they hadn't...

Mikhail shook his head, not wanting to think about it. The men in the botany expedition were fathers and sons and brothers. If they didn't come home, someone would miss them. And seeing how he'd spent the past eleven years of his life missing his own father, he couldn't turn his back on the botanists without knowing he'd done every last thing in his power to save them.

Mikhail paused for a moment beside a creek, noticing how the boot prints on the sandy bank and mossy earth sank deeper into the ground here, indicating the men had paused. There were even two indents where packs had been set in the sand for a bit. The men he was following were definitely prospectors. They'd left similar tracks indicating they'd stopped and searched for gold at the other creek he'd crossed yesterday, and at a couple geological formations.

Mikhail squatted next to a patch of flattened moss, rubbing it between his fingers, then scanned the dense trees surrounding him. Rain drizzled through the canopy, wetting his face and dripping off the brim of his hat, the persistent patter of water mingling with the rustle of the wind through the trees.

The prospector's tracks led him higher up the mountain toward where the falling rain would surely turn to snow, and at which point he just might lose the fading tracks.

Perhaps he was on a fool's errand, because even if the prospectors had crossed paths with the botanists, what were the chances there would be anything left of the botanists' tracks?

He clenched his jaw. It didn't matter. He knew his way through the mountains in snow, and he'd been sent on a mission to find the botanists and return them safely to Sitka.

He wasn't ready to give up just yet.

Order your copy of *Echoes of Twilight* on Amazon.

Author's Note

Established in 1798 by an act of Congress, the Marine Hospital Service's main goal was to provide medical care for sick and disabled seamen. Even though the United States was nothing more than a fledgling nation, Congress recognized the importance of trade and commerce if the nation was to grow. And it recognized the necessity of having healthy sailors, for both commerce and naval-defense purposes.

As the United States acquired more territory and grew into a much larger country than the original thirteen colonies—almost all of which were located on the Atlantic Ocean—the medical needs of its citizens expanded as well, but it took Congress more than one hundred years to act. The Public Health Service was officially created in 1912 by another act of Congress that broadened the scope of the original Marine Hospital Service to include all public health concerns, not just those related to sailors.

As with most acts of Congress, it can take many years of struggle, failed policies, and ignored problems before the government finds a good solution. In Nathan and Kate's story, I created a scenario where the health needs of the general populace in Alaska outweighed the needs of sailors. This was a growing trend in the United States as it became more obvious that the MHS couldn't address the health needs of an entire nation.

Surgeon General John B. Hamilton, who made an appearance at the end of this novel and was the real surgeon general in 1888, was known for establishing quarantine facilities to stop the spread of disease, and some of these measures involved the general populace, not just sailors.

The Russian influenza pandemic of 1889 and 1890 really did start in Russia. According to estimates, more than four hundred million people contracted it, and over a million people died from it.

As you may have guessed, medical care in the late 1800s was nothing like the medical care available today. The germ theory was just that, a *theory* about how disease spread, and only the most cutting-edge doctors saw validity in it. But without the existence of antibiotics, which weren't developed until nearly 1930, medical treatment was severely limited.

Sadly, options for female doctors in the late 1800s were about as limited as options for treating infections. While there were schools for female doctors, they were separate from schools for male doctors. So even though women could get medical degrees, treating patients was much harder. The prejudices and discrimination toward women were vastly different than today. Many people simply didn't believe that women could do the same work as a man, and those women who could find work as doctors were often relegated to treating "feminine complaints," some of which were caused by tight-lacing corsets. Women doctors could also treat infants and children, but very rarely would a woman go to a female doctor for something like asthma, and many male doctors treated feminine complaints by prescribing elixirs that often contained laudanum, an opiate that only served to dull the symptoms rather than treat the root cause of the health concern.

Researching and writing this book made me very grateful that I'm alive at a time when women have access to much better health care and have the option to pursue any career they want to.

If Kate were alive and practicing medicine today, she would probably be aware that her inability to sit still, her competence in high-stress situations, and her struggle to read social cues are symptoms of ADHD. While the first descriptions of ADHD appear in medical texts dating back to 1798, ADHD wasn't officially recognized until the late 1960s.

I didn't intentionally set out to write about a neurodivergent character, but my son was recently diagnosed with inattentive ADHD (formerly called ADD because his form lacks the hyperactivity component). This led to my husband being diagnosed ADD as well.

So when I sat down and looked at the female character who had already appeared in the first two books in the Dawn of Alaska series, it was quite clear I'd already created a neurodivergent character, and I couldn't take that away from Kate without greatly altering the character you've spent the past two novels getting to know.

As an author, I'm aware that *Above All Dreams* dives a bit deeper into historical details than most of my previous novels, but I have always loved the old TV show *Dr. Quinn, Medicine Woman*, and I have long thought about putting my own spin on a novel based on Dr. Quinn. In writing that story, I ended up addressing more complex issues than I originally anticipated, namely how common discrimination was for women in professions that society didn't see as appropriate for them. Another issue I ended up addressing was the poor condition of women's health care.

I find it inspiring that in spite of all the obstacles, there were medical schools for women and a growing number of female doctors who gradually ended up changing society's perception of them. The number of women in the medical field today shows just how far we've come in that regard. Thank you so very much for letting me share a story with you that highlights some of these early struggles.

If you're hoping for another story that demonstrates how American women in the late 1800s overcame significant obstacles to create a better place for themselves in society, you'll enjoy Bryony and Mikhail's story. It's coming next in *Echoes of Twilight*. Much like *Above All Dreams*, it will give you a small glimpse of some of the historical challenges that have shaped our lives today. (Plus, you'll finally get to know the mysterious Mikhail a little better—and meet the scientific woman who slips past his defenses and convinces him that falling in love might not be so terrible.) You can order your copy of *Echoes of Twilight* on Amazon.

Other Novels by Naomi Rawlings

Dawn of Alaska Series
    Book 1—*Written on the Mist* (Jonas and Evelina)
    Book 2—*Whispers on the Tide* (Sacha and Maggie)
    Book 3—*Above all Dreams* (Nathan and Kate)
    Book 4—*Echoes of Twilight* (Mikhail and Bryony)
    Book 5—*Against the Rain* (Yuri and Rosalind)
    Book 6—*Beyond the Dawn* (Alexei and Clarise)

Texas Promise Series
    Book 1—*Tomorrow's First Light* (Sam and Ellie)
    Book 2—*Tomorrow's Shining Dream* (Daniel and Charlotte)
    Book 3—*Tomorrow's Constant Hope* (Wes and Keely)
    Book 4—*Tomorrow's Steadfast Prayer* (Harrison and Alejandra)
    Book 5—*Tomorrow's Lasting Joy* (Cain and Anna Mae)

Eagle Harbor Series
    Book 1—*Love's Unfading Light* (Mac and Tressa)

Book 2—*Love's Every Whisper* (Elijah and Victoria)
Book 3—*Love's Sure Dawn* (Gilbert and Rebekah)
Book 4—*Love's Eternal Breath* (Seth and Lindy)
Book 5—*Love's Christmas Hope* (Thomas and Jessalyn)
Book 6—*Love's Bright Tomorrow* (Isaac and Aileen)
Prequel—*Love's Violet Sunrise* (Hiram and Mabel)

Belanger Family Saga
Book 1—*The Lady's Refuge* (Michel and Isabelle)
Book 2—*The Widow's Secret* (Jean Paul and Brigette)
Book 3—*The Reluctant Enemy* (Gregory and Danielle)

Acknowledgments

Thank you first and foremost to my Lord and Savior, Jesus Christ, for giving me both the ability and opportunity to write novels for His glory.

As with any novel, an author might come up with a story idea and sit at his or her computer to type the initial words, but it takes an army of people to bring you the book you have today. I'd especially like to thank my editors. Erin Healy's keen insight and ability to understand my characters and their worlds have made my novels shine in ways that I had never thought possible, and I count it a privilege to work with her. Jennifer Lonas's eye for detail helps me to deliver a polished, professional book to you every single time. And then there's Roseanna White, one of my longest friends and biggest encouragements in this industry. She answers my random emails, helps me brainstorm when I get stuck, and points out many ways to make my books stronger.

Many thanks to my family for working with my writing schedule and giving me a chance to do two things I love: be a mom and a writer.

Also, thank you to the hospitable people of Juneau and Sitka, Alaska, especially Rich Mattson with the Juneau-Douglas City Museum, and Hal Spackman and Nicole Fiorino with Sitka

History. The three of them answered question after question and provided numerous images and book recommendations to help me bring this small slice of Alaskan history to life. And finally, thank you to Susan Gorilla Benton, a resident of Alaska for over twenty years, who preread this novel looking for any mistakes or inaccuracies.

About the Author

Naomi Rawlings is a *USA Today* bestselling author of over a dozen historical novels, including the Eagle Harbor Series, which has sold more than 500,000 copies. She lives with her husband and three children in Michigan's rugged Upper Peninsula, along the southern shore of Lake Superior, where they get two hundred inches of snow every year, and where people still grow their own vegetables and cut down their own firewood—just like in the historical novels she writes.

For more information about Naomi, please visit her at www.naomirawlings.com or find her on Facebook at www.facebook.com/author.naomirawlings. If you'd like a free novel, sign up for her author newsletter.

Made in the USA
Las Vegas, NV
17 July 2025